ON FIRE

Matthew walked toward her slowly, as though testing his welcome. She stepped closer.

He paused, close enough to touch. "At your service."

Sharon breathed in his scent. Warmth and musk. Masculine. Her gaze drifted to his lips. Firm and full. He was Temptation. Sharon lifted her eyes to his and found the heat waiting for her. Her nipples hardened in response.

Slowly, Matthew lowered his head. Sharon's gaze wavered between his darkening eyes and his sensuous mouth. Instinctively, she recognized Matthew's warning—if this isn't what you want, step back now. She rose onto her toes to meet him halfway.

Matthew's lips brushed gently across hers. Sharon shivered at his tenderness. He pressed his mouth against hers and she opened for him. Matthew nipped at her lips as though sipping her. Stroked his tongue into her mouth as though tasting her. She felt like dessert.

On Fire

PATRICIA SARGEANT

Kensington Publishing Corp.
http://www.kensington books.com

DAFINA BOOKS are published by

Kensington Publishing Corp.
850 Third Avenue
New York, NY 10022

All Kensington Titles, Imprints, and Distributed Lines are available at special quantity discounts for bulk purchases for sales promotions, premiums, fund-raising, and educational or institutional use. Special book excerpts or customized printings can also be created to fit specific needs. For details, write or phone the office of the Kensington special sales manager: Kensington Publishing Corp., 850 Third Avenue, New York, NY 10022, attn: Special Sales Department, Phone: 1-800-221-2647.

Dafina and the Dafina logo Reg. U.S. Pat. & TM Off.

ISBN-13: 978-0-7582-1877-3
ISBN-10: 0-7582-1877-X

First mass market printing: September 2007

10 9 8 7 6 5 4 3 2 1

Printed in the United States of America

To my dream team:
 My sister, Bernadette, for giving me the dream.
 My husband, Michael, for supporting the dream.
 My brother, Richard, for believing in the dream.
 My brother, Gideon, for encouraging the dream.
 My friend and critique partner, Marcia James, for
 sharing the dream.
And to Mom and Dad always with love.

Sincere thanks to Tom Fee of the International Association of Arson Investigators and to Steve Meese, firefighter and paramedic, for answering my multitude of questions regarding fires and fire investigations.

Chapter 1

"I'm taking you off the fire department beat," Wayne Lenmore announced.

Her newspaper editor's words hit Sharon MacCabe like a leather palm. Hard. Stinging. Totally unexpected. Announcements like this shouldn't come on a Friday.

Sharon searched the older man's drooping features. She was too breathless to be hysterical, too numb to be outraged. She leaned back onto the hard, plastic visitor's seat, seeking support. "Why?"

Wayne shifted in his battered blue office chair. It squeaked under his weight. "The publisher is going to assign someone else to the beat. He thinks you're better with features."

Sharon flinched at the implication she couldn't handle hard news. She'd been covering the fire department for the *Charleston Times* for the past six months. The previous beat reporter had left the West Virginia daily for greater fame and fortune. The assignment had taken her one step closer to her dream of becoming an investigative reporter. That's why she hadn't resented the fourteen-hour days, or weekends in the office learning about firefighting and meeting department officials.

She'd worked for years to prove herself capable of handling a hard news beat. She'd finally been assigned to one only to have it snatched away from her.

She gripped the chair's cool, plastic arms. "Are you dissatisfied with my work?"

Wayne's pale gray gaze slid from hers. "Your work is fine."

His comment wasn't resounding praise, but neither was it criticism. Sharon clenched her fists in her lap to isolate her shaking. "Then why am I being demoted?"

"It's not a demotion. We're just shuffling personnel."

First, he demotes her, then he lies to her. The ice of shock melted under the heat of temper. "Who else are you shuffling?"

Wayne sat back and his seat screeched again. "At this time, no one. But additional reassignments may come later."

Something was wrong with this picture. Apparently overnight, Gus Aldridge, the publisher, had sprouted some wild hair and stomped her budding career into the ground. What was going on?

"Does Gus have a replacement in mind?"

Wayne finally looked at her. "Lucas Stanton."

Anger thumped in her chest, each pulse reverberating in her throat. "Senator Kurt Stanton's nephew?"

"He starts Monday."

The state senator from Institute, West Virginia, was up for re-election in November. He faced a tight race over the next seven months against his challenger.

What was Gus up to?

Sharon's voice shook as she spoke. "What newspaper experience does the senator's nephew have?"

Her boss sat straighter in his chair. "He received a degree in English from West Virginia State College."

"Oh, come on, Wayne." Sharon's chuckle held more scorn than humor. "You know there's a world of difference between a comp paper and a news story."

"Everyone has to start somewhere."

"I started six years ago transcribing police reports. Why can't Stanton's nephew do the same?"

"Because Aldridge wants him to start with the fire department." Wayne rested his forearms on the stack of press releases and news clippings on his desk. It wasn't quite nine A.M., but already the sleeves of his white shirt were dusted with newsprint.

Sharon swallowed her disappointment. "You told me it was my time to move up after Ernie went to the *Baltimore Sun*. Now you're taking that away?"

Shame joined regret in Wayne's tired eyes. "I'm sorry, Sharon, but Stanton starts Monday."

He spoke with finality. Sharon took a steadying breath. The musty scent of newsprint filled her lungs. Her gaze wandered her boss's office. It resembled a storage locker of newspapers. Rival papers. National papers. Small community weeklies. It was a definite fire hazard.

Wayne's room was one in a row of offices along one wall. Dim, dingy plasterboard formed three of its sides. The fourth was Plexiglas, which afforded the office's occupant a view of the reporters' cubicles. Were people watching them now and, if so, what was their interpretation?

She looked again at her editor. "What about the feature interview I scheduled with the new fire station captain today? And the fire department meeting this evening?"

"Features are your area. You can write up the captain's

interview. And go to the meeting. If anything comes from it, brief Stanton Monday."

Sharon's temper spiked. She counseled herself not to let her emotions take over. Nothing would be gained by creating a scene. "Do you expect me to train my replacement?" Her tone was hard but calm.

"Don't forget someone helped you when you first joined this paper, MacCabe."

"No, Wayne. I worked my way up from an intern. I wasn't *given* someone else's beat to curry political favor."

The flush started in Wayne's neck and rose to spot the scalp beneath his thinning gray hair. He dropped his gaze. "You have your assignment, MacCabe. Take it and be glad you still have a job."

Although muttered, the words stung. Sharon pushed herself to her feet and crossed the fraying gray carpet to the door. She clenched her jaw to keep from hurling words she could not take back.

She turned with her hand on the knob. "This newspaper is putting Stanton's political connections above my experience. How does that serve our readers?"

She turned her back on Wayne's guilty expression.

Sharon walked down the aisle, past the newsroom's gray-and-glass decor, and curious coworkers. Back at her cubicle, she continued to fume as she fired up her computer. A newspaper was no place for political cronyism. Among other things, people depended on the paper for information to actively participate in their democratic society. It shouldn't be used to advance someone's agenda, which was obviously Gus's intent.

"What did that keyboard do to you?"

Sharon looked up at the sound of Allyson Scott's voice. The political reporter stood in the entrance of

Sharon's cubicle, the inevitable mug of coffee cupped in her palms.

"I've been replaced on the fire department beat." Fresh anger spurted into Sharon's veins.

Allyson's hazel brown eyes widened in her tan, heart-shaped face. "Why?"

Sharon shrugged. "Gus wants to please his political buddy. Senator Stanton's nephew starts Monday."

The other woman's jaw dropped. In one fluid movement, she settled her mug on the corner of Sharon's desk and displaced the folders from the guest chair to the floor so she could sit.

The political reporter was a tall, willowy brunette. Her appearance was so feminine and unthreatening that new people at the capital usually didn't notice her sharp mind until it was too late.

Allyson reclaimed her coffee. "How long has this been in the works?"

Sharon glanced at her watch. She didn't want to be late for her interview with the new fire station captain, Matthew Payton. "I don't know." She jerked open her bottom desk drawer and grabbed her stash of pretzel rods.

"Is this a temporary assignment or is he going to be permanent staff?"

"I have no idea. I was too upset to think of asking those questions."

Sharon bit into one of the pretzels. Low sodium, low fat, very little taste. Once this bag was finished, her healthier eating habits would die an unlamented death.

Allyson leaned forward and touched the back of Sharon's wrist. "I would have been too. This is just so strange."

"I know." She offered the pretzels to Allyson, who

declined the snack with a shake of her head. "Gus is a registered independent. Why would he cozy up to a particular politician?"

"Money and power. That's what everyone's ultimately after."

Sharon pulled her oversized, overstuffed purse from her desk drawer and heaved it onto her shoulder as she stood. "It used to be about the news."

Arriving at Fire Station 11 almost thirty minutes later, Sharon followed the administrative assistant's directions to an office at the opposite end of the main floor. The room was devoid of personal effects. If it weren't for the nameplate on the wall beside the door, she wouldn't have known she'd found Matthew Payton.

Charleston's newest fire station captain looked over from his computer as Sharon paused in the doorway. With her reporter's eye for detail, she cataloged his dark brown skin, prominent cheekbones and strong jaw. Full, well-shaped lips softened features so sharply drawn they could have been sculpted from the mountains that made her state famous.

When he spun his chair forward, the woman in her caught the full effect of his broad shoulders, gift wrapped in a plain, white cotton shirt. He stood, smoothing his royal-blue-and-yellow tie.

His midnight eyes held her gaze for a long moment. Sharon wondered whether he was going to invite her in or if he expected her to conduct the interview from the hallway.

She made herself relax. The drive from the newsroom hadn't done much to improve her mood. She was still seething over her demotion. But this meeting wouldn't go well if she projected that anger on to her interview subject.

Sharon found a smile and strode forward, hand extended. The captain met her halfway and wrapped his long, blunt fingers around hers. His touch was firm and warm.

She tilted her head to meet his eyes. He was at least seven inches taller than her five-foot-five. "I'm Sharon MacCabe. Thank you for allowing me to interview you."

"You're welcome. Have a seat."

Matthew's deep, dark voice was even more compelling in person than it had been during their brief phone conversation. She watched him return to the large, brown executive seat behind his desk. He waited for her to sit before folding his lean body onto the chair. She was curious about the wariness in his eyes.

Sharon crossed her legs, pulling her reporter's notebook and mini-recorder from her bag. "Would you mind if I taped this interview?"

"No, go ahead."

She turned on the recorder, then found a blank page for her notes. "Why would someone born and raised in a big city like Pittsburgh decide to move to a much smaller one like Charleston, West Virginia?"

Matthew leaned back in his chair, propping his elbows on its armrests. "I was ready for a change."

It took a moment for Sharon to realize he wasn't going to elaborate. "What kind of change?"

Matthew paused as though considering her question— or maybe his answer. "The usual. A new place to call home and the challenges of a new job."

"This is your second week on the job. What challenges have you faced so far?" Sharon's hand sped across the page, transcribing his answers even as she continued to ask questions.

"Nothing I can't handle."

The captain's reticence to be interviewed fueled her curiosity. She was writing a harmless feature. To what could he possibly object? She'd lobbed softballs at him—as they said in the newspaper business—but he refused to relax. She switched her attention from her notepad to her interview subject.

"I'm sure you're up to these challenges, Captain, but could you give us examples of them?"

Matthew again appeared to weigh his response. "Re-creating a fire scene is always challenging."

"In addition to being the station's captain, you're also the lead fire investigator. How will the dual roles influence the station's fire inspection procedures?"

"I won't discuss that until we've completely reviewed those procedures."

The interview wasn't going well. Sharon smothered a sigh and went back to the basics: age, rank, and hobbies. How did he like the Mountain State? What tourist attractions had he seen so far? What was he looking forward to experiencing next? With each question, Matthew's answers became more relaxed.

Sharon was pleased with the interview's improvement as her pen flew across the notepad. "What was your job with the Pittsburgh fire department?"

"I was a firefighter."

She glanced up. "A lieutenant?"

"No, a firefighter."

"How did you jump from being a firefighter to station captain and lead investigator?"

Indignation flared in Matthew's midnight eyes. "I had the skills the fire chief and assistant chief were looking for."

"What are those skills?"

Matthew heard the incredulity in the reporter's

voice. He also sensed her anger. He didn't know why she was upset; he was the one on the hot seat.

He hadn't wanted to be featured in the *Charleston Times*. However, his new boss, Assistant Chief of Administration Brad Naismith, and Fire Chief Larry Miller insisted the story would help improve the department's image in the community. Deciding to save his energy for more worthy battles, Matthew had agreed to the interview.

The little reporter appeared harmless with her guileless ebony eyes. But he'd learned from bitter experience the press was capable of twisting answers to seemingly innocent questions.

Sharon pushed strands of her thick, dark hair behind her shoulder. She repeated her question. Her soft, Southern accent reminded him of warm summer nights. "What are those skills?"

"I have twelve years of experience as a firefighter."

She arched a winged eyebrow. "Do you have any experience running a station?"

"Ms. MacCabe, I don't have to give you my résumé. I've already earned my job."

"I realize that. But the community has a right to know their fire station captain's qualifications."

Matthew wasn't going to play the public's-right-to-know game. The press had a wicked winning streak compared to both the interview subject and the public whose interest they professed to protect.

He stood. "Chief Miller and Assistant Chief Naismith can vouch for my qualifications. Any other questions?"

The pint-sized reporter rose too. The modest cream dress shifted over her slender figure as she stepped closer to his desk. "Just one. Why are you so defensive?"

He couldn't believe her audacity. "This was supposed to be a personality story, not an interrogation."

Her eyes sparked with anger and vivid color dusted her cheekbones. "I wasn't interrogating you. I was asking simple questions."

"I'm sure that's what Woodward and Bernstein said before they brought down Nixon's presidency." He crossed his arms. "Not everyone you meet has a criminal intent."

The reporter's sharp intake of breath let him know he'd hit his target. "I'm not out to get you. I'm just doing my job."

"What is your job, Ms. MacCabe? I thought reporters were supposed to cover the news, not pass judgment."

She stepped back as though he'd struck her. He held her wide-eyed gaze, refusing to regret his words.

Sharon turned from him to lift her oversized purse from the floor. She pulled the strap over her shoulder. "Thank you for your time." She turned, back straight and head high. Long strides carried her from his office.

Matthew's temper chilled with the realization he'd just crossed the media. In a normal situation, he would welcome the attention of an intelligent, attractive woman. But, circumstances as they were, this woman's interest could burn him.

Sharon paused in a corner of the station lobby, shaking with fury. She skimmed her notes. She had pages of inane questions and answers. They were enough for a surface piece that would entertain her readers, but they didn't delve far enough to satisfy her.

She glanced down the hall toward the captain's office. There was a lot more to Matthew Payton, but she wouldn't find out from him.

She stuffed her reporter's notebook into her bag and wove her way past groups of people entering and exiting the government building. Beyond the glass doors of the side entrance, she saw Li Mai Wong, Brad's administrative assistant, sharing a smoke break with coworkers.

Sharon pushed through the revolving doors and approached the tall, slender woman. She ignored the odor of cigarettes that carried on the late spring breeze.

"Hi, Li Mai. Do you have a moment?"

"Sure." Li Mai drove her cigarette into a standing ashtray. "How'd the interview go?"

"Fine, thanks. But it needs some background." Sharon led her companion to a quieter section of the break area. She leaned against the side of the building, trying to appear more casual than she felt. "What can you tell me about your new captain?"

"He's very nice. He doesn't talk much, though."

"Is he a snob?"

"No, just quiet. He doesn't talk much about himself. But he does ask a lot of questions."

Sharon pounced. "What kind of questions?" *Questions about how to do his job, maybe?*

"He wants to learn about the department. Administrative details so he knows how we do things here."

Sharon nodded. Those were reasonable questions for a new manager. She searched her mind for a way to dig deeper into what the other woman knew about the recent addition to the Charleston Fire Department. Administrative assistants were a great source of information, if you knew the right questions to ask.

She tried a chummy tone. "Matt told me Brad and Chief Miller interviewed him. Did Brad tell you how many candidates they met with?"

"They talked to a lot of people. Several of them were from other states." Li Mai brushed a restless hand over the hips of her wide-legged black pants. The matching jacket hung open over a white shell.

"What was it about Matt that impressed them the most?"

The other woman glanced away. *Bingo.*

Sharon gave her a persuasive smile. "What?"

Li Mai combed her fingers through her short, black hair. The straight locks swung above her narrow shoulders. "I don't know if I should say anything about this."

Sharon held her hand over her heart. "I promise not to tell a soul."

Li Mai looked around, making sure no one was near enough to overhear. "Off the record?" She waited for Sharon's nod. "The assistant chief said Matt's father is a friend of Mayor West."

Sharon's smile froze. "Really?" Another person who was sneaking up the career ladder on cronyism rather than merit. Two in one day.

"Yes. But you have to promise not to tell anyone."

Sharon stood away from the building. "You can trust me, Li Mai. I won't tell anyone."

The fire department's meetings took place promptly at four o'clock in a community center room that looked and smelled like a classroom. Every time Sharon walked through its doors, she had flashbacks of her elementary school.

As she strode to the front of the room, she surveyed her sparse surroundings. Rows of wooden chairs made the space look even smaller. And Sharon knew they never had as many attendees as the number of seats implied.

She took her customary spot in the front and selected a pretzel rod from her bag to quiet her growling stomach before the meeting. As she bit into the snack,

she brooded over her horrible day and her options for
salvaging her career. Unfortunately, Charleston didn't
offer a lot of choices, and she'd rather not leave her
hometown.

There were several suburban weeklies, but applying
for a job with one of those companies would be a step
backward after working for a metropolitan daily. The
Charleston Gazette and the *Charleston Daily Mail* were the
capital city's other daily newspapers. She'd look into
opportunities there.

Sharon finished her pretzel and stood to dust crumbs
from the skirt of her cream dress. Minutes later, the fire
officials filed into the room.

The department served the sixty thousand residents
who lived in the thirty-three square miles covering
Charleston's hills, and the valleys the Kanawha and Elk
rivers created.

Having covered the department for six months,
Sharon had made the acquaintance of the fire chief, the
two assistant chiefs, and the eleven station captains. The
twelve men and two women took seats behind a row of
tables that had been pushed together. Nameplates were
already in place. Matthew's was shiny and new.

And directly in front of her.

In the hours before this meeting, Sharon had mentally replayed that morning's interview with Matthew.
When she'd put herself in the captain's shoes, she'd realized he'd had cause to be defensive. Her softball
questions for the puff piece had turned aggressive
when she'd asked about his professional background.

Sharon tried a conciliatory smile when she caught
Matthew's eyes. His expression remained somber. *Ouch.*
She obviously had a long way to go before she could
gain the captain's forgiveness. She switched her attention to her notepad.

Under Chief Miller's direction, the meeting moved quickly through the agenda. Sharon took exact quotes when she could and paraphrased when she wasn't able to keep up with the dialogue. This story would be the curtain call on her fire department assignment. She'd make it as thorough and informative as possible. The senator's nephew would have a hard time following in her footsteps.

When the meeting's momentum slowed, she flexed her writing hand and lifted her head. Matthew's midnight gaze snagged her own. There was suspicion in his eyes, as though he was trying to decide whether she was an ally or an enemy. Sharon fought a disquieted feeling as she held his gaze.

She'd already acknowledged that, during the interview, she had projected on to him her anger at being taken off her news beat. She'd been wrong to do that, and she would apologize. However, her behavior shouldn't label her public enemy number one.

Assistant Fire Chief Brad Naismith's voice broke her train of thought. "An electrical malfunction caused Tuesday's greeting-card store fire."

Sharon wasn't a fire expert by any means. But, based on her research, the event she'd witnessed earlier in the week seemed to move too quickly for an accidental blaze.

She glanced at Matthew and saw his questioning frown. Brad's ruling appeared to surprise him also.

The meeting adjourned less than an hour later. As Sharon stuffed her notepad into her large bag, she saw Matthew approach Brad. She slowed her movements to catch snatches of their conversation.

Matthew's warm baritone hailed Brad. "What information did you collect from Tuesday's fire?"

Brad's rural West Virginia roots were apparent in his voice. "The usual. Heat readings, photos, samples. Why?"

Sharon retrieved her notepad. With her back to the two men, she pretended to review her notes as an excuse to linger while they spoke.

Matthew's tone was casual. "The fire didn't have the characteristics of an accidental burn. I'd be curious to take a look at that information."

Sharon mentally patted herself on the back. It was satisfying to know her suspicions of the fire coincided with those of an expert. She'd spent a lot of hours reading about fires and fire investigations—for a beat that was no longer hers.

Brad sounded irritated and defensive. "The case is closed. My ruling is final."

"I'm not only the station's captain, I'm also the lead fire investigator. How do you suggest we work out our roles for the future?"

Sharon was impressed that Matthew was asserting his position in the station. Maybe the mayor's pet intended to take his responsibilities seriously. She crammed her notebook back into her purse and prepared to leave. She wanted information about the fire, but she wasn't interested in eavesdropping on a power play between the two men. She began working her way past the groups of friends and neighbors still congregating around the room.

Sharon was now in a hurry to return to the newsroom to file her story before dinner. The pretzel rod hadn't satisfied her hunger. Several times during the meeting, her empty stomach had spoken up.

Matthew saw Sharon leave the room and hurried after her. He caught up with the reporter as she crossed the parking lot. He called her name and she turned, her thick, wavy hair swinging behind her.

He jogged toward her, stopping an arm's-length away. "Hear anything interesting?"

The flicker of embarrassment that tightened her delicate features confirmed Matthew's suspicion she'd been eavesdropping on his discussion with Brad. He was still trusting enough to be disappointed that this reporter was like all the others.

Sharon angled her head to the right. "It was a good meeting."

"You know what I'm talking about. Are you going to give your readers the inside scoop on my conversation with Naismith?"

Indignation snapped her brows together. "I'm a reporter, not a gossip columnist."

"That's not an answer."

"I'm not going to report on your conversation with Brad."

A reporter shying from the scandal of intra-departmental discord? Not likely. He could even see the headline: SPARKS FLY IN FIRE DEPARTMENT.

Matthew crossed his arms. "I don't believe you."

"I can't help that."

He watched her tug her purse strap more securely onto her narrow shoulder. He wondered what she could possibly need to haul around in that misnamed suitcase.

Sharon folded her arms. "Off the record. Did Brad agree to your reviewing the information from the fire?"

Matthew hesitated. "He doesn't want to revisit cases he's already closed. We'll start the new investigation procedures going forward."

Sharon smiled, her eyes twinkling at him. "That's a diplomatic answer. I thought the fire was suspicious as well. It moved so quickly."

Reluctant admiration diffused most of his irritation. "That's true. How did you know that?"

"I wanted to know as much as I could about the fire department since it was my beat." She checked her wristwatch. Its thick, black plastic band looked awkward on her delicate wrist.

Matthew checked his own watch. It was almost six o'clock. "It's getting late. I don't want to keep you from dinner."

She adjusted her purse strap again. "I have to stop by the newsroom to file this story."

"You may want to eat first. Keep your energy up for the free and responsible press."

Sharon frowned. "What do you have against reporters?"

His irritation reawakened, the walls going back up. "You have your job to do, and I have mine. I just want to make sure your job doesn't make mine harder."

"You have trust issues, Captain. Have you been burned by the media in the past?"

Matthew froze, furious with himself for saying as much as he had. More than was safe. Sharon's expression held concern rather than curiosity. She searched his eyes as though looking for a door into him. He turned away before she could find it. He couldn't take the chance of a reporter learning anything about his past.

Chapter 2

Sunday morning, Sharon surfaced from sleep at eight o'clock. Toni Braxton's "Breathe Again" played softly on her radio alarm. Before she could convince herself otherwise, she rolled out of bed to go for a run. She was meeting her mother for brunch in a few hours.

Still tired, instinct helped Sharon find her wall-to-wall closet while Toni Braxton continued to hum in her brain. She exchanged her purple cotton nightgown for black running pants, an electric-blue jersey, white socks, and purple-on-white running shoes.

Sharon was more awake after brushing her teeth and splashing water on her face. She walked to her apartment's front door, collecting her Walkman, cell phone, and keys as she passed her hall table. She locked the door behind her, then jogged down the steps, tugging on her headphones and turning up the volume on the oldies music station. She clipped her cell phone to her waistband.

Sharon settled into a brisk pace while Gloria Gaynor insisted she would survive. Her route led her past her neighborhood's Victorian-style homes. Her thoughts took her back to Friday.

Since her editor's announcement he was taking her beat from her, Sharon had been wondering how to deal with the demotion. Her previous articles spoke for her. She was a strong writer with solid reporting instincts. And she'd achieved her success through her own hard work. She didn't have anything more to prove.

Sharon turned onto a narrow, tree-lined sidewalk that paralleled the Kanawha River. In the summer, the Kanawha hosted Charleston's Sternwheel Regatta, a festival that drew people from all over West Virginia and neighboring states. But on this mid-April morning, the river was a silent jogging companion. Distant hills formed a backdrop for the golden-domed state capital on the Kanawha's opposite bank. Sharon picked up her pace as Patti LaBelle sang about her new attitude.

This was Sharon's favorite part of the day. A sleepy silence coated the morning. Few cars roamed the streets. The community was just beginning to stir. Her community. She was a native West Virginian. She'd only left the state briefly, and even then she hadn't gone far. Just three hours to Columbus to attend The Ohio State University. Those four years were enough to confirm West Virginia—specifically Charleston—was home. She was suited to the easy pace of the big, little city. And she'd missed her mountains.

With the back of her hand, Sharon wiped sweat from her upper lip. A glance at her chronometer confirmed she'd completed the first half of her run. Thirty minutes. Three miles. She turned to begin the journey home while Taylor Dayne sang "Tell It To My Heart."

Another thirty minutes later, Sharon let herself back into her apartment. She was dripping with sweat and flushed with the success of a good run. She deposited her Walkman and cell phone on the hall table, and strode across her great room to her kitchen.

Sharon snagged a bottle of water from the refrigerator and chugged a third of the liquid. Twisting the cap back onto the bottle, she returned to the great room and used the remote control to tune the television to the Cable News Network.

As the pretty, plastic blonde recapped the top news stories around the world, Sharon pulled off her running shoes and socks, and eased into stretches. The newscaster touched on trouble in the Middle East, famine in Africa, floods in Asia, and corruption in Washington, D.C.

Completing her cooldown, Sharon pushed herself off the floor, turned off the TV and stripped her way to the shower.

About an hour later, dressed in hot-pink jeans and a mint-green jersey, Sharon was ready to meet her mother for brunch. She'd told her parent about her demotion, and Helen had been comfortingly outraged. She suspected her mother had suggested Sunday brunch in an effort to cheer her. She'd put on a happy face for Helen's sake, but the only thing that would lift her spirits was getting her beat back.

CNN was on the television when Sharon arrived at her mother's house. Helen had the volume up so high Sharon could hear it from the other side of the front door. After greeting her mother, Sharon walked to the coffee table. She used the remote to lower the TV's volume to more civilized decibels.

"Mom, I'm sure the neighbors appreciate your efforts to keep them informed, but they'd probably prefer to choose their own news station."

"You know I can't stay still, but I need to know what's going on even as I move around the house." Helen's ebony eyes were dark with maternal concern. "How are you?"

Sharon forced a smile. "I'll be fine, Mom."

Helen's frown didn't ease. "How about an egg-white omelet, turkey bacon, and wheat toast?"

"That sounds great." Sharon dropped her smile. She should have known the false expression wouldn't work with Helen. Her mother always knew how she was feeling. So why did Helen even bother to ask?

She followed her mother into the kitchen. Helen looked casually elegant in khaki pants and a ruby-red jersey. Matching red tennis shoes were a nice touch.

Despite her short stature, Sharon's mother rarely wore heels. Sharon didn't think Helen, who was a couple of inches shorter than she, needed the leverage. Her larger-than-life personality made up for her below-average height.

Helen took eggs, cheese, an onion, and a green pepper from the refrigerator. "So what are you going to do about your job?"

Sharon joined her mother at the kitchen counter and started chopping half of the onion. "I've been going in circles in my mind all weekend. The long and the short of it is, I have two choices: stay with the *Times* or go to another paper."

Helen separated the egg whites into a bowl. "What are the pros and cons?"

"On the pro side of staying with the paper, the salary is good. Not great, but good. So are the benefits. And I'm comfortable there."

"And the cons?" Helen liberally sprinkled spices into the bowl of eggs.

"There's only one. My assignment. Features are fine,

but you know I've always wanted to do investigative reporting."

"What about the other daily papers?"

Sharon sliced the green pepper, letting the cuts fall into the same bowl with the onions. "I wouldn't mind switching sides, but staff turnover at the newspapers is slow. I'd probably be ready for retirement before a spot opened up."

Helen dumped the chopped onions and sliced peppers into the bowl of egg whites. "It sounds like you may have to leave Charleston."

She heard regret in her mother's voice and, considering how deep her roots dug into the state's capital, leaving was a massive con on Sharon's list. "This is my home."

"I'm not anxious for you to go, either. But you shouldn't give up your dream just because you're comfortable." Helen poured the omelet mix into the heated frying pan.

"It doesn't seem fair that I should get chased out of the paper by someone far less qualified than me."

"No, it doesn't." Helen turned on the coffeemaker. "Have you met Lucas Stanton?"

Sharon popped slices of wheat bread into the toaster and pulled the turkey bacon from the fridge. "No, but Allyson, the political reporter, spoke to him briefly after one of his uncle's press conferences. She said he introduced himself as Senator Stanton's nephew, as though that was his name."

That was not a good sign. Obviously, the young Stanton intended to milk his family connections for all they were worth. And, at the *Times*, they appeared to be worth a lot.

"If the polls are any indication, he may need to change his name after the election."

Sharon tended to the frying bacon strips. "The special-interest money scandal is giving the senator's image a real beating."

"But it's early still."

Sharon flipped the bacon. "True, but this is shaping up to be the hardest campaign he's faced in his three terms."

"I've never liked that man. His solution for the state's budget deficit is to always cut funding for senior programs." Her sixty-two-years-young mother scowled.

"He cuts a lot of programs that support communities too. With the primaries in a couple of weeks, your group must be pretty busy."

After her husband, Sharon's father, had died five years earlier, Helen had joined a civic action committee that championed voter education.

"We've scheduled several registration drives. We could be registering people who'll reelect Stanton, but I can't worry about that. Our objective is to provide unbiased information so voters can make informed choices."

Sharon collected the bread from the toaster. "I wouldn't be sorry to see him voted out, though."

Her mother collected plates. "Neither would I. Then you'd get your beat back."

"And possibly lose it to another political favor." Sharon shook her head as she poured the coffee. "I'd rather get it back because my boss recognized my abilities and not because Aldridge's political flavor-of-the-month lost the election."

After brunch, they scanned the movie section of the Sunday *Times*. They settled on an action-adventure film, starring Wesley Snipes. Sharon drove them to the

Park Place Stadium Cinemas near the Town Center shopping mall in downtown Charleston.

They parked in the crowded lot and joined the long line in the lobby to purchase their tickets. As they searched the main area for their theater, a familiar baritone called Sharon's name.

She turned to see Matthew approaching her. His long legs, covered in tan Dockers, carried him with an athletic ease Sharon found mesmerizing.

He stopped in front of her, breaking the spell and prompting Sharon to wonder why he'd sought her rather than avoiding the encounter. She hadn't forgotten the accusations they'd made to each other after the fire department meeting. Had he?

"I'm surprised you're still speaking to me, Matt. We didn't part on the best of terms Friday."

Amusement stroked dimples into his cheeks. "Haven't you heard you should keep your friends close and your enemies closer?"

Sharon grinned. Score one for the dour captain. Maybe the man did have a sense of humor.

She put an arm around Helen. "I'd like you to meet my mom, Helen Davies MacCabe. Mom, this is Matthew Payton, the new captain of Fire Station Eleven."

Matthew's smile softened his features, making him look warmer, more approachable. Not like the man she'd interviewed Friday morning.

"I can see the resemblance." He extended his hand. The gesture called attention to his broad shoulders covered in a dark blue jersey.

Helen's gaze was curious as she accepted his hand. "Are you going to see the new Wesley Snipes movie too?"

"Yes, I am." Matthew looked surprised.

"Why don't you join us? There's no fun in going to

the movies by yourself. Don't you agree, Ronnie?" Helen asked, using Sharon's childhood nickname.

Sharon was amazed. She'd told her mother about her two uncomfortable encounters with the captain. Why would Helen then invite Matthew to join them?

Her gaze bounced from Helen's patient stare to Matthew's guarded look and back. She narrowed her eyes on her mother's guileless expression, certain she could hear Helen's thoughts. Add single, attractive man to marrying-age daughter. The sound of wedding bells and grandbabies was nearly deafening.

Sharon masked her resignation with a smile. "You're welcome to join us, but we'd better get moving if we're going to get popcorn."

She led the way to the concession stand. In her peripheral vision, she saw Matthew step aside so Helen could precede him. Her mother got in line to wait for the theater doors to open. But Matthew followed Sharon to the counter and changed her order.

"Make that three popcorns. The two small she ordered plus one large." He pulled his wallet from his front pants pocket.

"I can buy popcorn for my mother and myself. You can get your own."

"When I'm out with a lady—or two—I prefer to pay."

It was tempting to remind him they were in the twenty-first century. "This isn't a date."

"That doesn't matter." Matthew shrugged, a smooth movement of muscles. "Besides, if you change the order again, you're going to confuse the cashier."

Sharon glanced over her shoulder and caught her mother's attention. With a quirk of her brow, she tried to convey that Helen owed her an apology for inviting this escort. Her mother smiled without a hint of guilt.

Sharon glanced at Matthew. "Thank you."

He nodded in response.

The high school boy working the concession counter handed over their orders and gave Matthew his change. They joined Helen, who'd held their spot in the lengthening movie line. The trio munched popcorn in companionable silence. Helen and Matthew seemed to be people watching. Standing between them, Sharon was lost in thought.

She peeked at Matthew. Would this be a good time to apologize for her behavior Friday? She knew she'd taken him off guard by interrogating him as though he were a hostile witness rather than interviewing him for the agreed-upon personality profile. Couple that with his already low opinion of reporters and their relationship couldn't get any worse.

Maybe that's why Helen had invited Matthew to join them. She wanted to give Sharon the opportunity to express her regret in a nonbusiness setting. But, as she turned to Matthew, the line began to move and the moment was lost.

When he looked at her questioningly, she shook her head, exercising great self-control by not giving his long, well-toned body the once-over it screamed for. Their previous clashes hadn't prevented her from appreciating Matthew's physical fitness.

His appeal was even more pronounced in casual clothes. He'd captured her attention—against her will. How could she be attracted to someone who used political connections instead of ability to advance his career? There had to be more to a person than physical appearance. She needed depth.

The trio settled in to enjoy the movie. The plot was good although some of the dialogue was stiff. As usual, Wesley Snipes did a great job with his role. Unfortunately, even Wesley's talent couldn't help Sharon tune out Matthew's presence. He didn't speak. He didn't even fidget. But she felt him there beside her, making it hard to concentrate on Wesley's struggle to survive.

As the end credits rolled, the audience rose to leave. Matthew stepped out of their row and stood aside to let Sharon and Helen precede him out of the theater.

Helen stopped on the sidewalk in front of the building. "Does anyone have room for dessert?"

Sharon smiled at the reference to her mother's sweet tooth. "I do."

Helen looked at their companion. "You'll join us, of course."

Sharon turned toward Matthew, hoping he would be polite when declining her mother's gracious order.

The fire captain glanced at her before answering. "I'd like that."

Surprise wiped Sharon's mind clean. What was he thinking? She couldn't read his expression. Was he lonely? That made sense. He was new to Charleston and didn't know anyone.

Guilt shamed her. First her hostility toward him during the feature interview. Now she was trying to avoid him when all he sought was a few hours of companionship. She wasn't assigned to the fire department anymore, so there wouldn't be a conflict of interest in socializing with him.

Sharon followed Helen and Matthew to the Town Center shopping mall, hoping her truce with the fire captain would extend to Cinnabons and soft drinks.

Matthew adjusted his stride to keep pace with Helen as they walked the few blocks to the Town Center. Even as he listened to her description of the rebirth of Charleston's downtown, he was conscious of her daughter close behind them. Just as he'd been aware of Sharon beside him in the dark theater.

Helen swept an arm, encompassing the blocks around them. "All of this used to be empty buildings. Businesses had deserted the downtown area and moved to the suburbs."

Looking at the trees and red-brick pedestrian walkways, it was hard for Matthew to see the area as Helen was describing it, abandoned and neglected.

Sharon's voice carried over his shoulder as she followed them. "But the city council revitalized the area, and now businesses are coming back."

The two women led the way up the escalator to the mall's International Food Court. As the escalator rose, Matthew watched water rush three stories down a man-made fall to pool in the lobby's fountain.

The sweet aroma of cinnamon rolls found him before they found Cinnabon. Sharon scolded him with a look as he reached for his wallet. He gave the international sign for surrender and allowed her to go ahead of him. Was this how she asserted her financial independence with her boyfriend as well? *Poor guy.*

The cashier served mother and daughter their iced teas and cinnamon rolls. As he waited for his order, Matthew watched the women carry their trays to a table for three. Within minutes, he joined them, carrying a tray with two large cinnamon buns and a jumbo cola.

He paused when they stared at his food with identical expressions of amazement. Matthew shrugged, hiding his embarrassment as he took the remaining seat. "I'm hungry."

Sharon's teasing smile was her only response. Her ebony eyes danced with laughter.

Helen's question drew his attention reluctantly from her daughter. "What do you do to stay in such excellent shape?"

Matthew stilled, a cinnamon roll halfway to his mouth. "I jog and lift weights."

Was his face heating with a blush? He didn't think it was his imagination, based on the grin Sharon tried but failed to hide behind her iced tea.

Helen cut into one of the sticky buns. "Ronnie jogs and lifts weights too."

Matthew looked at the reporter. "I can tell."

Sharon's eyes shot upward to meet his. He smiled as he noticed the color rising up her neck. *Payback.* Satisfied, he returned his attention to his pastry.

Helen continued, apparently unaware of the silent exchange. "But young people still have to watch what they eat. They won't be young forever. How old are you, Matt?"

He swallowed a bite of the pastry. "I'll be thirty-three July fifteenth."

In Helen, Matthew could see where Sharon got her talent for questioning. But the older woman didn't have her daughter's edge.

Sharon appeared to have distanced herself from the conversation. Perhaps she was bored. After all, they'd done a lot of these getting-to-know-you questions during the feature interview. He tried not to think about the article, which would run in Monday's paper.

Helen placed her iced tea on the table. "Do you have any family nearby?"

"They're in Pittsburgh." Matthew forked up another bite of the bun, trying to ignore the tension spreading from his stomach.

Much to his relief, Sharon changed the subject. "During the meeting, Brad mentioned fire safety programs for the schools. Have those been scheduled?"

He swallowed soda, chasing the lump from his throat. "The schedule isn't final yet. Li Mai still has a few schools to contact. You can call her Monday for an update."

Sharon ate another bite of her cinnamon bun. "Who's going to do the presentations?"

"I will."

Her eyes widened. "You? I'm surprised Brad assigned you to do school presentations."

Matthew's back stiffened at the incredulity in Sharon's tone. "It's a good way for me to get positive exposure in the community. That's the reasoning they used to convince me to let you interview me."

Sharon's gaze dropped. If he didn't know better, he'd think their first meeting troubled the reporter.

She used a Cinnabon napkin to wipe the corners of her mouth. "I'd imagine you'd be too busy to do the programs."

That had been his argument as well. He wasn't going to admit that to the media, though. It was a headline he didn't need. "I'm looking forward to them. It's important for kids to know basic fire safety measures."

Helen sipped her iced tea. "That's true. And having the captain teach them about safety emphasizes its importance."

He smiled. "That's what they told me."

Sharon leaned back in her chair. "Did they talk you into doing the presentations?"

Matthew cursed himself for his off-the-cuff remark. He'd thought he'd learned the hard way not to make comments like that in front of reporters. "I wanted to do the presentations."

Thankfully, she dropped the issue. They talked about Charleston for a while before leaving the mall.

Sharon listened to Helen and Matthew's chatter, but her mind wouldn't move beyond the pending safety presentations. Why would the assistant chief sign off on their new station captain spending so much time in the community rather than doing inspections? Didn't Brad trust Matthew with compliance work?

Matthew strolled between Sharon and her mother. "Thank you for a nice afternoon, ladies. I've never had such a good time in a mall."

Helen looked up at him. "It was nice spending time with you, Matt."

They stopped beside Sharon's little yellow Honda Civic. She deactivated the car alarm, which unlocked the doors. With a farewell smile aimed at Matthew, Helen slid onto the passenger seat. Sharon turned back to him, unsure of what to say.

He filled the pause. "Your mother's very nice."

"Yes, she is." Sharon glanced away before meeting his eyes again. "Matt, I want to apologize for my behavior Friday. I know I came across like Johnnie Cochran for a simple personality feature, and that was unnecessary. I'm sorry."

The surprise in Matthew's eyes told her he hadn't expected her apology. She wondered about the people he knew that he wouldn't expect someone to admit when they were wrong.

He cleared his throat. "I'm sorry for my reaction too."

"No apology necessary." Sharon extended her hand and was pleased when his warm, strong grip closed over hers.

He gave her a tantalizing smile. "Enjoy the rest of your weekend." With a wave of his hand, he walked away.

Sharon stood beside her car, watching him cross the parking lot toward a Toyota Camry. She walked to her driver's door and slid into the car.

She inserted the key into the ignition. However,

instead of starting the engine, she sat staring at the Park Place Stadium Cinema. "Why did you invite him?"

"Are you telling me you didn't have a good time?"

She met her mother's gaze. "Please don't try to put me on the defensive. Why did you invite him?"

Helen sighed with more drama than suffering. "I was just welcoming a new neighbor."

"You didn't think I'd be a bit uncomfortable? I told you we had two unpleasant meetings."

"And you had plenty of opportunities to apologize."

Sharon returned to her view of the theater. The building would probably be more receptive to her opinion than her mother. "I did apologize."

"I'm glad. He's a very nice young man, and he seemed to enjoy our company."

Sharon recalled the relieved expression on Matthew's face when she'd saved him from Helen's questions about his family. Why didn't he want to talk about his relatives? Didn't he want to brag about his father's friendship with Charleston's mayor? Or had Mayor West asked him not to?

"A nice young man with nice connections."

"What? I didn't hear you."

"Nothing." Sharon started the car, hoping to distract Helen. She hadn't told her mother about Matthew's father and the mayor. She checked behind her before pulling out.

"He's not hard to look at, either." Helen's voice bounced with humor.

Sharon could agree with that. It was another thing that bothered her about the captain. He had looks *and* connections. Sometimes the universe just didn't play fairly. "Looks aren't everything, Mom. And not everyone is what they appear to be."

Chapter 3

Monday afternoon, Sharon returned to the newsroom seething over her interview with the director of the Senior Housing Authority. She pitched her purse into her desk drawer and snatched her phone to check messages. Still fuming, Sharon jabbed commands into her computer.

Allyson breezed into her cubicle, with the ever-present cup of coffee in her hand. "How'd the interview with Dickhead Donovan go?"

Sharon gave her friend a baleful stare.

"That bad?" The political reporter sipped her coffee.

Sharon's temper rose. "I asked him about the rumors of staff cuts, and do you know what he said to me?"

"Not a clue."

Sharon did a credible impersonation of Roger Donovan's nasal voice. "'Why don't you just make up the news, Ms. MacCabe? You reporters are so good at that.'"

Allyson's jaw dropped. "What did you say?"

"I told him I took my job at least as seriously as he took his. Therefore, I never have and never will make up the news."

"Good for you." Allyson glanced at Sharon's computer screen. "Why don't you take a mini coffee-break? Give yourself a chance to cool down before you work on that story."

After imparting that sage advice, the political reporter glided away. Sharon sighed a deep, calming breath. She rose to get the recommended cup of coffee, but Lucas Stanton was waiting outside her cubicle.

They'd been introduced during the morning staff meeting. Tall, lean, and blond, he had the stereotypical good looks of the privileged and powerful. Sharon didn't know how much of her cynical reaction to him had to do with his stealing her beat.

Lucas stepped toward her. "I heard what you told Allyson."

He'd eavesdropped on her conversation and was telling her about it. Sharon clenched her jaw. He was not making a positive impression on her. At least when she eavesdropped, she didn't tell the person about it—unless he cornered her in a parking lot after a fire department meeting.

She strained for an even tone. "What can I do for you?"

Lucas hesitated, his dark green eyes scanning hers. "Some reporters have made up stories."

Sharon almost stuttered with outrage. "In rare instances, unscrupulous people have fabricated stories. But the majority of reporters would never even consider doing that. Our community's trust is too important."

He arched a golden brow. "So you're saying you've never been tempted to embellish a story?"

"That's exactly what I'm saying. What about you?"

"Reporters have lied about my uncle. They're saying he's involved in this pay-to-play scandal."

Her friendship with Allyson triggered a fierce, personal

reaction to the newcomer's charge. "They've reported evidence linking him to the scandal. Your uncle hasn't explained those links."

The young man's voice sharpened. "So you think the press has the right to try an innocent man in the papers?"

"We have the responsibility to present the facts. If he has any facts to dispute the charges against him, we'll present those too."

Lucas sneered. "No, you won't. Because that won't be a sensational enough story."

"If you have such a poor impression of the media, why are you here?"

His smile was smug. "To provide balance."

Sharon withheld her caustic disbelief and didn't comment on his not answering whether he would embellish the facts. It seemed less torturous to change the subject. "The fire department is scheduling school safety presentations. Are you going to cover them?"

"No, you can handle those."

Lucas's tone and words stirred her resentment. She was a six-year veteran. He was an inexperienced political appointee. He may have the news beat while she'd been relegated to the catchall features, but she still considered him the junior reporter.

Sharon took another calming breath. "Before you make assignments, you should check whether Andre is going to cover the safety presentations."

The appointee frowned. "Who?"

"Andre Jamieson, the education reporter. You met him this morning." She moved past Lucas. "Since it's a school presentation, he may be covering it. I'll ask him."

Without waiting for Lucas's response, Sharon strode to Andre's cubicle. Her tension peeled away as the distance between her and the senator's nephew widened.

She stopped in the threshold of Andre's cubicle. "Excuse me, Dre." She interrupted, using her friend's nickname. "Are you covering the fire safety presentations at the schools?"

Andre typed a bit more before facing Sharon. The expression on his dark face was distracted, as though he was still in the story he was writing. "Hadn't heard of them."

"Would you mind if I covered them?"

Andre dragged his hand through his tight curls. "Did you check with the new guy?"

Sharon nodded. "He doesn't want them."

"Then go for it." He spun back to his computer, back into the story. "But I don't know how you find the time for extra stories."

Sharon smiled. "I can handle it. Thanks, Dre."

Delaying the recommended coffee, Sharon returned to her cubicle and called Li Mai for the presentation details, as Matthew had suggested.

The administrative assistant told her the first presentation would be at eleven o'clock on Wednesday at Fort Lee Elementary School. Sharon scribbled the information on her desk calendar.

"Let me put you through to Matt. He can give you more details."

Before Sharon could stop the other woman, a much deeper voice came on the line. "Matt Payton."

Sharon was chagrined to hear her voice emerge two octaves higher than normal. "Hi, Matt. It's Sharon Mac-Cabe. Li Mai said you could give me advance information about the fire safety presentations."

Caution entered Matthew's tone. "What would you like to know?"

Sharon was getting tired of the captain's media phobia. She flipped open her reporter's notebook and tucked the phone between her head and shoulder. "Are you doing the presentations alone?"

"No. Lieutenant Gary Dunleavy is going to join me."

"Oh, only the big names, huh?"

Sharon hoped the comment would lighten the conversation. She was rewarded with Matthew's chuckle, an intimate sound that clenched muscles in her stomach.

"Actually, I'm a little nervous." Matthew's tone was self-deprecating.

"Will this be your first public presentation?"

"No, but it's the first time I'll be addressing children."

She was more charmed than amused that elementary school students could intimidate a fire investigator. "Just pretend they're really short adults."

He laughed, and the muscles in her lower abdomen fluttered again. "What's your goal for the presentations?"

Matthew replaced his laughter with reluctance. "To teach young people about the dangers of fire."

She wrote quickly, splitting her attention between his answer and her next question. "What information will they learn during your presentation?"

"Who to call in case of a fire." His tone relaxed as he continued, as though his passion for his topic outweighed his caution with reporters. "What to do if they see a fire. I want them to know this information can save lives."

Matthew's voice seemed to tremble a bit on his last sentence. Sharon adjusted her shoulder to press the receiver closer to her ear. "What can children do to promote fire safety?"

"Tell their parents what they've learned. Help them remember to change the batteries in the smoke detector and recharge the fire extinguishers."

Matthew's voice was steadier now. Perhaps the phone connection had been distorted.

"This is great information, Matt. Thank you."

"You're welcome." He sounded surprised. "You'll be there?"

"Eleven o'clock on Wednesday."

"I'll see you then." He hung up.

Sharon recradled the phone and considered the different sides of Matthew Payton. He was hostile toward the press, but apprehensive around children. There must be a story there.

Matthew hung up the phone, wondering whether his admission to Sharon about being anxious over the school presentations would end up in the newspaper. He cursed silently. He had to remember to keep his guard up. Sharon kept making him forget he couldn't trust the press. A knock on his office door pushed those thoughts away.

His lieutenant, Gary Dunleavy, stood in the doorway. "Is this still a good time to meet?"

Matthew shook off his brooding and gestured for Gary to take one of the guest seats. He leaned back in his chair, contemplating his lieutenant's boyish features. "What was your reaction to Naismith's announcement Friday that the warehouse fire was accidental?"

Gary's eyes widened. The expression, coupled with his copious freckles, made him look like a startled Howdy Doody. Good. Matthew had intended to take Dunleavy by surprise.

The other man buried one hand in his explosion of red hair and scratched his scalp with nervous vigor. "Well, the assistant chief knows what he's doing."

Matthew tapped his pencil end to end against his desk. He spoke with careful deliberation. "I'm not questioning Naismith's abilities. I'm questioning the procedure."

"What do you mean?"

"Do you have a copy of the report?"

Gary shook his head. "Not yet."

"Do you know its status?"

Gary's brown eyes clouded with confusion. "No. I don't know who has it."

Matthew leaned forward. "Tuesday's fire took place in our station's community. Don't you think it's strange that Naismith pronounced it accidental before we saw the report?"

Gary frowned at Matthew's desk. "Well, maybe."

He regretted the lost expression on the younger man's face. But Matthew wanted a sense of Gary's regard for his position as station captain. "I have to be informed of these determinations in advance."

Gary nodded his understanding.

Still cautious of his second in command's loyalty, Matthew continued. "You've known Naismith a lot longer than I have. How do you think I should approach him about this?"

"You have to be straight with him. Even if he gets mad, you've got to talk to him, or he'll just continue to leave you out of the loop."

With Gary's response, a weight lifted off Matthew. He had his lieutenant's support. "Good."

But Gary gave him a puzzled look. "The assistant chief has never gone around his captains before. Why would he do it now?"

Perhaps Naismith had trouble accepting an outsider. Matthew kept that unfounded suspicion to himself. "We need a copy of the card-store fire's report."

"I'll ask Li Mai for it," Gary said referring to Naismith's administrative assistant.

Matthew nodded. "Great. But even with the report, I want to conduct my own investigation of the scene."

Gary's eyes widened again. "I don't know if that's a good idea, Captain."

Matthew felt his eyebrows knit. "Why not?"

The lieutenant's brown gaze flew around the room as though searching for hidden cameras. "Well, the assistant chief is a great guy. Really. But, he's also really, well, proud."

A new voice joined the conversation, coming to the younger man's rescue. "What Dunleavy's trying to say is Naismith's an arrogant asshole."

Matthew looked toward his office door and saw the speaker, Seth Gumble. Raymond Ford stood behind Seth. Both men were his most veteran firefighters.

Seth ambled forward, his lank brown hair falling over his blue eyes. He dropped into the spare visitor's chair. "But Dunleavy's too much of a Boy Scout to say it."

Raymond's thick shoulders quaked with silent laughter at Seth's comment. Matthew thought the man could pass for the older brother of Shaquille O'Neal, the professional basketball player.

Matthew looked at Gary. The younger man's freckles were even more prominent against his blush. His eyes crackled with irritation. "If giving the assistant chief respect makes me a Boy Scout, then give me a badge."

Matthew diffused the scene. "We need to investigate every fire that occurs in our station as a matter of procedure."

Raymond leaned against the wall beside Gary's chair. "Naismith's already called this one. We should let it go."

Matthew sensed political maneuvering behind that response. He didn't like it. "This isn't about stepping on toes. It's about making sure we made the right call."

Seth rested his right ankle on his left knee and folded his hands in his lap. "How 'bout making sure you keep your job."

Despite the amused smile on Seth's face, his answer produced a strong, negative reaction in Matthew. "If the fire wasn't accidental, we have an arsonist in our area."

Raymond crossed his arms. "What makes you so sure Naismith's wrong?"

"They have a point, Matt." Gary's eyes were troubled. "We don't know if the assistant chief is wrong, but it would embarrass him to have one of his captains double-check his work."

Matthew studied the three men who watched him with various levels of concern. He had a sudden flash of being on the outside of a very important circle. These coworkers knew each other and the assistant chief better than he knew any of them. It bothered him to think they might be giving an arsonist a free pass. But he'd have to trust his boss's judgment and ignore the little voice that claimed he was making a mistake.

"All right. Tuesday's fire investigation will remain closed." Matthew leveled a gaze at each of his subordinates. "But I'll handle the next one myself."

The bar was loud and crowded. That's why he'd picked it, Seth thought. He shoved his way through the mass of bodies, cutting through air heavy with cigarette smoke, booze fumes, country music, and cusses.

A decade and change ago, he would have gotten a charge out of the crush and the noise. Now, everything just pissed him off. Christ, he was getting old. That realization pissed him off even more.

He made it to the back and found Raymond hunched in a booth in a shadowed section of the room. Just like he'd told him.

Seth slid onto the bench seat on the other side of the table. "Can't back out, Ray."

The other man looked up at him, his expression anxious. "Payton isn't as useless as the Closer said he'd be."

Seth winced at the stupid nickname. He knew they couldn't use their contact's real identity, especially in public where they might be overheard. But he wished they'd come up with a code name that didn't sound like a Marvel comic book character.

"Doesn't mean he'll catch us."

Raymond's black eyes widened with incredulity. "You heard him. He's not going to rubber-stamp the fire investigation reports."

"We're professionals. We can cover our tracks. No one's connecting us to those fires."

Raymond held Seth's gaze. "I think we should end this."

"Too late." Seth enunciated as though speaking to the hard of hearing, which he believed he was. "Besides, we need the money. You forget you went bankrupt after your wife maxed your credit and left?"

The two men had bonded after their wives divorced them. Seth's wife had taken their two children and left him to find herself. Now, he was financially responsible for two households when he barely had anything left after paying expenses for one.

He was finding woman trouble and money problems were the only things he and Raymond had in common.

Raymond's long, black face looked stubborn. "I may be struggling, but at least I'm living honestly."

Seth should have followed his gut. He'd thought Raymond would be a good coconspirator, in part because he needed the money. And he looked trustworthy. No one would believe he'd be involved in criminal activities. But he had an honest face because he was basically an honest person. That's why he had so much trouble with his role in this scheme.

Seth slouched in the booth, resting an arm across the back of the seat. He ignored the stickiness of the wood. "You giving back the first payment?"

Raymond's gaze slid away from his. He ran a wide palm over his bald pate. "I can't. I've already used it to pay down my credit card bills."

Seth exhaled in relief. His partner was as caught up in this web as he was. If Raymond had been able to walk away from this pact, Seth would have had to continue on his own. He didn't think he could have done that.

Raymond turned back to Seth. "This is wrong."

Seth's irritation stirred. "We're not hurting anyone."

Drunken laughter from the table across the aisle yanked Seth's attention. Five young men were crowded in a booth. One member of the group was making rude noises, much to the brainless hilarity of his friends.

College students. Dumb asses. What were they doing getting drunk on a Monday night? Realization caught up with him. They must be on spring break. He looked around the bar again, this time with more scrutiny of the other patrons. They were mostly college students. Spring break explained the larger-than-usual crowd.

Raymond spoke again. "We have to call this off."

Seth considered his partner's near panic. He had to calm him down. If Raymond were released from his commitment, he might turn Seth in.

He kept his tone reasonable. "We're in too far. The Closer didn't pay for one fire. He paid for half the job. We quit, he's gonna send his people for his money."

The noise level at the other table rose to deafening volumes again when a pretty, little waitress approached the young men. Despite their beer-sodden brains—or, perhaps, because of them—members of the group

tried to win her approval with supposedly clever pickup
lines. Each attempt was more lame than the effort
before it.

Christ, had he ever been so stupid? Seth ran a tired
hand over his grizzled face. Probably.

When the waitress turned to their table to ask about
refills, he and Raymond just shook their heads. The
bottle of beer in front of each of them was still half full.

Raymond took a healthy swig. "We're going to get
caught."

Seth swallowed his beer. "No." How much more of
the other man's whining was he going to have to take?

"How do you know?"

"Only way we'll get caught is if one of us rats the
other out. And that won't happen, will it?"

Raymond finished his beer, left a tip on the table,
then told Seth good-bye. Seth waited a few minutes
after the other man had left before going to the back
of the bar and pulling out his cell phone. The Closer
picked up on the third ring.

Seth checked to make sure no one was standing too
close or paying too much attention to him. "He's crack-
ing. Don't know if he'll be reliable much longer."

The Closer's voice was cold. "He has to finish the job.
For both our sakes."

"Right." Seth ended the call, then pushed his way
through the mob of bodies to the bar's front door.

The Closer had stated they were both dependent on
Raymond to finish the job. But Seth would bet money
the Closer needed Raymond more than he did.

It was short of seven o'clock. Most of the other reporters had long since gone home. Sharon heard a few
coworkers wrapping up stories, hoping to get articles

reviewed by their editors and to the copy desk before press time. Occasionally, a comment or two would carry from the second-shift copy editors as they proofed news pieces before transmitting them to the production room.

Sharon logged on to the *Pitt Daily Times* Web site and typed a search for Matthew Payton. Something was behind his abhorrence of the media. She was fairly certain his reaction to her wasn't personal. The Pittsburgh paper was a good place to start.

Still, she was surprised when the search yielded multiple hits dated October 2006, six months prior. She was shocked at the headlines, which grew increasingly inflammatory with each article. She selected the first story, FIREFIGHTER QUESTIONED IN ARSON.

According to the reporter, fire investigators questioned Matthew regarding a suspicious fire that took place in a residential area of Pittsburgh. There had been extensive property damage but, even worse, someone had died during the fire. The identification was being withheld until officials notified the deceased's family.

The article quoted another firefighter and the fire chief. It also included several impassioned statements from Matthew declaring his innocence and insisting there'd been a misunderstanding.

"The department will find that I had nothing to do with the fire," he'd said. "I'll give my statement. Then they can continue to search for the real murderer."

Sharon's brows rose at Matthew's strong language. Not just *arsonist* but *murderer.* She couldn't picture the cautious captain speaking so frankly. Her curiosity hooked, she called up the second article, ARSON EVIDENCE POINTS TO FIREFIGHTER.

Her eyes widened. Was Matthew Payton an arsonist?

Her stomach growled, protesting the further delay of dinner. She liberated the remaining low-fat, low-sodium pretzel rods from her desk drawer, then returned to the second online article.

Sharon choked on a mouthful of pretzel when she read the life the fatal fire had claimed was that of another firefighter—Matthew's sister Michelle. She quickly scanned the news account. What evidence had investigators uncovered?

Apparently, they didn't want to share that information with the public. Something about protecting the integrity of the investigation. If they shared too many details of the case, it would make it harder to identify the criminal.

The article quoted the lead investigator calling Matthew a "person of interest." Sharon knew that translated to *suspect* in layperson's terms. She shook her head. The coverage must have done a great deal of damage to Matthew's career. Not to mention the pain of being accused of causing his sister's death.

She slowed her reading when she came to his quote. "I'm not an arsonist. I'm a firefighter," he'd said. "My job is to protect lives. I certainly wouldn't endanger another firefighter, and especially not my sister."

The feelings, the fervor in that statement resonated with Sharon. She felt the emotions behind his words. This was firefighter Matthew Payton, baring himself to the public—and being eaten alive.

The final article in the series, INVESTIGATION FOCUSES ON FIREFIGHTER, featured statements from the lead fire investigator and the fire chief. They hadn't asked to bring charges against Matthew. They were only talking with him. But they were anxious to close the case and find the person responsible for causing the death of "one of their own."

The reporter stated Matthew had no comment for the press. Sharon wasn't surprised.

There weren't any other articles referencing Matthew Payton. This implied the fire department had never closed the case. Unwilling to believe that, Sharon expanded her query of the *Pitt Daily Times* to cover all arsons during October 2006 that occurred in that area of Pittsburgh.

The search returned one new hit. It was a small article. It stated charges had been brought against a serial arsonist in connection with a suspicious fire that had resulted in the death of a Pittsburgh firefighter. Matthew wasn't referenced. It was as though the series of stories implicating him in the crime had never existed.

Sharon printed all of the articles and filed them in her desk drawer. Undoubtedly, the negative publicity had damaged Matthew's career and caused a strain with his coworkers at the Pittsburgh station. She could understand his wanting to start over.

Such reckless journalism made her ashamed to be a member of the media. Words carried a lot of power. Recognizing that, it was hard to accept that members of her profession could be so cavalier in their reporting.

Sharon logged off her computer. She took her purse out of her desk drawer and hauled it onto her shoulder. With a heavy heart, she turned to leave her cubicle.

No wonder Matthew was cautious around reporters. She had a lot of work to do if she wanted to gain his trust.

Chapter 4

The phone rang. The sound clashed with the John Coltrane jazz compact disc humming through Matthew's speakers. With relief, he closed the fire department's *Employee Handbook and Code of Ethics*. He switched his beer can for the phone on the end table beside him.

His mother answered his greeting. "How are you?"

"I'm fine, Mom. How're you and Dad?" Matthew stretched out on his sofa, half-reclining, half-sitting. He extended his jeans-clad legs and crossed his bare feet at the ankles.

"Fine." She brushed aside his question. "Have you settled in?"

"I've gotten into a routine." However monotonous. Get up. Go to work. Return to the house. Repeat. Each day seemed the same. He sighed, realizing today was only Monday.

He sensed his mother's concern and predicted her next words. "You can come home any time."

Matthew stared into the shadows of his living room, the darkness the single lamp beside his sofa couldn't penetrate. "I know, Mom."

At thirty-three years of age, Matthew was her second oldest child, but Evelyn Payton was still protecting him from bullies. That had been the worst part of the investigation. Having the media label him an arsonist had been bad for him and his career. But the pain his mother had gone through had been intolerable.

That memory brought to mind the article Sharon had written about him. The feature had run in the *Times* Lifestyle section today. He'd been prepared for a vicious piece, especially after their angry exchange Friday. Instead, the article's welcoming tone had surprised him. Surprised and alerted. He was braced for the proverbial other shoe to drop.

Evelyn's voice interrupted his thoughts. "Your friends are asking about you. I told them you'd call once you'd settled in."

"Okay."

"Is that all you can say?" Disappointment edged his mother's words.

More guilt. "I'll call them. I promise."

His mother didn't seem satisfied. "Are you making new friends?"

Matthew interpreted her question as, *have you stopped hiding in your house?*

"I went to the movies with some people this past weekend." He was relieved to be able to use that chance encounter with Sharon and Helen to reassure his mother he wasn't a complete hermit.

"That's wonderful." Evelyn's voice sang with relief. "Who are they?"

"Friends I met through work."

Why had he told Helen he was going to see the Wesley Snipes movie? Lucky for him the ushers hadn't checked his tickets. It would have been tricky explaining how he'd mistaken Snipes's action-adventure for Bernie Mac's comedy.

"I'm glad you're socializing again, Matt." His mother's words didn't mask her concern. "Mickey's death is hard on all of us, but you shouldn't punish yourself. The person responsible will rot the rest of his life in prison."

An image of the arsonist who'd killed his sister Michelle materialized on his mind. Everyone had wanted to protect her—the baby of the family—but in the end, it was Matthew who'd let her down.

He'd had this conversation so many times with his mother he could reenact it as a one-man show. "I'm not punishing myself, Mom. I'm starting over."

But the words even tasted like a lie. Bitter, insubstantial, fake. He wasn't starting over. How could he when he hadn't moved past Michelle's death?

"Why did you have to start over in a different state?"

Matthew spoke without inflection. "Because too many people still thought I was guilty. The others thought I'd lost my mind."

Her silence showed the memory hurt her also. He hated being the source of his mother's pain. When she spoke, her voice trembled with anger. "They blamed you, knowing you were innocent. And now you're doing the same thing to yourself."

"I enjoy my job here, Mom. Everything's going well."

His mother snapped her impatience. "What do you need to forgive yourself?"

"I don't know." Matthew blinked back stinging tears. He was five years old again, trying to convince his mother he could handle the neighborhood bullies.

He stared down the length of the sofa toward the cold fireplace on the opposite wall. Matthew needed to turn the clock back. He needed the words that would have convinced Michelle not to become a firefighter. He needed to stop the arsonist before he'd set the fire that had killed his sister.

"Has your self-imposed exile to Charleston helped?"

He whispered his response, unable to hide his grief any longer. "No."

Evelyn was relentless. "I lost Mickey. Now I feel as though I've lost you."

His mother's voice broke. The sound cut like a knife to his heart. Matthew rushed to reassure her. "You haven't lost me, Mom. I'm right here."

"No, you're not. I don't know where you are. You've cut yourself off from us and I can't reach you."

He searched for the right words but had to settle for much less. "I need more time, Mom."

Tuesday morning, Sharon studied her Metro section coworkers seated around the rectangular conference table. They were meeting to discuss the stories they'd run in Wednesday's paper.

Politics as well as crime and other disasters would feature prominently. She grew wistful. Charleston, West Virginia, wasn't the safe, quiet city in which she'd grown up. Crimes people once thought only happened in bigger cities—drugs, abductions, gang shootings—had migrated to the Mountain State's capital.

Wayne began the meeting without preamble. "What do you have on your plate, Jamieson?"

The education reporter sat beside Allyson at one corner of the scarred wooden table. Sharon again wondered when they'd admit there was more than friendship going on between them.

"The school levy." Andre adjusted his wire-rimmed glasses, but didn't refer to his notes. "Kanawha County

Schools has proposed combining two junior high schools. But they still need more money for computers and special programs, like foreign languages, music, and art."

Sharon listened with interest. She envisioned a series of articles on the topic before the May primary. Andre could present arguments from levy supporters and challengers. She compared the importance of Andre's story to her own and her heart shriveled with embarrassment.

"Great." Wayne turned to the police beat reporter. "What's on the police docket?"

Bill Meyer looked like he'd slept in his cream blazer and tan slacks. "A second student is missing from the Charleston Community College."

Sharon's alarm increased as Bill elaborated.

"They're both from St. Albans." The police beat reporter referenced a suburban community twenty minutes west of Charleston. "They're both sophomores. A source confirmed the police are working the cases together, but the department won't go on record that the events are related."

Sharon didn't know these students, but she was still concerned for their well-being. Their relatives must be devastated and other families frightened. Hopefully, Bill would include in the article personal safety tips to help university students better protect themselves.

A flush of excitement darkened Wayne's pasty cheeks. "Stay on that, Meyer." He nodded toward Allyson. "What's on the political scene?"

Sharon caught the quick glance her friend shot Lucas.

Allyson wrapped her hands around her coffee mug. "The Ethics Committee is investigating bribery allegations against Senator Stanton."

Lucas glowered at Allyson before cutting a glare to Wayne. What did the senator's nephew expect the editor to do?

Lucas leaned into the table, his neck extending forward as he growled at Wayne. "You're going to allow her to write this crap?"

The metro editor shrugged. "It's news."

Sharon exchanged a look of disgust with Allyson and Andre. Wayne's justification was the weakest she could imagine.

Allyson turned toward the senator's nephew. "The father of one of the coal miners killed in last month's accident has support for the investigation. The Ethics Committee is going to look into whether Stanton took bribes in return for cutting back on mine safety regulations."

Lucas sneered. "I'm so happy for the coal miner's father. What does that have to do with us?"

Sharon crossed her arms. "It's the media's responsibility to hold public servants accountable by keeping our communities informed."

Lucas redirected his glare to Sharon.

Before the political pet could speak, Wayne raised his arms to end the debate. "Tell them about the story you're working on, Lucas."

The editor's words distracted Sharon. Was Wayne helping Lucas develop story ideas for his beat? Other reporters came up with their own. More coddling of the well-connected.

Lucas's frown faded as the reporters' attention turned to him. "I'm working on a story about the proposed budget cuts for the city's emergency services, and how those cuts will reduce taxes and restore the city's fiscal responsibility."

Sharon burned with anger. She'd been researching that series before Lucas stole her fire department beat.

Lucas continued. "I called a couple of city council members and Fred." He glanced at the faces around the table. "The mayor, Fred West. He and several council members are friends with my uncle. They've been over for dinner many times."

Wayne glanced at Sharon, then looked away. "Get MacCabe's information on the budget."

Shock rolled over her. Hand over her hard work like a gift to the political appointee? Should she put a bow on it?

Lucas's smile made it worse. "You don't need those notes anymore, MacCabe. You might as well give them to me."

Sharon pictured the binder of information he referred to as "notes." "Sure. I'll get right on that."

"That's settled." Wayne pointed toward Sharon. "What are you working on?"

She regarded her coworkers. Budget cuts, missing people, political scandal, and her fire department beat. Sharon looked back at her notes and considered lying to spare herself the comparison.

It wasn't that her story didn't have value. It did. But it wasn't the investigative assignment she was working toward.

Wayne prompted her. "MacCabe?"

She took a deep breath, inhaling remnants of cigarette smoke trapped in the furnishings of the recently declared smoke-free building. "I'm interviewing Lettie Smith."

Wayne frowned. "The retiring city council member?"

Lucas chuckled. "That should be interesting. Not."

Sharon accepted Lucas's challenge. She turned to Wayne. "Did you know Ms. Smith was one of the earliest leaders of West Virginia's civil rights movement?

Were you familiar with her volunteer work and fund-raising efforts for the battered women's shelter?"

Interest flickered in Wayne's gray eyes. "No, I wasn't."

"You will be after you read my story."

Wayne nodded. "Okay, people. You have your assignments. Let's get moving."

Sharon walked out of the conference room without a backward glance. Allyson and Andre caught up with her before she'd made it to her cubicle.

With her hands on Sharon's shoulders, the political reporter turned her toward the break room. "I could use some coffee."

"You drink too much coffee." Andre fell into step beside Sharon.

"We can do without your nagging." Allyson released Sharon as they reached their destination. She made a beeline for the coffeepot.

Sharon trailed her friend. "I should be covering the emergency services budget, and that name-dropping windbag should be interviewing retiring council members."

Andre's tone was dry. "For Lettie's sake, I'm glad Stanton Junior isn't writing that feature. He wouldn't take the time to get to know her the way you would."

Sharon smiled at her friend's compliment. Behind his glasses, Andre's dark eyes were warm with understanding.

Allyson filled her mug before pouring coffee into Sharon's empty cup. "How much work have you done on the budget research?"

Sharon pictured the stack of documents she'd reviewed and the notes she'd taken. "A lot. I spent hours interviewing department and city officials."

Allyson rolled her eyes. "Adding insult to injury,

the Beat Thief didn't even come up with his own assignment."

"You noticed that too? And Wayne knew I was working on the budget story." Sharon tasted sour resentment.

Andre crossed his arms over his broad chest. "Have you looked for openings at other papers?"

Allyson scowled. "Why should she be the one to leave? Lenmore should come to his senses and give her back her beat."

Andre propped a hip against a nearby table. "That's a nice thought, but Lenmore's not going to come to his senses. And, if he could treat Sharon this way, he could do the same thing to us."

Allyson wrinkled her nose. "A depressing thought."

Sharon sipped her coffee. "Depressing or not, Dre's right. None of us are safe."

Sharon and her friends left the break room to return to their stories. Lost in thought, she sipped her coffee—and almost choked on it when she found Lucas waiting in her cubicle. She swallowed the coffee and took her seat behind her desk.

Lucas gave her a superior smile. "I'm here for those notes."

"I'll get them to you later." She turned her back on him and logged on to her computer.

"I want to start on my story now."

And I want you to go away so I can have my beat back. She freed a pretzel rod from her stash in her desk drawer as she considered a response.

The phone rang. Tension eased from Sharon's shoulders and she placed her hand on the receiver. "I have to take this call."

Lucas frowned at her phone before walking away.

She answered as the fourth ring faded. "Sharon MacCabe."

"It's Matt Payton." The captain's rich, dark baritone echoed across her stomach muscles.

"Hi, Matt. How can I help you?"

His pause was almost unnoticeable. "I liked the feature."

She looked behind her at the file drawer holding copies of the *Pitt Daily Times* news stories on Matthew's arson investigation. Did this call about her article on him have anything to do with those stories? Perhaps the gun-shy captain was starting to believe some reporters were after the truth.

Sharon indulged the urge to tease him. "What did you like most?"

"The fact you spelled my name right." Matthew's prompt response reflected a dry humor.

Sharon burst into laughter. She'd give the captain his due. "I suppose I deserved that. I'm glad you liked the piece."

"The positive tone was surprising, considering our first impression of each other wasn't good."

She smiled at his understatement. "I was writing a feature, not looking for revenge."

His warm chuckle wrapped itself around her. "Maybe that's the solution. You should stick to features."

Sharon's good mood went up in smoke. Was the entire city against her becoming an investigative reporter? "I can handle hard news. I can present facts without injecting personal biases."

"An unbiased reporter. That would be refreshing."

The rest of her pretzel rod snapped in her hand. "I can't speak on how other reporters work, but that's how *I* work."

"Why would you be different?" He didn't sound convinced.

Sharon dusted pretzel crumbs from her hands and

her desk into her wastebasket. "I'm in the majority. It sounds like you've had a bad experience. Care to talk about it?"

A heavy pause came in response to her turning the tables on him. Was he considering her invitation? Probably not. The experience would be too painful to share with a stranger.

There was controlled anger in Matthew's voice. "All you have to do is open a newspaper, or turn on the TV or radio to see what I'm talking about. You reporters love to vilify people. It's good for business."

Sharon stiffened. That shot had stung. However, it was hard to mount the high horse of journalistic integrity when her own paper was lowering the bar. Case in point: Lucas Stanton. It also was hard to argue with him when evidence to support his position was filed in her cabinet.

She called for a truce. "Why don't we agree we have a philosophical difference of opinion?"

"The harder you try to convince me you're a different kind of reporter, the harder it'll be for me to believe you."

Apparently, Matthew wasn't yet out of bullets. He still had a few rounds to clear and was targeting her integrity.

What had happened to the man who'd gone to the movies with her and her mother last weekend?

Sharon deliberately relaxed her grip on the phone. Her fingers stung as the blood began to circulate again. "Then I'll stop trying to convince you and let my work speak for me. Why don't you read some of my past articles? You want the press to give people the benefit of the doubt. Give *me* the benefit of the doubt."

Matthew ran his hand over his hair. The last reporter he'd trusted was a former classmate who wrote for the

Pitt Daily Times. The man had betrayed Matthew's friendship and joined in the feeding frenzy.

Anger rose with the memory and his grip tightened around the receiver. "What you did in the past doesn't matter as much as how you represent me and my department now."

"Excellent. You didn't have any complaints about the feature I wrote about you. That proves you can trust me."

Matthew crushed her argument. "It proves you can be fair with a feature. I've seen what happens to reporters with a real news story. Pour blood into the water and the sharks go mad."

Matthew heard her sharp intake of breath and knew the shot he'd taken had been unfair. He was striking at her in retaliation against the reporters who'd attacked him six months ago. But he couldn't seem to stop.

"You're wrong. I'm not looking for blood. I'm looking for facts."

Matthew shook his head. "I find that hard to believe."

"You have to put your past experience into perspective." Her voice took on an edge.

"What do you know about my past?" *She was too inquisitive, too smart.*

Damn it, why had he even called Sharon? He had to keep his distance from the reporter. It was only a matter of time before she found out about Pittsburgh. Then, like all reporters, she'd sink her teeth into the story and ruin the future he wanted to build in Charleston. Was he trying to sabotage himself?

"It's obvious you had a bad experience with the press. Why don't you just tell me about it instead of using me as your whipping boy?"

"That's not what I'm doing." *That's exactly what I'm doing. Why can't I stop?*

"Not every reporter is your enemy. We're looking for the truth just as you are. Lies only tear communities apart."

Her words were like a mermaid's song luring him toward the rocks. He had to get off this ship before he crashed. "You're a excellent salesperson, Sharon. But I'm not buying."

Chapter 5

More than an hour after the phone call, Sharon was still shaking with anger. She'd gone through her mail and responded to e-mails, but she was still in a temper.

No one had ever before questioned her integrity. How dare Matthew Payton? And then he'd hung up on her. The coward. She must have been getting to him.

It had been one heck of a morning, and Sharon still had to decide what to do with her emergency services budget story. In the end, she took the binder of information to Lucas. The research was useless locked in her cabinet. Her readers needed the information to understand the budget impacts to their community.

But when she got to Lucas's cubicle, she found his father posed behind the desk, assessing his manicure as he chatted on his cell phone.

Earl Stanton was the picture of wealth and self-importance. His designer suit hugged him even as he sat, legs crossed. His elevated foot tapped an imaginary beat. The ceiling light reflected off his expensive-looking wingtips.

Noticing Sharon, the older man abruptly ended his phone conversation, then rose to his feet.

Sharon stepped forward, extending her hand. "Mr. Stanton, I'm Sharon—"

"MacCabe. I'm familiar with your work." His handshake was firm. "My son has very large shoes to fill."

An opening like that was hard to resist. "Which is why he should have started with general assignments and worked his way up like everyone else at the paper."

Earl smiled. "Why work so hard when you have connections?"

"Because of the skills you'd learn along the way."

His smile widened unrepentantly. "Think of this as an advanced-placement program."

Sharon scrutinized the senator's older brother as he leaned against Lucas's file cabinet, which she'd bet was still empty. His stance was relaxed, but she sensed an impatience under the surface. She saw it in the tightness of his classic features and the watchfulness in his eyes.

Sharon propped her shoulder against the cubicle wall and crossed her arms, mimicking Earl's pose. "What's the rush?"

A spark of admiration warmed his cool green gaze. "You're a perceptive woman. I sensed that in your news stories." He nodded. "I want Lucas to learn all he can about reporters—how they think, the information they want, the way they cover events—so he can take over as his uncle's campaign communications director."

Sharon didn't think understanding reporters was as useful a skill for a communications director as learning to spin scandals such as bribery allegations. What wasn't Earl admitting?

"Wouldn't an internship with a public relations firm be more useful for Lucas? There are a lot of firms that would love to have a state senator's nephew on their payroll."

"He'll learn more from this newspaper experience."

The watchful expression had returned to Earl's gaze. It made Sharon uncomfortable.

"The election is less than seven months away. Isn't it late to change communications directors?"

"The switch wouldn't be made for this campaign. I'm referring to Kurt's bid for the U.S. Senate."

Sharon's eyebrows jumped in surprise. "Shouldn't you focus on winning this election?"

"Oh, we'll win in November. But we have to plan for the future."

Sharon was in awe of Earl's confidence in the face of the senate challenger's double-digit lead. "You're very ambitious for your brother."

"He has charm and charisma. It doesn't hurt that Kurt's good looking too. He'll go far." Earl's relaxed smile was at odds with the intensity in his eyes. "But I take it he doesn't have your vote?"

Sharon stared at Earl, incredulous. Looks and charm. How shallow. What about the issues? What were Senator Stanton's plans for the state?

She stepped forward and laid the budget binder on the desk between them. "I leave the pretty faces to television and movie stars. For my state representatives, I want a bit more substance."

Sharon turned her back on Earl and strode to her cubicle.

People like the Stantons amazed her. They believed they were entitled to their positions, regardless of who they had to screw over. She was certain she wasn't the only one who would suffer from the fallout.

At the end of the day, Matthew was still kicking himself for calling Sharon that morning. On the one hand, he felt better after voicing some of his anger. On the other hand, Sharon hadn't done anything to deserve his verbal abuse. Yet.

He shut his briefcase, logged off of his computer and walked out of the station.

Crossing the parking lot, Matthew saw Seth standing under the open hood of a beat-up Ford Escort. From yards away, he could see the frustration tightening the muscles of the other man's back.

Matthew approached with caution. "What's wrong?"

Seth didn't even glance up. "Starter. Engine won't turn." The firefighter met his gaze then.

His speech was spare, but the look in his eyes spoke volumes. It conveyed frustration, anger, and fatigue. Matthew imagined the untimely demise of his car had been the final straw added to a host of other problems burdening this man.

His attention moved from the engine back to Seth. "Is there anything I can do to help?"

Seth lowered the hood of his car. "Got tools in my trunk. Could use a ride to the store."

"Let's go."

Matthew led the way to his four-door Toyota. He stowed his briefcase on the floor in the back and neatly folded his suit jacket before laying it on the rear seat.

He couldn't read Seth's expression as the other man got into the silver sedan, but he thought he sensed resentment. Under the circumstances, Matthew could understand. His eleven-year-old Camry was in good condition. In contrast, it looked like it took a lot of work to keep the Escort running.

Seth snapped on his seat belt. "There's an auto parts store on Virginia Street."

Matthew put his Camry in gear and drove cautiously

through the parking lot. He waited for traffic to clear before merging onto Laidley Street.

Seth chuckled wryly. "I know every parts store in Kanawha County."

"Do you do a lot of work on your car?"

"Have to. Can't afford a mechanic. Can't afford a new car."

"You save a lot of money by doing your own repairs."

"Everything's expensive, especially when you pay for it twice."

"What do you mean?" Matthew glimpsed the other man's shrug before he switched his attention back to the rush-hour traffic.

For a time, Seth was silent. "My bills and my ex-wife's. Lost her job. Again. On top of alimony and child support, I'm making her car payments and paying her rent."

"That's rough." Matthew now knew the other problems that had added to the load on the firefighter's back.

"Don't mind. They're my kids."

Matthew turned onto Virginia Street. "Of course you don't mind. I understand."

He'd learned more about Seth during the ten minutes they'd been in the car than he had during the two weeks they'd worked together. Seth shifted in his seat. Had he grown uncomfortable with the personal conversation?

Seth paused. "Seems every time I save enough to go see them, something happens and the money's gone."

Matthew stopped the car at a red light. "Where do they live?"

"California. Los Angeles. Not even in the same damn time zone."

"When was the last time you saw them?"

"Fourteen months ago." Seth responded as though repeating a mantra. "Told her not to go. But she had to 'find herself'. Damn place is going to shake itself right into the ocean, my kids with it."

Matthew heard fear under the anger. "Why didn't you move to California with them?"

"Didn't have money to move. Didn't have a job there. When I have money, I'm going to file for custody of my kids."

They drove in silence the rest of the way to the auto parts store. Matthew navigated the lot, parked, then followed Seth inside.

His companion marched straight to the aisle that had Ford Escort starters. With his mind on their conversation, Matthew trailed after him. He wasn't a father, but it seemed to Matthew fourteen months was a long time to go without seeing your children. He could understand Seth's frustration. Especially since the firefighter hadn't wanted to break up his family.

Conversation was minimal on the way back to the station's parking lot. Matthew wondered whether Seth regretted his confidences.

He pulled in front of the firefighter's Escort. "Do you want me to wait?"

Seth started to get out even before Matthew had stopped the car. "If I can't get it going, I'll call a neighbor." Seth looked back at Matthew. "Thanks."

Matthew nodded, then drove off.

Half an hour later, he let himself into his house. Even as he started dinner—which meant tossing a frozen meal into the microwave—he couldn't stop thinking about Seth being away from his children for fourteen months.

The microwave timer went off. Matthew took the plastic container out of the machine and placed it on the counter. Instead of eating, though, he picked up the phone and dialed his parents' number. His father answered.

"Are you enjoying the basketball game?" Matthew hoped the familiar conversation would help pull him out of the darkness he lived in and lead him home.

John Payton's voice was big and booming, a perfect reflection of the man. "Are you kidding? If they keep it up, the Knicks are going to take the title."

Matthew grinned. His father lived for basketball. The only problem Matthew could see is that his father rooted for the wrong team.

"What about the Sixers?" It was an old argument about the home team, the Philadelphia 76ers, but one they both enjoyed. However, this time, the teasing didn't bring the satisfaction it had in the past.

John sighed in mock frustration. "I'm from New York. Once a Knicks fan, always a Knicks fan."

"But you've lived in Pittsburgh my whole life."

"You can take the man out of Brooklyn—"

"'But you can't take Brooklyn out of the man.'" Matthew forced a chuckle at the old joke.

They chatted for a while longer, his father as usual finding a way to work into the conversation the names of old Knicks greats. "It's not the same watching the games without you."

"I miss you too Dad." Matthew swallowed the lump in his throat. *Wait for me a while longer. I'll find my way home.*

The next morning, Sharon maneuvered her little yellow Civic through the winding roads of South Hills, a Charleston suburb. She was on her way to Fort Lee Elementary School for the first fire safety presentation. Part of her was looking forward to the assignment. Another part of her was working hard to overcome the dread of seeing Matthew again after yesterday's phone call.

She really had to stop rising to the bait of his attacks against the media. She couldn't afford enemies as she tried to rebuild her career. Besides, his antagonism wasn't directed at her. Matthew had formed his opinion on a very painful and very personal experience. She was sympathetic to his past.

But why did she feel as if the attacks were personal? And why did that matter?

Sharon pulled into the asphalt parking area, located an empty space on the outskirts of the crowded lot and got out of her car. She inhaled the scent of freshly mowed grass and spring blossoms. Battling the brisk, cool wind, she forged a straight path past the cars, trucks, and SUVs to the school's front entrance.

Sharon crossed the threshold of the elementary school and was transported more than twenty years back in time. She breathed in the familiar disinfectant smell and smiled. This was her alma mater. She was pleased to see it was well maintained.

The school was eerily silent as Sharon and her memories entered the front lobby. An official-looking older man sat at the unfamiliar security desk.

"Good morning." She handed him her media identification. "Principal Donna Walters is expecting me for the school safety presentation."

The guard checked his paperwork, then nodded his approval. "The auditorium is at the end of this hall." He turned and pointed to the hallway behind him.

Sharon walked past him, enjoying periodic flashbacks of her childhood. She scanned the display cases of paintings obviously created by very young artists. She smiled, drawn to the brilliant colors and free-form designs unfettered by realism. Once upon a time, her art-work had been displayed in those—or similar—cases.

At the end of the hall, the auditorium doors were propped open. Matthew stood in front of the stage with Lieutenant Gary Dunleavy and a woman Sharon guessed to be the school principal. The audience seats were empty since several minutes remained until the scheduled assembly.

Sharon walked toward the stage. The clicking of her low-heeled shoes echoed in the large room, heralding her approach. The trio's conversation ended as all eyes turned to her.

Sharon's smile wavered as she looked at Matthew. His expression was inscrutable as his eyes moved over her slim raspberry skirt suit. She couldn't tell what he thought about seeing her after their argument. But it wasn't his closed expression that caused her steps to falter. It was the way he looked in his uniform.

Matthew was handsome in a business suit. In casual clothes, he was hot. But in his formal, dark blue uniform, the captain took her breath away. He fulfilled her image of what a hero looked like. Strong. Bold. Confident.

The jacket emphasized his broad shoulders, contrasting them with his narrow waist and hips. His legs looked long and lean in the plain, dark pants.

Refocusing on the reason she was there, Sharon exchanged nods with Matthew and pleasantries with Gary before extending a hand toward the woman who stood with them. "I'm Sharon MacCabe from the *Charleston Times.*"

"Oh, yes. I spoke with you on the phone. I'm Donna Walters, the principal."

"Nice to meet you, Ms. Walters." She gave the presenters an encouraging smile, her gaze lingering again on

Matthew's chiseled features, before turning to select a seat in the audience.

Minutes later, the fifth and sixth graders filled the room relatively quietly and the presentation began. Matthew and Gary were informative and entertaining on a level that seemed to appeal to the students.

To look at Matthew on the stage, one wouldn't think he needed the moral support he'd mentioned to Sharon on Monday. He appeared natural and confident. Several times he recounted anecdotes that made the children laugh, easing the gravity of the presentation before returning to a more serious tone. Sharon would be certain to include those accounts in her article.

She took a lot of notes. At the end of the presentation, Sharon asked several of the students and some of the teachers for their reaction to the safety program. Everyone was impressed with the speakers. The teachers used terms like "highly educational" and "very informative." The students thought the presentation was "cool" and "fun."

Finally, Sharon asked the principal for her review. Donna's quotes were also positive. "Captain Payton and Lieutenant Dunleavy did an excellent job. I'm sure the students learned a lot today." She smiled and added, "I know that I did."

Excellent. Sharon took the quote and thanked the principal. She climbed the stairs to the stage where Matthew and Gary talked companionably while repacking their props. "Any words for the press?"

Gary shoved a fire extinguisher back into its case. "Those kids were great. They asked excellent questions."

"How about you, Captain?" Sharon braced for his rebuff.

Matthew returned the smoke and carbon monoxide

detectors to their case. "I was glad we had so much audience participation. They obviously wanted to learn."

Matthew's cell phone cut off Sharon's follow-up question. As he stepped away to take the call, she offered to help Gary repack the remaining props. It gave her an excuse to linger and perhaps learn the reason for Matthew's call. She and Gary were almost finished when Matthew's brief phone conversation ended.

Chapter 6

Matthew seemed preoccupied as he addressed his lieutenant. "There's a fire on the west side. The crews are on their way. Naismith wants us over there."

The announcement piqued Sharon's journalistic curiosity. "Are they suspicious of the fire?"

Matthew's expression closed, distancing himself from her. "Our policy is to investigate all fires in the interest of public safety."

The man was skilled at dodging the press. No doubt a lesson he'd learned in Pittsburgh. Sharon tugged her purse more securely onto her shoulder. "I'd like to tag along."

Matthew eyed her as though wondering how much trouble she was going to cause him. "We can't stop you."

It wasn't the warmest invitation she'd ever received, but Matthew wasn't standing in her way, either. She followed him as he hefted two of the bags and strode off the stage.

About twenty minutes later, Sharon pulled into a parking space beside the department car Matthew and Gary had driven. She'd lost them earlier as they'd raced through traffic with their siren blaring.

Standing behind the emergency tape, Sharon stared in nervous fascination at the wide, single-story building in front of her. It was ablaze in brilliant orange. Flames licked the windows as if trying to escape. Black smoke spiraled out, bringing blasts of hot air with it.

Sounds of the building's destruction mingled with firefighters' shouted instructions as they worked as a team. Acrid residue from the smoke caused Sharon's eyes to tear and stung her nostrils, leaving a strong, bitter taste in the back of her throat.

Despite her discomfort, Sharon remained across the street from the fire, ignoring the bodies jostling her just as she ignored the heavy heat from the flames.

During the six months she'd covered the fire department, Sharon had learned investigators factored in the color of the flames and smoke when trying to determine the origin of a fire. From the advanced stage of the burn, the orange flames and black smoke, it appeared the fire had help getting started. But it was too early to tell.

For almost another half an hour, the fire crews fought the blaze, each movement economical and efficient. Sharon took notes of the scene and interviewed spectators. Did they know when the fire had started? Had they seen anyone or anything suspicious near the building?

One woman taking an early lunch break to run errands said she'd seen a man walking around the building as though he were examining it.

"He was just walking up and down the block just staring at all these buildings," the woman explained. "Not like people do when they're just walking in a different neighborhood than they're used to. He was looking at it just in a considering kind of way. You know what I mean?"

"Yes, I think I do." Sharon's voice was calm even as her pen sped across her steno pad. "Can you describe him?"

"Well, he just looked normal." The woman squinted her eyes as though trying to pull the man's image from memory. "He had a ball cap. And a ponytail. And sunglasses. I really didn't pay him much mind." She shrugged apologetically.

"That's fine. Thank you."

Sharon moved on to see if anyone else had noticed this man or other strange activity in the area. No one had, leaving Sharon to wonder if the woman had made up the stranger, hoping to get her name in the newspaper.

Minutes later, Sharon found Matthew standing alone. She spoke loudly to be heard over the shouts and equipment noise as the firefighters battled the blaze. "What do you think?"

Matthew gave her a cautious glance. "I think this is a pretty bad fire."

He wasn't going to be any easier to interview this time than he'd been in the past. Sharon once again tried simpler questions with the intent of working up to the harder ones. "What type of business was this?"

"An office-furniture store."

"Have the owners been notified?"

"Yes." Matthew glanced around the crowd. "He may even be here now. His name is Reilly O'Conner."

"Will you question him about the fire?"

"We question everyone who might be able to help us identify the source of a fire."

Sharon heard the defensiveness in his tone. Was he reminded of Pittsburgh? "Do you have any idea how it started?"

Matthew slid a wary glance toward her notebook. "We don't have any theories at the moment."

Sharon pushed a little. "Not even an educated guess?"

Matthew scorched her with his glare. "We don't play guessing games. We do a thorough investigation before releasing information."

With an effort, Sharon ignored the rebuke. She was asking these questions for her readers. "When will you complete your investigation?"

"We'll have an initial report by end of day tomorrow. Based on that report, we'll decide whether we need additional analysis."

"Great. I'll call you tomorrow about the report." She started to leave, but Matthew's voice stopped her.

"Call my deputy, Gary Dunleavy. He'll have a copy of the report."

Sharon spun to face him. Why did his statement feel like a personal rejection? And why did that rejection hurt? "I'll present the facts as you give them to me, Matt. I don't have any reason to do otherwise."

Matthew's gaze was distant, as though he wasn't even seeing her. "I don't have time for the press."

Sharon flinched. "My job is not as dangerous and selfless as yours, but it's still a service for the community." Why couldn't she let the matter drop?

Matthew's lips thinned and his features went tight. "You don't serve the community. You serve an agenda."

Sharon stepped back from the sting of his attack. Matthew's eyes widened with surprise and he reached to steady her. She wrenched her arm from his touch. She bit back her initial response, tempering her words as she recalled his past experience. "You don't know me. Whatever experiences you've had with the press in the past, you don't know *me*."

She ignored the confusion in Matthew's eyes and started for her car. Why even bother trying to change his mind about reporters? Matthew Payton was never going to trust her.

* * *

It took Sharon a little more than half an hour to maneuver around the lunchtime traffic on her way back to the newspaper. Because of the fire, she'd skipped lunch. After this latest contentious exchange with Matthew, she wasn't hungry anyway. Instead, she'd spent the commute rehearsing her sales pitch to convince Wayne to let her write the fire story.

At the newsroom, she hurried past the copy desks, two long tables each with rows of computers attended by eagle-eyed copy editors. Sharon made a quick detour to the photocopier before continuing to Wayne's office. She knocked on the half-opened door and waited for his invitation to enter.

Two strides brought her across his small, cluttered space to his desk. Sharon hid her nervousness with bravado. "There was a fire on the west side. I'd like to cover it for tomorrow's edition."

Wayne studied her from across the pond of papers on his desk. "How did you know about the fire?"

"I was covering the school presentation when Captain Payton received the call."

He narrowed his eyes. "The fire department beat isn't yours anymore."

"But I was at the scene. I took notes." Sharon thought she'd been prepared for Wayne's denial, but the professional slight still stung, especially coming on top of the verbal bruises Matthew had given her.

Wayne turned back to his papers. A clear dismissal. "Stanton was on the scene too. I assigned the story to him when it came over the emergency scanner."

Sharon frowned. "I didn't see him there."

Wayne looked up at her. She held his gaze for a long moment before his wavered and dropped to his phone.

He picked up the receiver and jabbed several buttons. "Could you come to my office, please? I need to speak with you."

Sharon arched a brow. When had Wayne started framing his summons as a request? Or did he reserve those niceties for his politicos?

The senator's nephew sauntered into Wayne's office without knocking. His lanky frame was clothed in a sports coat and slacks. Sharon wasn't familiar with designer labels. She didn't have the time or inclination to peruse fashion magazines. But she knew expensive when she saw it, and Lucas's clothes were obviously from some designer's understated elegance line.

Lucas spared her a glance before claiming one of the chairs in front of Wayne's desk. Light from the dusty ceiling fixture shimmered on his golden hair. "What's up?"

"Did you go to the fire scene I assigned to you?"

Lucas balanced his right ankle on his left knee. "No. I left a message for the fire chief to give me a call when he got back to his office."

Sharon saw the astonished expression on Wayne's face and knew it matched her own. Lucas had called Fire Chief Larry Miller? What would Chief Miller be able to tell him before the news deadline? Surely, Wayne would let her cover the story now.

Wayne folded his hands on his desk. "You were supposed to go to the scene."

The younger man shrugged. "Why? By the time I got there, they would've been done with the fire. I thought this was more efficient."

Sharon leaned against Wayne's bookcase and folded her arms. "The crews were still working when I got there."

Lucas frowned at her over his shoulder. "Why were you at the fire?"

"I was covering the fire safety presentation when the call came in. You remember, the presentation you weren't interested in covering?" It was uncharitable of her, but she couldn't resist the dig.

"Give him your notes."

Sharon stiffened at Wayne's order. Her mind shouted no, but she held the protests and tried to reason her way out of an unreasonable demand. "It would be more efficient for me to write the story because I was on-site. A lot of it is already in my head."

Wayne gave her a steady stare. "You can't take stories from other reporters."

From her peripheral vision, Sharon noted Lucas's smug expression. She struggled to remain cool and professional. "An eyewitness account better serves our readers."

Wayne sighed and leaned back in his chair. "When you wanted the school presentations, you asked Jamieson. If you want this story, ask Stanton."

Hot anger threatened to melt her cool veneer. There was a world of difference between the situation with Andre and this one with Lucas. The biggest difference being Andre was a real journalist.

The smirk on Lucas's face deepened. "Don't bother asking. It's my beat. I'll write the story." He extended his hand for her notes.

Sharon's palms itched to smack the triumphant smile from his face. She pushed away from the wall. Her hands shook as she pulled her steno pad from her shoulder bag and ripped the pages of notes from the spiral binding. She ignored Lucas's outstretched hand. Stepping past him, she dropped the pages onto Wayne's desk.

Sharon gave Lucas a tight smile, finding small satisfaction in her parting words. "You're going to wish you'd been on-site. I don't think you'll be able to decipher my shorthand."

Back in her cubicle, Sharon tugged the photocopy of her notes from her bag. Not being able to write the story bothered her. But at least she'd been prepared for Wayne's decision and had thought to make the copy.

She stored her purse in her bottom desk drawer and grabbed a pretzel rod before logging on to her computer. She'd write the story on the fire safety presentation to the local elementary school and send that story to Wayne. Then she'd type her notes on the west side fire.

Sharon may not be assigned to the story, but that didn't mean she couldn't follow it. She wasn't a fire investigator, but her journalistic instincts assured her this was a story worth pursuing.

Chapter 7

Matthew stood in what remained of the office-furniture store and studied the powder-blue mid-April sky through the remnants of the burned and blackened roof. This would have been a greater tragedy if a store employee hadn't noticed smoke coming from the back of the store this morning. Thank goodness the woman had hustled her coworkers and customers out through the front.

Matthew set down his evidence kit. With the department's digital camera, he took several pictures of what remained of the roof. He lowered his gaze to the scorched walls and blown-out windows, and photographed those as well.

It had taken firefighters the better part of an hour to extinguish the blaze. But in that time, the flames had done a great deal of damage. The single-story structure was not much more than an unstable shell now. Matthew continued to photograph the scene as he advanced across the room, maneuvering around debris from the collapsed roof.

His steel-toed, rubber boots crunched over rubble. The extra eighty or so pounds he carried with his bunker pants and coat, boots, and other protective gear slowed his movements. The weight was reassuring, though. The threat of the fire becoming involved again was very real.

It also was the reason the suppression crew waited impatiently across the street. Once Matthew completed his on-site investigation, he would direct the crew regarding what materials they should preserve and what they could haul away without destroying evidence. If it turned out this fire had been deliberately set, Matthew wanted to make sure they'd have the evidence they needed for a conviction. He didn't want the torch to walk.

He turned when he sensed someone pause beside him. Raymond Ford wore similar protective gear. Behind his face shield, the lieutenant's dark face was shiny with sweat and lined with battle fatigue.

"Naismith said you wanted to talk to me." Ford's voice was muffled by his air mask. It was reasonably safe to enter the building, but the air still carried dangerous residue from fire-damaged furniture.

Matthew allowed the digital camera to hang from a strap around his neck. He readjusted his own air mask before pulling a small notebook and pen from his jacket pocket. "Your crew was first on-site?"

"Yeah. We were the first in."

"What was the scene like when you arrived?"

Raymond looked at him, then away. "The fire was burning pretty hot and fast. There were a lot of people on the street."

Matthew documented Raymond's observations. "What about the smoke?"

"It was dark." The big man shrugged.

"Darker than usual?"

Raymond's gaze wandered around the destruction. "Maybe."

"What kind of strategy did you take for engaging the fire?"

"We went on the defensive. Everyone was out of the building—workers, shoppers—so our concern was containing the fire and putting her out as fast as possible."

Matthew nodded his understanding. He visually surveyed the area again. A defensive approach to the fire was consistent with the condition of the structure. It didn't appear as though firefighters had battled into the building and ventilated it for a rescue.

He scanned the ceiling joists and beams, estimating the fire damage to the front of the building. In terms of floor space, the office-furniture store had been a large shop. "The employees I interviewed said the fire started in a back room."

Raymond shifted his stance. "Yeah. That's what it looked like to me too."

Matthew tracked the burn patterns on the walls and ceiling, letting them lead him toward the back room. Raymond followed, helping him with the evidence kit. Each step took them to areas of greater damage. The height of the scorch trails on the wall continued to decline. They were getting closer to the seat—the origin—of the fire.

Matthew photographed and documented the scene. "It helps that the employees noticed where the fire started. It cuts down on the investigation time."

"So you think this is arson?"

"It's too early to tell. Did your crew experience anything unusual putting out the fire?"

"No. She was stubborn, but she'd been burning for a while before we got the call."

Matthew glanced over his shoulder at Raymond.

"Did you notice whether any windows or doors had been left open?"

Raymond shook his head. "By the time we made it in, some of the windows had blown out. But the doors had been closed before the fire."

They walked in silence the rest of the way to the back room. The wooden door was severely charred—and closed.

Frowning, Matthew turned to Raymond. "Did someone close the door after you put out the fire?"

Raymond shook his head.

Still puzzled, Matthew put his hand on the scarred surface to test the temperature. He didn't want to open the door and find the fire had become involved. The door was cool to the touch, so Matthew opened it

Here was the seat of the fire.

Matthew looked around. The remnants of furniture. The mini-kitchen. He was standing in the employee lounge. He ran his finger over the scorched lettering on the door, filling in the missing letters. "Employees only."

He surveyed the room. The armchairs, tables, and sofa were badly burned. The two large windows facing the back parking lot were blown out. The tattered curtains danced frenetically in the breeze coming from the windows and missing roof.

Matthew stepped farther into the room. It was going to be a long afternoon and evening. "I'll need a hand sifting through this stuff."

Raymond's retreating footsteps crunched over debris. "I'll get the suppression crew."

Still tense from her confrontation with Wayne and Lucas that afternoon, Sharon went for a short jog after work. She usually walked through her problems. But this was more than a problem. She had challenged her demotion and lost. She needed to sweat out the anger and frustration of defeat. To paraphrase Patti LaBelle, she needed to find a new attitude. Or at least reclaim her optimism.

The sun was beginning to set along the Kanawha's banks. It was a quiet Wednesday night. The rhythmic echo of her footfalls, the cool evening air and the physical exertion worked to release her tension. Like a soothing massage. Until she heard the running footsteps behind her.

Sharon strained to gauge how far behind her the runner was without giving away the fact she was aware of the newcomer's approach. Perhaps it was another early evening jogger. But it was better to be safe than sorry. Sharon slowed and moved closer to the curb to let the other person pass. As she turned to look at the new arrival, her heart almost stopped.

"Matt, I didn't realize you lived in this area." Her inane greeting came out in a gasp.

Excellent. She'd gone jogging to ease the tension from her workday, and one of the causes of her stress had shown up.

Matthew paced with her. Sweat molded his gunmetal-gray T-shirt to his well-developed pecs. "I live on Bridge Road."

Sharon's eyes stretched in amazement. "That's on the other side of the bridge. Do you usually jog this far?" *Please say no. I don't want a repeat of this chance encounter.*

"Yes." Matthew looked forward. "Why are you jogging so late?"

She glanced around. There was still quite a bit of natural light. The streetlights were only now fading in, casting a glow on the sheen of perspiration on Matthew's rugged features.

"It's not so late." She kept her tone mild. "And you're out jogging."

Matthew raised a thick brow. "I don't have as much to worry about as a small woman like you does."

His baritone voice deepened with his dry comment. Sharon felt it stroke against her pulse. Her gaze met his, and she saw concern in the midnight darkness of his eyes. If he despised reporters, why did he care about her safety?

"I usually jog in the mornings, but tonight I needed the outlet."

"Bad day?"

Sharon frowned. "You ought to know. You were part of it."

In the fading light, she thought embarrassment washed over his features. "I apologize for what I said to you this afternoon. I shouldn't have attacked you personally."

Surprise cleared the scowl from Sharon's features. He even sounded sincere. Keeping his past in mind, Sharon gave him a small smile. "Apology accepted. Besides, I have other things on my mind."

"Like what?"

He sounded as though he wanted to know. Not like he was making conversation. Unexpectedly, a phrase from Patti LaBelle's "Right Kind of Lover" played in her mind. "A real man, strong but tender."

Sharon blinked away the mental image. "Personality conflicts at work."

"Do you want to talk about it?"

It dawned on Sharon that what she was going through was nothing compared to what he'd experienced in Pittsburgh. Did he have friends or family who'd helped him through it? She wasn't comfortable asking him. What would she say? *Matt, remember when the Pittsburgh press libeled you? How did you get through that nightmare?*

Instead she changed the subject. "There's not much to talk about. How was your day?"

Matthew studied the petite woman matching him stride for stride. What was it about this stubborn, strong-willed woman that kept pulling him back to her? And now he was inviting her personal confidences as though he could afford to get close to her. He needed to keep his distance for his professional—and he was beginning to think personal—survival.

For his own protection, he allowed Sharon's change of topic. "I'm getting into a routine. This is the first new job I've had in five years. I didn't realize how hard it would be to adjust."

"It's not just a new job. There are a lot of new things for you to adjust to."

Matthew smiled. "Yeah. New people, new city, new responsibilities. I have to get used to being part of management."

"I'm sure you miss your friends and family."

"Yes, but I don't regret the move. I needed a change."

"From what?"

Matthew shook his head with amusement. She asked that question every opportunity she got. But he'd be damned if he would answer it. If she wanted to know, she could find out on her own. He frowned, knowing disaster was just an Internet search away. "Don't you ever turn off your inner reporter?"

Sharon's apologetic tone was almost convincing. "I was born this way."

"No doubt."

A drop of perspiration trailed over her cheekbone

and along her jaw. He followed its path onto her collar-bone and down her neckline before he realized this indulgence wouldn't create the distance he needed between them.

Matthew followed Sharon as she turned back toward the South Side Bridge. Their silence was comfortable. The sound of their footfalls, the scent of the river . . . he'd never felt this relaxed during a jog before. He almost felt at peace. How much of that had to do with the company? A surprising thought, considering his companion was a reporter.

He looked ahead. They were coming up on the bridge. Considering his house was in the opposite direction, they should separate here to return to their respective residences. But he couldn't leave Sharon on her own. It may not have been dark when she'd started out, but it was certainly dark now.

Sharon spoke as though she'd heard his thoughts. "You don't have to come all the way home with me. I don't live that far from the bridge."

He kept his attention on the distance. "I wouldn't be able to sleep tonight if I didn't make sure you got home safely."

There was a smile in her voice. "That sounds a bit dramatic."

"That's me. I live for drama."

Sharon laughed at that, the sound as gentle as the evening breeze. "I suppose that argument could be made considering you're a fire investigator. But I don't think that's what you want in your personal life. I think drama just finds you."

Something in her tone made Matthew think there was more beneath the surface of her words. He caught the humor sparkling in her eyes. Perhaps he was imagining things. "Do you promise to usually jog in the mornings?"

Sharon laughed again. The soft, carefree sound was addictive. "I promise. And not that early."

Side by side, they crossed the bridge. Then Matthew dropped back to let Sharon lead the way to her home.

A block later, she turned with a challenging grin. "I usually sprint the last three blocks. Are you up for it?"

Matthew's competitive spirit woke from hibernation. "Bring it on."

Chapter 8

Slowly, Sharon increased the pace until they were at a dead run toward her apartment. She was short, but she was strong, and she pushed him to the limit. Several times, they vied for leadership. Matthew dug deep for more energy and freed a part of himself that had been restrained for a very long time—joy.

By the time Sharon called a halt in front of an old Victorian building, they were panting.

She walked past the residence, breathing hard. "I see how you work off those cinnamon buns."

Matthew followed her, taking deep breaths. "Same goes."

He was dripping with sweat. His muscles were shaking, heart racing and lungs straining. He had no idea where he'd find the energy to make it home. And he felt great. Better than he'd felt in months.

Sharon nodded toward his wet T-shirt. "It takes a lot of guts to wear a Pitt Panthers T-shirt in Mountaineer country."

Matthew glanced at the clothing under review. Sharon was referencing the rivalry between his alma mater, the University of Pittsburgh Panthers and the

West Virginia University Mountaineers. He paraphrased his father. "You can take the man out of Pittsburgh, but you can't take Pittsburgh out of the man."

"Is that why all of your ties are blue and yellow?"

"Blue and *gold*. Panther colors." He grinned proudly.
"You've noticed."

Sharon chuckled, turning back to the old Victorian.
"This is me." Her grin faded and a look of uncertainty
dimmed her glowing features. "Would you like to come
in for some water?"

"After what you just put me through, water would
help."

She laughed. This time the sound had a touch of
wicked intent. The tension that had gripped Matthew
for six long months eased.

Sharon sensed Matthew's presence behind her as she
mounted the steps and unlocked the building's front
door. The house had been renovated to accommodate
four apartments. Her unit was on the top floor. They
dragged themselves up the hardwood stairs.

Mentally squaring her shoulders, Sharon opened the
door to her roomy one-bedroom home and took the ir-
reversible step forward. Luckily, she was a neat person
by nature. Not that she was obsessively clean, but her
apartment was tidy. The only drawback was the furnishings. They weren't shabby. They were just excessively in-
expensive. You wouldn't find pieces like these in the
Stanton residence, for example.

A large, fluffy mango-orange sofa sat on the right.
Two matching chairs were kitty-corner against another
wall. Those three pieces were on their last legs when
she'd bought them almost six years before. Sharon had
refurbished them. Did her handiwork show?

The tall entertainment center had been refinished

and its original brown wood painted kiwi green. Did it scream *garage sale* to anyone other than her?

All the furniture seemed to merge into the wall-to-wall beige carpet. She wouldn't accept responsibility for the carpeting. It came with the apartment.

The only saving grace was the huge, rectangular windows beside the sofa. The streetlight in front of her building shone on the sturdy maple tree outside her apartment. Its branches could be seen all the way to the top of the windows. On lazy summer days, Sharon loved to lie on the sofa and watch the birds dance from tree branch to tree branch.

Matthew looked around. "Nice place."

Sharon squinted at him. Should she take his wide-eyed expression as a compliment or sensory distress? "Come on in."

He stared at a corner of her great room. "You have a weight bench."

"My mother mentioned I lifted weights."

Matthew's gaze traveled Sharon's figure in her sweat-soaked orange T-shirt and black running shorts. His smile released wicked dimples on either side of his mouth. "You certainly do."

Sharon arched a brow. Two could play that game. Her gaze skimmed his body. Unfortunately, she couldn't pull off her survey as casually as Matthew had completed his. She was getting turned on.

His hard, well-sculpted build made her tongue stick to the roof of her mouth. The man didn't have an ounce of spare flesh anywhere. His gray T-shirt clung damply to the carved muscles of his chest and stomach. Her palms trembled with a desire to stroke that hard surface.

Sharon turned away from temptation and sought a

reprieve in the kitchen. She took the jug of ice water from the refrigerator and filled two large glasses.

She returned to the living room and offered him the water. Matthew held her gaze as he took the glass. The rough pads of his fingertips grazed her skin.

He walked past her to examine her bookcase. It was a perfect match to her entertainment center. The shelves were neatly stuffed with magazines and books, both fiction and non-fiction. What was he thinking as he studied the contents?

"You have eclectic taste." He turned to her. His voice was soft, his dark eyes shadowed. "Will the real Sharon MacCabe please step forward?"

The vulnerability in his eyes confused her. "What were you expecting?"

He glanced back toward the bookcase. "I don't know."

Matthew finished the water. She watched his throat as he drank, the muscles moving smoothly up and down as he swallowed. He lowered the glass and licked beads of liquid from his lips.

Sharon's mouth went dry.

He disappeared into the kitchen, then returned without the glass. He seemed to hesitate on the threshold between her kitchen and her great room. "Thanks for the water."

She sensed a conflicting energy surrounding him, as though he needed to leave but wanted to stay. Sharon wanted him here, if only for a little while longer.

"Thanks for protecting me tonight." She tried a smile.

Matthew walked toward her slowly, as though testing his welcome. She stepped closer.

He paused, close enough to touch. "At your service."

Sharon breathed in his scent. Warmth and musk. Masculine. Her gaze drifted to his lips. Firm and full.

He was Temptation. Sharon lifted her eyes to his and found the heat waiting for her. Her nipples hardened in response.

Slowly, Matthew lowered his head. Sharon's gaze wavered between his darkening eyes and his sensuous mouth. Instinctively, she recognized Matthew's warning—if this isn't what you want, step back now. She rose onto her toes to meet him halfway.

Matthew's lips brushed gently across hers. Sharon shivered at his tenderness. He pressed his mouth against hers and she opened for him. Matthew nipped at her lips as though sipping her. Stroked his tongue into her mouth as though tasting her. She felt like she was dessert.

Sharon pressed herself tighter against him. He wrapped his arms around her and straightened, lifting her with him. Her feet left the ground and she clung to his broad shoulders. Their sweat mingled and his musky scent fogged her brain. She trembled as his hard, wet muscles strained against her. He opened his mouth wider and took the kiss deeper.

Her mind was spinning with the smell and feel of him. An ache was building inside her, and Sharon dug her fingertips into Matthew's shoulders to relieve the pressure.

Too soon, her inner voice shouted. Even as her body arched into his, her mind warned her, *he doesn't know me yet.*

Sharon pulled her lips from Matthew's and knew the pain of separation. He looked as dazed as she felt. "Matt." Her voice quavered. "Put me down."

She slid against him as Matthew returned her to her feet. Her body shuddered with desire as it came into contact with a particular muscle. Matthew braced his hands on her waist as though sensing she was still a little shaky. Or perhaps he wasn't steady on his feet, either.

Sharon took a deep breath, searching for a transition. "I—"

"It's late. I'd better get home."

She looked up with gratitude at his words. "Do you want me to drive you?"

His full lips twisted in self-deprecation. Heat still simmered in his eyes. "I think another jog will do me good."

Sharon trailed him to the door. "Be careful getting home."

"I will be." He turned to her. "I hope you work out whatever was bothering you tonight." And then he was gone.

It took Sharon a moment to remember the crisis that had precipitated her nighttime jog in the first place.

Sharon shoved aside the Thursday edition of the *Times*. It left a bitter taste in her mouth. Lucas's west side fire article was worse than she'd expected. It was disjointed and incomplete. Wayne's decision to run those wasted column inches rather than let her write the news piece further undermined her position at the paper. Was that his intent, or was she being paranoid?

And what had happened to her notes from the fire? Lucas hadn't used any of them. Perhaps he hadn't been able to read her shorthand. Sharon scowled. Even more reason to allow her to write the article.

What concerned her most was her suspicion the article wasn't accurate. That some information was deliberately misstated. At several points in the article, Lucas referred to the fire as an arson. However, during her interview with Matthew, he'd stated the cause of the fire wouldn't be confirmed until this afternoon. What made Lucas think the fire had been purposely set? Had the test results come through sooner?

Without stopping to consider her actions, Sharon called the fire department. She asked for Gary Dunleavy, but Li Mai suggested Sharon speak to Matthew.

"He read the article in the paper. He'll want to speak with you."

Sharon grew apprehensive at the administrative assistant's somber tone. "But, Li Mai, I didn't write that article."

"He'll still want to speak with you. I'll put you through."

Excellent. This wasn't going to be the morning-after scene she would have chosen. Sharon took a deep breath as she waited for Matthew to answer the transferred call.

He didn't sound happy. "Who is Lucas Stanton?"

Her heart sank. Where was the man who'd kissed her senseless last night? "He's the new reporter assigned to the fire department. I take it he didn't call the station yesterday?"

"I've never spoken with him, and yet he has more information about my investigation than I do. When did the paper assign him to my department?"

"Monday." It was still hard for Sharon to talk about having her beat taken from her.

"Then why were you at the fire yesterday?"

"Because I was there when you got the call."

Sharon sensed Matthew working out the chain of events. When he spoke again, his anger was gone. "But they had him write the article. Is that why you went jogging last night?"

He was perceptive, but Sharon didn't want to talk

about her career problems right now. "When will you have the test results?"

"The lab should have that information this afternoon. Gary and I are walking through the site again later this morning. The preliminary report won't be ready until tomorrow."

"Great. I'll call Gary tomorrow."

"Why, if it's not your beat?"

Sharon didn't need another person reminding her she'd been displaced. "Since I was on the scene, I'd like to know how the investigation turns out."

"Call me instead. I'll go over the report with you. For now, could you transfer me to your editor? I'd like to discuss this article with him."

Sharon complied with Matthew's request with a mixture of trepidation and triumph. She regretted the paper would have to run a retraction. However, Wayne knew Lucas didn't have the experience to cover hard news. He should know the results of his decision.

Sharon was wrapping up a preview piece on the upcoming May Day celebration when Wayne called her to his office. Curiosity blossomed into the hope that, after Matthew's call, her editor had decided to give her back her assignment.

She beat back that hope as she strode the narrow aisle formed by the other reporters' gray cubicles. She knocked twice on Wayne's office door—two quick raps—then entered at his summons. He waved a hand toward the battered plastic visitor seats. Sharon took one, crossing her legs and folding her hands to quell her nerves. She couldn't read the thoughts behind his expression.

Wayne's chair moaned as he leaned into it. "I don't tell Payton how to run his fire investigation. I won't let him tell me how to run this newspaper."

With that simple statement, Sharon's hope died. She clenched her hands more tightly together. "Lucas's story was factually incorrect. Did you realize that?"

"So Payton said. I told him we'd run a retraction."

"How many retractions are you willing to run before you accept Stanton's nephew is not ready to cover hard news?"

A flush darkened Wayne's homely face. "You're out of line."

"How? Because I care about this paper's reputation?"

"And you think I don't?"

Sharon uncrossed her legs and leaned forward in the chair, gripping the arms tightly. "What am I supposed to think when you put an untrained, inexperienced political appointee on a news beat?"

Wayne leaned toward her, his chair groaning with the shift of weight. "You're supposed to think, 'He's the boss.'"

Sharon narrowed her eyes. If that's the best he could give her, he must realize he and the publisher, Gus Aldridge, had made a mistake. "What did you think of Lucas's article?"

The older man scowled at her. "I ran it, didn't I?"

"But what did you think?"

"MacCabe, I'm going to tell you this just once more. You're no longer assigned to the fire department. Do you understand me? It's not your beat anymore."

Sharon stood. "What I understand is that you're making a mistake. What I don't understand is why." She turned to leave.

"Listen, MacCabe, I know how unhappy you are with covering features. But you can't let your disappointment affect your professionalism."

Sharon's anger spiked. No one could question her

professionalism. She'd worked too hard for that. "What do you mean?"

"Perhaps you could work with Stanton. Help him develop his reporting skills."

Sharon's lips parted with shock. "Why don't you help him, Wayne? You're the boss."

Wayne called after her, but she left his office. She could kick herself for being stupid enough to think Wayne had seen the error of his ways.

Sharon marched back to her cubicle and dropped into her chair. Wayne's request had been the final straw. She wouldn't work for a newspaper that devalued her reporting skills by demoting her to general assignment, then suggested she train her replacement. That was just too much.

She was going to take a page from the Patti LaBelle song, "Stir It Up," because she wasn't going to take this anymore.

Chapter 9

"Forensics confirmed an accelerant was present." Matthew spoke over his shoulder to Gary. He moved closer to the fire scene photos tacked to the case board in his office. The images recalled memories of other fires. Memories of Michelle. His hand shook as he pushed past those flashbacks, his voice carefully controlled. "Test results from the temperature and burn rate indicate the substance was kerosene."

Gary joined him at the case board. "Ford said he'd send his report over this afternoon."

Matthew angled his body so Gary could see the pattern his pencil traced above the three-by-five color pictures. His hand was steadier now.

"Here's the pattern. The fire started in the employee break room, then flashed over to the showroom." Matthew waved the pencil over deeper burns apparent in several photos. "It sped along the baseboard, then rose up the wall before the next flashover."

He stepped back from the photos, distancing himself from the scenes so similar to his nightmare. It hadn't bothered him yesterday while he'd taken the photos. He'd been focused on the investigation then. But studying the site now brought back the bad dreams he'd held at bay for weeks.

Gary leaned closer to the pictures. "It looks like the arsonist concentrated on the north side of the building. That's where most of the damage is."

Matthew walked to his desk. The late-morning sun shone through his office window, drawing patterns of light and shadow across his desktop. "We don't have enough evidence to prove a torch caused the fire."

"But we have a burn pattern and the kerosene."

Matthew opened a file folder. "Those things suggest arson, but without more, we can't be certain. Unlike the press, I have to base my report on facts that will hold up in court." Anger over that morning's article on the fire was still close to the surface.

He returned his attention to his lieutenant, noting the pink tint rising in the younger man's cheeks. "What's wrong?"

Gary rubbed his face as though trying to remove the blush. "I should have realized what you said about needing solid evidence for the courts."

"The press enjoys embellishing stories. We can't do anything about that."

Gary looked uncomfortable but nodded his understanding.

Matthew flipped through the folder. "Forensics estimates the fire started between eleven and eleven-thirty A.M."

Gary glanced at a page of handwritten notes. "The owner, Reilly O'Conner, had an eleven A.M. meeting with a supplier."

"He could have used a time-delay device." Matthew stood. "Let's go talk to Mr. O'Conner."

* * *

Sharon drove her little yellow Honda along the streets of Charleston's west side searching for a parking space. The closer she got to Reilly O'Conner's home, the more run-down the streets became.

In the background, the National Public Radio station's statehouse reporter updated her audience on Charleston's political scene.

"Senator Kurt Stanton refuses to hand over documents from meetings with coal industry lobbyists." The broadcaster spoke without inflection. "Stanton, chair of the Senate Mining Committee, says releasing the documents would hamper legislators from having candid consultations with outside experts in the future."

Sharon shook her head in disgust as she maneuvered her Civic through the narrow streets. She didn't think the country's founding fathers would agree with governments operating in complete secrecy.

The reporter continued. "Meanwhile, Henry Rush, the father of one of the workers killed in the recent coal mining accident, continues to speak out against Stanton's alleged dealings with lobbyists."

Sharon heard a slight pause as the station switched to a tape of Rush's latest public statement. The father's voice shook with an anger that thickened his southern West Virginia accent. "We need better enforcement of safety. Too many miners have died these past few months. Stanton's district is smack-dab in the middle of our mining families, but he puts his greed ahead of my boy's life."

Sharon's heart went out to the grieving father. She hoped the Senate Ethics Committee would force the senator to hand over his meeting notes.

As the news segment ended, she finally spied a space that would accommodate her compact car. She wedged her Civic between a decades-old white Lincoln Town Car and a battle-weary silver Ford Taurus. She stepped onto the broken sidewalk and turned in the direction of Reilly's apartment. When she'd called him yesterday to request this morning's interview, the office-furniture store owner had agreed to provide her with a list of vendors and creditors.

Sharon's self-doubt pinched her as she hopped over a raised section of the street. Was there more to this fire, or had it been an unfortunate accident? At this stage of the investigation, she couldn't answer that question with any degree of certainty. But her reporter's instincts wouldn't let her ignore any part of a possible lead.

Minutes later, she knocked on Reilly's apartment door. A short, slender man in wrinkled brown slacks and a cream-colored, long-sleeved shirt opened the door. Tired brown eyes squinted at her. A coffee mug shook in his right hand.

"Mr. O'Conner?" At his jerky nod, Sharon extended her hand. "I'm Sharon MacCabe from the *Charleston Times*. I appreciate your agreeing to meet with me."

The frown vanished from his pale face, and he shook Sharon's proffered hand. "Oh, yes, Ms. MacCabe. Please come in." Reilly smoothed what remained of his straight brown hair and stepped aside to allow Sharon to enter.

"Please call me Sharon." She walked past Reilly. As she glanced around the tiny living space, she tried to hide her dismay.

Sharon had decorated her apartment like someone on a tight budget. Reilly's apartment looked like someone who didn't have any money. Or someone who preferred to invest his money in other interests. How much had yesterday's fire cost this man, and what would it take for him to recover?

Her concerned gaze took in the threadbare olive carpet straining to cover what appeared to be an all-purpose room. The only pieces of furniture were a worn green-and-brown–patterned sofa, a coffee table littered with papers, a fourteen-inch television, and an overstuffed bookcase.

On her left, a half-bar and two backless stools formed the boundary between the main area and the snug, gleaming white kitchen. A bedroom probably hid behind the scarred, half-opened door before her.

Sharon took off her spring coat and turned to Reilly with the silent question.

He stopped chewing his nails long enough to gesture toward the sofa. "You can lay it over there. And have a seat." He lifted himself onto one of the stools.

Sharon warily lowered herself onto the lumpy sofa and took out her reporter's notebook. She noted his grizzled jaw and reddened eyes. He must not have slept the night before. Her gaze fell to the papers strewn in organized chaos across the table.

"Mr. O'Conner—"

"Reilly." He hopped off the stool to sift through the papers on his coffee table. He shoved a sheet toward her. "I made the list of vendors and creditors you asked for." He climbed back onto the stool.

Sharon scanned the names on the page he'd given her. "Reilly, do you have an estimate of the property damage from the fire?"

The wiry man got to his feet and thrust his fingers through the hair rimming his head. "A lot of money."

In addition to his caffeine buzz, Sharon felt Reilly's anxiety and frustration. "How much?"

He paced to the half-opened bedroom door, naming

a figure that made Sharon cringe. She wrote the information on a fresh sheet of paper. "Are you insured?"

She wasn't ruling out the possibility the small-business owner had been involved in the fire. Businesses had been destroyed for insurance money. However, Reilly's distress appeared genuine.

"Yes. But it's not just the money." He clenched his fists, staring into the distance. "Having my own business was my lifelong dream. I've always wanted to be my own boss. Since I was a child."

Sharon saw the anger tightening his thin features. "Perhaps with the insurance money, you'll be able to start over."

Reilly sat on the bar stool, his anger draining. Now defeat slumped his shoulders. "I don't have that much coverage. I couldn't afford it. Most of the money will go to repay the mortgage and business loans."

Sharon didn't know what to say, so she listened.

His words were muffled, as though he spoke to himself. "All these years of sacrifice to start a business and, overnight, I lose it all. Isn't that just my luck?"

Sharon surveyed the clean but shabby surroundings. She could only imagine how devastating this experience was for him. "Does anyone have a grudge against you?"

Reilly looked up, his frown puzzled. "No."

"Have you laid anyone off recently or had any arguments with competitors?"

He shook his head. "Why are you asking these questions?"

Sharon forced a casual shrug. "It's possible someone might be trying to get even with you."

His tired eyes widened. "By burning down my store? Isn't that extreme? I thought the fire was an accident."

"The fire department is investigating. Can you

think of any reason someone would want revenge against you?"

He stumbled off the bar stool and began pacing his familiar route. "Of course not."

"No disgruntled employees? Bitter ex-girlfriends? Former business partners?"

"With the hours I put into my business, I don't have time for a social life. And I've never had a business partner. I wanted to be my own boss."

Sharon could sense his mind trying and discarding possible connections. A knock on the door broke the silence. Reilly crossed the room and opened the door without checking who waited for him. Sharon read that as an indication of his distraction.

She stiffened when she recognized Matthew on the other side of the threshold. Their surprised gazes met. Sharon's face heated with embarrassment. Matthew's eyes frosted with anger.

He recovered first. "What are you doing here?"

"Mr. O'Conner granted me an interview."

Reilly interrupted their exchange. "Who are you?"

Matthew's gaze freed hers and turned to Reilly. "I'm Captain Matthew Payton. This is Lieutenant Gary Dunleavy. We're with the fire department's investigation unit. We'd also like to ask you about yesterday's fire."

Reilly glanced from Sharon to Matthew. "Sharon said you guys think it was arson."

Sharon's mouth parted with surprise. "No. I said—"

Matthew's cold stare quieted her. "I'm afraid Sharon has misinformed you."

Sharon stood and collected her coat. Time for a strategic retreat. "I should probably leave. I don't want to be in the way." She once again extended her hand toward the business owner. "Good luck, Reilly."

Sharon turned toward the door, avoiding Matthew's

eyes. But when his imposing figure didn't grant her room to pass, she was forced to look at him. His internal struggle reflected in his dark eyes. He was probably wondering whether he should let her go for maximum damage control or tie her up so she couldn't get in his way again.

Sharon debated her next move. Thankfully, Gary stepped aside so she could leave. But Sharon sensed Matthew's hostile stare following her down the hallway. Why was he angry? They were after the same thing, weren't they?

Sharon logged on to her computer and started transcribing the notes from her interview with Reilly while it was still fresh in her mind. She could use the information to further her investigation. This was a lot of work for a story she wasn't allowed to cover, but it wouldn't go to waste. Of that much she was certain.

She spent the next two hours returning e-mail and voice mail messages and revising her feature articles before filing them. Anything to chase away her boredom and the memory of Matthew's anger. She hadn't thought about the impact her interview would have on his investigation. Or had it been that, in her quest to prove her worth as a hard-news reporter, she hadn't cared? She shook that thought off. Her readers were what mattered most, not her byline.

Sharon looked up at the sound of footsteps approaching her cubicle. Allyson and Andre slipped into her small work area.

Surprisingly, Allyson wasn't carrying a coffee mug. She moved the folders from Sharon's guest chair to the floor and claimed the seat for herself. "How was your meeting with the man with two last names?"

Sharon frowned her confusion. Then the connection dawned on her. "Reilly O'Conner?"

Allyson nodded. "Did he burn his place down?"

Sharon shook her head. "He seems genuinely devastated by the setback."

Andre leaned against Sharon's cubicle wall and crossed his arms. His biceps flexed beneath the sleeves of his white dress shirt. "Are you sure it's arson?"

Sharon met his eyes through his thin, wire-rimmed glasses. "I never said it was arson. Lucas did. Matt's still investigating."

Allyson crossed her long legs. "What makes the Beat Thief think it's arson?"

"He quotes an unnamed source."

Andre shook his head, disbelief in his tone. "An unnamed source for a fire report? Lenmore let him get away with that?"

Sharon nodded, deciding against snagging a pretzel rod from her desk drawer. She would get through this conversation without giving in to emotional eating.

Allyson leaned forward to touch Sharon's wrist. "What are you going to do?"

Sharon read the concern in her friend's hazel eyes. "I want to cover hard news. If I can't do that here, I'll have to go somewhere else."

Andre's brows knitted. "Even if it means leaving Charleston?"

That image wasn't easy for Sharon to accept. "This is my home. Community is very important to me."

Allyson sighed. "I feel the same way. We were both born and raised here."

Sharon drew on Allyson's empathy for this difficult discussion. "It's that sense of community that made me want to be a reporter." She caught and held Andre's gaze. "I have a responsibility to my neighbors to keep them informed."

Andre gave her a wry smile. "That's an idealistic goal. Numbers show newspaper readership is dropping. It seems as though our neighbors don't care what's going on."

Allyson rolled her eyes at him. "You're always so negative."

Sharon leaned forward, caught up in her enthusiasm for the debate. "Just because some people may not care doesn't mean we should give up or even compromise on our responsibilities."

Allyson nodded. "Readers are disillusioned."

"I agree." Andre crossed his ankles. "And who could blame them? Look at the crap Lenmore lets Lucas pull. Who does that help?"

Sharon thought of Matthew. "They don't trust us. We have to continually prove to them that we can provide the information they need to strengthen and protect the community."

Allyson stood and returned the folders to the visitor chair. She glanced over her shoulder at Andre before turning back to Sharon. "Do you want to have lunch with us?"

Sharon smiled her decline. "I packed."

As much as she enjoyed her friends' company, Sharon didn't feel like being the third wheel. They made a good-looking couple. Allyson with her fair and misleadingly fragile appearance. Andre with his tall, dark *GQ* good looks. Sharon could go for Andre herself, if his interests weren't so obviously in another direction. Obvious to everyone but Allyson.

Allyson squeezed Sharon's shoulder before turning to leave. Andre gave Sharon a wink and a smile before disappearing.

Her stomach growled. Sharon spun her chair around and reached under her desk to pull her sandwich and soda from her lunch cooler. Moments later, when she heard footsteps stop outside her cubicle again, she dropped her lunch back into her cooler. Thinking her friends had returned, she pushed her hair from her face and looked up with a smile.

Her expression froze at the sight of a very annoyed Matthew. The civilized cut of his slate-gray suit did next to nothing to soften his dangerous appearance. His jacket hung open. He'd loosened his cobalt-and-lemon tie and freed the top button of his white shirt.

Matthew scanned her cubicle before reclaiming her gaze. "Is there someplace we can speak without being overheard?"

Sharon considered for a moment introducing him to Lucas with the hope of redirecting his anger. But that scheme smacked of cowardice.

She stood, smoothing her skirt, and led the way to a small conference room at the other end of the floor. She tried not to become agitated by Matthew's brooding presence behind her. Sharon maneuvered the row of reporters' cubicles. As usual, many of her coworkers were working through lunch. She felt their curiosity as she escorted Matthew past them.

At the conference room, Sharon allowed Matthew to stalk past her into the overly bright, strikingly shabby little room. She closed the door and waited for him to begin.

Chapter 10

Matthew turned to confront Sharon but was momentarily distracted by her appearance. She looked cool and professional in her red blouse and narrow, knee-length black skirt. The fluorescent lights shone on her black hair as it curled past her slender shoulders. It was an extreme makeover from his sweaty, disheveled jogging partner of two nights before.

How many sides were there to Sharon MacCabe? And which, if any, could he trust?

Matthew checked his disappointment. "You interfered in an open investigation."

It was only an instant before Sharon responded. "I was interviewing a source."

"For what? You aren't assigned to this story."

"Not officially, no."

"Your unofficial interference prejudiced our interview."

"What do you mean?"

Matthew's gaze wandered over her knitted eyebrows and ebony eyes. Did she really not know or was she trying to play him?

He'd wanted to believe she was different from those other reporters. The ones so driven to be the first with the news that they didn't care about consequences, either to the people or processes involved. But today she'd given him an abrupt and disillusioning reminder that she was in fact the enemy.

He stepped toward her. His attention dipped briefly to the pulse thumping at the base of her throat. "While you're trying to get your name in print, I'm trying to investigate a fire that endangered lives."

Sharon flinched as though he'd slapped her. *Good.* He wanted her to remember this exchange the next time she was tempted to muddy his cases.

But she wasn't through defending herself. "I didn't stop you from interviewing Reilly. In fact, I left so you could speak with him in private."

Matthew's patience strained. "After you prepped him."

Sharon stepped forward. Her eyes snapped with outrage. "I did not prep him." Her temper rose to match his.

"You alerted him to the investigation before Dunleavy and I could interview him." Matthew turned to put distance between them. Was she so focused on her own agenda that she couldn't see what she was doing? "You gave him time to prepare."

He sensed her hesitation. Her next words came with persuasion instead of anger. "He couldn't have done it. That store was his dream."

"So he told you."

"I'm sure he told you the same thing."

Matthew turned from his view of the stained, white wall. "What was O'Conner's reaction when you told him we were investigating the fire?"

"He was surprised and confused."

He recognized triumph in her expression. She still didn't get it. His impatience mixed with disappointment. "Was his reaction genuine?"

Sharon started to respond, then seemed to reconsider her answer.

Matthew pounced. "Was it so important for you to get that reaction for a news article that won't even make it to print? I needed to make that call for an investigation that will prevent further property damage and protect lives."

Matthew saw when her mistake finally registered with Sharon. He watched her drag one of the scarred orange plastic chairs from under the table and sink into it.

Sharon looked up with regret in her eyes. "I wanted to cover the news. But the more important goal—for both of us—is protecting the public. I'm sorry. I didn't think."

"I know. I wish you had."

"What will you do now?"

He shrugged. "Continue our investigation."

"Is there anything I can do to help?"

"Stay out of our way. If you want to check the progress, call Dunleavy. He'll give you whatever information we can release without compromising our work."

Sharon hesitated. "Do you think it was arson?"

She still couldn't let it go. Resentment curdled in his stomach. "We haven't come to any conclusions at this time."

Her wide ebony eyes held earnest appeal. "Matt, I didn't mean to cause problems. The only reason I ask about the arson is that Reilly needs the insurance money to pay off his debts. If the insurance company learns the fire was deliberately set, it'll withhold payment. Meanwhile, Reilly will have to continue paying on his loans. Unless he's cleared as a suspect."

Matthew shook his head as he walked to the door.

"You don't even realize you've just given O'Conner a motive for arson."

"But I—"

He paused with his hand on the doorknob. "I know. You had the best of intentions. But the road to hell is paved with them."

Friday's *Charleston Times* shook in Sharon's hands. Her anger grew with each word she read under Lucas Stanton's byline. When had *he* spoken with Reilly O'Conner?

Sharon was out of her cubicle and down the aisle before her next thought. She found her nemesis at his desk, downloading songs from the Internet onto his iPod. On company time. When did he actually work?

She spotted the silver band of his wristwatch. Designer. She thought of the Timex Ironman she wore, which doubled as a chronometer when she went jogging. She and Lucas were worlds apart, forced together by a news beat she'd worked for and he'd stolen. A news beat he was shredding by playing fast and loose with journalistic integrity.

She looked around his cubicle. It was more spacious than her work area. Personal effects were prominently displayed. Framed photographs showed Lucas with his father and uncle, and with prominent state and federal politicians. However, Sharon didn't see either a dictionary or a copy of the *Associated Press Stylebook and Libel Manual*, otherwise known as the reporter's bible.

"When did you interview Reilly O'Conner?"

The senator's nephew frowned at her over his shoulder before returning his attention to the Internet. "Who?"

He'd written a whole article based on an interview with someone he didn't remember? Sharon rubbed her forehead. "The owner of the office-furniture store that burned down Wednesday."

"Oh, yeah. I talked to him yesterday." Lucas pounded computer keys to download more music.

Sharon arched a brow. He'd talked to Reilly yesterday but couldn't remember the man's name this morning?

She addressed the back of Lucas's head. "Did Reilly call you?"

"Yeah."

"When?"

Lucas's distraction turned to irritation. "Why are you badgering me? Can't you see I'm busy?"

"You weren't at the scene. You didn't even mention him in your initial article."

"I talked to the guy after I wrote the first story."

Did he actually believe his lie, because she certainly didn't. That he thought she would offended her. "Reilly didn't mention you when we spoke yesterday."

Lucas gave her his full attention. "Are you snooping around my beat again? You know, all I have to do is say a few words to Wayne and he'll have you delivering the newspapers instead of writing for them."

Anger simmered in her blood. Was that supposed to scare her? She stepped forward, leaning closer. "How long do you think Wayne will cover for you when he has to run retractions for every story you write?"

Lucas's smile was confident. "For as long as my uncle is senator."

Sharon straightened and stepped back. "How long will that be? Have you read the papers lately? Your uncle is trailing by double digits."

Sharon marched back to her cubicle and made a beeline for her bottom desk drawer for her stash of pretzels. Almost immediately she shoved the drawer closed. She was too agitated to eat.

Yesterday's confrontation with Matthew gave her a greater appreciation for the fine line reporters balanced between covering news and interfering with an investigation. However, part of her frustration grew from the fact she'd discussed the fire with Reilly yesterday. This morning, an interview with the businessman ran with Lucas's byline. Meanwhile, her notes would never see newsprint.

Sharon couldn't—just could not—believe Lucas had spoken with Reilly. She glared blindly at her desktop. She'd call Reilly and ask him.

She took several calming breaths. Then, with deliberate movements, she lowered herself onto her chair and picked up the phone. Reilly answered on the second ring.

"It's Sharon MacCabe."

His disappointment was less than flattering. "I was hoping you were the insurance company. I left a bunch of messages asking them to return my call."

Sharon held a mental image of the store owner's threadbare quarters. How could Matthew believe anyone who'd invested as much money into his business as Reilly obviously had would burn that business to the ground?

She cast aside that question and focused on the present concern. "I won't keep you. Have you seen the paper today?"

His voice took an excited tone. "Is there an update on the investigation?"

"No, but there's an interview with you on page two."

Reilly sounded confused. "You wrote an article about me?"

"No, Lucas Stanton did."

"Who?"

Sharon's heart skipped. "Did you talk with Lucas Stanton?"

"No, I only spoke with you. And those investigators."

"Are you sure?"

"Yes. I'm sorry, but I really need to keep this line open. I'm waiting for some important calls."

"Of course, Reilly. I'm sorry." She wished him luck and ended the call.

Sharon sat still as her mind whirled. If Lucas hadn't spoken with Reilly, where did he get his information? She skimmed the article again. He hadn't fabricated the story. All the details matched the statements Reilly had shared with Sharon.

Her eyes widened in disbelief. Her gaze instinctively shifted to her computer. Lucas couldn't have gotten into her system. It was password protected.

She remembered the ease with which Lucas typed commands into his computer. Could he have hacked into her system? Even as she dismissed that thought, she rolled her chair over to her computer and reset her password.

Her phone rang twice before she completed her security upgrade. "Sharon MacCabe."

"You ran the interview?" Matthew's anger hit her with the fury of a natural disaster.

Sharon's grip on her receiver tightened until her palm hurt. "Did you even bother to look at the byline? Or do you think I write all of the paper's articles using a variety of pseudonyms?"

"You must have provided the background."

"Do you honestly believe I would give my notes to the person who stole my beat?"

"Maybe not voluntarily." Matthew sounded as though he were working out a puzzle.

Sharon stiffened. Now she was offended. "I didn't give Lucas my notes, voluntarily or otherwise."

"Then how did he get them?"

Sharon glanced at her computer screen, then away. "What makes you think they were my notes?"

"Only two people interviewed O'Conner yesterday. You and me. We both know I wouldn't share those notes with the press."

She was getting tired of being Matthew's media punching bag. "Three people. You're forgetting Gary."

Matthew's temper was on the rise. "No one in my office would give sensitive information to the press."

"It makes as much sense for someone in your office to give Lucas information as it makes for me to give him my notes."

"Why would someone on my team leak information?"

Sharon enjoyed having the arrogant investigator on the defensive for a change. She relaxed into her chair. "Oh, I don't know. Perhaps one of your firefighters is trying to curry political favor with the senator's nephew."

"What?" With that single word, Matthew conveyed his lack of faith in her sanity.

"Didn't you realize, Captain? There's no lack of cronyism in the Mountain State's capital." Sharon replaced her receiver, letting it slip softly from her fingers.

The sun sparkled on the water, dazzling Seth as he and Raymond stood fishing on the banks of the Elk River. On the north side of Charleston, Coonskin Park was almost deserted this early on a Saturday morning. Seth remained vigilant, though. He wanted to make sure no one was near enough to hear Raymond's latest bitch fest.

"The Closer said Payton wasn't experienced enough

to put two and two together during an investigation."
Raymond's voice quavered. "But he was wrong."

"Payton's looking at the owner." Seth shifted his balance, lifting his leg to break the mud's hold on his foot.

"And what about the next fire? Is he going to keep looking at O'Conner?"

"Why not?" A casual glance around the panorama of newly budding trees and bramble assured Seth they still had their privacy.

Raymond stuttered. "Because there won't be anything to connect him to both fires."

Seth flicked a bland look at Raymond. The big, bald man threw more fits than his kids. "What connects us?"

Raymond quaked with frustration. "This is just too risky. Payton's not going to give up."

"How's he goin' to catch us? You were at the station when it started."

"And it's not just Payton." Raymond continued as though Seth hadn't spoken. "Sharon MacCabe's nosing around too. Dunleavy said she spoke to the owner."

Seth grinned, picturing the curvy, little reporter. "She's a hot number."

Raymond snarled like a rabid dog. "Will you focus, man? What are we going to do?"

"Finish what we started." Concentrating on the sunlight dancing on the waves kept Seth from reaching over to punch Raymond out of his hysteria.

Raymond lifted his baseball cap to scratch his bald scalp. "Listen. Payton's not just trying to close this case. He wants to solve it. He's interviewing people, doing background checks, reviewing old cases for similarities."

"Nothing links us."

"Maybe not right away."

"Not. Ever." Seth ground the words.

The soothing waters weren't keeping his temper at

bay any longer. He was tired of the constant whining. From Raymond about the Closer, from his wife about her bills. All he wanted was to care for his children. To see them. It had been more than a year.

If he had to set a few fires in exchange for money to get things for his kids—for a plane ticket to Los Angeles—so be it. His kids were worth it. And he wasn't hurting anyone. "We don't like it, but we were paid. Suck it up or return the money."

Seth turned back to the riverbank. A deep breath carried the scent of clean mountain air and moist earth to him. With a snap of his wrist, he sent the bait back into the water.

"You know I can't give back my share of the money."

"Then suck it up." He felt Raymond's incendiary stare boring into him.

"We're going to get caught."

"Only if you keep crying about it."

Sharon was curled on the plump love seat, perpendicular to the matching sofa on which her mother lounged. The game between the Cleveland Cavaliers and the Detroit Pistons basketball teams was almost over.

Without a home team to root for, Sharon had long ago declared herself a Cavaliers fan. The Cavs had made good use of their home-court advantage and won, albeit in overtime. Sharon basked in the victory.

"Good game." She stretched, then stood to help her mother clear the remains of their snack—chips and salsa.

"Hopefully, they'll be able to win again Monday." Her mother was a Philadelphia 76ers fan. But tonight she cheered on the Cavs.

Sharon followed her mother into the kitchen. "Preferably without going into overtime. I don't think I could handle the stress."

Helen chuckled as she bent to put the dirty dishes into the dishwasher. "How are things at work?"

The glow from her team's victory dimmed slightly. "It's hard to get enthusiastic over an interview with the oldest living graduate of Fort Lee Elementary School."

Helen's wide ebony eyes telegraphed concern. "Have you applied to other newspapers?"

Sharon returned the bag of nacho chips to the cupboard and the leftover salsa to the refrigerator. "I'm looking. But most of the listings are with papers outside of the state."

"That shouldn't stop you." Helen transferred the seasoned chicken from the refrigerator to a broiler pan before slipping the pan into the oven in preparation for dinner.

"Why should I be the one to leave to get the position I've earned at that paper?" Sharon chopped fresh vegetables for a medley.

"You can always come back." Her mother leaned against the counter beside her. "A position with the *Gazette* or the *Daily Mail* will open sooner or later. While you're waiting, build your name with another paper."

Sharon smiled reluctantly. "Or maybe the *Times* publisher will come to his senses and offer me a big raise to return."

"In the meantime, don't let other people define you, Ronnie. You know who you are. Go after what you want."

Sharon's eyes widened with realization. "You're right, Mom. I am allowing other people to tell me who I am. And they've labeled me a general assignment reporter. I need more of a challenge." She paused as the memory of last week's confrontation with Matthew came to her. "Like the fire investigation story."

"The fire on the west side?"

"Yes. The fire investigation bureau is looking into it. But I've probably lost my welcome with Matthew."

"Why are the two of you always fighting?"

"He hates the media. But I need his cooperation to cover this story."

"Is the senator's nephew covering the story?"

Sharon shook her head. "It's his byline but someone else is doing the legwork. I'm certain of it."

"That doesn't sound fair."

"It's worse than unfair. It calls into question the article's integrity. Where is he getting the information?"

Helen pilfered one of the baby carrots and popped it into her mouth. "Is he even writing the articles?"

Sharon paused in midchop. "That question had occurred to me."

Chapter 11

The phone rang and Seth cursed. Who in the hell would call in the middle of the basketball game? Granted, it was the second game of tonight's double-header, but still. . . .

The caller hung up on the answering machine and Seth relaxed. Immediately the phone began to ring again.

He snatched the receiver and answered with even less graciousness than usual. "What?"

"Have you seen the newspapers?" The Closer's voice was clipped with anger.

"Yeah." Seth leaned over and hit the RECORD button on the tape recorder attached to the phone.

"I thought you could make the fires look like an accident. Now they're investigating them as arsons."

"You said you'd handle the investigator."

There was a tapping noise in the background. Was the Closer drumming his fingers against a desk? "He's more experienced than I thought. And the papers have picked up on it." It sounded as though the Closer was speaking through clenched teeth.

Drumming fingers and grinding teeth. The guy was

falling apart. Seth took a swig of beer and leaned back in his recliner.

The Closer continued. "Obviously, we're going to have to try something else."

Seth didn't think it was obvious.

The game was just starting. The guy must not have the game on or he'd have realized it himself. Seth opened his mouth to end the conversation, but his caller spoke over him.

"You'll have to get rid of Payton."

Seth frowned. "What?"

The Closer's voice hardened. "You heard me."

"No misunderstandings." He drank more beer.

There was a long pause. Seth hoped the other man was using the time to pull his head out of his ass.

"Kill him." The Closer's tone was final.

Seth's gaze shot to the tape recorder. He thanked the survival instinct that had prompted him to get the thing. If he was going to get burned over this scheme, he wouldn't fry alone.

The voice on the other end of the phone may call himself the Closer, but Seth knew who he really was. He'd followed the guy's stooge after he and Raymond had agreed to the deal. Seth had seen the man to whom the go-between had given the photographs and list of locations. He'd been shocked—and a little afraid. He'd almost called it off. But the payoff had been too tempting.

Seth's gaze skimmed the photos of his kids arranged around the room. The pictures chronicled family events—birthdays, holidays, fishing trips—from the day they were born.

"You want me to kill Matthew Payton?"

"Are you deaf?" The Closer was running out of patience.

Well, so was Seth. "Nope. Not stupid, either."

"What does that mean?"

"I'm not killing anyone. And neither is Ray."

"I'm paying you—"

"For fires." Seth drained his beer. "You want someone killed, do it yourself."

Seth replaced the telephone receiver and took the tape out of the recorder. Insurance.

He studied the pictures of his kids again. Murder. He and Raymond still had two targets, but maybe his partner was right. Maybe it was time to walk away. He couldn't get caught up in murder. He wouldn't be able to face his kids with blood on his hands.

Sharon entered the break room for her first cup of coffee. She found Allyson already there, staring at the pot. "How are you?"

The other reporter spared her a glance before returning her attention to the brewing coffee. "Do you really need to ask? It's Monday."

Sharon's lips twitched. "Sorry." She stood beside Allyson to help guard the coffee. "I read your article on the Ethics Committee's investigation. Do you think Stanton's telling the truth about lobbyists not paying him for votes?"

Allyson shrugged. "He sounds sincere, but the facts speak for themselves. He got a ton of money from the mining industry, and the industry got a lot of legal breaks."

"What are his party leaders saying about it?"

The pot stopped dripping and Allyson poured herself a cup of coffee. "So far, they're standing by their man. They want his seat back. But as Stanton's fund-raising ability shrinks, so will their loyalty."

Sharon heard the bitterness in Allyson's voice. It echoed her own feelings as she thought of the miners who'd lost their lives. "Of course he'll lose support. People died because he chose to relax the safety regulations."

Allyson filled Sharon's mug with coffee. "Whether the committee finds a connection between the money and Stanton's voting, he can't escape the consequences of his decision." She was silent a moment. "But I wonder how many other members of the legislature the coal industry lobbyists have bought off."

"Good question."

Allyson returned the carafe to the coffeemaker. "What's going on with you and Matt Payton?"

"Nothing."

"Oh, come on. I heard he stormed in here Thursday, looking for a fight."

Sharon sipped her coffee. "He's always looking for a fight. But I have to convince him I'm not the enemy. I need him to trust me."

Allyson folded onto one of the break room chairs. "It's not easy to get someone's trust but very easy to lose it."

The look in Allyson's eyes grew distant, as though she was focused on events years in the past. Was she thinking of her late husband? When Sharon had broached the subject before, Allyson had shut down.

Sharon took the seat opposite her friend and propped an elbow on the table. "How do I get him to trust me?"

"Be yourself. Everyone knows you're a Girl Scout. In time, he'll see he can trust you."

Sharon stared into her mug. "But I need his help now for the fire investigation."

"What is it about this story that has your panties all in a bunch?"

Sharon shook her head. "It doesn't feel like malicious mischief, but the fire didn't burn like an accident, either."

"Are your Spidey senses tingling?" The political reporter referenced the Marvel Comics superhero, Spiderman.

Sharon smiled. "Something like that. Wayne and Lucas aren't interested, but I'm not willing to walk away. There's something under the surface, and I'm going to keep digging until I find it."

Sharon paused on her way to Wayne's office. With his door partially open, she heard his end of a phone conversation, presumably with Lucas.

Her editor's voice was terse. "It's another fire on the west side. I want you to go to it this time. Talk to some of the bystanders. Get a couple of quotes from some firemen. Real quotes. I don't want to have to run another correction. Do you hear me?"

Another fire on the west side? This was the second fire in less than a week. Sharon glanced at her watch. It was almost noon. Same location. Approximately same time. Coincidence? She had to know.

Sharon heard Wayne hang up the phone. She knocked on his door and waited for him to invite her in. "These are press releases for potential features for Sunday's edition. Let me know if you have a preference for what I write."

She laid the photocopied releases on a relatively clear corner of his desk and started to leave.

Wayne's voice stopped her. "I don't care. Write what you want."

Sharon took the papers from his desk, trying not to let her anger show. She'd read her editor's game. She was being made to feel as though her contributions to the paper weren't of value. Why? "Thanks for your input."

Wayne gave her a speculative stare. "Did you hear my phone call?"

Sharon held his gaze. "I don't eavesdrop on other people's conversations."

It wasn't exactly a lie. More like a prevarication. In any event, she didn't feel compelled to be direct with him.

Wayne turned back to his computer. "Good. Because I don't want to tell you again to stay away from Stanton's beat."

Sharon returned to her cubicle, grabbed her purse and her bag of pretzels—she didn't know when she'd get lunch—then strode to her car. She didn't have the exact address, but instinct told her it wouldn't be far from the first west side fire. The smoke, fire trucks, and crowd should help her find it.

About thirty minutes later, she'd parked her car on a side street and jogged the two blocks back to the incident site. Sharon scanned the crowd for Lucas. She didn't want to be caught doing what she still considered her job. She frowned at that irony.

The building was a coffee shop and bakery. Or it had been. One story tall and twice as wide. Her heart skipped with concern that people may have been hurt or killed. Wayne had told Lucas about the report around eleven-forty A.M. The call must have come over the emergency scanner not long before then.

Had the customers been dwindling from a breakfast rush or ramping up for a lunchtime swarm?

Sharon surveyed the scene. The fire was burning too fast. Just like the first one. And, just like Wednesday's fire, the smoke was dark. Almost black.

Businesses on either side of the coffee shop were in danger of being destroyed. The shop was flanked by a quick-copy store and a cellular phone outlet, which sat on the corner of the block. Judging by the size of the crowd, those buildings also had been evacuated. Firefighters were working to keep the blaze from jumping to the other structures.

"Does your editor know you're here?"

Sharon turned to find Matthew standing close behind her. Perhaps too close. She ignored the leap in her pulse. Surprise? Or something else?

She kept in mind her conversation about trust that morning with Allyson and told the captain the truth. "No, and I'd rather he didn't find out." She broke free of his piercing gaze and returned her attention to the fire. "Was anyone hurt?"

"No, thankfully." His response came after a predictable pause. "Several people—employees and customers—were treated for smoke inhalation."

Sharon's shoulders relaxed at the good news. They tensed again when she saw he was still watching her and not the fire. She hadn't forgotten their argument Friday over Lucas's story stating Reilly O'Conner was a suspect in the first west side fire.

"Are you checking out the possibility that this fire was deliberately set?"

Matthew looked from the notepad in her hands to the coffee shop. "It's procedure. Have you been here long?"

"Long enough to realize this fire is burning much too quickly."

His gaze swung back to her face, more piercing than before. "You know quite a bit about fires."

"I covered the beat for six months."

"I don't know many reporters who bother to learn about the beats they cover."

"There are a lot of differences between me and the

reporters you know." Sharon arched a brow, adding emphasis to her reminder.

Matthew stepped back. "I'd better get back to work." He turned, moving into the crowd.

Sharon assumed Matthew was going to question bystanders and photograph the crowd. She watched him for a while, enjoying his easy panther's stride. His tan overcoat emphasized his broad shoulders. The rest of his figure was obscured as the coat swirled around him in a gentle breeze. Such a handsome package. Too bad it was wrapped so tightly.

She set out in the opposite direction to find her own interview subjects and take her own pictures.

Sharon was photographing the crowd when she noticed a man at its edge fixated on the fire. He was tall. His baggy clothes made him seem thin. But it was his dark baseball cap and wraparound sunglasses that roused her curiosity. They screamed "disguise."

She watched his brisk strides carry him toward the yellow tape that separated the crowd from the crisis zone. When he ducked under it, Sharon stepped forward.

Chapter 12

Matthew stopped beside Gary, who'd positioned himself next to the fire truck. "What have you got?"

Frustration darkened Gary's brown eyes. "No one saw anything or anyone suspicious before or after they found the fire. How 'bout you?"

"The owner said a customer saw the smoke coming from a back room. Her employees ushered the customers out as she called nine-one-one."

A spark of interest lit Gary's gaze. "A back room? Like the other fire?"

"Let's not jump ahead of ourselves." But Matthew had made the same connection. Were the fires related? "The owner said her shop's been here for almost two years." Another similarity to the first fire.

"How was she?"

Matthew recalled the middle-aged woman's flood of helpless tears as she watched her livelihood go up in flames. "Upset. But she could be faking it."

Although Matthew didn't doubt the owner's tears were genuine, he'd question her. And, if there was evidence of arson, she'd lead his list of suspects.

Matthew turned to scan their audience, pretending

he wasn't looking for Sharon. He located the reporter staring at something in the distance. He followed her line of sight and saw a man duck under the emergency tape. When Sharon followed him, Matthew's heart bounded into his throat.

"Damn it." He turned to Gary. "I need you at my back."

Where is he going? Sharon bent under the police tape and straightened on the other side. She monitored the stranger's progress toward the back of the cellular phone company—the building the crews were trying to keep from also catching on fire.

He walked with his head bent. A dark sweat jacket masked his build. A thick, brown ponytail emerged from his black ball cap and swung between his shoulder blades. Dirty, baggy blue jeans hung limply from his hips.

A cap, sunglasses, and a ponytail. A witness from the first fire observed a suspicious person matching that description.

Sharon followed him. She was close enough to the fire to feel the waves of heat rolling over her. She blinked against the sting of smoke. She trailed her target, hanging back as he turned the corner.

Her heart beat like dance club music. She'd read arsonists often returned as spectators to their events. If this fire was an arson—and Sharon suspected it was—this man could be the perpetrator. Or torch, as firefighters called them.

Sharon timed it so she turned the corner moments after her target. But when she entered the parking lot, all she saw were cars. She hadn't seen a vehicle leave the lot, so where had her target gone?

She walked farther into the lot with cautious steps.

Her eyes scanned the area searching for movement. Her ears strained for sounds other than the battle waging on the street between the fire and the firefighters. She heard nothing above her pounding heart and nervous breathing.

Across the lot, Sharon saw the back entrance to the cell phone company. She squinted toward the building. The door appeared to be slightly open. Had the stranger entered the building despite the inferno next door?

Her mind racing, she wanted to move forward, to see whether he stood on the other side of that door. To check the risky impulse, she took a deliberate step back. The fire hadn't reached that building yet, but it could. And soon. Why would he have taken the risk and gone inside? What could be so important?

Sharon spun back the way she'd come. The firefighters had to be told someone may have reentered the cell phone store. She'd advanced perhaps a yard when a blow to the back of her head cut off the communication between her brain and her muscles. Her vision wavered, then everything went black as her body crumpled to the asphalt.

Sharon awoke in what appeared to be a hospital room. The last time she'd opened her eyes she'd been in an examining room and a doctor had been poking at her head. He'd given her painkillers and disappeared before she could ask him what had happened.

Frightened and disoriented, her gaze traveled from Allyson, who hovered over her, to Andre, who stood at the foot of her bed. It calmed her to know she wasn't alone.

"You're supposed to *report* the news, not *become* the

news." The worry in Allyson's eyes softened the sting of her rebuke.

Sharon's throat hurt as though she'd inhaled a lot of smoke. But how? "I have to call my mother." Her voice was a croak.

"I already did. She's on her way." Allyson turned to the table beside the bed and poured Sharon a glass of water. She helped Sharon sit up and gave her the drink.

Sharon took a careful sip of water through a straw. "How did you know I was at the hospital?"

"Matt called the paper. The receptionist couldn't find Wayne, so she transferred Matt's call to me. What were you doing in that building?"

It hurt to swallow. "What building?" Her voice was still raspy.

Allyson's expression reflected the confusion Sharon felt. "Matt told us you went into the cellular store next to the burning building."

"No, I didn't." Events were a little confused. It didn't help that she had a killer headache. But Sharon was certain she hadn't gone into any building.

Andre walked around the bed to stand beside Allyson. "Then how did you get into the store?"

"I don't know." But she could guess. She raised her hand to gingerly finger the back of her head. It ached. The knot was pronounced, although the skin wasn't broken. "I was in the parking lot."

Andre exchanged a look with Allyson. "Why?"

Sharon gave the glass back to Allyson and watched her friend return it to the table. "I was following someone, a man who was acting strangely."

Andre's brows furrowed. "Why didn't you tell a fireman?"

Sharon rubbed her temples, trying to ease the throbbing in her head. "They were busy."

"I wasn't too busy." Matthew entered the room and took up Andre's previous post at the foot of her bed. "As part of my investigation, I would have taken the time to hear about a suspicious person."

The captain's thumbs were hooked into the front pockets of his black slacks. The top two buttons of his white shirt were undone above a loosened blue-and-gold tie. But his relaxed appearance was at odds with the tension radiating from him.

Sharon's heart sank as she wondered how much more ground she'd lost while trying to gain his trust. She tried to explain what she now realized was inexplicable. Her actions were just that stupid. "He was moving quickly. I was afraid I would lose him."

Matthew seemed unimpressed by her reasoning. "You did lose him. And you were almost killed. If I hadn't seen you slip under the tape—which was clearly marked *do not cross*—you would have died."

Sharon flinched at that thought. The drumming in her head sped up. "I didn't go into that building."

Matthew's brows met above confused dark eyes. "I found you there."

An image of herself being carried from a smoking building teased her mind. Strong arms had cradled her. An anxious voice had whispered in her ear, assuring her she'd be all right. The next thing Sharon remembered was waking in an ambulance.

Allyson's words interrupted the memory. "Sharon should rest. She has a slight concussion. The doctor wants her to stay overnight."

Matthew's gaze released Sharon as he addressed her friends. "I have some questions about the man she followed."

Andre shifted to face Matthew squarely. "She's tired and in pain."

Matthew was stubborn. "It won't take long."

Allyson and Andre wore identical looks of concern. The only thing her protectors lacked were suits of shining armor.

Sharon gave Allyson's hand an encouraging squeeze and tried to draw Andre's attention from Matthew. "I'll be fine, Dre."

Andre looked at her before returning his attention to the fire investigator. "We'll wait outside." He placed his hand on the small of Allyson's back.

Allyson gave Matthew a stern glare. "Remember, she's been through a lot." Without waiting for a response, she followed Andre from the room.

With her protectors gone, Matthew's attention returned to Sharon. "What did the man look like?"

Sharon closed her eyes, straining to bring forward a picture of the mystery man. "He tried to hide his identity. He was tall and seemed thin under his baggy clothes. Black sweat jacket and dirty blue jeans that were really baggy and too long. Long, unkempt brown hair pulled back into a ponytail. He wore a black ball cap and wraparound black sunglasses. But they were cheap. As though he'd bought them at a discount store."

Matthew arched a thick brow. "Impressive." His praise surprised her.

"I'm a journalist. I'm trained to observe."

The reminder seemed to cool his regard. "Are you also trained to act irresponsibly?" He didn't wait for an answer. "Did you see him go into the building?"

Sharon pondered his latest insult. Perhaps she'd been irresponsible, but it had seemed like a good idea at the time. "No, but he wasn't in the parking lot. I was leaving to tell the firefighters I thought he'd gone into the building. That's when someone hit me from behind."

Matthew's square jaw tightened. He moved closer and stood beside her. "Hard enough for you to lose consciousness?"

Without asking permission, he brushed his hand over the back of her head, his fingers gently searching. Sharon tensed, trying not to get excited. She hadn't been affected by the doctor's examination. But then, he'd been an elderly man who'd reminded her of Captain Kangaroo. Matthew reminded her of a wet dream.

His probing fingers found the bump on the back of her head. He traced it gently, his tender touch trailing electricity from the wound down her spine. Quickly, she reached behind her and grabbed his hand. Just as quickly, she released it.

"It's still tender." Her voice shook.

"Do you think the man you followed hit you?"

She looked away, clearing her throat. It still hurt. "He must have hit me. Who else could it have been?" She met his gaze again. He didn't seem affected by her at all.

Matthew sat on the edge of her bed. He took her hand, the connection adding emphasis to his words. "This isn't a game, Sharon. It's not a TV show or a movie. It's real. People who are crazy enough to burn buildings aren't above killing anyone who tries to stop them. What you did was incredibly dangerous."

Sharon stared at their clasped hands, finally facing what she'd begun to fear in the ambulance—someone had tried to kill her. And Matthew had jeopardized his life to save her.

She lifted her eyes to his and found fear and concern churning in the dark depths. "Thank you for saving my life."

He started to speak, but a commotion at the door

drew her attention from him. Her mother rushed in, eyes wild with fear until they settled on Sharon.

"Oh, my goodness." Helen flew to her daughter's side. Matthew stood to give her mother room.

"Mom, I'm fine." Sharon covered her mother's hands as they cupped her cheeks.

Helen blinked. "What happened to your voice?"

"Smoke inhalation."

"These scratches don't look too deep." Helen traced Sharon's cheeks, her voice soft as though she spoke to herself.

Startled, Sharon lifted her hand to her face. She hadn't realized it had been cut during the ordeal.

Helen gently tipped Sharon's head forward, carefully probing through her hair. "The bruise isn't very big." She felt Sharon's arms and shoulders as well. Her examination complete, her mother wrapped her in her arms. "Oh, my goodness. I was so scared when Allyson called me."

What had Allyson said? "I'm sorry, Mom." She saw Matthew watching them. "Matt saved my life."

His eyes widened in surprise, his attention swinging to her mother.

Helen released Sharon and walked to Matthew. The top of her head just cleared his chest. "Thank you." Her words were thick with emotion.

Helen wrapped her arms around his waist. Sharon smiled as Matthew awkwardly returned the embrace.

He looked at Sharon as he patted her mother's back. "You're welcome."

Sharon held his gaze, letting herself drift back into the memory of his arms around her, carrying her to safety as he whispered words of comfort in her ear.

* * *

When Sharon arrived at work Tuesday morning, she found Allyson and Andre waiting in her cubicle. Andre moved aside so she could enter her work space.

Allyson rose from Sharon's desk. "You're sure it's not too soon for you to come back to work?"

"Positive. My headache's pretty much gone." And it didn't hurt as much to speak. Sharon laid her purse and newspaper on her desk, and the cup of coffee Allyson handed to her. "Thank you for everything you did for me at the hospital yesterday."

Allyson waved her hand in a dismissive gesture. "I hope Matt wasn't too hard on you after we left."

Sharon sat. "No, he wasn't." She thought of her mother hugging Matthew.

Andre crowded farther into the small space. "What did he say about the attack? Does he think it's isolated to yesterday's fire or will this guy come after you again?"

Sharon shook her head. "I don't think he'll come after me. At least that's what I told my mother."

Andre didn't look appeased. "Are they going to circulate his description?"

Sharon sipped her coffee. "They sent a sketch artist to the hospital. I wasn't able to give her much to draw, though. The man did a good job masking his appearance."

Allyson stepped closer to Andre, putting a hand on his upper arm. "Every bit helps. We should get back to work. Let us know if you need anything."

Sharon nodded. "Thanks again. For everything."

Andre stepped aside so Allyson could precede him from the cubicle. "No problem. See you later."

Sharon spun her chair around to store her purse in a desk drawer. Turning back to her desk, she opened her paper to Lucas's article on the latest west side fire. She took a fortifying sip of coffee before diving into the story.

By the end of the lead paragraph, Sharon's head was spinning. She struggled to finish the article before marching to Lucas's cube. "Were you at the fire yesterday?"

The young usurper was hunched over his computer. His Cartier watch winked from the wrist poised over the keyboard. The screen displayed a download dialogue box from a music Internet site.

"Yeah. Sure." He jabbed the commands that would transfer the music files to his iPod.

"I didn't see you there."

He turned to face her. "Were you trying to take a story from my beat again? What's it going to take to get you to stop?"

"The last time you filed a story from a remote location, the paper had to run corrections for several claims you made."

Anger ignited the cold green eyes. "And yet they haven't taken me off the beat. It's a pity you can't say the same."

Sharon ignored the sting. "Who's doing your work for you?"

"What makes you think I'm not doing it myself?"

"It's obvious you're not taking the responsibility seriously. Instead of following up on the fire, you're downloading music. What's the matter? Did your father pull your allowance and make you get a job? Having trouble paying your bills?"

The anger in Lucas's eyes glowed brighter. "Careful, MacCabe. Your jealousy is showing."

Sharon started to fire off a blistering reply, but her words were cut off by Wayne's greeting.

"MacCabe, glad you could join us. Jamieson and Scott said you went home sick yesterday. The next time you leave early, call me yourself."

Sharon turned toward her editor. She knew she was taking a risk, but she couldn't stand by mutely while the credibility of the paper she worked for was continually undermined. Her readers were the ones who would suffer. "I need to speak with you."

Behind her, she heard Lucas's taunting voice. "You're out of your league, MacCabe."

She glared at him. "And you're still in training camp."

Wayne frowned at her. "What's this about?"

"Could we speak in your office?"

The older man's gaze swung between Sharon and Lucas. With heavy irritation and marked reluctance, he turned back to his office. Sharon followed, closing the door behind her.

Wayne stood behind his desk. "Make it quick."

Sharon came farther into the cramped office. "Lucas wasn't at the fire scene yesterday. This is the second time he's reported on an event without being on-site or talking to any of the principals."

Wayne's gray gaze narrowed on her. "How do you know that?"

Sharon's shoulders stiffened with nerves. She tried to make her boss stick to the point. "You told him to go to the fire. He ignored your assignment."

Wayne lowered into his chair. "Did you go to the fire, MacCabe?"

Sharon couldn't bring herself to answer his direct question. A deep breath drew the stench of aging newsprint. "Why does Lucas have this beat?"

"Because I gave it to him." Wayne's aggravation was rough in his voice. "I'm the boss. I can do that."

"Who told you to give it to him?"

Wayne shot out of his chair, causing Sharon to take a startled step back. "The beat isn't yours, MacCabe.

How many times and how many ways do I have to tell you that?"

Sharon's suspicions grew. She stepped forward, regaining ground. "One day, you're satisfied with my work. The next day, you replace me. Whose decision was that?"

Her editor's face darkened with anger. "If you interfere with that assignment again, I'm going to reassign you to the calendar section."

More threats against her career. Sharon clenched her damp fists to keep anger and outrage from tearing her apart. "What was behind the decision to give Lucas my beat?"

Wayne, beet red and shaking, reclaimed his seat. "Not another word."

"Seven months ago, I was good enough for you to promote me. Now, you're doing everything imaginable to undermine me."

"MacCabe." Wayne said her name in warning.

Sharon ignored him. "You demoted me. Pulled my stories. Threatened to demote me further."

"MacCabe, stop—"

She took note of Wayne's rapid breathing, his flushed cheeks and the sweat on his upper lip. "Why are you doing this?"

"Not one more word. Understand?"

"No, Wayne. I don't." Her boss was too much of a coward to tell her what was really going on. He must have promised someone something. Was she in the way?

Clenching her teeth, Sharon marched from his office. She rounded into her cubicle and restrained the urge to pound her desk. Why was Wayne keeping Lucas on the beat? What was the point? He wasn't even doing the work. Or was he?

Lucas's comment about reporters making up stories

returned to her. It was followed almost immediately by an image of the suspicious stranger at yesterday's fire. The stranger had a long, brown ponytail. But that could have been part of his disguise, a wig. Under the baggy clothes, the stranger's body type could have been similar to Lucas's build.

Sharon frowned. Was she letting her imagination get away with her? Or was it possible Lucas was the assailant who had pulled her unconscious body into a burning building?

Chapter 13

Matthew rounded the corner of Elizabeth Street onto Kanawha Boulevard, completing the first half of his run. He filled his lungs with the cool evening air as he headed back toward the South Side Bridge.

Tuesday's after-work rush hour had been over for some time and traffic was sparse. Matthew jogged in place beneath a lamp and checked for cars before dashing across the street. Nagging questions followed him.

Who'd dragged Sharon into the cellular phone store yesterday while a fire had burned nearby? Was it the arsonist or was someone else trying to kill her? If it was the torch, would he come after her again? Matthew wiped the stinging sweat from his eyes.

As he'd carried Sharon's unconscious body from the building, she'd stirred in his arms. That proof of life, in addition to her soft breaths against his neck, had reassured him. He'd held her closer in a reflexive gesture that had steadied him as much as he'd hoped it had comforted her. That's when he'd realized how hard his heart was pounding. Part fear for her and part anger against whoever had tried to harm her.

Matthew crossed the street, squinting into the distance.

Sharon's apartment building was less than three blocks away. All day, he'd tempered his urge to call her with his need to keep his distance from the curious journalist. But wasn't it only natural he'd want to make sure she was all right?

Matthew turned onto Ruffner Street before he could change his mind. He slowed as he approached Sharon's home. How would she react to his showing up at her door in the middle of the night unannounced and dripping sweat? He practiced what he would say to explain his impulsive visit.

His thoughts broke off at the sound of rapid footfalls behind him. They were too fast for a recreational runner. For some reason, the approach unnerved him. He shifted to the right, closer to the street, giving the other person room to pass on his left.

But the stranger didn't pass.

A powerful blow to his right calf drove Matthew to the sidewalk. He landed on his hands and knees. Shock, confusion, and anger exploded in him. He felt a rush of adrenaline that quickened his reflexes and heightened his senses.

Matthew rolled onto his back, barely avoiding a second blow. He grunted with pain as the concrete tore the exposed flesh of his legs and arms. The club emitted an almost deafening crack as it connected with the sidewalk.

His assailant straightened. In the dim glow of a nearby streetlight, Matthew had the impression of a tall, young black man in dark, baggy clothes. Thick braids were combed back from his round face. Then Matthew saw the club—a baseball bat?—swinging for his head. He rolled again, this time kicking out to connect with his attacker's knee. The force of his kick sent the stranger to the sidewalk beside him.

Matthew straddled the younger man, pinning him to the ground. "Who are you?"

His attacker remained silent. Matthew watched contempt build in the young man's eyes.

He hauled the stranger to his feet, gritting his teeth as the movement breathed fire into his scratches. He gripped the front of his assailant's hooded sweatshirt, preparing to interrogate him further. The piercing screech of a whistle cut him short.

"Whoever you are, I've called the police." Sharon's voice carried from her front steps. "You can either spend the night in jail or take whatever problem you have out of my neighborhood."

"What are you—" Matthew stopped in midsentence, gasping when his adversary used Sharon's interruption to sucker punch him.

Doubled over with the breath driven from him, Matthew lost his grip on his combatant. He listened to the stranger's running footsteps as the younger man escaped into the night.

"Matt?" Sharon sounded surprised.

Matthew regained his breath. "Yeah."

He glanced at his wounds. He'd have to clean them. He took a cautious step toward Sharon and winced again.

She met him halfway. "What happened?"

"Some punk with a baseball bat came at me from out of nowhere."

Sharon slid under his arm to brace him as they walked toward her building. "How badly are you hurt?"

"Nothing's broken." Matthew stopped walking and looked down at her nestled in the crook of his arm. Her oversized West Virginia University jersey nearly swallowed her whole. She was a foot shorter than he, yet she was trying to half-carry him toward her home.

It was almost as ridiculous as her trying to stop a fight between two grown men.

"What made you confront two angry men by yourself?"

Sharon's eyes widened with amazement, then narrowed with determination. "I won't allow violence in my neighborhood. Not two angry men. Not two fighting boys. Not some kid kicking a dog."

Matthew's reaction balanced between annoyance and admiration. "Why didn't you wait for the police?"

She glanced toward the street and back again. "For how long? I don't think an unarmed fight in this neighborhood is a high priority for the police. Besides, everything worked out."

Matthew snorted. "Easy for you to say."

"Sorry." Sharon seemed regretful.

"Next time, think before you act." He started moving again but pulled up short when Sharon hung back.

Her lips parted in surprise. "I did."

"At best, you thought *while* you acted."

"I can't believe you're going to be mean to me and then expect me to help you."

Matthew hesitated. That is what he expected. He'd never considered she wouldn't help him. Nor had he realized he'd developed expectations where this woman was concerned. When had that happened?

Disappointment rose like poison in his system. But the sound of Sharon's laughter was his antidote. It spilled from her like a freshwater spring. Mischief gleamed in her ebony eyes, inviting him to laugh at himself. He compromised with a smile.

Sharon helped him up her front steps. "Stop sulking, Captain. I was just teasing you."

"I wasn't sulking."

She let him into her apartment and gestured to a chair at her dinette table. She disappeared into the kitchen, then reappeared offering him a glass of water. "I'll be right back."

Sharon strode to her bedroom, mentally listing the items she'd need. She crossed to the connecting bathroom and grabbed the bag of cotton balls and a bottle of antiseptic before returning to her dining area. Matthew sat in a chair, his long, muscled legs bent at the knees. Her mouth went dry.

She walked to him and lowered herself to a kneeling position to tend his injured leg. She looked up into Matthew's midnight eyes. "I'll try to be gentle." Her small joke fell flat in her husky voice.

"I leave myself in your hands."

His sexy smile made her heart skip. What would Florence Nightingale do?

Sharon braced Matthew's left leg against her right side. The short hair along his thigh brushed damply against her fingers. She ignored the press of his knee against her hip—to the best of her ability—and used a cotton ball and antiseptic to clean dust and gravel from the injured area. Matthew's leg muscle flexed against her. Her fingers trembled above his leg, but she kept her eyes lowered.

What was the matter with her? How could she react this way to a man who didn't even trust her?

Sharon poured antiseptic onto a fresh cotton ball and gently swabbed her patient's wounds. Most of the scratches were surface, but two or three were deeper.

She took another cotton ball from the bag. "What did he want?" She cleaned the scratches and abrasions again before putting Band-Aids on the deeper cuts.

"Probably money."

Sharon looked up, finding the heat of anger in Matthew's eyes. "Someone tried to kill me yesterday. Then someone tries to beat you senseless tonight. I think it's safe to say we won't be voted king and queen of the prom."

"You think the attacks are connected?"

Sharon ignored the doubt in Matthew's voice as she bandaged his wounds. "I don't believe in coincidences."

"Why would someone try to kill us?"

She rose to her feet. "What do we have in common?"

It took Matthew a second to make the connection. "The fire investigation."

"Until we figure out who's behind these attacks, no more night running for you."

Matthew seemed startled. "You sound like my mother."

She faked a smile. "That's the most seductive thing a good-looking man could say to a woman."

His eyes widened even more. "You think I'm good looking?"

"I remind you of your mother?"

Matthew rubbed a hand over his close-cropped hair. "That came out wrong."

Sharon took the antiseptic and cotton balls back to her bathroom. When she returned, she found Matthew limping circles around her table. "How do you feel?"

"Sore." He gave her a crooked smile. "Thanks for playing nurse."

"What are neighbors for? I'll drive you home."

Sharon collected her keys and cell phone from the hall table on her way out. She unlocked the passenger door before walking around her Civic to the driver's side. She buckled her seat belt and made sure Matthew was strapped in before starting the car.

Matthew's voice broke the intimate silence. "I was on my way to your place to see how you were doing."

"I'm fine." Sharon glanced at him. "Did you get a good look at the guy who attacked you?"

"A young black guy with braids."

Sharon's brows knitted. "The guy I followed was white with a brown ponytail."

"If two men are involved, maybe these attacks aren't connected."

Sharon shook her head. "Do muggers carry baseball bats?"

"Good point. If they do have a weapon, it's usually a knife or a gun."

"Exactly. Besides, I don't think a mugger would target a jogger. How many joggers carry wallets?"

"All right, Nancy Drew." Matthew pointed toward the windshield. "Take the next exit."

Sharon turned off at an exit that led to the middle-class neighborhood of South Hills. "You need to get a description to a sketch artist."

"I will." Matthew gestured toward the windshield again. "The last house on the right. There's only one torch, though. The MO for the fires is the same."

"Then only one of them is setting the fires, but they're both involved." She stopped the car in front of Matthew's house and climbed out to help him.

"I can manage."

"Sure you can, tough guy." She took his arm to help him gain leverage.

Matthew unfurled from the Civic and stood beside Sharon on the sidewalk. "If you're right, it's not safe for you to investigate the arsons."

Sharon released Matthew's arm, her fingers lingering on his skin. "It's not safe for you, either."

He stepped closer, his presence surrounding her, the sky a blanket of diamonds above her. "It's my job."

"It's my job too."

Thankfully, Matthew didn't repeat that the fire department wasn't her beat any longer. Instead Sharon listened to the bullfrogs and crickets who provided theme music for their impasse.

Matthew raised his hand to cup her cheek. The warmth from his palm filled her whole body, chasing away the evening's chill. "This isn't a game, Sharon."

She frowned. He just didn't get it. "My readers need to know there's an arsonist—or two—threatening our community."

He lowered his arm. "Is getting that information to them worth your life?"

Sharon met the challenge in his midnight gaze. "I hope it doesn't come to that." She wasn't a fool. But she couldn't sleep at night if she walked away from this responsibility.

"So do I."

Matthew limped to his house and up the staircase that led to his front door. As Sharon tracked his painful progress into his house, she had a new urgency to find the arsonist.

Matthew would have better appreciated Fire Chief Larry Miller's office if this had been a social call. Instead, he barely registered the dark wood and red accents as he waited to defend his job performance.

He slid a glance at Brad Naismith, admiring the assistant chief's apparent calm. But then, what did his boss have to worry about? If Miller brought the heat to bear on the investigation, Naismith could put the blame on Matthew. That was called delegating.

Matthew had firsthand experience with that management technique. His supervisor at the Pittsburgh station had felt pressured to close the investigation into the arson that had killed Matthew's sister. Instead of insisting they follow procedure, the other man had caved in to the media and thrown Matthew to the sharks.

Matthew shook off the past. Ignoring the soreness in his leg from last night's fall, he rose with Naismith when the fire chief finally joined them.

Miller didn't acknowledge his subordinates until his long strides carried him to the other side of his desk. He lowered himself into his executive chair.

A tall wiry black man with fair skin, Miller's soot-gray gaze bore into Matthew. "What the hell is taking so long with your investigation, Captain?"

Nothing like getting to the point. Matthew resumed his seat. "Sir, it's only been a week. The first arson occurred last Wednesday. The second occurred a few days ago."

The older man frowned, his heavy eyebrows knitting above his narrowed eyes. "How many arsons are there? You're quoted all over the papers bragging about a string of arsons, causing a panic all over the city."

"Sir, I'm investigating two. But I wasn't interviewed for those articles. The reporter fabricated those quotes, and the paper ran corrections."

"I never saw any corrections."

Matthew clenched his teeth, mentally cursing the *Times*. Once again, a newspaper's overzealous pursuit of revenues and readership was jeopardizing his reputation.

Naismith crossed his arms over his chest. "I don't think it's arson."

Miller's gaze ricocheted to the assistant chief. "Why not?"

The burly man shrugged. "My men worked that fire. They didn't see anything to indicate arson."

Matthew didn't want to contradict his boss, especially

in front of the fire chief. But Naismith was wrong. "My lieutenant and I found evidence of an accelerant and a clear burn pattern."

Miller dragged his hand over his hair, which was cropped so close, it appeared like a thin layer of smoke on his scalp. "Were the scenes similar?"

Matthew felt the sting of Naismith's gaze. "Yes, sir. These aren't accidental fires."

Naismith interrupted the exchange. "You think we have a torch?"

"The evidence points to one." Did Naismith doubt the evidence, or was he trying to get out of the investigation? If his goal was to end the investigation, what was his motive?

Naismith shook his head. "It's all circumstantial."

Matthew could add that someone tried to beat the crap out of him last night. But in the clarity of a new day, he heard the paranoia in that claim. The only substantiating evidence he could offer were Sharon's thoughts, which didn't sound so reliable this morning.

Matthew stayed with the tangible evidence he had. "Circumstantial or not, we can't ignore it."

His boss gave him a hard stare. "What's the motive? Who are your suspects?"

"We're talking to everyone associated with those companies, as well as witnesses."

Naismith snorted. "Your evidence against the furniture-store owner is weak."

What was Naismith getting at? The evidence may not have pointed to O'Conner, but it pointed to someone. "We're also checking into a report of a suspicious person at the location."

Miller stopped swinging his chair and sat forward. "Enough." He glared from Matthew to Naismith and back. "I'm getting calls from people on the west side complaining about how long it's taking to find this torch. They're afraid their companies will be next."

Naismith drummed his fingers on the chair's arm. "We can't rush to judgment. We have to be sure before we claim arson."

Miller's glare turned fierce. "You'd better figure this out soon. I need this case closed."

"Understood, sir." Matthew considered Naismith's glower.

Would his boss be a help or a hindrance during the investigation?

Chapter 14

Hours later, a knock diverted Matthew's scowl from the arson interview reports to his office door. Sharon stood in the threshold, looking warmly seductive and coolly professional. Her bronze skirt brushed her knees while her matching jacket traced over her waist to her hips.

He straightened in his chair. "How did you get past Li Mai?"

Sharon glanced at her watch. "She must be at lunch."

The hint of a humid Southern day in her voice evoked memories from the night before when she'd knelt beside him to clean his injuries. Matthew blinked the images away. That's when her words registered.

He checked his own watch. "Lunchtime?" It was almost a quarter to one. Wednesday was speeding away from him. "No wonder I'm hungry."

"Mind if I join you? I haven't eaten, either."

The little reporter looked harmless. Matthew the man would welcome her company. But Matthew the fire investigator reminded him what happened the last time he'd trusted the press.

He couldn't read the thoughts behind her wide

ebony eyes. "Would it be a social visit or a working lunch?"

Sharon leaned against the doorjamb and shrugged a shoulder. "Both. How's your leg?"

The image of her tending his thigh returned. "Fine. Thanks again for your help."

Sharon's grin signaled mischief. "I must have latent maternal instincts."

Matthew smiled. "Ouch."

She stood away from the door and paced farther into the room. "We need to talk about the fire investigation."

"If I find anything of interest, I promise I'll tell you."

Sharon started shaking her head before he'd finished his sentence. Her dark, wavy hair swung with the movement. "That's not good enough, Captain. We agreed last night that the attacks against us are connected to the arsons."

Matthew rubbed his hand across his forehead. "That's one theory we tried last night. I'm not so sure it's valid."

She sank into the chair in front of his desk and crossed her legs. "Someone threatened both of us. That makes us equal partners on this case."

"You're chasing a conspiracy while I'm looking for a torch."

"You may not agree with my theory, but we actually want the same thing."

Matthew checked his watch again. The numbers ticked closer to one P.M. He pushed out of his chair. "Let's get lunch. I don't like to argue on an empty stomach."

Sharon stood. "It doesn't have to be an argument."

"When you're involved, everything becomes an argument." He was only half-joking.

She laughed. "Funny, I was thinking the same about you." She preceded him out of his office.

Less than thirty minutes later, they were riding the escalator to the Town Center's International Food Court. Sharon stepped off the mall's escalator and a bevy of culinary scents hit her at once. Her mouth watered and her stomach sent up a roar of approval. She felt her face flame with embarrassment.

Matthew chuckled. "Not a moment too soon."

Due to the lateness of the hour, the food court was almost empty. Sharon carried a tray with her chicken sandwich and lemonade past abandoned tables and chairs to a setting farthest from pedestrian traffic. Matthew followed.

He removed his suit jacket and settled it on the back of his chair before taking his seat. "How's Helen?"

Sharon switched her attention from his broad shoulders to his dark gaze and recalled the afternoon she and her mother had spent with him. "She's well. Busy organizing voter drives."

Matthew unwrapped his steak sandwich. "Did you get your interest for public service from her?"

Sharon laid her napkin on her lap. "You're very observant. It comes from both of my parents."

Matthew drank his root beer. "Why journalism? Why not some nonprofit organization or something?"

"News is my passion." She sipped her lemonade. "It's important for people to know what's going on around them so they can make informed decisions. Or, in the case of this arsonist, protect themselves."

"I'm beginning to think *tenacious* is your middle name." There was subtle sex appeal in his smile.

Sharon felt her lips curve in response. "You'd be close."

She was comfortable with the silence that followed

and too hungry for casual conversation. The meal filled the gaping hole in her stomach.

She finished her sandwich and wiped her hands. "What did the café owner tell you about the events before the fire?" She tossed out the question as she pulled her reporter's notebook from her bag.

Matthew's gaze traveled a skeptical path from her eyes to her notebook and back. "I thought you couldn't cover the fire beat? What are you going to do with your notes?"

"I'll worry about that later."

Matthew set aside his empty tray and drank the rest of his root beer. "You're going to work your full-time job and investigate an arson on the side?"

Sharon thought of all the work she'd done on the local jazz band feature only to have it pulled due to lack of space. It wasn't the first time that had happened, and she was certain it wouldn't be the last. Wayne's campaign to undermine her in the newsroom was in full swing. Why was he doing that? What was behind his actions?

"I'll make the time."

Matthew studied her for a long moment. Sharon could almost hear his internal debate. *Should I trust her? She's a reporter. Are any of them trustworthy?* She held his gaze and her breath, willing him to take a chance on her.

Matthew wiped his large hands on a paper napkin. "We're not investigating one arson. We're investigating two."

Matthew sat back in the metal-and-plastic chair. "At both events, the smoke was a darker black than usual and the fires were burning too quickly for an accidental blaze. The flames left a distinct path across the employee break room in the furniture store. Same with the café's supply room. The torch didn't even try to make it look like an accident."

"You sound as though you wish he had." Sharon furrowed her brows, trying to concentrate on the words she wrote as well as those she heard.

Matthew dragged a hand over his hair. "That's not it. Torches usually try to mask their work, and they usually set their fires at night. This one set his fires in broad daylight and left a clear trail. He's cocky. That's what worries me."

Sharon shared his concern. A torch who thought he couldn't get caught. "What does he want?"

"I haven't figured it out yet." He paused as though working on the puzzle. "There are six identified motives for arson."

Sharon set down her notebook and used her fingers to count the reasons. "Revenge, profit, vandalism, thrill-seeking, political or social statements, and concealment of another crime."

Matthew's brows jumped in surprise. "You've done your research." He paused, watching her closely. "You've also interviewed witnesses and one of the business owners. Any thoughts on which motive fits?"

Sharon shook her head. "I don't have enough information." She searched Matthew's features. "Have you ruled out the possibility Reilly may have burned down his furniture store for the insurance?"

"Not yet. Insurance scam is a common reason for arson. It fits the profit motive." Matthew leaned back in his chair, tilting his head contemplatively. "O'Conner was having lunch with a business colleague around the time the fire was set, but he could have had someone set the fire for him."

Sharon nodded, reluctantly, at the truth of his words. Her gaze tracked his thumb's path up the side of the drink container. "I don't think it was profit. Reilly's business meant too much to him."

"I have to build my case on evidence, not feelings. Unfortunately, arson is one of the hardest crimes to solve because often the fire destroys the evidence."

Sharon wrote his comment as a direct quote for the article she would eventually write. "It's the leading cause of property damage. But only two percent ever lead to convictions."

"That's right."

Sharon saw the admiration in Matthew's eyes. It wasn't such a leap from admiration to trust, was it? She hoped not. She really wanted his trust. She needed it.

She placed her food tray on top of his. "Do you think it's possible the arsonist is done? Maybe he won't set another fire."

"He will. He's too obvious. It's as though he wants to get caught."

"But if that's true, if we don't catch him this time, will he continue setting fires until we do catch him?"

"Probably." Matthew must have seen the concern in Sharon's expression. He covered her hand with his. "I don't mean to cause a panic. I'm trying to explain why the department doesn't treat suspicious fires as though they're isolated cases of mischief. We can't afford to."

Sharon stared at the large, dark hand covering hers. She wanted to record his statement as a direct quote, but she didn't want to lose this connection to him. His skin was so warm.

She pulled her gaze up and away from his touch to settle on his eyes. "What kind of liquid did the arsonist use to start the fire?"

Matthew chuckled, sliding his arm back and breaking the connection. "Good effort, Sharon, but we aren't divulging that information at this time."

Sharon battled her disappointment and tossed him a smile. "I had to try."

His lips quirked. "I know." He checked his watch. "It's after two. I'd better head back to the office."

Sharon waited while he shrugged into his suit jacket, then followed him as he carried their trays to the trash bin. "Thanks for the interview, Matt."

"I still don't know how you're going to use it."

They walked together toward the parking garage. Sharon had driven, promising to return Matthew to the fire station, which was on her way back to the newspaper.

Sharon huddled in her coat as a cool spring breeze slipped past her in the mall garage. "I can't meekly accept management's decision to derail my career. To paraphrase Patti LaBelle, I have to stir things up."

Matthew paced beside her. "Patti LaBelle?"

"Yes. Lately, my life has resembled one of her greatest hits albums."

"Which songs?"

Sharon looked at him, deciding against listing "The Right Kind of Lover." "Well, I already mentioned 'Stir It Up.' And there's 'New Attitude.'"

"I don't recognize 'New Attitude.'"

She gave him a look of exaggerated horror. "How is that possible?"

Matthew stopped beside her car. "Sing it for me."

Startled laughter burst from her. "No, I won't sing it for you."

"I'd really like to hear it."

"I'll loan you my CD."

Still laughing, Sharon started to walk past him, but Matthew curled his hand around her forearm. "Please."

Her amusement died. His whispered word seeped into her chest and melted her heart.

She pulled her gaze from his and looked around the

empty parking garage. At two o'clock in the afternoon, it was too late for the lunch crowd, but too early for the after-work shoppers.

Turning back to him, she saw the warmth in Matthew's eyes, the hint of a smile softening his firm lips. Dignity be damned. She took a deep breath, closed her eyes and channeled LaBelle.

Sharon belted out the opening lines, swinging her hips and pumping her arms. She was lost in the moment when she got to the chorus. Then a sound, similar to a gasp, broke her concentration. She opened her eyes and found Matthew almost doubled over with laughter.

She gaped at him. "You tricked me."

With two steps, she was close enough to punch him. Sharon gave in to the temptation with a hard shot to his upper arm. Her knuckles hit firm muscle.

Matthew grunted but kept chuckling. "I couldn't resist." His voice was breathless. "I'm sorry."

His humor was contagious. A few giggles escaped her even as she pulled her arm back to slug him again.

"Ouch." Matthew straightened and cupped her shoulders to hold her at arm's length while he controlled his hilarity. "I'm sorry. I was just teasing you."

Sharon watched him wipe tears from his eyes. Coupled with his broad grin, the tears seemed to weaken his credibility.

"You snake." Her own smile and lingering chuckles drained the heat from her response.

Sharon sensed the moment his humor changed to something warmer, thrilling. She no longer felt the chill of the parking garage.

Matthew's hands tightened on her shoulders, drawing her in as he lowered his head. She smoothed her palms up his chest and raised onto her toes. She rested her hands on his broad shoulders to keep her balance.

His lips moved over hers, investigating their shape and texture. His hands stroked from her shoulders downward to the small of her back. Sharon moved forward, still on her toes, letting Matthew bring her closer to his long, hot body.

She shivered when he stroked the corner of her mouth with the tip of his tongue. Her arms curved around his shoulders to steady herself. She tilted her head and parted her lips to invite him in. Matthew's tongue entered her mouth with one long, deep stroke. Sharon gasped, opening wider. She caressed his tongue with her own, sucking it deeper.

Sharon realized the humming she heard came from her. Her entire body was singing and she was one pulse beat away from grinding herself against Matthew. This was neither the time nor the place. She drew her arms away from Matthew's neck, letting her palms slide down his chest before gently pushing her hands against him. Instantly, Matthew stepped back, allowing some space between them.

Sharon took a deep breath before opening her eyes. She smiled at him. "Public displays of affection, Captain?"

"You draw me like a moth to a flame." His voice was rough.

Her smile faded. "I don't know whether to be flattered or insulted. Do you really think I could destroy you?"

"You could if you wanted to."

She shook her head. "I don't want to."

"Then I have nothing to worry about." His lips bore down on hers again. He gave her a hard, quick kiss before releasing her.

Sharon's knees weren't quite steady as she walked to

the driver's-side door. She deactivated her car alarm. Matthew may think he had nothing to worry about, but perhaps she did. The cautious captain was carefully working his way into her heart.

Chapter 15

Sharon leaned against the break room counter and stirred her afternoon coffee. She didn't really need caffeine. Her system was still charged from the lunch she'd had with Matthew a couple of hours before. Well, from the kiss they'd shared in the mall parking garage. She'd had several positive breakthroughs that afternoon. She also felt more optimistic about her prospects for working with him on the investigation.

The possibility of a personal relationship between them looked promising as well. Sharon blushed, remembering the kiss they'd shared. Her behavior amazed her. It had been so out of character.

"Why did you have lunch with Matthew Payton today?"

Sharon glanced up at the sound of Lucas's voice. He stood on the other side of the break room, suspicion tightening his features.

She tossed the coffee stirrer into the trash and sipped the hot drink. "I was hungry."

With a stiff-legged gait, he marched farther into the room. "You know what I mean."

"Who I have lunch with doesn't concern you, Luke."

"Stop calling me Luke." His scowl darkened. "What did you talk about?"

"That doesn't concern you, either." Sharon sipped more coffee. Nothing and no one would burst her happy bubble, especially not the Beat Thief.

"It does if you were discussing my beat." Lucas seemed to relish the last two words.

Sharon refused to react to his statement, instead taking the offensive. "How do you know I had lunch with Matt?"

"My father and I saw you. We were at the mall looking for suits to wear to my uncle's fund-raiser next weekend."

Sharon assessed his designer pants and expensive shoes—Italian?—and wondered in which mall stores he usually shopped. "Did you find anything?"

Mild distain crossed Lucas's features. "No. We're going to a tailor tomorrow. We'll have to pay extra because of the rush charges, but we can afford it."

"Well, that's good news." Sharon hoped he'd caught her sarcasm. "If your father is still paying your bills, why are you working at the newspaper?"

Far from being offended, Lucas looked amused. "I don't have to work, but it gives me something to do with my time. Frankly, I don't know how you survive on the pocket change they call a paycheck. You must live in a dump."

Sharon thought about her one-bedroom apartment with the furniture she'd refinished and the view of the grand old maple tree through her front windows. "I like it." She contemplated the pampered young man who spent more time downloading iTunes than working his beat. "Let's be honest, Luke."

"Don't call me Luke."

Sharon continued, unfazed. "You don't have any

interest in the news. Whose idea was it that you work for the *Times*?"

Lucas gave her a gloating smile. "Are you jealous of me? Is that why you were having lunch with Payton? Are you trying to get your beat back?"

Sharon scowled at her nemesis. "If you worked the beat properly, you wouldn't have to worry about my taking it back."

"If you'd worked your beat properly, no one could have taken it from you."

"That's a response guaranteed to convince me *not* to help you."

"Do you want me to talk to Wayne?"

His smug tone gave the impression he expected Sharon to capitulate out of fear.

She chuckled. "And tell him what? That I had lunch with a fire investigator? As you've pointed out, it's not my beat anymore. I can socialize with any member of the fire department, if I so choose."

"You weren't socializing."

"Can you prove that?"

Footsteps interrupted them. Sharon glanced toward the entrance and smiled when she saw Allyson. The tall, slender political reporter looked elegant in a black-and-white checked jacket and pencil-thin black skirt.

Allyson nodded at Lucas and winked at Sharon. "Tell me there's java and I'll owe you my soul."

Sharon grinned at her friend's dramatics. "I made a fresh pot."

Allyson's sigh was more suited to the bedroom than the newsroom. She clutched her soup bowl-sized mug in both hands. "You're a goddess."

"Allyson, I have to talk to you." Lucas jabbed a finger in her direction.

"I bet." Allyson muttered the sarcastic remark as she floated ever closer to the coffeepot.

"I want you to stop lying about my uncle in your articles."

Allyson poured coffee into her mug. "I'm not lying." Her movements were relaxed, her tone casual.

"My uncle did not take bribes from the coal industry."

"I never said he did."

"Yes, you did." Lucas's voice was harsh and angry.

Sharon found the contrast between Allyson's calm and Lucas's agitation disturbing. His behavior seemed extreme, as though he was on his way to a meltdown.

Allyson turned to the red-faced young man. "I said he was accused of accepting bribes, which he was. It's up to the Senate Ethics Committee to determine if the accusations are valid."

"But you implied the charges are true." Lucas's voice grew more strident with his anger.

"How?"

"By reporting on it."

Sharon almost choked on her coffee. "If your uncle didn't accept any bribes, he doesn't have anything to worry about."

Lucas shifted his glare to Sharon. He made several attempts to speak before giving up. He spun on his heels and stalked from the room.

Allyson muttered an uncomplimentary phrase about the senator's nephew. Her hazel eyes snapped with suppressed anger. "What's that kid doing here?"

"I was wondering the same thing." Sharon turned to her friend. "What is he doing here, and why was he assigned to the fire department beat?"

Seth's phone was ringing when he entered his apartment Wednesday evening. Ignoring the irritating summons, he locked his front door and carried the auto-parts bag to his living room.

The answering machine activated on the fourth ring and the computer voice read his phone number. Before the recorder clicked on, the caller hung up. Seth sat on his sofa, opened the box containing the oil filter and reacquainted himself with the installation directions.

Seconds later, his phone rang again. Seth rose to check the caller identification. The number was blocked, but he knew who was calling. He could tell from the tension building in his shoulders.

He picked up the receiver and pressed the RECORD button on the attached tape machine. "Yeah?"

There was a series of clicks and a whir before the distorted voice responded. "He got away last night."

Seth trudged through confusion until he realized the Closer referred to Matthew Payton. "So?"

"That's all you have to say? This is serious. You'll have to get rid of him."

Tension crept upward to Seth's neck. He carried the cordless phone to his sofa, stretching the recorder's extension, and took the television remote control from the coffee table. "No." He hit the remote's power button and adjusted the volume.

"It's in your best interests to get rid of him."

Seth doubted adding murder to arson charges would be in his best interests. "How?"

"Payton is pursuing the investigation. It's a matter of time before he connects you and Ford to the arsons."

Seth smiled without humor. "And to you."

"Get rid of him before that happens."

Seth heard the threat in the Closer's voice, but he wasn't fazed. The answering machine continued to record the conversation. "Why couldn't you?"

Seth sensed the Closer's anger on the other end of the line. Was it directed toward him or the fire investigator? Either way, he couldn't care less.

"I hired someone to take care of Payton, but some woman called the police."

Seth's eyebrows flew up. "Your guy get caught?"

Irritation snapped in the distorted voice. "Of course not. Do you think I'm stupid enough to hire someone who'd get caught?"

Seth's gaze strayed to the recorder, but he ignored the question. "We agreed no one gets hurt."

"That was before Payton and his investigation."

If you're afraid of getting caught, don't add to the charges. "Nothing's changed."

"If it's more money you want, that can be arranged."

"No." *You'd have more luck pissing up a tree.*

The Closer's anger snapped. "Are you toying with me? You know that you can use the money. Why are you against this idea?"

Besides the fact that I'm not a killer? Seth thought of his kids. He'd already crossed the line by committing arson. He didn't want their father to be a killer too.

Seth held down the remote's CHANNEL UP button. "Find another way to get rid of him."

The silence on the other end of the line was contemplative. Seth pushed the CHANNEL UP button again. Alex Trebek, the *Jeopardy!* game show host, read the answer centered on the television screen. "He was the third man to walk on the moon."

Seth searched his memory. *Who was Pete Conrad?*

The buzzer sounded, signaling the contestants had run out of time. "The correct question is 'Who was Pete Conrad?'" Alex Trebek said.

Seth's smile was self-mocking. *Jeopardy! was safer than working for the Closer.*

"Do you think Payton would back off if I spoke to him?" the Closer asked.

No. "Try."

"All right. But if it doesn't work, will you take care of him?"

"No. Last fire and I'm done."

The Closer sighed heavily. "What about Ford?"

Seth snorted. "He's no killer."

"I'd like to remind you that you two have the most to lose."

Seth glanced at the recorder. "I'll chance it."

It was after seven o'clock Thursday evening, but the newsroom was just as hectic and noisy as it had been at eight o'clock that morning. Maybe even more as copy editors verified text and hustled to get last-minute stories to production. Coworkers were shouting questions and comments from one end of the room to the other.

"Where's that story on the convenience-store robbery?"

"Are you sure the Kanawha County schools' budget numbers are right?"

"The next person who asks for the status on my column is dead."

Sharon only half-listened to the exchanges as she logged off her computer. She'd worked a long day, gathering information on the two arsons in addition to her features work. But now she needed dinner. The pretzel rods were barely keeping the edge off her hunger. And there was an NBA play-off game tonight. Sharon took her purse and left her cubicle, but her mind remained on the information she'd collected.

She'd had to wait until Lucas had left before calling the arson victims. Luckily, Lucas always left promptly at five o'clock. Apparently, no one had corrected his misperception that news was a nine-to-five business. Or perhaps she was the one misinformed.

In any event, both Reilly and Angie Stover, the café shop owner, were eager to talk with anyone willing to help them find out what had happened to their businesses.

Sharon dodged a frantic police beat reporter as she crossed the newsroom. She dug her car keys from her purse before pushing through the front doors.

The mountains were silhouetted against the night sky as they stood guard over downtown. Sharon hurried down the steps to the parking lot. She felt spring in the air. The season of renewal. Starting over. That's what she had to focus on, finding a way to start over at another paper—or even another city if that's what it took to find a job as an investigative reporter.

The sound of rapid footsteps behind her made Sharon spin around. A tall man was rushing toward her. She turned to run. Her fear might have been irrational, but she would rather be a live fool than a dead one.

She'd only gotten a few yards before he caught up with her. He grabbed her left upper arm from behind and spun her hard against a nearby car.

Sharon felt the impact against her ribs. She screamed and struggled to pull free. She strained to twist away even as she kicked back toward his legs, aiming for his kneecap. Her assailant pulled her arms back and up. Hard. The white-hot pain took her breath away, stopping her screams. She couldn't move without making it worse.

The stranger leaned into her back. Sharon screamed again, long and loud, fearing the worst. He slapped his hand against her lips, pushing so hard her teeth ground against the inside of her mouth. The back of her head came to rest against his chest.

Now her breath was coming too fast. Sharon smelled

alcohol and mints. Her heart slammed against her ribs, shaking her entire body. The pressure of his weight on her back added to the pain shooting up her arms. She thought they would snap.

He lowered his head beside her face. Sharon squeezed her eyes shut and tried to pull away, but his hand over her mouth kept her in place. The stubble from his jaw grazed her temple.

His voice was low and rusty in her ears. "Walk away from the arson stories or I'm going to bust you up."

Her eyes widened in shock.

With a shove, he set her free. Running footfalls tracked his departure. Sharon slid to the parking lot's broken blacktop. Her body was shaking. Her armpits were sweating. Her mind was screaming, *Who are you and why did you do this to me?*

She huddled against a coworker's car and rocked herself.

Chapter 16

At almost eight o'clock that evening, Matthew's doorbell rang. Who would be coming by so late? He set aside the arson reports he'd brought home and pushed off the sofa. He checked the peephole first. The crown of the woman's bent head looked familiar. His heart bumped once with dread as he opened the door. The expression on Sharon's face scared all thought from his mind.

Matthew slipped an arm around Sharon's waist and drew her gently into the house. "What's wrong?"

Her voice shook as though she were cold. "I was attacked in the newspaper's parking lot."

Matthew froze at her words. His arm tightened reflexively around Sharon's waist before he remembered not to hurt her more. "Are you all right?"

"No." Her voice broke, making her response two syllables.

Matthew looked her over as he helped her onto the sofa. Sharon's clothes were dirty, but they weren't torn. Her face was pale, but she wasn't bruised. One step at a time.

He knelt in front of her and held her hands. "Can you tell me what happened?"

Anger rose within him as Sharon described trying to run from a tall man who'd chased her down in the parking lot. He rose to pace the room as she described her attacker slamming her against a car.

Sharon gripped her hands. Her voice quavered. "I was so scared."

In Matthew's gut, anger battled fear for supremacy, but the need to comfort proved stronger.

He returned to kneel beside Sharon and drew her gently into his arms. He felt her trembling and pulled her closer. The outside of Sharon's right thigh pressed into his hip. Her fingers dug into his upper arms as though she were trying to draw on his physical strength. He gladly let her.

They were silent for several minutes. The stereo made the only sound in the room. Matthew ignored the Al Jarreau CD, focusing instead on Sharon's needs. He held her even after her trembling subsided.

Matthew knew she didn't intimidate easily. When she'd realized someone had dragged her into a smoldering building, she'd been shocked and angry, but not afraid. To see her so badly rattled now scared him.

"How did you get away from him?"

Sharon tensed in his arms again. "He released me and ran away."

This was unexpected. Matthew stopped rubbing her back, but left his cheek pressed to her hair. "Why?"

"Because his purpose had been to deliver a message."

He leaned back to look at her. "What message?"

Rage replaced the shattered look in her eyes. "He wants me to stop investigating the arsons."

"The attack was about the arsons?" Matthew waited

for Sharon's nod. "This is the second time. Was it the same guy who attacked you outside of the café?"

Sharon shook her head. "He reminded me more of the man who assaulted you outside of my apartment."

Matthew's surprise chased away his frown. "Are you sure?"

"It was dark, and his hood was up. But he had the same build and, when he ran away, he had the same loping gait."

Matthew stood. Was it possible the same man who had attacked him had come after Sharon? "Why would he harass you? I'm the one in charge of the investigation."

Sharon rose too. She was a bit shaky at first but soon found her balance. "And I'm the reporter covering it."

He quirked a brow at her. "Lenmore took you off the beat."

She threw him a look. "I'm still at the sites and I'm still questioning witnesses."

Matthew watched as Sharon paced his living room. She seemed to be trying to walk off the effects of the assault like an athlete walking off a hamstring pull. "But your information isn't being printed."

"Perhaps he doesn't know that. Whoever the thug works for doesn't want people paying attention to the fires."

Matthew crossed his arms, still tracking her journey around his living room. "What makes you think the thug works for someone? He could be doing this on his own."

Sharon gave Matthew an impatient glance. She'd already worked through that part and was trying to fit other pieces into the puzzle. "The arsonist wants to hide his identity, so he wouldn't come after me himself. It would be too big of a risk that I would see his face. No.

Someone sent that thug to scare me. Someone who lets others do the dirty work while he reaps the benefits."

Someone like Lucas Stanton, she thought.

Matthew nodded. "What's his motive?"

"Money always seems to work."

With her fear alleviating, Sharon stopped pacing and studied her surroundings. A dark brown sofa, coffee table, and brown armchair kept a big-screen black television and sound system company. Did the captain have something against primary colors or was he just more in tune with his Goth side?

Matthew turned off the stereo. "Money is one of the motives for arson. Which one of the business owners needs money more?"

"I don't think either of them is the arsonist."

"Then who is it?"

"Lucas Stanton."

Confusion settled on Matthew's features. "Stanton? I haven't seen him at any of the scenes."

"That's my point. He's writing the stories, but he's not doing any of the legwork."

"That might make him lazy, but it doesn't make him a torch."

"And he gets very upset when he learns I've been at the site or that I've spoken with you."

Matthew dragged his hand over his hair. "That's because it's his beat. I would be upset too."

"Imagine how I feel." Sharon took a calming breath and began again. "He saw us having lunch yesterday and demanded to know what we'd been talking about."

"Did you tell him?"

"No, and that made him angrier. Then, tonight, some punk assaulted me."

The anger that crossed Matthew's face startled

Sharon. He stroked her arm, one long, comforting caress. Was he reassuring her or himself?

Matthew took her hand. "But the thug never mentioned Stanton's name and you don't have proof of a connection. Just a suspicion."

"Lucas has no interest in the news, but the publisher gave him the fire beat. Why?"

Matthew released her hand and turned to pace across the room. "Now you think your publisher is involved in this?"

Stubborn man. Sharon tried another calming breath. "You have to admit something is going on here."

Matthew turned back to her. "Yeah. There's a torch loose in the community and someone is terrorizing you. But I think it's a leap to involve Stanton in this."

"I disagree."

"I realize that. Have you reported your assault to the police?"

Sharon frowned, trying to keep up with Matthew's change of topic. "No. I came straight here." She looked away. The admittance made her feel strange.

Matthew walked into the kitchen. She heard the jingle of keys before he returned to the living room. "You have to report this. I'll go with you." He stopped in front of her. "Just promise you won't bring up your theory about Stanton."

She scowled at him. "I know I need something more tangible than my very reliable instincts before I accuse someone of a crime."

"Imagine that. A reporter who bases her story on facts."

Sharon arched a brow at his sarcasm. It lacked its usual punch. "All good reporters do."

His barbs were getting weaker. Sharon smiled. Her cautious captain was mellowing.

* * *

The next morning, Sharon placed her hand on her apartment's front doorknob for balance as she lifted onto her toes to look through the peephole. Matthew smiled back at her from the other side of her door. Her lips trembled with humor.

Not surprisingly, she hadn't slept well the night before. Flashbacks of the encounter in the newspaper's parking lot had kept her on the fringes of wakefulness. She'd planned to swing by Starbucks on her way to work, but Matthew's playful expression energized her more than a tall, skinny café mocha could.

She unlocked her door and gave the fire captain a mock scowl. "Are you lost?"

Matthew straightened away from her threshold with an exaggerated grace that at once amused and attracted Sharon.

He winked at her. "Good morning, sunshine. Are you ready to go?"

Sharon blinked. "Go where?"

"I'm taking you to work." His tone implied she should have known that.

"Why?"

He dropped his teasing manner and lifted her hand, pressing it to his warm, hard chest. His voice was as gentle as a lover's touch. "Because I don't think either of us wants a repeat of last night's attack."

Matthew's words resurrected her fears. She stepped back, leading him into her apartment. "How long are you planning to play chauffeur?"

Matthew shrugged, releasing her hand. "Until we both feel more comfortable with your driving to and from work alone."

He was right. Someone had threatened her last

night, shoved her around and threatened her because of a story she wasn't even officially working. She wasn't going to lie to herself and pretend the incident didn't affect her.

Sharon studied Matthew as he stood in the middle of her great room. He looked like an executive in his navy-blue dress suit, white shirt, and sapphire-and-bronze tie, but Sharon had seen him fight the same thug she believed assaulted her. "Strong but tender," a line from Patti LaBelle's "Right Kind of Lover," repeated in her mind.

Sharon moved to collect her bag and suit jacket from the dining table. She tugged her purse strap onto her shoulder as she walked back to Matthew. "Thank you."

Matthew had parked his sedan in front of her building. He held the front passenger door open while she slid onto the seat. The scent of coffee had her senses on high alert.

Sharon dragged her attention from the cup holders to Matthew as he entered the car. "You brought coffee."

"This is a full-service operation. Cream, sugar, and sugar substitute are on the tray."

Her morning was complete when he tuned in the NPR station before pulling into traffic.

The male newscaster updated them on developments from the evening before. "The Senate Ethics Committee has scheduled meetings to discuss allegations of bribery against three-term State Senator Kurt Stanton. Meanwhile, Stanton announced last night he would return the hundred-thousand-dollar campaign contribution he received from the coal industry lobbyist. However, the senator insists this is not an admission of wrongdoing on his part."

Matthew stopped at a red light and sipped his coffee. "It doesn't matter whether he did anything wrong. It's the appearance of wrongdoing that has the media in a feeding frenzy."

Sharon's enjoyment of her morning coffee dimmed. "You don't think it was wrong of him to accept money from the group that drafted a bill he sponsored?"

"If that's what he did, he was wrong. But it's the media coverage I disagree with. Who are they to judge?"

Sharon noted Matthew's tense jawline. "The anchor didn't judge Stanton. He reported the news."

"His report was biased."

The traffic light turned green. Sharon watched Matthew put the car in motion. His run-in with the *Pitt Daily Times* had left deep scars. Would his resentment continue to handicap their relationship, or would he let her through that protective wall even with her media credentials?

Matthew got her to the news building a little before eight A.M., giving her almost an hour before Lucas arrived. Her nemesis usually strolled in closer to nine o'-clock.

As she waited for the wannabe reporter, Sharon finished her coffee, reviewed her notes for an upcoming feature, and checked other news sites on the Internet. Finally, a little after nine o'clock, Lucas ambled by her cubicle on the way to his own. She followed him past the two work spaces that separated them.

Sharon watched as he hung his designer suit jacket on the back of his chair, hooked his iPod to his hard drive, then sat behind his desk.

She crossed her arms. "I received your message last night."

Lucas paused in the process of putting on his earphones. "What message?"

Sharon didn't believe Lucas's confusion. "The message you sent through the punk who attacked me in the parking lot. Where did you find him, by the way?"

"You were attacked in the parking lot? When?"

She leaned against the modular wall, hoping to hide the fact her muscles were shaking with fury. "Last night, just as you arranged. Or did he arrive early?"

"What? I didn't arrange for anyone to attack you. You've lost it." He started to lift the earphones to his head, but hesitated when Sharon strode toward him.

She stopped on the other side of his desk, no longer caring if he saw her wrath. She wanted the truth. "Why are you warning me off the arsons?"

"Because it's my beat."

Sharon heard the resentment in his tone. Good. She leaned forward, lowering her voice. "Who are you working with? You can't set the fires on your own. You're not that smart."

His eyes snapped with indignation. "You're crazy. I don't have anything to do with the fires. And I didn't have someone come after you in the parking lot."

Lucas was convincing, but Sharon didn't believe in coincidences. "You saw me having lunch with Matthew Wednesday. Thursday, some two-bit thug pushes me around in the parking lot. Am I supposed to believe that was random?"

Ugly emotion twisted his classic good looks. "Prove it was me."

Sharon started to respond but Wayne interrupted her. "What's going on here?"

She looked over her shoulder to find her editor planted in the threshold. Why was it Wayne always

happened to appear when she was trying to shake
Lucas down for information?

Antagonism deepened Lucas's voice. "Your star girl
reporter has gone nuts."

"What's the problem, MacCabe?"

Sharon held Lucas's glare. Matthew hadn't bought
her theory last night. She had no reason to think her
boss would believe her this morning, especially since
Wayne's political appointee was doing such a convincing job of denying any part of the crime. As Matthew
had said, she needed concrete evidence before she
went public.

She stepped away from Lucas's desk. "There's no
problem. We were just discussing the fire department
beat."

"Are you still trying to cover stories on that beat?"
Wayne frowned. "Back off, MacCabe. I'm not kidding
about busting you down to the calendar department."

Sharon glared at Wayne's retreating back. How could
he threaten her with further demotion after the years
she'd spent with the company? She turned her scathing
expression to Lucas.

Wayne's pet gave her a smug smile before tucking
in his iPod earplugs. He leaned back in his wheeled
chair and stacked his ankles onto his desk.

Sharon marched back to her cubicle, her body stiff
with irritation. There was a connection between Lucas
and these arsons. She was absolutely positive of that.
She wouldn't rest until she exposed him and everyone
else involved.

Chapter 17

Matthew stared at the photos of the office-furniture store and café fires spread over his small conference table, then turned back to the reports. "The burn patterns in both fires lead back to employee-only areas."

Gary scanned his notes. "So an employee was involved in the fires."

Matthew glanced at his lieutenant seated across from him. "We don't know that." He flipped through his notes. "The furniture store and café don't employ any of the same staff. We'll have to find out if any of the employees know each other."

"It might have been a break-in."

Matthew wondered if he imagined the excitement in Gary's voice. "There wasn't any evidence of that at either location. Although the fires may have destroyed those signs."

"So we can't rule it out?"

"Not yet. Follow up with the lab to see if they've found anything to support or dispel the break-in theory."

"All right." Gary scribbled more notes on his writing tablet.

The lingering smell of the French fries he and Gary had eaten while they'd worked through lunch briefly distracted Matthew. He'd offered to get something for Sharon, but she'd told him she was having lunch with friends.

His attention drifted to the phone on the other side of his office. Should he call to make sure she'd returned safely? He shook away the thought. She hadn't gone alone. There was no reason to worry.

Matthew returned his attention to the investigation. "The standard arsonist profile. They're antisocial. Ninety-four percent are male. The majority are white."

Gary continued the listing. "Most aren't well-educated, and eighty-seven percent were previously arrested for some other felony."

"That means we're looking for a white male with a record. One who lives near this area since most torches set the fires within two miles of their home."

"Well, that's something to go on." Gary made some notes.

"We need to take another look at the owners. What's their money situation? Have they recently refinanced? How deep in debt are they?"

"So you haven't ruled them out?"

"Not yet." Matthew reexamined the site photos.

"But you have a profile of the arsonist as a white male. Doesn't that at least rule out Angie Stover from the café?"

"We're not ruling anything or anyone out yet." Matthew's attention shifted between the fire scene photos from the café and those from the furniture store.

"Maybe the furniture-store owner burned up his company, then set fire to Angie's business to throw suspicion off himself?"

"Let's not stray too far from the evidence." Matthew fought the Pittsburgh flashbacks.

"But you've said the evidence doesn't really show anything."

"It definitely doesn't show O'Conner setting fire to his store and Stover's café." Matthew was getting the same uncomfortable feeling he usually had when a reporter interviewed him.

"It could happen."

Matthew slid the pictures toward Gary so his lieutenant could get a better look. "There's something different about the burn patterns in these photos. At first, they seemed the same. But, if you look more closely, the one from the café has a single origin. The furniture store has multiple origins in the employee break room."

Gary nodded his understanding. "It's as though the person who started the fire at the store stopped and started a couple of times. As though he wasn't certain where to pour the accelerant." He looked up. "Two different people? Maybe the first torch was an amateur."

"Or maybe it's the same person who wants us to think the fires aren't connected. Let's not make any assumptions."

Gary collapsed against his chair, his frustration showing. "We have to have something to go on."

Matthew held the other man's gaze. "We're not trying to close a file. We're trying to solve a case."

"But there are too many options."

The hint of a whine in the younger man's voice bothered Matthew. "If we make assumptions this early in the process, we close ourselves off to other possibilities. We have to consider everything before we can rule out anything."

* * *

Sharon checked her Timex again. It was a little after six o'clock in the evening. She'd promised to meet Matthew in the *Times* front lobby. She sighed and crossed her legs, getting more comfortable on the bench across from the guard's desk.

She hated waiting. Living on her own gave her more control of her schedule. If she wanted to work late, she did so. Then, when she finished working, she'd drive herself home. But, after last night, she'd choose caution over control. Two physical attacks per news story was her limit.

The front door sighed open, and Sharon felt a finger of cool air brush against her calves. Matthew entered the building and walked toward her. His eyes were tired, his tie was missing and the top button of his shirt was undone. He looked incredible. Good enough to give any movie-star idol serious competition.

Matthew stopped in front of her. His smile made her knees shake. "Are you ready to go?"

Sharon put her hand in his and allowed him to help her up. His grip was firm, a little rugged and warm. Their footsteps clacked against the tile, tracking their approach to the front doors. Matthew released her hand and settled his palm against the small of her back. He held the door open for her and Sharon glanced around before stepping into the evening.

At his car, Matthew opened the passenger door, and she settled into the seat. Then he rounded the car and slid behind the wheel.

Sharon shifted in her seat to face him. "How was your day, honey?"

Matthew's head jerked toward her. His wide-eyed stare dropped to her grin and he relaxed. "It was fine."

"Just fine. What happened?"

He didn't answer right away. Disappointment dimmed

Sharon's good humor as it seemed he wouldn't respond at all. She'd hoped he was beginning to see her first as a partner in this investigation, a reporter second—and a woman always.

When his answer came, his voice wasn't guarded as it had been in the past. "One out of every three fires is arson. But no one can confirm that statistic because arson is difficult to prove."

Sharon deadpanned Han Solo's line from one of the *Star Wars* movies: "Never tell me the odds."

Matthew's grin revealed his dimples. "All right, Captain Solo. But it would help if we could find similarities between O'Conner and Stover's shops."

"You mean besides the neighborhood and the fact both were nearly burned to the ground?"

He arched a brow. "Yes, besides those. Until we have evidence connecting the two events, we have to treat them as separate cases."

Sharon pondered the surrounding mountains as Matthew's car logged the miles down Lee Street. "I might be able to help you there." She glanced at him. "Reilly and Ann have the same business lenders, and their loans are insured by Peak Protection."

"How do you know this?"

"Business licenses are public information. But it's amazing what else you'll learn with the right connections."

Matthew changed lanes to pass a slow-moving SUV. "Like what?"

"They took out policies at the same time for almost the same amounts. But I can't find any evidence they know each other. Different schools, different banks, different neighborhoods. I'll keep looking, though."

Matthew signaled to turn off Lee Street toward the neighborhoods along the Kanawha River. "Gary and I will follow that lead."

"Okay. I'll look for a personal connection— churches, fitness clubs, Tupperware parties. Whatever."

He glanced at her before returning his attention to the streets that led to her home. "They still do Tupperware parties?"

"I don't know, but I'll find out."

Matthew stopped the car at a red light. "I don't think it's a good idea for you to make those inquiries."

"Just relax and say thank you."

"Someone's trying to kill you."

Sharon heard the strain in Matthew's voice and felt guilty, but not enough to change her mind. "I promise to be careful."

He didn't have a response. The silence remained unbroken until Matthew pulled his Camry into an open space at the curb a few paces from Sharon's building.

She nodded toward the old Victorian. "Do you want to come in? I make a mean spaghetti."

"A homemade meal that I don't have to cook myself? I'd be a fool to say no."

Sharon led him into her apartment, then took his coat. "Make yourself at home. I'll fix dinner."

Matthew followed her into the kitchen. "I'll help."

Sharon contemplated him, then her tiny kitchen. She handed him a spare apron. "Sure."

Matthew hesitated before putting on the red-and-white–checked garment. "So, honey, how was your day?"

Her smile came and went with the reminder of the day's events. "I confronted Lucas about last night."

"What happened?"

Her anger stirred as she recalled the conversation. "He denied knowing anything about the attack or the arsons."

"That shouldn't have surprised you."

"It didn't." Sharon filled a large pot with water. "You

know, I was certain you wouldn't approve of my speaking to Lucas."

"If Stanton is involved, some people would say you've given away your advantage." He took the pot from Sharon and set it on a rear burner to boil. "Now that he knows you're on to him, he'll be more careful and you'll have a harder time catching him in the act. Some people would think confronting him would make him more likely to make mistakes that would help you catch him."

"What do you think?" Sharon took a packet of ground turkey from the refrigerator.

He leaned against the kitchen counter beside the stove. "I think you're reckless. That's why I intend to stick to you like glue until we catch this torch."

Sharon bent to pull a pan from a cupboard, then straightened to place it on a front burner. Her back was to him as she cooked the ground turkey. Hopefully, he wouldn't notice the flush of pleasure heating her cheeks. "So how are you handling the investigation?"

"Carefully."

She waited, but Matthew didn't add any more. "The longer he's out there, the more dangerous he becomes."

"We have to be thorough so that, when we get to court, we can show that we took everything into consideration." The water came to a boil and Matthew fed spaghetti into the pot.

They cooked in silence. Sharon was deep in her own thoughts. She drained the fat from the cooked ground turkey and began adding spices and sauce. "So the community is left to fear the next event?"

"I realize we're running out of time, but I'm not going to compromise the investigation. This is a felony case. I'd rather be right than fast." He stirred the spaghetti. "Do you mind if we talk about something else?"

"Of course not." Sharon wondered whether his

commitment to being right rather than fast was born of his own experiences in Pittsburgh. "How 'bout those Cavs?"

Conversation about the NBA play-offs carried them through setting the dining table and serving the spaghetti with turkey-meat sauce.

Matthew sampled the meal and sighed. "This is the best spaghetti I've ever had."

Sharon smiled. "I told you so."

"Did you learn to cook from your mother?"

"From both of my parents. They taught me to cook and they taught me the importance of civic duty."

In between forkfuls of spaghetti and sips of iced tea, Sharon shared anecdotes of her mother's media watch-dog campaigns in which she flooded Charleston's daily and weekly newspapers with criticism or praise for their news coverage. Some of her complaints were so scathing they were amusing. Several times, she and Matthew wiped tears of laughter from their eyes. The stories continued as he helped her clear the table.

"She really wrote that?" he asked, setting a newly washed dish onto the drain board.

"She really did." Sharon took the dish from the board and dried it before storing it in a cupboard. "So you see, with a mother like Helen Davies Mac-Cabe, I have to make sure my articles are accurate and balanced."

"Do you think she'd send her own daughter a flaming letter?" Finished with the dishes, Matthew dried his hands.

"No. She'd deliver her criticism in person." Sharon turned to face him. "Enough about my family. Tell me something about yours."

Matthew stilled. "What do you want to know?"

"Whatever you're willing to share." Sharon waited through a long silence.

"My family lives in Pittsburgh. My parents, an older sister, and a younger brother." Matthew's smile looked forced. "My father's a misguided Knicks fan. My brother and I give him a hard time about that."

"That's not very nice."

"He brings it on himself."

There wasn't much humor behind the small joke. Sharon sensed a strain in him, as though he wanted to run but knew he needed to stay.

Matthew shoved his hands into his front pants pockets. "My mother's a worrier."

"What does she have to worry about?"

"She's worried about me. About why I left Pittsburgh."

Sharon held her breath. "Why did you leave Pittsburgh?"

Matthew felt a muscle jump in his jaw. He didn't want to relive the memories, but keeping silent only fed his nightmares. He needed something—or someone—to help him. In Sharon's eyes, he saw compassion and concern. He turned away, took the few steps to the dining area and dropped into his seat. Sharon sat across from him. How far would she be willing to follow him?

He squeezed his eyes shut against the firestorm of anger, guilt, and regret flashing over inside him.

"I told you I had an older sister and a younger brother." He opened his eyes. "Until about a year ago, I also had a younger sister. Michelle."

He waited for Sharon's questions. He was grateful when none came. "Mickey and I were very close. We were always getting into trouble, either together or on our own."

Matthew smiled and dropped his gaze to the dining table. "One night, when I was a senior in high school, I went out with a group of friends. I missed curfew and knew my parents would bring the pain on me. I got to my bedroom without detection and undressed in the dark. But, when I got into bed, it felt like someone was in there with me. I almost blew my cover. Came this close to screaming like a girl."

Sharon laughed. "What did you do?"

"I flew out of bed and turned the light on, ready to either defend myself or run for my mother." Matthew chuckled. "The companion in my bed turned out to be a pile of clothes Mickey had stuffed under my sheets to look like me in case my parents did a bed check."

"How did you know it was Mickey who did that?"

"She'd pinned a note to one of my shirts, 'Hope you had fun. Mickey.'" Matthew swallowed the lump in his throat so he could continue. His gaze remained on the table. "I knew part of what Mickey felt for me was hero worship. I think that had something to do with her becoming a firefighter."

"Not many women go into that field." Sharon's tone reflected her surprise.

"I tried to talk her out of it. She was twenty-two, but she was still my baby sister. The thought of her facing the dangers firefighters experience—that *I* experience—scared the . . . scared me. But she was stubborn."

"That must run in the family."

Matthew heard the smile in Sharon's voice and managed a small one of his own. "At first I was protective of her. I made sure she was on my crew when she went into a building. We argued about that."

"I can imagine." Sharon's tone was dry.

He arched a brow at her, then looked away. "She said

I was making it hard for her to be accepted as an equal. I told her to find a safer job."

"How did she take that?"

Matthew snorted and met Sharon's gaze. "Mickey is—was—a lot like you. How do you think she took it?"

Sharon pursed her lips. "Not well."

"She threatened to go to another station. The idea of not being able to keep an eye on her scared me enough to make me give her some room."

"That must have been hard for you."

"It was. But when I stepped back and watched her work, I realized my sister was a damn good firefighter. The kind you want at your back when you go into a blaze. I stopped breathing down her neck and made sure everyone treated her with respect. After all, I'm still her brother." He paused. "I *was* still her brother."

Matthew stopped, embarrassed by his mistake. He rose from the table and paced into the great room. Sharon followed him. "We never talked about it, but I could tell she knew how I felt."

He paused in front of Sharon's bookcase. "Years went by. Everything was fine. Then one day about a year ago a call came in." Matthew spoke haltingly as he forced himself to continue. "Fire in a retirement home. Mickey went in. She got caught by a backdraft and was severely burned."

Matthew barely heard Sharon cry out. There was a roaring in his ears. He braced himself against the bookcase as he struggled to banish the images burning his eyes. He hadn't been on-site when Mickey fell, but the thought of her in pain, on fire, tortured him.

He had to continue to speak, if only to drown the memory of Mickey's moans of pain as she lay in the intensive-care burn unit. The same moans he heard in his nightmares. "She was in the hospital for a week before she died from her injuries."

"Matt, I'm so sorry." Sharon's voice was a whisper.

Matthew walked restlessly around the great room, trying to move away from the memories. "I felt as though I had let her down. As though I'd failed my family. I should have talked her out of staying in the department."

"What did your family think?"

Matthew shook his head and paced to the other side of the room. "They never blamed me."

"And you can't blame yourself." Sharon stood. "Your sister wanted to be a firefighter. She worked in a job she loved. It just so happens that job has devastating risks. But she knew those risks when she became a firefighter."

"I shouldn't have let her. I should have found a way to protect her."

Sharon's wave dismissed his remark. "Matt, do you enjoy being a firefighter?"

His answer was automatic. "Of course."

"How would you have felt if someone had told you that you couldn't be a firefighter because it was too dangerous?"

Matthew stepped back as she moved toward him. He didn't want her touching him while Mickey's sobs whispered in his head. "I would have ignored them. But I'm a man—"

Sharon's eyes widened with incredulity. "Does that make you immortal? Mere danger can't touch you? You could never get hurt?"

He turned from her and the questions she fired at him, his hands balled into fists of frustration. "Of course not."

"Then what's your point?"

Matthew was silent for long seconds. "Sharon . . . my God, I miss her so much."

"I understand." Her voice seeped soothingly through the chaos in his mind. "But don't blame yourself for your sister wanting to do something she loved."

Matthew's muscles bunched as he struggled to keep it together. But when Sharon's warm, gentle hand rested on his tense shoulder, he came apart.

Chapter 18

Matthew turned and gathered Sharon to him. She crossed her arms behind his neck and lay her cheek against his shattered heart. Burying his face in her hair, he let his cleansing tears fall. He pulled her closer, trying to lure her light into the yawning darkness. But he needed more.

His lips sought and settled against hers. Her warm softness pulled a swift, sharp response from his gut. He nibbled along the curve of her mouth, silently begging for her healing touch. With the tip of her tongue, she stroked the seam of his mouth. Matthew groaned and parted his lips.

Sharon cured him. With every touch of her tongue, her lips, her hands, the darkness receded and Matthew's heart grew whole again.

Matthew's hands traced Sharon's taut figure, over her trim waist to settle on her rounded hips. He pulled her closer, molding her body to him. Sharon moaned against his mouth, and he chased her tongue with his.

Her body heat warmed him. Her fragrance, powder-fresh and feminine, clouded his mind. He wrapped his arms around her waist and lifted her to him. Sharon gasped and he slid his tongue deeper, stroking the roof of her mouth. Sharon caught his tongue and sucked it. His body throbbed against her.

Matthew lowered Sharon to her feet and tugged her blouse free of her skirt. He'd moved his hand up her bare back when he felt her small palms nudge his chest.

"Matt, wait." She rested her forehead on his chest.

Matthew tilted her face up. His fingers shook with the need to keep touching her. "What is it?"

Sharon's cheeks were flushed, her lips swollen. "It's too soon. I'm sorry."

His mind spun like a merry-go-round, accepting her wishes, rejecting her wishes, wanting to hold her, having to let her go. He jumped off the ride before he did something they both would regret. "I'm the one who's sorry. I didn't mean to rush you."

Sharon started to speak. Matthew waited, mentally urging her to help him understand her rejection. *What do you need from me to make you feel right about us?* But she walked away to retrieve his suit coat.

Sharon held the garment out to him. "Thank you for understanding."

Matthew's steps felt heavy as he walked to the front door. He slid into his jacket, then turned to her. "I'll pick you up for work Monday."

"Thanks."

Matthew hesitated, but the confusion in her eyes convinced him it was time to go home. With clear and simple directions, he instructed his body to walk out the door.

Matthew stood in front of his fireplace, studying the pictures on the mantel. Cautiously, he dragged his gaze to the photo of him, Natalie, Gregory. And Michelle.

The Payton offspring caught on film. It was a good time. They were together, and they were happy. Sunday afternoon sunlight kissed the frame, leaving the picture in shadow.

He waited for the rush of crippling guilt. It didn't come. Instead he was restless, as though he'd forgotten to do something. Matthew turned from the fireplace and prowled his family room. In his mind, he heard Sharon challenging him to stop blaming himself for Mickey's death.

His sister had been good at her job and happy with her career. Isn't that all that mattered? The answer helped him let his sister rest in peace. Guilt moved on, although the restlessness remained. There was more he had to do. He strode to his kitchen phone and dialed his parents' number.

His mother answered on the third ring. "Matt? Are you all right?" Evelyn sounded ready to climb through the phone if her child needed help.

Matthew smiled. "I'm getting better, Mom."

She absorbed his news in an almost prayerful silence. "I'm so glad, Matt. I'm so glad."

"How are you?"

She laughed, sounding more worry-free than she had in months. "I'm fine, but I think your father's going to have a heart attack if the Knicks don't win tonight."

Matthew chuckled, remembering his father's pre-basketball game jitters. "The Sixers are always happy to welcome another fan."

"Good luck trying to change his loyalties." His mother's tone was dry. "Now, are you eating well?"

"Yes, ma'am."

"And getting enough sleep?"

"Yes, ma'am." Matthew stretched out his legs and

crossed them at the ankles, getting comfortable for his mother's twenty questions on his welfare.

Sharon had curled up on the ottoman in her mother's living room to read the Sunday edition of the *Charleston Gazette*. If she had to leave her job, the *Gazette* was a good place to further her career.

Helen reclined on the matching sofa with the *Times*. She turned the page and refolded the paper's State section. "Your friend Allyson reports that Senator Stanton is lagging behind in the campaign fund-raising battle. He lost a lot of ground when he returned the coal industry lobbyist's contribution."

"The *Gazette* reports the same thing." Sharon read further from the article on the state senate race. "Polls show the pay-to-play scandal has hurt Stanton. And he doesn't have much of a record to stand on."

Helen hummed her agreement, apparently still on the *Times* article. "He's been running on name recognition. But his challenger also has name recognition as well as a long list of accomplishments."

Sharon regarded her mother. "I wonder if other state reps are reconsidering donations from coal industry lobbyists?"

Helen arched a brow. "I think they should reconsider donations from all lobbyists."

Sharon nodded her agreement. "The Ethics Committee will want to make a ruling on its investigation as soon as possible before the November election."

Helen's eyes sparked with curiosity. "Speaking of investigations, what's the latest on the arsons?"

Her mother's question sent Sharon back to Friday night and Matthew's kisses. "With every answer, I end up with several more questions."

Helen lowered her paper, giving Sharon her complete attention. "Is Matt working with you?"

"We've discussed the investigation a couple of times." Sharon wondered whether Helen heard her answer over the "Wedding March" playing in stereo in her mother's mind.

"Oh?" Helen sounded like a backup singer in a sixties Motown band. "Any progress on the personal front?"

"There's been some."

"This is like pulling teeth." Helen sighed gustily. "Will there be more?"

Sharon looked out the picture window. From her vantage point, she could see a profusion of treetops in the distance. Leaf buds were unfurling.

She loved the spring. The earth had weathered the winter, and nature was coming out of hibernation. Everything was new again. A fresh start. She was going through a winter, looking forward to that fresh start. But her personal and professional futures were uncertain.

"It's hard to get close to someone when he's keeping secrets from you."

"What kind of secrets?"

Sharon heard the concern in her mother's voice and gave Helen a reassuring smile. "He hasn't committed a crime or anything, but I don't feel comfortable telling you about it since he hasn't confided in me."

Helen looked puzzled. "If he's not the one who told you, how do you know you can trust your source?"

"I can trust my source. You know I double-check things like that."

"Have you asked him about it?"

Sharon shook her head. "I want him to trust me enough to tell me."

Helen chuckled. "Darling, take it from a retired schoolteacher, love shouldn't have pop quizzes. But, if you're going to test your relationship, you should at least give him a cheat sheet so he isn't completely in the dark."

Sharon gave her mother a dubious look. "But if I give him all the answers, how do I know he's telling me the truth?"

Her mother looked wise. "You'll know. Trust me."

When Matthew entered Sharon's apartment Sunday evening, he knew she was the cause of his restlessness.

Her brows knitted as though she sensed his tension. "What's wrong?"

Matthew walked past Sharon and into her great room, before turning to face her. "I wasn't able to protect Mickey. I'm afraid I won't be able to protect you, either."

Sharon's frown was blatant confusion. "From what?"

Matthew blinked. "From the torch who's tried twice to warn you off the story." What else would he be talking about? "Don't you realize you're in danger?"

Sharon fisted her hands on her hips. Steely determination settled in her eyes. "Don't even think about talking me out of this story."

Matthew rubbed his face, trying to scrub away the memory of carrying her from the smoking building and the image of her attack in the *Times* parking lot. "It's too dangerous."

"I'm not the only one in danger. Whoever we're searching for sent someone to beat you up. Remember?"

His gaze slid over her small frame. "I think my odds are significantly better."

"I'm not dropping this story."

Matthew stepped closer, crowding her. "Is it worth your life?"

She spun from him, dragging her hands through her thick, dark hair. "You know we can accomplish more together than we can separately."

Matthew felt her frustration like steam from a boiling pot, but he held his ground. "I can't accomplish anything if I'm worrying about you." His answer seemed to surprise her.

Her response was more measured. "I'm worried about you too. Does that mean we're going to walk away from the case?"

This woman redefined *stubborn*. "I'm on the job. You're on some kind of crusade."

She folded her arms. "Bottom line, I'm on this story with or without you."

Matthew pinched the bridge of his nose, clinging to patience. "These people are trying to hurt you."

Her tone turned coaxing. "They're trying to hurt *us*. I can help you find them. Together, we can stop them."

He shook his head at her change in tactics, from schoolyard bully to foreign diplomat. Matthew closed the short distance between them. He rubbed his thumb over her full lower lip. Her gaze heated. He lowered his head, touching his lips to hers once. A tender salute. Undemanding and gentle, but not enough. He touched her mouth again. A whisper against her flesh. It could never be enough.

"I won't lose you." His voice was gruff with emotion.

She put her palm against his chest. "We'll take care of each other."

"All right, partner. I'll watch your back if you watch mine."

"Deal."

"And no more following strange men into deserted parking lots."

Beneath the humor in his midnight eyes, Sharon read Matthew's desire and felt her body respond to it. His heat wrapped around her and into her, spreading down to tighten her nipples and loosen her thighs. His scent was a drug, clouding her thoughts.

Matthew stroked his knuckles lightly down her right arm. He took her fingers into his hand and lifted them to his mouth. His lips sipped at her skin. His tongue slid across her fingertips. A new pulse awakened inside of her. A restless energy pulled her closer to him.

He lowered himself onto the sofa, and Sharon sat on his lap. Warm, strong fingers massaged the back of her neck, conveying to her the message to touch him. Taste him. She closed her eyes and lowered her head to rest her mouth against his.

Sharon drew her tongue across the seam that separated his lips and, when he opened for her, she cupped the back of his head to keep him steady for her exploration. Sharon kissed him deeper, harder, trying to satisfy the craving inside her.

She gasped when the heat of his palm seeped through her T-shirt to scorch her breast. Matthew caressed her. Stroked her. Kneaded her. She felt wild, pushing her breast harder into his hand.

Matthew tilted her over his arm. Her head fell back. His lips followed the length of her neck, licking, nibbling, biting her flesh as his hand continued to caress her breast. He lifted her T-shirt and reached for her bra. Sharon's eyes flew open at the intensity of her reaction to his intimate touch.

Her vision focused on her ceiling. She shifted her gaze to the dark tight curls of Matthew's hair as his head rested above her bare breast.

"Stop." She wedged her hands between them and pushed against his chest.

He lifted his head and, for Sharon, the loss of his touch was a physical pain.

"I'm sorry. Am I too rough?" Matthew's features were tight, sharp with desire.

Sharon stared into the fire in his eyes, loath to deny them both this pleasure, but knowing they deserved more than a physical release. "No, Matt. It's just . . . this is too soon."

He frowned, his eyes clouded with hunger and confusion. "I'm moving too fast?"

"Yes." Sharon relaxed with his understanding. She rearranged her clothes.

He pulled her into a sitting position. "Sorry. I'll slow down."

Sharon's eyes widened as she lifted her hands to his chest. "No. You misunderstood. *This* is too soon." She waved one hand between them.

Matthew's brows furrowed. "Why?"

Sharon took a deep breath and tried harder to find reason in the fog of sexual arousal. "Making love is more than a physical expression for me." That was true enough. At twenty-eight, she could count her lovers on two fingers. "It's an emotional commitment. I can't make that commitment to someone who's not honest with me. Who can't confide in me."

Matthew's eyes regained focus as her message became clear. "I have confided in you. I've told you about Mickey. That was a big step for me."

Sharon adjusted her clothes and slipped off his lap to sit beside him. "I'm honored you felt comfortable discussing your sister with me. It shows we have a basis for a friendship."

"I want more than friendship."

"I'm attracted to you too." Sharon folded her hands in her lap. "But, before we go any further, I need to know we trust each other."

Matthew seemed to stiffen. "What are you holding back from me?"

Sharon stood. "Nothing. But you're holding something from me."

His eyebrows rose in surprise. "I am?"

Sharon recalled her mother's advice that she provide Matthew with a cheat sheet if she gave him a relationship quiz. She tried to lead him in her direction. "Do you trust me, Matt?"

He didn't hesitate. "Yes."

"Can you honestly tell me that you can separate me—the woman—from my job?"

His answer wasn't as certain this time. "Yes."

"But you think I would leak sensitive information you share with me?"

Matthew looked down. His silence hurt her more than she would have imagined.

Sharon walked to her front door. "Before I share my body with you, I want you to know who I am." She rubbed her chest above the heart Matthew had crushed.

Matthew stood to follow her. "I trust you, but I'm not comfortable with your job."

Sharon stopped in front of her door. "My job is one part of me. But there's more to me than the reporter."

"I know that."

Sharon tried to read her future in Matthew's eyes. Her body still pulsed with desire, but her mind hesitated to take the next step. She wouldn't make that commitment without trust. "Are you sure, Matt?"

He ran a hand over his hair. "How can I prove it to you?

Sharon spoke gently. "You have to first prove it to yourself."

Chapter 19

Sharon entered the *Times* break room Monday morning and found Allyson scowling at a stream of brown liquid brewing into the coffeepot. She looked from the slowly filling pot back to her friend's disgruntled expression. "What's wrong?"

"I'm wondering if I should wait for the pot to brew or slip my mug under that stream."

Sharon considered those options. "Do you think we drink too much coffee?"

"You sound like Dre."

"Does he think we drink too much coffee?"

Allyson took a chair at a table next to the coffee machine. Her eyes never left the pot. "I don't know about you, but he thinks I do. He's such a nag."

"He cares about you." It was the strongest hint Sharon felt comfortable giving the other woman.

"All the men in my life are nags." Allyson pushed a chair toward Sharon.

Sharon sat, crossing her legs. The hard plastic seat squeaked. "How's your father?"

Allyson smiled. "When he first retired a couple of

months ago, he was so bored and I was worried. But now, he's excited about the elections."

"My mom's excited too. It's going to be a tight race, especially since Stanton's working with a smaller budget."

Allyson leaped from her chair the moment the coffee had brewed and filled her cup to the rim. "This is the first time money has been an issue for Stanton." She poured Sharon's coffee, leaving room for creamer. "Even with his first campaign, his brother, Earl, used money he'd inherited from his late wife for financing."

"I'd heard rumors that Earl had married for money."

"That's what his late wife's family thought." Allyson sipped her coffee and sighed. "Dad thinks a big voter turnout could cost Stanton the election."

Sharon stirred skim milk and sweetener into her coffee. The scent of the strong Colombian blend made her mouth water. Andre could be right. Maybe she should try cutting back on the caffeine.

"If your father's interested, he could call my mother about working on the voter registration drive. This is about getting more effective representation in our state legislature."

Allyson swallowed another sip of coffee. "I'll tell him." She leaned against the break room counter. "Henry Rush showed up at another one of Stanton's photo ops yesterday demanding answers from the accident investigation."

Sharon's heart felt heavy at the mention of the father of one of the coal miners who'd died in the recent accident. "How did Kurt handle it?"

Allyson shrugged a graceful shoulder. "He basically blew him off. Told Rush he didn't know when the investigation would be over."

Sharon's brows snapped together in disapproval. "That's not a good way to handle a grieving parent."

"I agree."

Sharon started toward the break room door. "It's been more than a month, and we haven't heard anything. I can understand Rush being agitated. He wants to know why his son died."

Allyson walked with her. "And what about your investigation?" She lowered her voice. "Have you learned anything more?"

Sharon stopped near the door. "Not yet. On the surface, there doesn't seem to be anything connecting the fires."

Allyson paused beside her. "Then maybe they're not connected."

Sharon shook her head. Frustration made her movements choppy. "They must be. I don't think there are two torches."

"Then what are you going to do?"

Sharon frowned. "Keep digging."

Sharon hurried to the fire station's reception area, hoping to catch the chief's administrative assistant before lunch. She smiled with relief when she spotted Li Mai seated behind her desk.

"Hi, Li Mai. May I have copies of the last four weeks' meeting minutes?"

"Sure. I have them right here." Li Mai reached for a thick envelope on her desk. "Your replacement doesn't seem to want them. I was going to stop printing the extra copy."

"Thank you." Sharon took the package, irritated at Lucas's lack of interest in the beat she'd loved.

"What's his problem, anyway?"

Sharon flipped through the stack of meeting notes looking for references to the last two arsons. "I wish I could answer that question." But her stubborn loyalty to the *Times* kept her from speaking poorly of her employer.

Li Mai leaned forward on her folded arms. "I even left a message telling him I could provide notes for meetings he'd missed. I thought maybe he didn't know that. He never returned my call."

"I'm sorry, Li Mai. I don't know what to say." Sharon returned the notes to the envelope. Perhaps she'd find mention of the arsons when she took a closer look later.

The assistant's eyes sharpened with interest. "Why are you taking the notes? Are you coming back to us?"

Sharon was saved from answering when Gary's door flew open and he rushed passed Li Mai's desk on his way out of the station.

"Li Mai, there's another fire on the west side," he called over his shoulder. "Get Matt."

"Thanks, Li Mai. See you later." Sharon hurried to catch up with Gary. The scent of the story stirred her blood.

She rushed down the hallway in Gary's wake and managed to slide through the front door before it closed after him. "Is this fire in the same location as the first two?"

"A block away. That's all I know. Call just came in."

"Where's Matt?"

"Meeting with the chief." Gary jumped into an official station vehicle at the front of the parking lot.

Sharon raced to her Civic. The fact this fire was located in the same area and occurred at the same time of day as the first two wasn't lost on her.

Fire crews were battling the blaze by the time she

arrived. Sharon pulled into a nearby parking lot, grabbed a pen and her reporter's notebook, then made her way as close to the activity as she could.

The burning building was a dry cleaner. It was one-story tall with a glass facade and a narrow doorway. The sign, partially obscured by smoke and licking orange flames, read KEEP IT CLEAN in red letters on a gray— or perhaps white—background. It stood beside a city parking lot, which was framed by a three-foot-plus chain fence.

Sharon pushed back strands of hair blown forward in the breeze from the high-pressure fire hoses. Moisture carried on the wind and kissed her face. Shouts from the crew created the impression of confusion, but these men were in complete control. Sharon had quickly realized that when she'd had the beat.

She scanned the area. One block east was the charred remains of Angie Stover's bakery. Reilly O'Conner's office-furniture store wasn't too far from Angie's shop. These three events had to be connected. But how?

People were streaming out of nearby businesses to watch the firefighters in action. Sharon canvassed the crowd, but no one had seen or heard anything or anyone suspicious before the fire.

Continuing her search for information, Sharon neared a familiar, broad-shouldered back in a tan over-coat. "How'd the meeting with Chief Miller go?"

Matthew looked at her over his shoulder. He carried his frustration like a second coat. "Not well. He said Dunleavy and I aren't moving fast enough. I agree."

Sharon was indignant for him. "But you're only two people searching for a serial arsonist. How fast can you work?"

He nodded at her notepad. "What do you have?"

Sharon allowed him to change the subject. "Nothing. What about you?"

He surveyed the scene. "The owner saw the smoke coming out of the supply room. One of her employees called it in. She rushed everyone out, then tried to put the fire out with an extinguisher."

Startled, Sharon looked up. "It started in the supply room? Where they store the chemicals?"

Matthew nodded. "She said the fire kept growing despite her attempts with the extinguisher, then accelerated when it made contact with the cleaning supplies. That's when she ran out of the building."

Sharon rushed to take down the information. "What do you think about the proximity of this fire in relation to the other two?"

Matthew's answer was interrupted.

"Captain Payton."

Matthew and Sharon turned to find Reilly O'Conner.

Matthew stepped closer to the furniture-store owner. "Mr. O'Conner, how can I help you?"

"I want to know the status of the investigation. What's going on?"

Reilly looked thinner than Sharon remembered. Her concern grew as she noted his gray pallor and reddened eyes. When was the last time he'd gotten a full night's sleep?

"The investigation is ongoing, sir." Matthew's manner was patient and empathetic. "We're doing everything we can to find the person or persons who destroyed your property."

Reilly's guard dropped, revealing his shattered expression. He was a man who'd lost everything, and Sharon thought he looked the part. "Destroyed my property? How about destroyed my life?"

The businessman's strident voice drew an audience.

Sharon sent a worried look in Matthew's direction, but his attention remained with Reilly.

"I poured everything I had into my business. I come back every day to see what's left of my dream. Nothing. I don't have anything. But do you think the bill collectors care?"

The crowd began to murmur. Their stares shifted between the fire investigator and the devastated business owner. Sharon sensed where the audience's sympathy rested. She shifted closer to Matthew.

"They don't." Reilly continued without giving Matthew a chance to respond. His volume increased in seeming proportion to his fury. "But because I'm the victim of arson, the insurance company won't pay the collectors. I've been victimized twice."

Matthew's voice and expression conveyed his sympathy. "Mr. O'Conner, I'm very sorry for your loss. I assure you, we're not going to stop looking until we find whoever's responsible."

Sharon stepped forward. She gave Reilly's thin forearm a gentle squeeze, winning his attention. "You're not alone in this, Reilly. The fire investigation unit is working long hours and following up every scrap of information to get justice for you and the arsonists' other victims."

Tears chased unchecked down his cheeks. "I'm so tired."

Sharon gave his arm another sympathetic squeeze. "Then get some rest. Captain Payton is taking care of things here."

Reilly pulled shaking fingers through his thinning brown hair and glanced at Matthew. The store owner nodded before he left. Sharon noted his slow gate and rounded back. Her heart ached for him. With the show over, the crowd dispersed.

"You're very good at that."

Sharon turned at Matthew's words. "At what?"

"Reassuring people. It's like you have some kind of light that draws them to you."

A blush heated her cheeks. She stared over her shoulder in the direction Reilly had taken. "It's not fair what's happened to these business owners. They've worked so hard to build something for themselves only to have a coward destroy their dreams."

"We'll find the torch."

Sharon smiled at Matthew. "I know. I'll see you later."

She returned to her car, trying to fit the puzzle pieces together. What did the arson victims have in common? The people involved held the key to the arsons. They just didn't realize it yet.

Sharon was adding information about the latest west side fire to her arson summary when she felt someone watching her. She tensed when she spotted Lucas looming in the entrance to her cubicle.

His glare could have burned a hole in her desk. "You were at the fire earlier this afternoon."

"Who told you that?" Sharon rewrapped the twist tie around her half-empty bag of pretzels and shoved it aside.

"You can have your beat back when I'm done. This job is just a stepping-stone for me anyway."

"To the communications director position on your uncle's U.S. senate campaign?"

His narrow-eyed stare was sharp with suspicion. "How do you know that?"

"Tell me, Luke—"

"Don't call me Luke."

Sharon ignored him. "Why did your uncle want you

to have the fire department beat? Why not general assignment? Or city council or police? Why did it have to be fire?"

"Maybe that's where Aldridge decided they needed the most help."

Sharon noted the hatred in his smug smile. Did he hate her enough to try to kill her? "Who's your informant at the department? *You're* not doing the work."

"You know I can't reveal my sources."

Sharon snorted with disdain as her nemesis left her cubicle. Lucas didn't have to tell her his source's identity. Through process of elimination, she'd figured out who'd provided the information. But why was the informant helping the Beat Thief, and how involved was this person in the crimes?

Chapter 20

"What's this?" Matthew took the pages Sharon had pulled out of the carry-on luggage she called a handbag. *What does she have in there?*

"A report comparing and contrasting the arson victims." Sharon sipped her second glass of homemade iced tea. They'd finished clearing the remains of the dinner they'd made in her kitchen.

Matthew set aside his own iced tea to flip through the document, skimming the neatly typed and logically formatted charts. He was impressed. "How did you get all of this information?"

"I know people in the community. Remember, I've lived here all my life. It took about two weeks of research and networking to compile this report, including interviewing Candi Lipton, the dry cleaner owner, this afternoon."

"You've listed that O'Conner, Stover, and Lipton use the same insurance company for their businesses."

Sharon leaned closer to Matthew. He breathed in her scent as she pointed to the column under the business financing heading. "And the same lender. But look." She drew his attention to one of the other columns. "At the time of the loan application, Angie and Candi had poor credit, and Reilly had no credit."

Matthew pictured the furniture-store owner's threadbare apartment, outfitted with milk crates and other people's discarded furniture. "Reilly must pay for everything with cash."

"But all three were approved for their loans and given reasonable rates."

Matthew had a mental image of a caution sign flashing on the side of the road down which Sharon was headed. "Do you think either the insurance company or the business lender is involved in the arsons?"

Sharon frowned, and Matthew feared his voice revealed more skepticism than he'd intended.

"If money is the motive, why wouldn't either or both be involved?"

"You're still looking for conspiracies. A lender wouldn't burn down one of its holdings just to call in a loan, and an insurance company wouldn't torch a building so it wouldn't have to pay on a policy."

"Think outside of the box." Sharon shifted in her chair, moving even closer to him. "If it was ruled an accidental fire, the lender would get a lump-sum payment. Ready cash. If it was arson, the insurer would cancel the policy and keep the money, including all that interest."

"That's pretty far outside the box."

She ignored his interruption. "That's at least three policies that have been active for more than two years. That's hundreds of thousands of dollars."

Unwelcome flashbacks of the *Pitt Daily Times* coverage of the fire that had killed his sister returned to him. Reporters had turned an arson investigation into a prime-time drama and, in the process, tried to railroad him while the real torch almost walked.

"Your theory is too complicated. The simplest explanation is usually the right one."

Sharon tapped the report. "Could you at least give it some consideration before you dismiss it out of hand?"

Matthew sighed, staring at the charts. "I'll discuss it with Dunleavy in the morning. But I'm not promising to do more than that."

Sharon lifted her hands in the universal surrender sign. "That's all I'm asking. Will you keep me posted?"

Matthew nodded toward the report. "Are you sure you're not going to write an article on this?"

"I was taken off the fire department beat. Remember?"

"What about the article on O'Conner?"

Irritation dampened Sharon's excitement. "I told you, I didn't have anything to do with that article. Have you checked your department?"

Matthew scowled. "My people know better than to discuss an ongoing investigation."

"Are you certain?"

"What? No shoe sizes for these suspects?"

Matthew smiled at Gary's joke. "Sharon's report is very thorough."

He glanced at his office phone before checking his watch. Eight thirty-seven A.M. Wednesday morning. Eight minutes later than the last time he'd looked at his phone and marked the time. Where was she?

Sharon had an early meeting this morning before she went in to the paper. She'd told him she'd drive herself to work and had promised to call him again after the meeting. In the meantime, she had her cell phone with her in case she had any trouble.

In addition to being worried, Matthew also was disappointed. Granted, it had only been a few days since they'd starting riding to and from work together, but he'd really come to enjoy their morning routine. He hadn't realized how much.

Matthew forced himself to concentrate on the work. "This report shows what the business owners have in common and some of their differences. As we already knew, none of them has a criminal record, which torches typically do."

Gary raised his hand, palm out. "Which doesn't mean they haven't committed a crime. It just means they haven't been caught."

"Good point." Matthew returned to the document. "They use different banks. Have different life and health insurance providers."

"And different accounting systems. O'Conner uses a software program. Stover goes to a service, and Lipton's father does her taxes."

"But they have the same business insurance and lending company." Matthew skimmed the report. "We need to see if there's anything that implicates either of those companies."

Gary frowned. "You mean like they're doctoring their books or something?"

"Something."

"Like a conspiracy?" Gary shuffled the papers. "Stover and Lipton went to the same high school. Isn't it easier to believe they cooked this up for profit than to believe an insurance company or bank would go after their small change?"

Matthew scanned the narrative again. "Stover and Lipton both attended George Washington High School, but Lipton enrolled three years after Stover graduated."

Gary looked sheepishly at Matthew. "Oh. I didn't catch that."

Matthew thought of his encounter yesterday with O'Conner. "We're going to check every possible lead—thoroughly—no matter how far-fetched. These people deserve justice."

"What if one or more of them is the torch?"

"We'll arrest them."

"Do you still want to look at the file of convicted arsonists?"

"Yes. We need to check their alibis. And they may be able to give us information that could help with the investigation."

"I'll get the paperwork. It's going to take us a while." Gary pushed himself out of his chair.

"I know." Matthew leaned back in his seat. "Naismith and Miller don't want to spend the overtime on a special task force. It's just you and me."

Gary paused on his way to the door. "By the way, I was wondering if you and Sharon MacCabe had something going?"

Matthew stared at the younger man. The lieutenant appeared close to Sharon's age. Had she ever mentioned Gary to him? Once again, Matthew checked the time and looked at the phone. Eight-forty-seven and still Sharon hadn't called.

Gary shifted his feet. "It's just that she probably won't be able to write about the investigation."

Matthew's eyes narrowed. Sharon's words echoed in his head like a siren he was hearing too late. *Have you checked your department for leaks?*

Gary's freckles blended into his rising blush. He shrugged a little too casually. "You know, since she doesn't cover our department anymore."

Matthew kept his voice low and measured. "How long have you been giving Lucas Stanton confidential information about the arson investigation?"

"I—"

His voice sharpened. "How long?"

Gary's Adam's apple bobbed. "He called me after the first one. But he exaggerated the information for the story."

Matthew wanted to punch the wall or kick his chair. He remained seated. "I have to be able to trust you."

The younger man looked away. "I'm sorry. I just . . . He's the senator's nephew."

With Gary's every word, Matthew's blood ran hotter. "We're not here to do political favors. Our responsibility is to protect the people of Charleston. Leaking confidential information to the press doesn't help the people we serve."

"I'm sorry. I—"

"This torch has already threatened Sharon twice to scare her from the story Stanton is supposed to be covering. Do you know anything about that?"

"Me?" Shock drained the heat from Gary's face. "*No.*"

Matthew gave his lieutenant a hard stare. "Are you certain?"

"Yes. Positive. I swear it."

Matthew noted the increasing shine on Gary's forehead as the younger man began to sweat. "In the future, refer any questions about the investigation to me."

"Yes, sir." Gary spun and hurried from Matthew's office.

Matthew marked the time again. It was almost nine o'clock. Between Sharon's silence and Gary's betrayal, his temper was on a fast boil. He grabbed the phone and dialed Sharon's direct work number. She answered on the first ring.

"Sharon MacCabe."

"It's Matt."

"Matt." He heard the smile in her voice and his temper instantly cooled. "I was just about to call you. Did you think I'd forgotten?"

Yes. "No, but I thought I'd check on you."

Sharon made a chiding noise. "I don't think you're telling me the truth. I think you were checking your watch every five minutes and getting increasingly irate."

He chuckled, the lightness of her personality pushing against the darkness edging closer to him. "You think you know me so well. How'd the meeting go?"

Some of the enthusiasm left her voice. "It was for a May Day feature I'm working on. It went well. Any big news on your end?"

"How long have you known Dunleavy was the leak?"

"Not long. Only the three of us had that much detail about the interviews with the business owners, and I knew you and I wouldn't have told Lucas."

Matthew rubbed his fingers and thumb across his eyes. "Why didn't you say anything?" He could almost hear Sharon's shrug.

"I suggested twice that you check your department for leaks, but it was easier for you to believe I was passing out information."

Matthew winced. "That's because of my experiences with the media."

"I'm not just the media, Matt. I'm also Sharon."

He thought of their conversation last night. Had he made matters worse? "I'm sorry. I wasn't being fair."

"You can apologize over dinner."

His mood lifted. It unnerved him just how much peace he'd found in her presence. What would he do without her? He didn't want to think about that.

Then he remembered the stack of files he and Gary had to go through. Disappointment hit him like a prizefighter's punch. "I have to work late. Can I have a rain check?"

"Of course. But you can cook this time."

Matthew grinned. "You're a risk taker, Ms. Mac-Cabe."

"Do you think Gary knows more about the arsons than he's telling us?"

Sharon's question was unexpected. Matthew instantly went on the defensive. "No, I don't."

"Why not?"

He deliberately relaxed his grip on the receiver. "Dunleavy's working with me. He would've told me if he had information about the case."

"He didn't tell you he was feeding Lucas information."

She had a good point. He hated that. "There's a big difference between leaking information and committing a felony."

Sharon's sigh blew across the phone line. "You may want to check your blind loyalty to the department. That trait may actually hurt the investigation."

"We're done. Quit bellyaching." Seth gulped his beer, wishing for something stronger to take the edge off of Raymond's complaints.

Damn, the guy whined like a bitch in heat. And had he lost weight? Seth stared hard at the other man. Damn. Raymond was starving himself. Not good.

Seth scanned the bar. What a sty. A burden lifted from his chest when he realized he'd never have to come here again. He was tired of breathing the second-hand smoke. Tired of peeling himself out of the beer-soaked booths. He shifted in his seat, afraid he'd picked up a splinter from the worn wooden bench.

Raymond rubbed his meaty hands back and forth over his clean-shaven dark head. "You're a fool if you think we're off the hook just because we're done setting fires. Payton's going to keep looking until he finds us."

Seth studied his unwilling partner in crime. He was especially glad he'd never have to listen to Raymond's bitching. Ever again. "Nothing links us."

The other man's eyes narrowed. "Do you think we've committed the perfect crime? That's stupid."

Seth watched the spittle from his coworker's mouth shoot across the table. It barely missed his beer. Perfect.

He shoved his bottle aside. "Stupid was setting the fire in the cleaner's storage room. It burned too fast. Could've killed someone."

That truth had been weighing on Seth since yesterday. Anger flashed through him again. Sloppy. Careless. Thoughtless.

Raymond heaved a sigh. "You're right. I was too anxious. I wanted to get out of there fast. I didn't think. I'm sorry."

"It's done." Seth looked around, wondering if he should order another beer. The first one hadn't been that good, though. No point ordering a second.

"I'm glad no one was hurt." Raymond spoke with tired relief.

"We'll get the final payment and move on."

"Man, we're not going to be able to move on. This shit is going to follow us for the rest of our lives. We're always going to be looking over our shoulders."

"Long as we can pay our bills."

Seth stared at the scarred wooden table. The next time his kids asked when they would see him, he wouldn't have to say, "Soon." Or worse, "I don't know." Next time, he'd say, "I've booked my flight." He wanted to laugh out loud with joy.

Then he'd be able to see where his irresponsible ex-wife was raising his kids. Fear clenched his gut. Seth released the emotion. If he didn't like her neighborhood, he'd sue for full custody. He'd have enough money for the court battle. And he'd win. Then his ex-wife could call *them* long-distance. He smiled.

"Payton's not going to quit."

Raymond's words shattered Seth's happy thoughts.

Seth returned his attention to the other man. "They can't connect us unless one of us turns rat. That won't happen."

Matthew's office smelled of grease and onions. He and Gary ate the deli sandwiches and French fries in his office as they reviewed the profiles of Charleston's convicted arsonists.

Matthew closed another folder. "A lot of these guys use accelerants." He put the folder on top of his growing "possibilities" pile and took another one.

"Most of them are still in prison." Gary reached for a fry while he skimmed his latest profile.

Matthew swallowed a healthy bite of his roast beef sandwich. "That narrows it down. The ones who've been released, we'll bring in for questioning."

Gary wiped his fingers on a napkin before writing a note. "There are quite a few repeat offenders."

Matthew closed the last of his files. He finished his fries and sandwich, and tossed the empty containers into his trash. "Torches like to watch their work. He'd either work or live somewhere nearby."

"I've got a few on the west side."

"So do I." Matthew wiped his mouth and hands on a paper napkin.

"But you don't think any of these guys set the fires," Gary said hesitantly.

"No, I don't think they're involved. But we can't skip any steps."

The atmosphere between them had started awkwardly because of Gary's role as media informant. Luckily, they'd quickly returned to their comfortable working relationship. They had a lot of work to do. Matthew had to trust that his lieutenant had learned from his mistake and wouldn't repeat it.

Matthew got up and paced to the wall map they'd posted that afternoon. Three blue tacks sketched the path of the arsons. The pins were concentrated in a small area of a west side neighborhood.

Behind him, Matthew could hear Gary throwing away the remains of his dinner. He turned to find his lieutenant organizing his desk. "Leave the files as they are. We're picking it up again in the morning."

"All right." Gary joined Matthew in front of the map. He traced the tacks. "Do you see a pattern?"

Matthew shook his head. "They're just locations on the west side." He checked his watch. It was after ten o'clock. His mind and body were slowing down. "Let's call it a night."

"Yeah. Tomorrow's another day. We got a lot done today." Gary started for the door. He looked back at Matthew before crossing the threshold. "We'll catch this guy. It'll just take a while."

"That's the problem. We're running out of time."

Chapter 21

"Have I got a scoop for you."

Matthew smiled as Sharon's used-car-salesman impersonation came over the phone line. "It must be some kind of scoop if it can't wait for me to pick you up in . . ." he checked his watch, "just over an hour."

"Believe me. When you hear it, you'll be glad I didn't wait. It'll make your entire Thursday."

His smile grew into a grin. "Then let's hear it."

A dramatic pause preceded her revelation. "Do you remember the fire that occurred on the west side three weeks ago? Early April?"

Matthew narrowed his eyes in concentration. "The greeting-card store."

"Right. I just found out the owner, Stu Grisham, had the same business loan lender and insurance company as Reilly, Angie, and Candi. What do you think about that?"

Matthew frowned. "The greeting-card store wasn't arson."

"You and I were suspicious of that fire. But Brad signed off on the report without letting you do a walk-through."

"I remember." He also recalled Dunleavy talking him out of pushing Naismith to reopen the inquiry. Had he been wrong to take his lieutenant's advice?

"The card store could be a part of this." Sharon's tone was contemplative. "If it is, then we've had at least four arsons."

Matthew rubbed his fingers over his eyes. "You're jumping to conclusions."

"The same section of the city. The same lender. The same insurer. Connect the dots, Captain."

His mind fought against her compelling evidence and sought shelter in reason. "Experienced firefighters ruled out arson."

"What if they're wrong? Then this arsonist has been around a lot longer than we suspected."

Matthew sat in awe of her stubbornness. "You're in full conspiracy mode, aren't you?"

"There's one way you could put an end to my latest theory. Take another look at the file. If the file doesn't support what I'm saying, then I'll drop it."

Matthew considered her proposal. What would it mean if Naismith had signed off on a false report? Why was he so reluctant to find out?

Matthew's thoughts raced, trying to digest the ways this potential new lead could change the perspective of his investigation. "If we add this older event, it could widen the pool of suspects."

"Will you take another look at the report?"

"I'll have to."

Matthew ended the call, recradling his phone. Tension built within him. Was the past repeating itself? He didn't want to believe a firefighter had suppressed information about an arson.

He pressed buttons for Li Mai's intercom number.

"This is Li Mai."

"It's Matt. Could you get me the file for the Grisham's Greetings and Gifts fire?"

Matthew didn't have long to wait before Li Mai brought him the information. The thinness of the folder was a bad sign. His concern was verified after leafing through the contents. He took the folder with him down the hall to Naismith's office. The assistant chief grunted acceptance of the interruption.

Matthew crossed the threshold, lifting the thin folder in his hand. "The file on the greeting-card store fire is missing information from the scene."

Naismith barely spared him a glance. "Like what?"

"Site photos, descriptions of the damaged areas, test results from site samples."

Naismith autographed the forms he'd skimmed and tossed them into his out-box. "So?"

"On what information did you decide the fire wasn't arson?"

The assistant chief braced his thick arms on his desk. "My crew's statement."

"You closed the file without getting evidence?"

The other man shrugged. "I didn't need it."

"What?" Matthew couldn't believe what he was hearing.

"My men told me the fire wasn't set. That's good enough for me. And, if it's good enough for me, it's good enough for you."

Matthew's face tightened with anger. "No, sir, it isn't. You and Chief Miller want this investigation closed yesterday. So do I, but we can't take shortcuts."

Naismith's casual regard became a cutting glare. "Are you calling my crew sloppy?"

Matthew lifted the folder in his hand again. "If the torch has set other fires, I need to know. Starting with this one." He flipped open the folder to reference the report. "Ford was first on-site. Dunleavy and I'll walk the site with him in the morning."

Sharon slid another glance in Matthew's direction. She'd sensed his controlled temper as soon as he'd walked into the newspaper's front lobby. Now, in the confines of his Camry, it was like a heat shield between them. His monosyllabic answers to her innocuous how-was-your-day-honey questions weren't positive predictors to his answers for her how's-the-investigation-going-honey questions.

But they were blocks from her home and the silence had lasted long enough. "Are you going to tell me what you found in the card-store fire's file?"

"Nothing."

Sharon waved away the hurt. "You promised to include me in the investigation."

"I am." He found a parking space a few houses from her building.

"Then tell me what you found in the file."

"Nothing." He parked the car, cut the engine and turned to her. "The initial incident report but no details. No evidence." Matthew slammed out of the Camry and walked around to her side of the car.

She held his hand as he helped her out. "What does this mean?" Her hand remained in the warmth of his as they walked to her apartment.

His brow furrowed above his sharp, dark eyes. "I don't know. Dunleavy and I are going to walk through the site in the morning."

"But it's been a month. Isn't the site contaminated now?"

Matthew paced beside her up the few steps to the

front entry. "If an accelerant was used, there'd still be trace evidence in the floorboards and walls."

Sharon considered his explanation. Releasing his hand, she led the way up the narrow staircase to her apartment.

She opened the door and watched him walk past her into her great room. "If you can salvage the situation, why are you so angry?"

He caught her gaze. Temper snapped in his eyes. "Because Naismith lied when he said he'd looked into the fire."

Sharon still didn't understand. "But now you're going to look into it."

He spun away from her. Agitated steps carried him across the room. His voice was low, rough, and reluctant. "I've been in this situation before."

Sharon froze, finally realizing what this was about. What his words meant. "Tell me." *Trust me.*

Chapter 22

Matthew moved past his present anger and into bitter memories. The heat of old flames. The stench of choking smoke. The pain of a loss so devastating it still buckled his knees.

He'd tried to lock away those memories, buried the key and took off running. A new city, a different job. But as fate would have it, he'd run right into the pain he'd prayed to forget. Fate had found the key and forced him to carry a burden too heavy to bear alone. But was he alone?

He turned and found Sharon watching him with anxious eyes. Through his gathering gloom, he sought her light. "Last October, there was a string of fires in my station in Pittsburgh. It seemed like one every week."

Sharon sank onto her sofa. "Over what period of time?"

"Five weeks. But, by the second fire, I was getting suspicious."

"That it was arson?"

Matthew nodded. "All the signs were there. Rapid burn, distinct burn pattern, black smoke."

"What did your station captain say?"

"He didn't believe me." His frustration was as fresh as the day he'd met with his captain. It was the same feeling he'd had speaking with Naismith hours earlier. "He wouldn't even consider an investigation."

"What about the fire investigators?"

Sharon looked as baffled as he'd felt six months ago, as baffled as he still felt when he remembered that time.

Matthew clenched his fists as the long-ago anger rekindled. "They supported his decision. There was a torch in our area, but we weren't even looking for him. Every time my crew went in to one of those fires, I thought this is a risk we shouldn't have to take. We should be trying to stop this guy, not cleaning up after him."

The silence felt heavier this time as he struggled with his grief. He was grateful Sharon waited patiently for him to continue. She didn't stand in judgment of his actions—or lack thereof. She didn't rush blindly to his defense. What he sensed instead was an understanding of his concern. A shared dedication to community. And that empathy allowed him to open up.

"And then Mickey's company got the call." His bone-deep sigh didn't ease the constriction in his chest. "It was a risk she shouldn't have had to take." He turned away, scrubbing his face. His palms came away wet with tears.

"Oh, Matt. I'm so sorry." Sharon's voice was thick with sorrow.

Matthew sensed her approach. Her hand settled lightly against his upper arm. He cupped her palm and drew it closer to his heart, hoping her healing warmth would ease his pain.

"I lost my mind and blamed myself. I should have done a better job of looking after her. I should have forced those brain-dead bureaucrats to listen to me."

Sharon rested her cheek against his shoulder blade. "But you don't blame yourself anymore."

"Not so much anymore. But, at first, I also blamed my captain and the investigators for Mickey's death." He turned to face Sharon, still holding her palm to his chest. "They knew those fires were arson but refused to investigate them. I called them out during a public meeting."

Sharon's winged eyebrows took flight. "What happened?"

"They punished me for it."

"How?"

He released her hand, needing to pace off the remnants of his rage. "By accusing me of being the torch."

"On what evidence?" Fury trembled in Sharon's words.

"They didn't have anything to tie me to the arsons, but that didn't stop them from lying to the press about evidence that put me at the scene."

"That's outrageous."

Her outburst grabbed Matthew's attention. She looked ready for battle.

Matthew dragged a hand through his hair. "They couldn't press charges against me without proof and, eventually, they caught the torch."

"I'm glad, but they ruined your reputation and your career. And for what? Petty revenge? Shame because they didn't do their job?"

Matthew shrugged. "All of the above and probably more. It's because they ruined my reputation that I had to leave Pittsburgh."

"It's a good thing your father knows the mayor. And that he was able to help you get a job with Charleston's department."

Matthew frowned. "Fred West? My father doesn't know him. What makes you think he does?"

Sharon looked startled. "A rumor I'd heard. I'll have to check my sources."

"Yeah. You should do that." He crossed his arms and propped a shoulder against the threshold between her great room and her bedroom. "I don't know why Naismith and Miller hired me. I'm sure they had stronger résumés. But I'm glad they took a chance on me."

Sharon pondered that question. Why had Naismith and Miller hired Matthew if cronyism hadn't played a role?

Sharon shoved that mystery aside. Now that he'd told her what she'd already learned through the Internet, she could ask the question she'd wanted to ask almost from the day they'd met. "How did you find the strength to survive that experience?"

Matthew's eyes widened in surprise. "I wasn't strong. I ran. After the media was done with me, there wasn't a firehouse in Pittsburgh—probably all of Pennsylvania—that wanted me."

Sharon stepped closer to him. "You may consider it running, but I see it as fighting for your career. They tried to ruin you—the press, the investigators and your boss—but you wouldn't let them."

Matthew looked away as though her praise embarrassed him. "Sort of like what you're going through with your job at the paper."

"Not as extreme, but we do have more in common than we originally thought."

Matthew's lips curved into the sexy smile that made her crave him. "Yeah. We're both survivors."

Beneath the heat glowing in Matthew's eyes was a wary question. Sharon knew he wondered whether this time as the others she'd pull away. Not now that she knew he trusted her. She had more confidence in their relationship. There wasn't a need to hold back any longer.

Sharon stopped within touching distance from him. "Thank you for trusting me enough to share this part of your past with me."

His trust was a gift more precious to her than she could possibly describe. She would take very good care of it.

Sharon braced her palms against his well-developed chest—the man obviously weight trained regularly—and stood on her toes to kiss him. Matthew met her halfway and she walked him backward to her bedroom, letting him know there would be no stopping tonight.

Chapter 23

Sharon sighed as Matthew's lips moved on hers. Softly. Sweetly. Coaxing her mouth to part for him. Her knees trembled as she pressed her body against him, using the contact to guide him down her short hallway to her bedroom.

She breathed his name and Matthew's tongue swept inside, a bold, daring stroke that sent a current through her system. She dug her fingers into his biceps, and he brought her closer. His large palm explored her body with the same bold moves his tongue used to explore her mouth.

Sharon cupped the back of his head with her hands. Matthew lifted her and she wrapped her legs tightly around his waist.

Sharon felt herself falling with Matthew above her. Her eyes popped open and her startled search recognized her bedroom. "I see you've found my bed." Her body tensed beneath him. "Did you bring a condom?"

He smiled, a sensual promise. "Yes."

Her gaze dropped to Matthew's full, moist lips. Her mind switched off and her body reclaimed control. Her arms wrapped around his neck to draw his mouth to hers. Matthew's eyes glowed hot enough to make her sweat. As his lips met hers, Sharon closed her eyes in ecstasy and freed the hunger she'd held in check for so long.

Matthew's blood roared in his ears, a tsunami of need that had built up over weeks of wanting. Now, Sharon lay beneath him, her limbs entwined with his. His hands shook and he urged her even closer to him.

His lips moved along her neck, nibbling, licking, kissing. He breathed in her scent and his groin tightened. He ran his fingers over the silky feel of her blouse and gently squeezed the hot, heavy weight of her full breast. She moved against him.

Matthew groaned. "I need you now, but I want this to last."

She chuckled, breathless. "Me too. But who says we can only do this once?"

A lightbulb went off in his head. *Good point.*

With a dizzying mixture of reluctance and haste, he drew away from her to unbutton her blouse and unfasten her bra. Her breasts bounced free. He dipped his head to suckle her nipples. Sharon gripped his hair, pulling him closer as she pressed against him.

He helped her remove his shirt. Her teeth nipped into the curve of his neck. Her nails raked his back. He rubbed his chest against her breasts, feeling her hardening nipples press into him.

They discarded the rest of their clothes with an emphasis on speed rather than seduction. Matthew pressed Sharon onto the mattress, but she pushed against him until he rolled over. She straddled him, her knees on either side of his waist, her hands on the pillow on either side of his neck, her nipples grazing his chest. She smiled into his eyes, licked his mouth, then lay above him for a full-body caress.

Matthew's head pressed into the pillow. He squeezed his eyes shut, concentrating on maintaining control of his body. He felt himself move against Sharon's taut belly.

"I don't know how much more I can take." He raised his hands to reach for her, but she was already lifting away from him.

Sharon kissed the pulse at the base of his throat. Her tongue came out to circle the area. Then she continued the caress in one straight line down his torso. When her lips wrapped around his straining member, he almost jackknifed off the bed.

He groaned, drilling his fingers into the mattress, arching his spine to give her more of him. Her mouth was hot, moist. Heaven on earth. She moved him, sliding her fingers along his length. She spiraled her tongue around his tip. He was on sensation overload. The scent of her that lingered in her room. The feel of her tongue on him. The sound of his heart galloping in his ears. But he needed to add the taste of her. He hungered for her flavor.

Matthew pulled himself away from Sharon, his body shuddering at the sudden loss.

Confused, Sharon opened her eyes in time to see Matthew reach for her. With one fluid flex of muscle, he switched places with her. He wrapped his fingers around her wrists like tender bands and kissed her deeply, making her every nerve ending sizzle. He lifted his head and locked his gaze with hers as he rubbed his hair-roughened chest against her breasts.

Sharon bit her lip. Her arousal made her nipples extremely sensitive. Her body shifted restlessly among the sheets. Matthew slid his body lower, skimming against her belly. His tongue licked the pulse at her neck, detouring to feast at her nipples before resuming its course over her stomach.

She strained against the gentle restraints at her wrists. "Matt, let me go."

He paused only long enough to answer. "No."

"I want to touch you."

"You already have. More than anyone I've ever known."

His hot, damp tongue stroked her waist, pausing to play in her navel. Sharon's restless movements increased. She gasped and pulled against Matthew's hold. Finally, he released her. He ran his large hands down her body, molding them to her breasts, tracing her waist, then cupping them over her hips. He lifted her and kissed her intimately.

Sharon's eyes flew open and she cried out. Her spine arched reflexively, pressing her tighter against Matthew's mouth. He stroked her, licked her, fed on her. Sharon felt her juices flowing.

She was torn between passion and embarrassment. She'd never experienced such an intimacy. She wanted to pull away. She wanted to draw closer. She wanted Matthew to stop. She prayed this magic would never end. How could something be wrong when it felt so completely right?

But, as Matthew had given her his trust, she'd trust him. She gave her body over to the incredible sensations his lips and tongue created.

A pressure built deep inside her. A tightening and a stretching, almost painful in its pleasure. She squeezed her eyes shut and gripped the bedsheet, pulling it from the mattress. Her heart rate accelerated until she was gasping. Colors exploded behind her eyelids. Her body went taut, tense, then flew apart as she screamed Matthew's name.

He kissed her deeply one last time before pulling his body up and over hers. Matthew covered her parted lips with his own and she tasted her desire on his tongue.

They made quick work of putting on the condom. Sharon's body still pulsed from the aftershocks when he entered her, smoothly, deeply. She cried out again at the intense desire. He was full and thick. Sharon licked her lips at the pleasure of his movements. She arched her back, matching his rhythm. Matthew dipped his head and sucked first one, then the other nipple into his mouth. She cupped the back of his head and pulled him closer.

Her muscles tensed. She felt the now-familiar anticipation of her climax. She wanted to prolong the ecstasy. More and more. She wanted to charge toward it. Tighter and tighter. She began to pant. Closer and closer. Finally, she flung her arms wide and dove toward the end. Her muscles shook and shattered. Matthew's body moved with her. He groaned softly into her ear, his limbs tensing, then relaxing against her. She felt him kiss the side of her neck, soft and sweet. As she drifted into sleep, Patti LaBelle's "Right Kind of Lover" again whispered across her mind.

"Raymond Ford is dead." Matthew had called Sharon after lunch. This wasn't the conversation he'd anticipated having with her after last night, but a lot had happened since he'd taken her to work that morning.

"The firefighter you were going to do the walk-through with?" Surprise lifted her voice several octaves.

"Yeah." Matthew massaged his temples with his thumb and fingers. "The police are calling it a suicide. They said he shot himself in the head."

Naismith had come to Matthew's office first thing that morning with two homicide detectives to give him the news. Matthew had been satisfied and relaxed, enjoying memories of his new closeness with Sharon. That sense of well-being had been replaced by a deep unease. Once some of the shock had worn off, Matthew had wondered about his boss's lack of emotion. But he'd set aside that mystery to talk with Dunleavy.

"Matt, that's terrible. I'm so sorry. How are you handling it?"

"I'm okay. It's hard when someone you know dies. People who've worked with him longer than I have are really shaken up. Li Mai went home."

Perhaps he should've suggested Dunleavy go home as well. The young man had worked with Ford for several years, almost as long as Naismith had. The lieutenant had taken the news hard. That's why Matthew hadn't told him everything.

"Did Ray leave a note?"

Matthew rubbed his hand over his hair. Answering that question was almost as difficult as talking about Ford's suicide. It felt like he was disrespecting the dead. "Yes, but it's not common knowledge. The detectives gave me a copy for my case file. Ford typed the note. He confessed to being the west side torch."

"What?"

Matthew rolled his pen between his fingers while Sharon stuttered her surprise.

"Are you closing the case?" She whispered the question. Probably didn't want any other reporters overhearing their conversation. Good. He didn't want anyone getting wind of this story, either. At least not yet.

Matthew contemplated the fire scene photos pinned to the case board in a corner of his office. "No."

"Why not?" Sharon's voice conveyed some of the surprise and confusion Matthew felt toward his actions.

He set down his pen and drummed his fingers on his desk. "I still have questions."

"You don't believe Ray's confession, do you?"

Matthew stopped drumming. "No, I don't."

"Why would he lie in a suicide note?"

"Maybe it wasn't suicide."

She dropped her voice to a whisper again. "You think someone killed him? Who?"

"The real torch."

"And you call me a conspiracy theorist. This has got to be the mother of all conspiracies."

"Ford was a firefighter."

"That doesn't mean he couldn't be an arsonist." Sharon spoke gently. "A lot of arsonists are thrill seekers, and you know some firefighters are too."

Matthew pictured the quiet man who blended into the background. "Ford wasn't a thrill seeker." He scanned the case board, recalling details of the events. "He was first on-site for two of those fires. He wouldn't have had time to set them, then return to the station to go out with his crew."

"Maybe he was working with someone." Sharon paused as though collecting her thoughts. "Matt, I understand you don't want Ray railroaded the way they railroaded you in Pittsburgh. But there wasn't any evidence against you. The detectives showed you Ray's confession."

Matthew leaned into his desk. "Who types a suicide note?"

Sharon sighed her exasperation. "Maybe he was already on his computer."

Matthew ran his hand over his hair again. He knew he wasn't crazy. "So he typed a confession, printed it, dug out his gun, walked into his kitchen, sat at his table, laid the note beside him, then blew his brains out?" He imagined Sharon mulling over the scenario.

"That does seem strange."

His shoulders relaxed. He wasn't alone. "Now we have to convince Naismith and the homicide detectives."

Chapter 24

Matthew followed Sharon into her apartment. They'd picked up Chinese food on their way home.

That morning, Matthew had woken grateful it was Friday. He'd taken a step toward rejoining society and anticipated spending the weekend with Sharon doing pretty much what they'd done last night. But with Ford's death and alleged confession, he'd plummeted from excited anticipation to numbed disbelief. Add to that, he was struggling with flashbacks of his own bitter betrayal.

Questionable confession aside, Matthew couldn't accept the idea of a firefighter committing arson. He turned to Sharon. They'd get to the bottom of this. Together.

Sharon took plates from her cupboard. "What did the detectives say when you asked them to check Ray's note for fingerprints?"

Matthew helped her serve the sweet-and-sour chicken, vegetables, and steamed rice. Since they'd started ending the day together, he'd become as comfortable in her kitchen as he was in his own. Maybe more. "They didn't want to at first. But I got their attention when I explained we might have two torches."

Sharon chuckled. "The next time you're tempted to call me a conspiracy theorist, I want you to remember how I supported this latest development in your investigation."

He gave her a reluctant smile. "I guess this is something else we have in common."

The look in her eyes grew warmer, heating him. "The list keeps growing."

He put down the serving spoon and crossed his arms. "It does, despite our bad first impressions of each other."

"I knew I'd win you over with my wit and unquenchable élan."

"Élan?" Matthew chuckled. "Can't you say *confidence*, like everyone else? Why the one-dollar words?"

"Sorry." She batted her lashes, a teasing light shining in her eyes. "A large vocabulary is a hazard of my profession."

He arched a brow. "Is that so?" Matthew rounded the table toward her.

"And they're two-dollar-and-fifty-cent words now. Inflation."

"Thanks for the update." He cupped her shoulders, then ran his palms down her arms in one, long caress. He felt the goose bumps raise along her skin and grinned. "You didn't win me over so much as you wore me down. You're as tenacious as a starving dog with a bone when you want something."

Sharon threw back her head and laughed. Matthew loved the sound. It warmed him. Relaxed him. Lured him to her.

Her amusement died down. "It's a good thing you're so cute because your compliments suck."

Matthew's shoulders shook with humor. That was another reason he needed her. She brought joy back into his life. Laughter and light. When was the last time he'd laughed so freely?

Matthew reached up and drew his fingers through the wavy locks of her hair. "Do you want me to tell you what drew me to you?" Besides her light. He couldn't tell her that. She'd think he was crazy. "You're smart and funny. I love your passion." He smiled into her eyes. "Both in and out of bed. Your courage and determination."

Sharon's cheeks were flushed. Her voice was warm and husky. "I see all those traits in you, as well." She touched his cheek. "I was afraid you'd never get past my being a reporter."

Matthew dipped his head to kiss the side of her neck. As she shivered in his arms, he drew her closer and lost himself in her. Her scent. Her taste. Her touch. "None of that matters now. None of that matters."

Matthew sighed and pushed himself away from his desk. He felt, as well as heard, his joints as he flexed his neck and shoulders. Mondays were always brutal, and this one still wasn't over. He checked his watch. It was after six o'clock. He'd promised Sharon he'd be at the paper by six-thirty.

Matthew piled folders into his briefcase—the furniture store, coffee shop, cleaners, and card-shop fires. He'd bring Sharon up-to-date with his search for Ford's theoretical partner. He still didn't believe Ford had been involved with the arsons, though.

A quick tap on his office door interrupted him. He looked up to find Naismith filling his doorway.

"I haven't seen your final report on the west side arsons."

Matthew shut his briefcase. "I haven't closed the case yet."

The assistant chief's heavy eyebrows lowered. "Why not?"

"I still have some questions."

"Like what?"

Matthew braced his hands on his hips and considered the frustration and anger in his boss's eyes. Why was Naismith so anxious to close this investigation? He'd wanted it over before Matthew had even begun.

"I'm not convinced Ford was the torch." Matthew watched for his boss's reaction.

Naismith's nostrils flared and angry color filled his cheeks. "You have his confession, for pity's sake. What more do you want? For Ford to pop out of the ground and give it to you in song?"

"That's just it. Ford can't give me his side of the story. But I have to make sure that what we think happened is the truth." Matthew paused. "You knew Ford for years. Do you think he was a felon?"

A flicker of doubt winked in Naismith's gray eyes. "Ford was a good firefighter, but maybe I didn't know him as well as I thought."

How quickly Naismith's loyalty for his firefighters disappeared under pressure. It was easier to accept the information presented to him than to verify the truth. *Is that how my station captain had justified the false accusations against me?* "Or maybe someone's setting him up."

"For the love of Pete, what more are you looking for?"

Matthew dropped his arms. "Why are you in such a rush to close this case?"

Naismith's frown darkened. "Why are you dragging your feet? Believe me, we'll have plenty for you to do even after you're done with this case."

Matthew dragged his briefcase from his desk and

walked toward his boss. He stopped to pull his jacket from the hook behind his door. "It's not enough to close it. We have to get it right."

"Dammit, you've got a typed confession."

Matthew stood before his boss. For the moment, he wasn't seeing Naismith. He saw instead his former captain who'd stared through Matthew while reading the accusations of the ultimate firefighter's betrayal. "Is it really that easy for you to believe one of our own would break the law and endanger lives?"

"Don't test me." Naismith's nostrils flared as he took an angry breath. "This is nasty business. Hard to swallow. Your leaving the file open on this is just making it worse."

Matthew shrugged into his jacket. "I should have the forensics report from the police department in a couple of days."

"Forensics from what?"

"The typed confession found with Ford."

A vein throbbed in Naismith's forehead. "You didn't tell me you were going to request a forensic exam."

"Is there a problem?"

"Hell, yes." Naismith's tone again simulated a growl. "You should have told me before you asked another agency for help with your investigation."

Matthew faced the snapping indignation in Naismith's gray gaze. "You're right. As my boss, I should have told you. I'm sorry."

Suspicion replaced Naismith's indignation. "Then withdraw your request."

The order didn't surprise Matthew. But it did disappoint him. "I need that information before I can close the case. If there's another set of prints on the paper, it could mean we're dealing with a second torch as well as a homicide."

Naismith shook his head. "Ford acted alone and he killed himself. Accept it, close the case and move on."

"If you're right, the evidence will prove it."

With one last glare, Naismith stormed away from Matthew's office.

Matthew looked at his watch. Six-seventeen. He was going to be late meeting Sharon. He pulled his office door closed behind him and strode briskly down the hall.

What would Sharon say when he told her about his exchange with Naismith? She'd probably move his boss to the top of her suspicious persons list.

Sharon was amazed at Matthew's stubbornness. "I know it bothers you to think a member of your department could be behind the arsons, but why else would Naismith try to block the investigation?"

She waited until he'd put away the dish he'd just dried before handing him the last dripping plate. They'd finished dinner—at his place this time—but still debated Naismith's position on her suspicious persons list.

"Why would a firefighter commit arson?"

She dried her hand on a kitchen towel, then gave it to Matthew. "Why would a reporter make up the news? Why would a politician accept a bribe? There are desperate people in all walks of life."

Matthew returned the towel to its hook beside the sink. "I just can't see it."

Sharon rested her hand on Matthew's shoulder. "Are we going to spend the entire evening discussing whether your boss is an arsonist?"

He turned to her with a sexy smile. "What else is there for us to do?"

Sharon shrugged and tilted her head flirtatiously. "What are you up for?"

Matthew's smile widened. He took her wrist and drew her hand from his shoulder to the zipper of his dress pants. "Just about anything."

Her body temperature jumped at least ten degrees. She was on fire. Sharon felt her lips curve. She kept her palm cupped over him and took his hand with her free one. Holding eye contact, she walked backward, leading him out of his kitchen. They'd need more room. But apparently Matthew couldn't wait.

He stopped in the living room, pulling her into his arms. Matthew licked his way from the soft, sensitive hollow behind her ear to the pulse racing in her throat. His tongue left a hot, wet trail across her skin and sent her body into convulsive shivers. She rubbed her palm against his pants, feeling him growing warmer and harder through the cotton material.

Matthew grabbed her knee and raised her leg against his thigh. She gasped. Her skirt pulled up. Through the nylon of her hose, his pant leg scratched her inner thigh. The man was a master at providing a complete sensory experience.

Matthew cupped his other hand around her hip, holding her to him. A breath caught in her throat as his hand stroked up her thigh, pushing her skirt farther aside. Her stomach muscles knotted in anticipation as his fingers climbed the path.

Sharon knew he needed access. Greater access. And she would give it to him.

Reluctantly, she shifted away from Matthew to remove her shoes and hose. She swayed on her feet. They unbuttoned each other's shirts. He tossed his shoes, socks, and pants aside as she slid out of her skirt.

She stepped closer to him, rubbing her hands down the hair covering his chest and abs, the sensation creating erotic images across her mind. Her eyes squeezed shut.

Matthew lifted her knee again. This time she pressed herself hard against him. He stroked her leg, his hand on an unerring course for the curls at the juncture of her thighs.

Sharon felt the pool of moisture even before Matthew slid his fingers inside her underwear and parted her curls. "Matt, I can't stand any longer."

Releasing her leg, Matthew lowered them both to their knees beside his coffee table. Sharon eased her grip on his forearms. She ran her fingertips over his chest, massaging his pecs. His muscles shook beneath her touch.

Sharon's tongue slipped between Matthew's parted lips to caress the roof of his mouth. His tongue found hers and drew a moan from her. She arched her back to more fully press her sensitive breasts into his large palms. Her whole body strained toward his.

Sharon pushed him into a prone position and straddled his hips.

"You like to be on top, do you?" Matthew's hands moved possessively over her thighs.

"You can be on top if you want."

"Honey, you can have me any way you want me." His invitation fed Sharon's need.

She dipped her head to graze her tongue over the rigged line bisecting his chest. Matthew's groan was like applause. Sharon charted a course toward his abdomen, trailing her nails down his sides. She paused just above the waist of his briefs and helped him shed his final article of clothing. As she crawled back over his legs, she lowered her head and dragged her tongue over the length of him.

Matthew jerked in response. His blood rushed

through his veins. His heart raced in his chest. He was hungry, and it was his turn to feast.

Reaching behind her, Matthew unsnapped Sharon's bra. Her breasts sprang free. His cravings grew. He hooked his hands under her arms and drew her breasts down to his mouth. Sharon rubbed herself against him. He felt her moisture seeping through her underwear and he suckled deeper. Low, pleading moans broke free of Sharon's throat.

Matthew rolled them over and lowered himself between her legs. "I'll be on top."

He kissed Sharon deeply, wanting that connection. He trailed his tongue to the pulse dancing at the base of her throat and lower to her chest. Sharon's body arched off of the floor, lifting her breasts toward his face. Matthew pulled her arms up and held her wrists above her. He wrapped his lips around her nipples. Sharon writhed beneath him, undulating her body in a way that made his eyes cross. He let her pull her arms from his grasp. She cupped his head and kissed him.

With a reluctance that tore at his soul, Matthew drew away to search his wallet for the condom he'd tucked within.

"I've never felt this way before."

Startled by Sharon's words, Matthew's gaze jumped to her. She made him feel clean after the filth he'd left in Pittsburgh. She made him feel like he belonged after his community, his peers, and his friends had shut him out.

He rolled on the condom and returned to her. Laying between her thighs, he propped himself above her and looked into her heavy-lidded eyes. "I've been happier with you than I've been in a long time. You've filled a hole in me and chased away the cold."

Matthew covered her mouth with his and slid his

tongue past her lips as he entered her. She was hot and wet and tight. She was home. The journey was slow and tender, quenching more than a physical need.

Loving the feel of him, Sharon closed her eyes and arched her back, matching Matthew's rhythm. His hands stroked her from her hips to her waist and back, guiding her, caressing her skin.

She stroked her breasts against his chest and rubbed herself against him. Feeling Matthew quicken the pace, she wrapped her legs around his waist and sank further under his spell.

Sharon's heart pounded in her chest. Her breath locked in her throat. Her blood was on fire. Time stopped as she strained toward him, hungry, aching.

His skin felt hot beneath her fingertips, above her breasts, between her thighs. His breath came short and fast in her ear.

A moan started deep in her throat in a voice she didn't recognize. Her muscles pulled tight, tighter. Her body bowed beneath Matthew's. Reaching. Begging. Matthew slipped his hand between them and touched her there. Her body froze on the brink of snapping, and she exploded with him in completion.

It was a while before Sharon stirred. She rested her head on Matthew's chest and listened to his heartbeat as she lay in his arms. "At least we managed to have dinner first this time, even if we didn't make it to the bed." She curled closer to his side, enjoying the feel of his large hand stroking her bare back and the warm scent of his skin beneath her cheek.

"You'd put food first?" Matthew feigned incredulity.

"I've got to keep my energy up."

"You had plenty of energy a while ago."

She heard the sexy humor in his sleepy voice and

smiled. Sharon rolled over and listened to the rain fall softly outside Matthew's home.

She glanced at the clock on his cable box and groaned. "It's getting late, but I'm too comfortable to move. And I bet it's cold out there. It's nice and cozy in here." She relaxed back into the crook of Matthew's arm and kissed his chest.

"You can stay the night." Matthew's invitation came quickly. So quickly, it was as though he'd been waiting for an opening.

Sharon considered the change in their relationship. She'd despaired of the media-phobic fire captain ever trusting her enough to allow their relationship to grow, and now he was inviting her to spend the night.

Matthew shifted toward her. "Too soon?"

"Maybe."

"Sorry."

"It's okay." She rubbed her hand over the crisp hair liberally covering his chest. "Have you ever wondered about the karma that brought us together?"

"What do you mean?"

"I mean what outside factors worked together to bring us to this place in our lives?"

"Well, since I was there when it happened, I know exactly how I got here. Interstate Seventy-nine South from Pittsburgh."

"Very amusing." Sharon propped her chin on the hand she'd rested on his chest and stared down into his face. "I believe everything happens for a reason—usually."

Matthew grinned, his eyes still closed. "And what do you think brought us to this place?"

She read between his lines. "I know what brought us to your living room floor, smart aleck. But what brought us together? You pulled up your Pittsburgh roots to become a Charleston fire investigator at the same time I was removed from the fire department beat, but we still got together. Why is that?"

Matthew opened his eyes and looked at her with almost comic alarm. "Is this one of those relationship questions?"

Sharon laughed and lay back on the carpet beside him, staring up at the ceiling. "No, chicken, it's a karma question. If everything happens for a reason, for what reason were you and I brought together despite these obstacles?"

He rolled to face her. "I told you why I left Pittsburgh."

"I know." She smiled at him. "I guess it will take years before we know what brought us together."

Matthew pulled her toward him. "I'm not in a hurry."

Chapter 25

Sharon stared out the front window of Matthew's Camry. Her left hand rested on his thigh. She was absently listening to the NPR newscaster's update on Tuesday morning's traffic patterns and almost missed his transition to the top news stories.

"The *Charleston Times* is reporting that the identity of the west side torch has been revealed." The newscaster paused dramatically. Sharon felt Matthew's thigh tense beneath her fingers.

The newscaster continued. "Firefighter Raymond Ford confessed to the arsons in a suicide note he left behind Thursday night. This radio station has not been able to confirm the information but will update you as the story unfolds. In other news, the father of one of the coal miners killed—"

Sharon stared in disbelief at the car radio before lifting her gaze to Matthew. "Do you think Gary spoke to Lucas?"

A muscle jumped in Matthew's jawline. His attention remained fixed on the traffic. "Dunleavy stopped leaking information. Besides, I didn't tell him about Ford's confession. He was too upset over his suicide."

"I can't see Naismith talking to the press."

Matthew shook his head. "Neither can I. But we definitely have another leak." He turned into the newspaper's parking lot.

Sharon's thoughts raced. They needed a plan. "We'll know more once we read the article."

Matthew stopped his car in front of the *Times* building. "You're right."

Sharon gave him a quick kiss good-bye. "I'll call you if I learn anything more."

Battling the spring breeze, she hurried up the front steps and into the lobby. Her heels played a rapid staccato against the tile.

"Ms. MacCabe."

Sharon stopped at the sound of her name. Earl Stanton stood across the lobby. It had to be a breach of etiquette for a member of a political campaign to speak to someone before that person had her second cup of coffee. She searched for and found the clock above the lobby. It wasn't even eight A.M. yet.

Sharon smothered a groan and pasted on her I'm-alert-and-interested expression as Earl sauntered toward her, his steps slow taps across the floor. She'd survived having her wisdom teeth pulled—all four at one time. She'd survive this too.

"Good morning, Mr. Stanton."

"Please call me Earl. May I call you Sharon?"

No. "Of course."

"So they've identified the west side torch."

"That's what I've heard."

"My son's article is on the front page." Earl handed her a copy of the paper.

She noticed the gold-and-silver Montblanc watch peeking from beneath his white shirt cuff. It looked exactly like the model the actor Nicolas Cage promoted in an ad that ran in a recent *Newsweek*. Was that the reason Earl had bought the watch?

Sharon switched her attention to the newspaper. The story with Lucas's byline was spread across the top half of the front page. The banner headline read WEST SIDE TORCH COMMITS SUICIDE. A frisson of anger ran through Sharon. Matthew was going to explode.

"This information isn't supposed to be public yet."

Earl laughed. "When have you reporters ever let that stand in your way?"

Sharon gave the campaign manager a cool stare. "Every time we've needed to verify the accuracy of our information." Did he even realize how obnoxious he was?

He chuckled again, stepping closer. Sharon caught a hint of his cologne, cool and vague, reminiscent of the man.

Earl pointed to a paragraph in Lucas's story. "The information must be correct. The fire chief is quoted."

Lucas's father must not be aware of his son's penchant for attributing quotes to people he'd never spoken to.

Sharon returned Earl's paper. "The case is still open. The lead investigator has additional questions."

Earl's amusement wasn't as exuberant this time. "It sounds as though my son has scooped the fire department in its own investigation."

Sharon forced a smile. "That would be funny, if it were true. I just hope we don't have to run another correction on one of Lucas's reports."

Earl's cool green eyes chilled, but his smile never wavered. "If the fire chief says the investigation is over, it's over. Payton should listen to his boss."

That's if *Matthew's boss actually made the statement Lucas attributed to him.* Sharon watched Lucas's father leave the building. If Earl didn't want his son to retract another article, he should encourage Lucas to spend more time fact-checking and less time downloading music from the Net.

On her way to her cubicle, Sharon grabbed a copy of the *Times* from the lobby. She tossed the newspaper on her desk, logged on to her computer and locked her purse in her bottom drawer before going for her second cup of coffee.

As usual, Allyson was there before her, absently stirring her brimming mug.

Sharon studied her friend's solemn expression. "What's wrong?"

Allyson glanced up, then away. "Henry Rush left a message for me here last night."

Sharon recognized the name of the father of the coal miner killed in the mining accident earlier in April. "How is he?" She poured herself a cup of coffee and added cream and sugar substitute.

"He's coming unglued. The last time I spoke with him, I suggested he get grief counseling. He wouldn't even consider it." The political reporter shook her head. "He said the Ethics Committee would give him all the grief counseling he needs when it recommends expelling Senator Stanton."

Sharon frowned. "But suppose it doesn't make that recommendation?"

"That's what worries me." Allyson straightened from the counter to walk with Sharon out of the break room. "His son was the only member of his family left. Now he's alone. And he's not in good health."

Sharon wondered if her friend was thinking of her own father. If anything happened to Allyson, Edison Scott would be alone.

Sharon stopped and put a hand on Allyson's forearm. "You can't put this on yourself. You've listened to him when he's called. And you've given him good advice. It's his choice whether he acts on it."

Allyson tried a smile, but shadows remained in her eyes. "I saw the Beat Thief's article on the front page. What are you going to do now that the investigation is over?"

Sharon turned toward her friend. "But it's not over."

Surprise chased away Allyson's frown. "You mean our front-page story is wrong?"

Sharon nodded, mentally connecting dots. "Someone's going to a lot of trouble to cover up this case."

Allyson's brow knitted. "Who?"

Sharon started toward the door. "That's what I intend to find out."

Back at her desk, Sharon drank her coffee and read Lucas's article more carefully. It was short on details. She read the quote from Chief Miller.

"I'm disappointed in Firefighter Raymond Ford's criminal behavior, but he had become increasingly frustrated about his life after his divorce."

She'd never heard of frustration as a motive for arson. And how did the chief know about Raymond's divorce?

She reread the quote. The tone didn't seem right.

Sharon had spoken with the fire chief on several occasions during the six months she'd covered the fire department. That quote was far too personal for the just-the-facts-ma'am public official. Alarm bells jangled in her head as she rose to find Lucas. The Beat Thief was in his cubicle sprawled in his usual pose—legs stacked on his desk, earphones tucked into his ears.

Sharon waved her folded newspaper at him. "You didn't speak to Chief Miller, did you?"

Lucas pulled out one of his earplugs. "He's quoted, isn't he?"

She refused to dignify that response. "Who contacted you about this story?"

Lucas made a tsking sound. "You know I can't give up my sources." His eyes glittered with spite.

"Has it occurred to you your source might be the torch?"

His lips tightened. "It's not the torch."

"How can you be sure?"

"I know it makes you feel better about yourself to think I don't know what I'm doing, but I do." He pushed the earplug back into his ear and returned to the Internet.

Sharon went back to her desk. She considered retrieving a pretzel rod, but she was too agitated to snack. Instead, she called Matthew. "Have you read the article?"

"Miller would never say something like that."

Sharon circled the quote and wrote *Why?* in the margin next to Lucas's news story. She sipped her coffee and grimaced as it went down cold.

"Lucas won't give up his source." She kept her voice low. Walls had ears, especially in a newsroom.

Matthew sighed. "There aren't that many people who knew about the note. Just Naismith, the detectives, and me."

"And the torch." Sharon added the names to the margin, then drew lines connecting each one to a single question, *Torch?*

"What are you getting at?"

Sharon was encouraged that Matthew didn't shoot her theory right away. "Whoever leaked the story wants to stop the investigation. Who has the most to gain if that happens?"

"The torch. And that puts us right back where we started."

"I know this circular reasoning is frustrating, but let's talk it through. Who are likely suspects?"

Matthew's answers came quickly. "O'Conner, Stover, and Lipton."

"I don't think it was any of the business owners." But, to maintain the integrity of the investigation, she wrote the names of the arson victims in the margin. "My likely candidate is—" Sharon cupped her hand around her mouth and the receiver to further mask her voice. "Lucas Stanton."

"I didn't catch that."

She cupped her mouth and receiver again, and spoke more slowly. "Lucas Stanton." She wrote *S.* in the margin.

"You're accusing the senator's nephew?" Matthew's inherent skepticism made its long-anticipated reappearance.

"He requested the fire department beat. He's written the arson stories without going to any event sites, and he's made up information he's included in his reports." She wrote quick notes on the newspaper.

"He's on your list because Lenmore gave him your beat."

Sharon scowled, hissing into the phone. "Will you focus? I listed three reasons."

"I can't see a senator's nephew being an arsonist."

"Don't you watch *Hollywood Justice*? Public figures aren't immune to criminal behavior."

His skepticism audibly increased. "You're basing an investigation on a cable TV show?"

"Focus, Payton."

Matthew sighed. "What's his motive?"

"He's a thrill seeker." Sharon added that to her list. "I don't think it's profit. He comes from money. And it couldn't be frustration. I've never heard of that one."

Matthew chuckled at her reference to the chief's alleged quote. His reaction eased the gathering tension. "Now, if we only had some proof to back up your theory."

Her irritation rose again. "Do you remember your conspiracy theory? Remember how supportive I was?"

"Sorry. Since we're thinking outside the box, maybe we should add Naismith to the list. He's also pressuring me to close the case."

Sharon wrote Naismith's name without comment. It must have been difficult for Matthew to add his boss to their suspects list. "When will you get the forensics report?"

"The detectives said I should have it tomorrow."

Sharon looked at her list of notes. A lot of names. Some questions. No real direction.

A chill raced through Sharon as she made an unwelcomed connection. "If the torch wrote Ford's confession, he probably also killed him."

Matthew's words came haltingly. "That means our torch could also be a murderer."

In his voice, Sharon heard the dread she felt. Still, she added that possibility to her notes.

Chapter 26

"I'm suspending you with pay, pending a full investigation into these charges of past criminal behavior." Naismith shoved the Wednesday *Times* across his desk.

Matthew stared at his boss, baffled. Naismith had ordered him to his office about ten minutes after he'd gotten in. Matthew stepped forward to take the paper. A bad premonition twisted his gut. His attention fell to the front page. Shock numbed him. He couldn't feel the newspaper in his hands. The headline above Lucas Stanton's byline shouted FIRE INVESTIGATOR'S PAST PUTS HIM IN SPOTLIGHT.

The blood rushed from Matthew's head, making him dizzy as the past and present collided. "This . . . is . . . bullshit."

Naismith spoke without emotion. "The *Times* is a very reputable publication. I doubt they'd print bullshit."

Matthew glared at the other man. Vicious anger cut away at icy shock. "You know I don't have a criminal record. You did a background check before you offered me this job."

Matthew's gaze returned unwillingly to the front-page article like a witness to a heinous car accident. How?

Who? His hand shook with stunned realization. Sharon. Could it be? She was the only person he'd told. He dragged his attention back to Naismith.

Satisfaction gleamed in the other man's eyes. "We can't allow even the impression that the department's doing something wrong. Miller agrees with me. You're on suspension. Effective immediately."

Sharon worked for the *Times*. That gave her the opportunity. She had motive; she wanted a spot as an investigative reporter. But would she betray him?

Matthew tossed the paper across Naismith's desk. "What am I supposed to do in the meantime?"

Naismith shrugged. "Hell if I know. Watch Oprah."

Matthew ground his teeth. "You want me to watch Oprah while there's a serial arsonist—possibly a murderer—at large?"

Naismith never blinked. "We can't have you investigating a case you could be involved in."

Matthew clenched his fists. "You know this is bullshit. You've checked my records. You know I'm clean." He raised his arm toward the newspaper. "You should be defending me. Why are you going along with this?"

Naismith's lips curved into a cold smile. "The power of the press, my friend."

Matthew turned on stiff legs and marched from Naismith's office. He was familiar with the power of the press. Once again, they would drag his name—his family's name—through the mud. And all because someone had lied. But it was worse this time. This time, he'd been betrayed by the woman he loved.

Sharon stared in disbelief at Lucas's contribution to the Wednesday *Times* front-page, FIRE INVESTIGATOR'S PAST PUTS HIM IN SPOTLIGHT.

It was Pittsburgh all over again. Sharon couldn't believe Matthew was reliving the nightmare because of her own newspaper.

The article, the most exhaustive Lucas had ever written, resurrected the arson allegations brought by Matthew's former fire station captain and its lead investigator. It quoted liberally from the archival articles, including attributions to prevent the Pittsburgh paper from bringing charges. Matthew was again referred to as a "person of interest" in the investigation.

Lucas quoted Chief Miller. "I'm disappointed in Captain Payton's past. We weren't aware of these criminal allegations, but we're investigating them thoroughly and any relation they may have to our city's recent string of arson fires."

The article raised the possibility that Raymond Ford had had a partner helping him commit the arsons.

Sharon was speechless with outrage. First, Lucas libels a dead man because, as far as Sharon was concerned, Raymond Ford did not commit those arsons. Now, Lucas went after an innocent man—with her newspaper.

Sharon ignored the phone ringing on her desk. Rage propelled her to Wayne's office. She knocked twice as a warning prior to her entrance. Wayne was meeting with Lucas. Perfect. They were both there.

She shook the newspaper in her fist. "Did anyone bother to fact-check this before printing it?" Her voice was stiff with controlled fury.

Wayne's expression shifted from surprise to irritation. "MacCabe, I'm in the middle of a meeting. Come back in an hour."

Sharon stalked forward on wooden legs. "We'll discuss this now."

Wayne's eyes expanded with indignation. "I don't like your tone."

"And I despise your lack of integrity." She turned to Lucas. "Where did you get this trash?"

The Beat Thief's usual cocky smile wobbled under the force of her anger. "You know I won't give up my sources."

Her vision was coated in a red haze of rage. "That's because they're fake, and you're holding on to the slight hope that if we don't know who they are, we won't realize they don't exist."

She thought of Matthew standing alone in Pittsburgh while the establishment—the newspapers, fire department, city officials—made him a scapegoat for speaking out to protect his community. She'd be damned if he stood alone this time.

"MacCabe, what the hell has gotten into you?"

Sharon turned on Wayne. He'd stirred himself to stand. She threw the paper onto his desk. "Did you even check to see if your political connection had anything right in that story? Did you know there weren't any charges brought against Matt?"

The blood drained from Wayne's face. "The information in the story came from already published articles."

"Articles that were wrong. There was no evidence to connect Matt to the arsons." Sharon clenched her fists to keep the fury swirling within her from breaking free. "But you were too blind and lazy to protect the integrity of the information printed under your watch."

She rubbed her chest, her heart hurting when she thought of the pain and shame Matthew had gone through before and how hard he'd worked to recover from that experience. Now he'd have to go through that all over again.

Blood rushed back into Wayne's cheeks, turning his

skin from pale to near purple. "Now wait just a damn minute. How was I supposed to know Pittsburgh got it wrong?"

"You should have called." Sharon snatched his receiver from his desk. "Pick up the phone and call." She slammed the phone back into its cradle.

Wayne slapped the paper. "Miller is quoted in the article."

"As saying he wasn't even aware of the allegations. Shouldn't that have been a clue?" She swung her attention back to Lucas who'd remained wide-eyed and silent through the venomous exchange between Sharon and her boss. "Did you interview the chief?"

"I can't—"

"Did you?" Her question rose to a near roar.

"No, I didn't." Lucas's response was barely audible.

Sharon shifted her contempt from Lucas to Wayne. She pointed a finger, shaking with anger, toward the political appointee. "How many times are you going to run retractions before you realize you can't trust him?"

Wayne dropped back into his seat. "You've gone too far."

"With this subject, no." Sharon took a deep breath, trying to soothe herself. "With this paper, definitely."

Lucas shifted in his seat, his confidence appearing to return. "What? Are you taking your toys and going home?"

Sharon stared at him. The enormity of his actions, the gravity of the situation had not touched him at all. In the span of two days, he'd shredded the reputations of two men. Didn't he realize that? Lucas slid his attention away from her to a spot on Wayne's wall.

Sharon held Wayne's gaze. "My resignation is effective immediately."

Wayne sputtered. "You can't leave like this. You have

to give me at least two weeks' notice, otherwise I won't give you any references."

"A reference from this newspaper would probably hurt my chances of getting another job." Sharon looked at the two men. "For the past month, I've questioned my reporting abilities. Why was I demoted? Do I ask the right questions? Am I thorough enough?"

Sharon picked up the paper she'd tossed across Wayne's desk. "You pull my stories but print crap like this. Lies and innuendos that ruin innocent people. Garbage that could get this company sued. I've stopped doubting myself." She tossed the paper again. "I'm a damn good reporter. I always report the truth. You're the one who isn't fit to cover the news." She started for the door.

Wayne blustered. "You're insubordinate."

Sharon gripped the doorknob. "If you have any integrity left, you'll take steps to repair the damage you've done to a very decent, honorable man, beginning with a front-page retraction of that piece of crap you call reporting. But I don't have a lot of hope you'll do the right thing. This paper has really changed and not for the better."

Sharon swung the door open and walked out, deciding against closing the door after her. It was past time to air out the stench.

Her anger spent, Sharon walked with weighted steps to her desk. Her message light indicated she had voice mail. She went through the series of codes to retrieve the call.

"Sharon, it's Matt. Call me."

Her lover's voice was curt in the extreme. She was certain he'd read the article. Her anger stirred again. She would counsel him to get a lawyer and sue the pants off the *Times* for defamation of character. He wouldn't stand alone this time.

She glanced at her watch. It was almost nine A.M. The date and time stamp on the message had been twenty minutes prior.

Sharon dialed Matthew's number and sat while her call rang through.

He picked up on the second ring. "Payton."

"Matt, it's Sharon. I'm so sorry—"

"You told them." Matthew sounded as though he were clenching his teeth.

"What?" She must have misheard him.

"You told them about Pittsburgh."

Ice rose from Sharon's chest, spread across her shoulders and down her arms. She shivered violently. "No, Matt, I—"

He mowed down her denial. "I trusted you with that information and you used it against me."

Chapter 27

Sharon's arms began to tremble. She gripped the receiver with both hands to keep from shaking apart. "Matt, I didn't—"

"Did you barter the information in exchange for the investigative position you've been pining for?" His voice was coldly polite, like a stranger asking for a bus schedule.

"How could you think that?" Sharon tasted blood and realized she'd bitten her lip to hold back her tears.

"I'm glad I could service you." He struck a nasty emphasis on his words. "I hope your job was worth it. I never want to see your lying face again." He disconnected the call, the sound like a sledgehammer in her ear.

Sharon stared at the receiver as though it were a cobra. What had just happened? Did Matt actually believe she would give Lucas anything, much less information that would hurt him?

With her hands shaking violently, she managed to replace the receiver on her second attempt. The magnitude of what she'd been through sapped her energy. In less than an hour, she'd thrown away her career and lost the man she loved.

Fighting the tears, Sharon upended the cardboard supply box she used as a recycle bin and shoved the arson investigation files into the box. She turned to her computer to check her backup compact disk before deleting the electronic copies of her research.

By checking items off her mental to-do list, she kept her emotions under control. She grabbed her half-empty bag of pretzel rods, coffee mug, spare hose, box of tissues, and her *Runner's World* magazine wall calendar.

Her task list complete, she called Allyson on the intercom. "Could you take me home?"

"What's wrong?"

Sharon felt Allyson's concern wrap around her and the tears almost won. "I just quit."

"I'll be right there."

Sharon recradled the phone, then dug out her box of tissues—just in case.

As Sharon suspected, Allyson came with reinforcements. Andre took the supply box from her while Allyson helped her with her coat. Without comment or question, her friends formed a perimeter around her to shield her from curious stares and discourage prying questions as they walked to Andre's vehicle.

Andre put Sharon's belongings in the back of his Jeep. He held the door open so she and Allyson could climb into the backseat while he chauffeured them to her apartment. Her friends had visited often enough not to need directions.

Allyson put her arm around Sharon's shoulders. "Is this about the article in the paper?"

Sharon had stopped trying to hold back the tears. She pulled one aloe-coated tissue from the box on her lap and mopped her eyes. "He thinks I told Lucas about Pittsburgh."

"Who does?" Andre spoke from the driver's seat.

"Matt, of course." Allyson patted Sharon's shoulder.

Andre drove out of the parking lot, merging with traffic. "Start from the beginning."

Sharon felt her temper stir as she described her confrontation with Wayne and Lucas. Allyson often interrupted with exclamations of "You said what?" and "No way." Sharon ended her recount with Matthew's call.

Allyson was incensed. "Is he crazy? Men are such jerks."

"Excuse me, there's a man in the car." Andre waved his right arm as though alerting them to his presence.

Allyson inclined her head. "Present company excluded, of course."

"I don't like having my manhood set aside at your convenience."

Sharon frowned. Was she mistaken or did Andre's words carry a double meaning?

Allyson smiled. "Sorry."

Andre continued. "Matt wasn't thinking straight when he called."

Allyson interrupted again. "That's what I said. He's lost his mind."

Andre exited the freeway. "He also should have let you explain."

Sharon pulled another tissue from the box and blew her nose. "I thought he trusted me. Why would he think I would betray him?"

"Because he's crazy." Allyson squeezed Sharon's shoulders. "He's Mad Matt."

Andre steered the car through the winding curves of Sharon's neighborhood. "He'd trusted his bosses in Pittsburgh. He'd known them a lot longer than he's known you, and they set him up."

Sharon clenched another tissue in her fist. "But I'm not his bosses. And I'm not those Pittsburgh reporters, either."

Andre glanced at her in the rearview mirror. "He knows that, Sharon. He just forgot because he's angry."

Allyson snorted. "Then he'll apologize for temporarily losing his mind and expect you to forgive him. And, before you know it, you'll get sucked into a vicious cycle of him losing his mind and begging forgiveness. My advice to you is to give Mad Matt the boot before you get trapped in that losing situation."

Sharon stared at her friend. Still waters ran deep. What baggage had been dumped into Allyson's pond and by whom?

Andre parked two houses from Sharon's apartment. "Sharon can make her own decisions based on what's best for her. She doesn't need to strike a blow for brokenhearted women all over America."

"That's not what I'm saying," Allyson protested.

Andre got out of the car and opened the back passenger door to help Sharon and Allyson out. "Yes, you are."

Sharon silently agreed with Andre. Allyson's arguments reminded her of a line from "On Our Own," Patti LaBelle's duet with Michael McDonald. Her friend had her and Matthew talking about divorce and they weren't even married.

Sharon's shoulders shook on a watery sigh. Another event from her life captured in a Patti LaBelle song. Perhaps she should review her collection to learn what LaBelle predicted would happen next.

Sharon led Allyson and Andre to her building. Andre carried Sharon's box of belongings into her apartment and settled it on the table by the door.

Allyson followed him in. "Call me if you need to talk."

Sharon embraced her friend. "I promise." She turned to Andre and hugged him also. "Thanks for your help."

He patted her back. "Anytime."

She locked the door behind her friends, then turned and stared at the phone. Should she hope Matthew called or pray that he didn't?

Why wouldn't Matthew listen to the truth? This time, her watery sigh ended with a hiccup. Her body shook from the tears. Matthew didn't love her. How could he possibly when he didn't trust her? Accepting that hurt so much.

Matthew jogged the hilly roads of his suburban neighborhood under the late morning sun. He wiped the perspiration from his brow with his forearm and started another lap. His muscles burned and his breath hitched. But anger clung to him as closely as his sweaty T-shirt.

Had that been Sharon's plan all along? Get him to trust her—perhaps to fall in love with her—and then use sensitive information about the investigation to advance her career? She must have thought she'd gone to heaven when he'd told her about Pittsburgh.

But why hadn't the story appeared with her byline? Had Lenmore insisted on giving the story to the senator's nephew? Matthew smiled bitterly. That must have pissed her off.

He wiped the sweat from his eyes and ran a little faster, increasing his speed until he was running flat-out. Anger chased after him. He pushed his muscles to the limit to outdistance his multiplying questions. The strategy didn't work.

How involved was Sharon? Was she the torch? Matthew's mind, body, and soul rejected that idea.

Sharon's primary motivation might be personal gain,

but she cared about her community. Matthew had read that even in her feature articles.

She might be an ambitious liar, but she wasn't a murderer. She wasn't the torch. Which meant a felon was still out there, looking for another target to destroy. Another life to end.

Matthew slowed when he got to his street. Head down, hands on hips, he walked the rest of the way to his house, allowing his muscles to relax and his body to cool. Two doors from his house, he raised his head— and saw someone sitting on his steps. Someone with curly red hair.

Matthew mounted his steps. "Dunleavy." His breathing hadn't normalized yet.

His lieutenant stood. "Captain."

"What are you doing here?"

The younger man's expression was solemn as he handed Matthew a box. "Li Mai and I thought you'd need these."

Matthew recognized the west side arson files. "You're going to get into trouble if they find out you've taken these."

Dunleavy blinked away tears. "Ray was our friend. He didn't commit suicide. Whoever typed that confession killed him."

Matthew heard the conviction in his lieutenant's voice. "How do you know that?"

"Li Mai and I have known—knew—Ray for a long time. He wasn't depressed. He may have seemed tense and anxious, but not depressed." Dunleavy scratched his head. "You're the only one who can help us find his killer. No one else cares."

Matthew felt the protective wall he'd resurrected during his run start to crumble. He hadn't expected this steadfast faith in him. "What about my suspension?"

Anger heated Dunleavy's face. "The suspension is bullshit. You had nothing to do with those fires."

Matthew lifted his brows as pressure rose from his shoulders. "Watch your language, Lieutenant." He preceded Dunleavy up the stairs. "Order us a pizza. I'm tired of sandwiches and fries. Extra large, extra cheese, pepperoni. I'll take a shower."

"I don't know if the extra cheese is a good idea, sir. All that cholesterol."

"We're going to need the fuel. We've got a lot of work to do, and we're running out of time."

"Hi, Mom. It's me." Sharon swallowed the lump in her throat.

Helen's mommy radar was fully operational. "It's the newspaper, isn't it? Tell me what happened."

Sharon gave her mother a complete report on the morning's events, including the one-sided argument with Matthew. Helen listened quietly until the end.

"You did the right thing in leaving the paper, Ronnie."

"I hope so." Sharon pulled a tissue from the box. When would the tears stop?

"Your talents were being wasted there. Find a paper that will allow you to grow professionally." Helen's steadfast support helped Sharon pull herself together.

She gave her mother a shaky laugh. "I hope you still feel that way when I can't find another job and have to move back in with you."

"You know you're always welcome. But everything will work out, Ronnie. Have faith."

Sharon wiped her nose. "Even things with Matt?"

Helen took a moment before answering. "I'm sorry he reacted that way, but not really surprised. Lucas's story is very damaging. Remember, Matt's been through this before. He knows just how bad it will get. Last time, it cost him his reputation, his job, and his home."

"I understand that, Mom. But why would he think I'd have any part of this?"

"He's scared and he's angry. It's easier to show those emotions to people you care about because you hope they'll understand and forgive you."

Sharon drew another tissue. "Should I forgive him?"

"That's for you to decide. But if you do forgive him, you have to trust him enough to believe he won't make the same mistake again."

Sharon took a shuddering breath. "Trust. It always comes back to that."

Sharon and her mother talked a while longer, but she declined Helen's lunch invitation. She wanted to be alone. Instead, she updated her portfolio of news stories and prepared for a more serious job search. Since losing her beat, her efforts had been halfhearted at best.

She ate a bowl of cereal for a late lunch–early dinner while she searched the Internet for job openings. When the phone rang after six o'clock, she let the answering machine pick up. Allyson's message explained she'd just gotten home from work and would be up late if Sharon needed to vent. Sharon hadn't wanted to talk, but it was good to know someone would be there if she changed her mind.

She shut down her home computer and snuggled under an afghan on her sofa to spend the rest of the evening channel surfing. The cable news stations were repeating themselves. There wasn't anything funny on the Comedy Central channel and no music videos on the music television stations.

The phone rang again. She ignored it. That's what

answering machines were for. But the caller didn't leave a message. Sharon clicked through the channels in reverse order this time. More than a hundred stations. And . . . nothing was . . . on.

The phone rang for a second time in almost fifteen minutes. Sharon frowned at it. The answering machine switched on and the caller hung up. Was it Matthew?

Sharon tried to shake the disquieted feeling. She struggled not to let her gaze stray to the phone. She wasn't ready to talk to Matthew yet. Images flashed by as she ran the channels for a third time. Perhaps she should give up on television and get a book. She tossed the afghan aside and stood up.

The phone rang.

She hesitated. The second ring faded. Sharon walked to the other end of the sofa and picked up the receiver on the fourth ring. "Hello." She tried to sound composed.

"Ms. MacCabe?" The male caller was unfamiliar.

Sharon ignored the part of her that was disappointed at not hearing Matthew's voice. "Who's calling?"

"This is Seth Gumble, ma'am. I'm a firefighter with Fire Station Eleven."

Matthew's station. "How can I help you, Mr. Gumble?"

Hesitation. "Well, ma'am, you can help me catch the guy who killed Ray Ford."

Chapter 28

Sharon dropped onto her sofa, her reporter's instincts on high alert. Grabbing the notepad she kept beside her phone, she started taking notes. *Seth Gumble. Firefighter. Station 11.* "Mr. Gumble—"

"Seth."

"Seth, the police believe Mr. Ford committed suicide. What makes you think someone killed him?"

"Well, ma'am . . ." His nerves were showing.

"Please call me Sharon."

"Yes, ma'am. Well, first, I knew Ray. He wouldn't give up. He was a responsible person."

"I understand." Her pen sped across the paper.

Seth breathed a relieved sigh. "Next, well, this part is hard to explain. It's complicated."

"Take your time."

"I know who killed Ray."

Sharon's eyes stretched. Her pen was poised, ready to write the killer's name. "Who?"

"The real torch."

I knew it, her mind shouted. "Who is the real torch?"

"That's the complicated part. The torch paid Ray and me to set the fires, so we were the torches. Ray wasn't comfortable with the plan, but we both have money troubles. See, we're both divorced and women can bleed you dry. They take everything."

Sharon hurried to write down everything Seth said, with the exception of his comments regarding divorces. She sensed his nervousness was behind most of his chatter and his hurried speech. Her mind filled with questions. But she had to get the most critical one answered first. "Who paid you to set the fires?"

"I can't tell you that over the phone."

Sharon's hand stilled above the paper. "Why not?"

"This is too important. I have to meet you."

Suspicion furrowed her brow. "How do I know this isn't a trick?"

"I'm not a killer, ma'am. The Closer wanted me to kill Payton. But, when I refused, he hired someone else to do it. The same person who was supposed to scare you."

Sharon clenched her fist around the pen until her short nails dug into her palms. This person Seth called the Closer had hired someone to kill Matthew. "Who is he?" She heard the anger in her voice.

"We have to meet. I have proof of everything I'm saying."

"Then why don't you go to the police?"

"You can keep my name out of this." He sounded desperate. "I don't want my kids to know their father's a felon. I did it for them. I needed the money to take care of them."

There must have been another way. A better plan that would not have gotten him involved with a murderer. "I'm not coming alone."

Seth sighed. "I won't hurt you, but I understand if you want Payton with you. He'll find out what I did soon enough." He sighed again. "It was never supposed to get this far. No one was supposed to get hurt. Ray and I were supposed to get paid so he could get out of debt and I could take care of my kids. Then we weren't looking back. Now, Ray is dead and Payton's being framed."

Sharon's temper sparked again at the reminder of the *Times* article. "Where and when do you want to meet?"

Sharon didn't plan to meet Seth alone, but neither was she ready to see Matthew. Instead she conference-called Allyson and Andre to tell them about Seth and ask them for backup. Less than an hour later, they arrived outside her apartment building in Andre's Jeep.

By eight P.M., it was dark and drizzling. Sharon searched the shadows before jogging down the front steps to meet her friends. The attack in the parking lot was still fresh in her mind, especially after her conversation with Seth.

Andre rounded his vehicle to help Sharon into the backseat. The light rain had sprinkled his glasses. "How do you know you can trust this guy?"

Sharon closed her umbrella as she settled into the Jeep. "I don't. That's why I asked you two to come with me."

Allyson laughed with wry humor. "So we're your show of force? As long as we're in agreement that, if he pulls a gun or something, we're running the hell out of there."

Andre returned to the driver's seat and wiped the raindrops from his glasses. He pointed his vehicle in the direction of the storage company, the location Seth had chosen for the meeting.

He turned the windshield wipers to a slow speed. "I

still think we should have called the police. Are you willing to go to prison to keep his name out of this?"

Sharon stared out the window at the shadow of great mountains and the drizzle of light rain. "Hopefully, with the evidence he gives me, the courts won't need his name to prosecute this Closer."

Allyson turned from the front passenger seat. Her honey-brown curls framed her face. "Why does he call this guy Closer?"

Sharon shrugged. "I wondered that too. Someone who closes a deal, maybe?"

Andre stopped the vehicle at a red light. "You've left the paper. Why are you still working this story?"

Sharon found his gaze in the rearview mirror. "I have to clear Matt's name."

Allyson's eyes widened. "After the way he treated you this morning, you still want to help him?"

Sharon was stubborn. "What happened to him in Pittsburgh was wrong. I won't let it happen here."

They were silent as they drove the rest of the way to the storage facility. It was almost half-past eight when they arrived. They were a few minutes early. At that late hour, they passed only one other car as they searched for 1231, the storage garage Seth had chosen for the meeting. Andre parked at the end of the row designated for that number.

The rain fell faster now. It tap-danced against the Jeep. Here and there, drops pooled into puddles. The asphalt shone like a blanket of black diamonds under the security lights.

Sharon scanned the lot through the Jeep's windows. She didn't see any other vehicles, but this was the correct address. Was Seth running late?

Andre turned off the windshield wipers and the Jeep's engine. Sharon strained to see or hear anything in the deserted lot. She rolled down her window slightly. Beneath the distant traffic and the steady rain was perfect silence. Too perfect. It was still and eerie, like a scene from a Lifetime made-for-TV movie. Sharon gave silent thanks for her friends.

She looked around their surroundings again. "Maybe we should drive over to the storage garage."

"I have my cell phone." Allyson rummaged in her handbag. "Maybe we should call the police."

Sharon frowned at the back of her friend's head. "And tell them what? That a parking lot is freaking us out? They'll just tell us to go home."

Andre started the engine. Sharon leaned forward in her seat.

He looked at Allyson, then over his shoulder at Sharon. Light from the security lamps obscured his eyes. "Stay alert."

Allyson sat straighter. "I'm ready."

A tense silence permeated the Jeep. Andre drove slowly down the row of storage units. The tires splashed through puddles. Through her open window, Sharon smelled damp earth and stale garbage. She kept a constant surveillance on the lot. Why did she have the creepy feeling someone was watching them?

Chapter 29

Maybe this wasn't a good idea. Why did she suddenly wish Matthew were there? He'd made it clear he never wanted to see her again. Why would she still yearn for his company? How long would it take for her to stop loving him?

Andre stopped the car and leaned toward the wind-shield. "Is that Seth?"

Sharon pushed forward between the driver's and passenger's seats. She followed the direction of Andre's gaze to what appeared to be a man sprawled on the ground in front of garage number 1231.

She would have rushed out of the vehicle if Andre hadn't reset the door locks. She scowled at him. "We have to see if he's all right."

"I know. But let's be smart about this." He turned to Allyson. "Al, get your cell and be ready to call nine-one-one."

Allyson's teeth chattered as she pulled her cell phone from her bag. "Suppose we're not alone?"

Sharon led the group out of the car toward Seth. She crouched beside him and her heart froze when she saw the trail of blood washing away in the rain.

Sharon pushed at his shoulder until his body rolled onto his back.

Allyson gasped. "I don't think we're supposed to move the body."

Sharon felt for a pulse. Her fingers shook with cold fear. "He's gone. I think that's a gunshot wound in his chest." She looked up at her friends' frozen, shocked expressions. "He just wanted to take care of his kids."

There was regret in Andre's eyes. "He won't be able to do that now."

Sharon looked at Seth's body. He'd been a big man, brought down by a single bullet. His gray eyes stared up at the wailing sky. His clothes—worn blue jeans, brown bomber jacket, gray sweatshirt—were sopping wet. How long had he been here, bleeding out?

His sweatshirt had the Charleston Fire Department emblem across the chest. The fatal bullet had pierced the emblem and probably his heart. The gunman was either an excellent shot or he'd been standing very close.

Sharon stood. "Call nine-one-one, Al."

Andre looked around. "I thought he had information for you."

"Whoever shot him must have taken it." The implications of her statement made Sharon's mouth dry.

Allyson made quick work of the emergency call while Sharon and Andre kept watch over her.

Sharon waited until Allyson had closed her cell phone. "Maybe we should go back to the Jeep."

Allyson dropped her phone into her purse. "Good idea."

They returned to the Jeep, walking close together. Sharon peered into every shadow, unable to shake the feeling of being observed.

They boarded Andre's Jeep, wet and cold, to wait for the police and emergency vehicles.

Allyson's voice was small. "I never want to go through anything like this again."

Sharon hugged herself. She was cold from the inside out, and it wasn't just from the rain. "I'm sorry I dragged you into this."

"We weren't going to let you come alone." Andre started the engine and heat slowly filled the vehicle.

"No way," Allyson agreed.

Sharon surveyed the lot again. "Where's Seth's car?"

Allyson looked around. "Maybe he came in a cab." Her words didn't carry much conviction.

Sharon shivered. "Or maybe whoever killed him took the evidence as well as his car."

Matthew stared at the front page of Thursday's *Times* while he waited for the telephone connection to go through. He'd read the article, FIREFIGHTER SHOT TO DEATH. First Ford and now Gumble. That couldn't be a coincidence. But what really rocked him was the fact Sharon had found the body. What had she been doing there?

The call transfer went through and a male voice answered. "Andre Jamieson."

Matthew took a moment to compose his thoughts. He didn't know what kind of reception he'd get from Sharon's friends. "This is Matt Payton. The receptionist told me Sharon no longer worked for the *Times*. Do you know why she left?"

Dry laughter preceded Jamieson's response. "Man, you have completely messed up."

Well, now he knew what Sharon had told her friends. Everything. At least her version of everything. "Why did Sharon leave?"

"Why don't you ask her?"

Matthew rubbed an agitated hand over his hair. "You know why not. I just want to know if she's okay. I read about the shooting. Damn it, is she all right?"

Matthew paced his living room, dining room, and kitchen while he waited for Jamieson's answer. The muscles in his back were screamed with tension.

"She's fine. She's home."

Relief made him weak. Matthew braced his left arm on his kitchen counter to stay upright. "Good. Thank you." Through his kitchen window, he saw cherry blossoms blowing in the breeze. Chunky clouds bobbed in the pale blue sky. "Why did she leave the paper?"

"Why do you think?"

Did all reporters have the annoying habit of answering questions with questions? "I don't know. That's why I'm asking."

"You're asking the wrong person. This is between you and Sharon. But there are some things you should consider before you call her."

Matthew turned away from his window. "I don't know if I should call—"

"When Lenmore took her beat from her, she stayed. When he pulled her features from the paper, she stayed. When he ran that bullshit article about you, she left."

Matthew clenched the receiver so hard it hurt almost as much as the pain in his heart. "She left before she went to the storage company last night?"

"That's right, genius. Now do you understand why she left?"

Matthew hesitated, afraid to hope. "No, I don't."

Jamieson snorted. "Then she's better off without you."

The call disconnected before Matthew could think of a response. He returned to his living room to hang up his phone.

What was Jamieson trying to tell him? Why would Sharon give up her job—her career—after the paper ran that story on him? Was it because of the harm those lies would cause him? If that were true, then Sharon hadn't betrayed his trust.

It was disconcerting how quickly hope took root. He had to know if it was justified.

Matthew reached for the phone again. Sharon was the only one who could answer his questions. Why had she left the paper? Why would she risk her life to meet with Gumble? Could she ever forgive him for doubting her?

Matthew stopped, returning the phone to its charger. He needed a strategy. If he called Sharon, she'd hang up on him. Matthew jogged upstairs for his shoes. It wouldn't be as easy to shut him out if he showed up at her door.

"Mom, I told you last night, I'm fine." Sharon poured herself a second cup of coffee. Mothers were masterful at stirring their children into guilt frenzies. And she hadn't even done anything wrong.

Helen was almost squeaking in her agitation. "You're quoted as saying you believe Seth Gumble was killed because he had evidence pointing to the real west side arsonist."

Sharon was glad Bill Meyer, the police beat reporter, had included that quote. She'd called Bill while she, Andre, and Allyson were waiting for the police. With press time looming, Bill had worked magic to get the story for the morning's paper. Because of the speed with which the article had to be handled, Sharon's provocative quote slipped past editors and the copydesk.

She stirred cream and sugar substitute into her coffee. "I want this guy to know we're still looking for him. He's not going to get away with framing innocent people, much less committing murder."

Her mother didn't sound appeased. "Ronnie, if he knows you're looking for him, he's going to come after you."

Sharon cupped her mug, absorbing its warmth through her suddenly cold hands. "I'll be careful, Mom."

"I know you want to fight for truth and justice, but you're not a superhero."

Sharon knew the risks she was taking with that news story. Last night, Andre and Allyson had made her aware of all of them. But she wouldn't sit blindly while a sociopath got away with killing a misguided father, murdering a desperate firefighter, and implicating an innocent man. She couldn't.

Sharon returned to her seat at her dining table and spoke gently. "Sometimes the right thing is the hardest thing to do. You taught me that, Mom."

The silence was long and weighty. Sharon wished she could see Helen. She worried about her mother's reaction to witnessing the result of the life lessons she'd successfully instilled in her daughter.

Helen's voice was low with emotion. "It's also hard to stand back and watch your children do the right thing."

"I understand."

"Your father would be proud of you. I am too. But I also worry about you."

Sharon chuckled, rubbing her fingers over the West Virginia University Mountaineer emblem on her mug. "I'm not saying I'm not scared. I am. But I couldn't live with myself if I didn't do something."

"Maybe you should move in with me until all this is over. I'd feel better knowing you weren't alone."

And endanger her mother if the killer tracked her to

Helen's house? "No, Mom. I have neighbors all around me. I'll be fine."

"At least think it over."

"I promise." *But my answer won't change.*

"What are you going to do now?"

Sharon sipped her coffee, frowning at the pile of folders on her coffee table. "Since I've lost my partner in this investigation, I need to regroup."

"Do you think Matt's read the story?"

Sharon grimaced. "Considering the hatchet job the *Times* did on him yesterday, he's probably canceled his subscription."

"If there's anything you want me to do to help, let me know."

Sharon heard the excitement in her mother's voice. "I will. There are a couple of things I want to look into." Such as Lucas's familiarity with firearms.

"I'd better go. Eddie will be here soon."

Eddie? Sharon pictured Allyson's father. A tall, broad, attractive man. "What's on your agenda for today?"

"We're going to the mall to hand out fact sheets on the ballot issues. You can reach me on my cell if you need me."

They disconnected the call after telling each other to be careful. Sharon recradled her phone.

A knock on her door stopped her progress toward her kitchen. She returned her mug and coaster to her coffee table and strode across the room. She checked her peephole, concerned with security more now than ever before. Her jaw dropped. Matthew.

He stood with his head bowed and one hand braced against the doorjam. Sharon's heart leaped before shattering in her gut.

"I know you're in there, Sharon. I heard you come to

the door." His voice carried softly through the wood. "Please let me in."

Sharon stepped away from the door and considered her options. She could let him in and risk more heartache or she could hold off the inevitable a little longer.

Matthew rang the bell again.

Chapter 30

Sharon didn't feel up to this confrontation—would she ever?—but she opened the door anyway.

Matthew looked up. His clothes—black jersey tucked into faded blue jeans—made him look long, lean, and sexy. Sharon's mouth went dry.

He straightened from the threshold. "May I come in?"

Why was he being so polite? This was a 180-degree switch from their last encounter. She felt even less prepared now, not knowing which Matthew she was dealing with. She hesitated before stepping aside for him to enter. Sharon locked the door and leaned against it while Matthew walked farther into her great room. She wanted as much distance as possible between them.

Matthew faced her. With his fists bunched in his jeans pockets and his legs braced, he seemed ready for whatever happened. What was he expecting?

"Why did you leave the *Times*?"

Sharon raised a brow. "You're willing to listen now?"

A muscle flexed in Matthew's jaw, a sign that her words had gotten to him. "I'd like to know what happened."

Sharon's legs were shaking. She pushed herself off the door, knowing she wouldn't be able to hold herself upright much longer. With measured steps, she made it to an armchair beside her sofa and sank into its soft cushions. "I've told you that I'm worried about the direction the *Times* is taking. Lucas's articles are playing fast and loose with the public's trust."

Matthew watched her with narrowed eyes. "Did you leave because of the article they wrote about me?"

Her anger helped steady her. "That piece crossed every line, right into another time zone. I can't work for a paper that knowingly passes off lies as the truth."

Matthew sat on the sofa. He braced his forearms on his spread knees. "I thought you gave him that information. That you'd told him what I'd confided in you."

More anger. She was even steadier now. "I know you did. What I don't understand is how you could possibly think I would do something like that."

"Where else would he get the information?"

Sharon leaned into the armchair. "The same place I got it. The Internet."

Surprise wiped all expression from Matthew's face. "You found out about the Pittsburgh arson on the Internet?" He waited for Sharon's nod. "I was afraid you would. But you never said anything. How long have you known?"

"About three weeks before you told me."

"Why didn't you say anything?"

"I wanted you to tell me." Sharon pressed a fist against her chest. "I wanted you to trust me with information the wrong person could misuse. I wanted you to know I was the right person. That I would protect this information with you."

Matthew leaned into the sofa and looked at her as though from a fresh perspective. As though he were seeing more than the person in front of him. He saw her words, her actions, her beliefs, and her convictions.

Was he finally seeing Sharon the woman and not just the reporter?

"What would you have done if I'd never said anything?" He posed the question hesitantly.

Sharon's shaky smile bloomed with bittersweet memories. "I never would have slept with you."

"What?"

She saw that was the very last response he'd expected. Perhaps it wasn't even on the list. Despite her mood, Sharon almost laughed out loud. "I told you, for me, sex is more than a physical release. It's a commitment. I can't make a commitment to someone who doesn't trust me."

Matthew let his gaze drift away from Sharon's cool regard. How was he going to explain that he did trust her? She'd probably laugh in his face, thinking he just wanted to get back into her bed. And he wouldn't blame her. But it was the truth. He'd called her in a moment of blind emotion, when he'd felt too vulnerable to think straight.

He'd taken away her trust. Did he have any hope or had he lost her forever? "Why were you meeting with Gumble?"

"So you did see the *Times* article." Sharon crossed her long legs. "He said he had evidence about the real arsonist. He wanted to give it to me."

"But why would you take the risk of meeting him?"

Her frown cleared. "You think I took the risk for you? In a way, you're right. I want to help clear your name. Just like I would try to prove the innocence of anyone I thought was being unjustly accused."

Translation—he wasn't special. She would help anyone. Matthew felt the hurt and knew he deserved it. How much had his words hurt her when she hadn't deserved it?

Matthew stood and paced across the room to her bookcase. He spoke with his back to her. "I wish you had asked me to go with you."

"I'm sorry. I thought you never wanted to see my 'lying face' ever again."

Matthew flinched. She was batting every painful barb he'd lobbed at her back to him. It took a lot of courage to face her and the wrong he'd done. "I'm sorry. I was angry when I said that."

Her eyes glittered with bitter humor. "I wasn't angry when I chose not to call you. In fact, I didn't feel anything."

Desperate for a way to reach her, Matthew strode across the room and went down on one knee in front of Sharon. He took her hands in his, holding fast when she tried to pull away. He was on a level to look directly into her ebony eyes. "I know I hurt you, and I'm sorry. I was wrong. It's hard to explain but, after reading that article—"

"Which Lucas wrote." Sharon's tone was inflexible.

Matthew nodded. "After reading it, I had . . . a flashback is the only way I can describe it. It was like Pittsburgh again."

Sharon stopped tugging at his hold. "I understand that."

Matthew tried to build on her understanding. "I was angry. I wasn't thinking. I'm sorry, Sharon. I was wrong. Can you forgive me?"

Sharon lowered her head. Matthew stared at her dark, wavy hair, silently pleading for a second chance.

He wasn't sure he'd expressed himself well. He wasn't good with words. He was better with math and science, the skills needed to fight fires and investigate their origins. He'd rather charge into a burning building than talk about feelings.

Did she understand where his head had been after he'd read Stanton's story and where he was now?

I've been stupid. Yell at me. Curse me, but please, please don't leave me.

Sharon looked up. Her cheeks were wet with tears. Matthew reached out to cup her face and wiped them away. She closed her eyes and sighed. Her breath stroked the palm of his hand. He felt a shiver down his spine and knew he couldn't live without this woman.

It was much more than physical, more than emotional. He needed the light she brought to keep his darkness at bay.

Sharon opened her eyes. "I can forgive you."

Matthew's relief was so great it was almost painful. He started breathing again. With gentle pressure he tipped her head to kiss her, but Sharon raised her hands and laid her fingers against his mouth. He looked at her, confused.

"I'm sorry, Matt, but I can't go back to a relationship with you."

He sat back on his heels. "Why not?"

Sharon bit her lower lip. "As your friend, I can forgive your outburst. I understand your anger. But as your lover, I expected more from you. I can't forgive you for doubting me. If you cared about me, you would trust me and there wouldn't be any room for doubt."

Matthew furrowed his brow. "But I explained what happened."

"Yes. You were upset. You've had time to get over it. I haven't had time and may never get over it." Sharon stood, forcing Matthew to scramble out of her way. "This wasn't 'Honey, I worked late and forgot to call you.' This was 'I never want to see your lying face again.'"

Matthew heard her rising temper and stood. "I'm sorry. I was out of line."

"That was more than out of line. You didn't trust me." Sharon crossed her arms. "If you did, you would never have made that call."

"But I made the call, and I've admitted it was a mistake. What can I do to make it up to you?" His mind was a whirl of confusion and frustration. Simplify. Simplify.

She appeared to be vibrating with the same frustration he felt. "I've told you. Nothing. You're the best lover I've ever had, but I need more than great sex. I need the relationship that comes before and after. The foundation of that is trust, and we don't have that."

Matthew extended his hands, palms up. "All I can give you are the words. I do trust you."

Sharon watched him with sad eyes. "Actions speak louder."

Matthew ran an agitated hand over his hair. He braced his free hand on his hip as he considered her carpet. "Fine." He raised his gaze and found her eyes. "Then listen up."

"The forensics report came back on Ford's suicide note." Matthew stood in Sharon's doorway the next morning balancing coffee and fast food. In his lightweight ruby-red sweater and tan khakis, he looked delicious.

Sharon's attention shifted from him to the McDonald's bag. She was certain she smelled sausage biscuits. And hash browns. He was exploiting her weaknesses.

"What did the report say?" Sharon stepped aside to allow the food in.

Matthew headed straight for the dinette table. "There are prints on the paper used for the confession, but none of them are Ford's prints."

Sharon's eyebrows lifted. "So how does someone write a suicide note without leaving any prints?"

Matthew hummed pensively, the sound making Sharon's toes curl into her carpet. "That's what the detectives want to know."

Sharon watched Matthew's economical movements as he served the fast-food meal. "So they're working Ray's case as a homicide?"

He nodded. "We've given them information on the arsons in case they can find a connection."

"They're connected." Sharon sat across the table from him. "You timed this well." She'd just changed into her jeans and jersey when she heard the knock on her door.

Matthew grinned, uncovering the Styrofoam container for his hotcakes and sausage. "I've paid attention to your schedule. Morning run, shower, then breakfast while you read the paper."

Sharon resisted the memories of their lazy weekend mornings. So few, but no less precious. She unwrapped her breakfast sandwich. The scent of the hot biscuit and spicy sausage made her mouth water.

She swallowed her first bite. "I've already taken a look at the paper. Even for a Friday, there isn't much news." She stirred her coffee. "Lucas doesn't have any bylines. No statement from fire officials about Seth's murder. Not even an update on the emergency services budget, which goes to committee soon."

Matthew cut into his hotcakes. "And no mention of my suspension. I glanced at the paper too."

Sharon coughed as her coffee went down the wrong way. "You were suspended?"

"Wednesday. Naismith wants to make sure I don't have a criminal record." He chewed a forkful of hotcakes.

She couldn't believe he spoke so casually. But there was a hardness in his eyes that told her Matthew was holding back a lot of emotion.

"Wednesday. That was the day Lucas's story ran. They didn't waste any time, did they?" She bit into her biscuit.

"Naismith told me right before I called you."

Sharon nodded. He definitely hadn't been in his right mind when he'd called her Wednesday. This whole situation was so unjust. "Didn't they check your record before they hired you?"

"Apparently, they want to check it again."

"In the meantime, you're off the investigation." Sharon arched one brow. "You know I don't believe in coincidences."

"Neither do I."

A contemplative silence hung heavily in the room. Matthew's bombshell took away her pleasure in breakfast. What were Matthew's supervisors after?

She cleared the remains of their guilty-pleasures breakfast and offered Matthew a glass of ice water. He wasn't the only one who'd paid attention during their weekends together.

She shared the sofa with him, tucking into the opposite corner and curling her legs under her. "I'm certain Lucas is involved somehow. He didn't write about your suspension because he doesn't care. He has what he wants. He thinks you and I are off the investigation."

Matthew sighed, the sound soft, sexy, and a little sad. "Naismith wanted me to close the investigation too. I don't want to believe he had anything to do with the fires, but this suspension is a joke."

"I agree." Sharon plucked at the fabric covering the top of the sofa. "Does this mean the business owners are off your list?"

Matthew's lips tilted in a wry smile. "Not completely.

But I've checked their backgrounds. I don't think any of them are capable of murder. Stover has a couple of speeding tickets and O'Conner regularly commits parking violations, but that's it."

Matthew stretched his legs, angling them away from the coffee table. Sharon studied the indentation in her carpet, left behind when she and Matthew had repositioned her table to allow more room for his legs.

He turned his head toward her. "I wish we knew what evidence Gumble had."

"Seth said the Closer paid him and Ray." She stood to pace. "It must have been a substantial amount of money to tempt firefighters to commit arson."

Matthew sat up, watching Sharon prowl her great room. Her compact body exuded a vitality that mesmerized him. "He must have paid them in installments. You wouldn't give someone all the money up front if it was going to take a while to complete the job."

"But even the initial payment must have been a lot of money." Her cloud of dark hair, still damp from her shower, swung as she turned to retrace her path. "Where did the Closer get it?" Sharon paused. "Initially, we were looking at arsonists and people who were connected to the businesses. But I think we were looking in the wrong place."

Matthew stood to pace on the opposite side of the room from Sharon. The coffee table separated them. "Based on what Gumble told you, we're looking for someone who had a lot of money."

"But if he has money, why would he get involved in this arson plot?" She began to pace again.

"Because he wants more. His motive is greed. If he were after the thrill, he'd set the fires himself."

Matthew's mind raced to fit the puzzle pieces that would show him the suspect's face. He felt the synergy flowing between him and Sharon as they lobbed theories to each other.

Sharon paced past him. "He's not trying to make a statement and it doesn't feel like revenge."

Matthew ran a hand over his hair. "No. It feels like greed."

"If we follow the money, I think we'd have to remove Naismith from our list of suspects."

Matthew had to be sure. "Anything is possible. He might have saved up a lot of money from investments and other accounts."

Sharon frowned. "Then why spend it bribing firefighters to commit arsons? If you need more money, why not reinvest it?"

"You can ask the same about Stanton."

"That's true, but he still seems like a better bet than Brad for the role of the Closer." Sharon came to a stop on the other side of the coffee table. "I can see Lucas bribing two firefighters."

"How would he have known about Gumble and Ford's money problems?"

She rubbed her chin, the gesture slow and pensive. "Good point. Someone must have told him about them."

"Who?" Matthew held up a hand, palm out. "Before you suggest it, it wasn't Dunleavy. He was devastated when he found out about Ford's supposed confession." He didn't know how he was going to tell his young lieutenant about Gumble and Ford's role in the arson plot.

"Well, I'm glad it wasn't him. I like Gary." Sharon tapped her chin, staring off into space.

Matthew's gaze slid over her bright yellow sweater and dark green jeans. The strong, cheerful colors reflected the woman within.

When the *Times* had failed to meet the standards her

community deserved by hiring an inept but politically connected reporter, she'd fought for her readers. When her editor had compromised the paper's integrity by printing lies about him, she'd stood on her principles and left.

And when he'd questioned her loyalty in a moment of colossal stupidity, she'd put distance between them—but she hadn't walked away. Instead, she was contributing a great deal of time and energy—and jeopardizing her safety—to help him.

"Sharon, I appreciate everything you're doing for me."

Her enthusiasm seemed to dwindle. She wandered to her window. "What are friends for?"

Matthew tracked her progress. "You're a good friend." *I wish I would have realized it sooner.*

Sharon spoke to the windowpane. "And you're a good person. I'm sorry your reputation is being attacked. Again."

"At least I'm not going through it alone this time." Matthew risked a step closer. "Dunleavy told me about the forensics report. He also brought over my files."

She turned with a smile. "Gary's a good guy, despite his misguided association with Lucas."

He closed the distance between them with cautious steps, ready to give her space at her slightest indication. Her smile dimmed, but didn't fade. Wariness mixed with wanting in her eyes. Matthew reached for her, running his hand over her rich, dark hair. "Sharon, I know it's too soon—"

"Way too soon."

"But would you give me the chance to repair the hurt I've caused you?"

She stepped around him and away. "Please don't rush me." She spun to face him, pain in her voice. "Don't trivialize what I'm feeling."

"I'm not. I realize I hurt you. I want to make it up to you."

Her eyes widened with incredulity. "How, Matt? Do you think if you bring me breakfast every day for a week, all will be forgiven?"

He was in dangerous territory. "Well, I—"

She stepped toward him. "Maybe jewelry, but something unusual. A diamond ankle bracelet or a jade toe ring."

He realized now he hadn't thought this through. "If that will convince you that I trust you."

She was close enough for him to catch her fragrance. She smelled like soap, fresh from the shower. With the scent of Sharon underneath. Soft and warm. At odds with the cool anger in her eyes.

"Or maybe you should have my name tattooed on your chest. Sharon." She planted her left hand over his right pectoral. "MacCabe." Her right hand covered his left pectoral.

Matthew's eyes held hers as his heart beat against her right palm. How had he allowed things to get so far out of his control? "How am I making you feel trivialized?"

Sharon dropped her hands and crossed the room, creating enough breathing space for both of them. "Do you often sleep with women you don't trust, Matt?"

Matthew resisted dropping his head into his hands. The gesture wouldn't go over well with the ticking time bomb across the room. "You are not some nameless, faceless lay, if that's what you're thinking."

"That's exactly what I'm thinking." Her glare heated several notches. Matthew felt it singe his soul.

"Sharon, I care about you."

"But you don't even know me."

Matthew spread his arms in frustration. "Yes, I do. You've tried and convicted me on one phone call." He held both palms out when she parted her lips. "Yes, it was the worst call I've ever made and probably one of the worst calls you've ever received. But it was one call, and I've admitted I was wrong."

"I wanted you to separate me from the press and to get to know Sharon. But when you picked up the phone Wednesday morning to accuse me, I realized you didn't know me at all. Because, even as a member of the press, I would never have betrayed you." Sharon sighed and her shoulders slumped.

Matthew felt the ice collect in the pit of his stomach. She was done with the argument. Was she also done with him? "How can I prove to you that I do know you?"

She blinked away tears. "I don't think you can."

Chapter 31

"How's it going, Super-Sleuth?" Allyson's call was a welcomed interruption on Friday afternoon.

"Pretty well." Sharon balanced her cordless phone between her cheek and shoulder as she worked her laptop's Internet connection. "I answered a couple of job ads earlier."

"Anything good out there?"

Sharon grimaced. "Not much. But I'm not panicking yet. There's plenty of time before I have to move in with my mom."

Allyson laughed. "Your mother wouldn't mind."

"But I couldn't face the shame."

"I know what you mean. I love my dad, but I'd hate to give up my independence. I'd feel like a failure."

"Exactly." Sharon glanced at the notes in her arson investigation file and typed in another search term.

"Have you heard from Matt?" Allyson's tone was in the best-female-friend safe zone. Regardless of the answer, she wouldn't pass judgment.

"We've talked."

"How'd that go?" A hint of concern laced her friend's words.

"Not well." Sharon's hands stilled above the keyboard. "He can't understand why I'm upset, and I can't bridge that men-are-from-Mars-women-are-from-Venus gap."

"It's the nuances. Men don't always understand them."

"We're still working together on the investigation, though. We're going to follow the money."

"You mean like Woodward and Bernstein? *All the President's Men*?" Allyson referenced the *Washington Post* reporters who'd followed the money to find evidence incriminating then-president Richard Nixon in the Watergate scandal.

Sharon pulled up another Web page. "We're not going to take down a presidency. But I think money is the key to finding this serial arsonist turned serial killer."

"What do you have so far?"

"All four business owners had the same business insurer and financing company." Sharon scanned the Web page she'd just loaded. "I'd researched the business lender before I left the *Times*. There wasn't anything interesting there. I'm looking at the insurer now."

"Anything good?"

"I don't know yet."

"Well, call me if you find anything."

Sharon promised to do that, and she and her friend rang off. She went back to the business insurer's home page. Peak Protection was owned by a limited partnership, Main Coverage LLP.

Strange. The lender also was part of a limited partnership. Flipping through her file folder, Sharon found the information she'd collected on the business lender. It was a subsidiary of Bright Ideas LLP.

She didn't believe in coincidences.

Sharon searched for information on Main Coverage

and was directed to Bright Ideas. She waited impatiently for her high-speed Internet connection to load Bright Ideas's home page. That page explained that Bright Ideas's limited liability partnership had only one principal, Earl Stanton.

Sharon reached for her phone. It was a quarter after six P.M., but she was certain her friend was still at work. "Allyson, do you have the campaign financing statements for Kurt Stanton?"

"Yes. I think they're current as of Wednesday." Computer keys clicked in the background as though Allyson was pulling up a file. "His office e-mailed it to me. I love technology."

"Perfect." Sharon vibrated with excitement. "Could you forward it to me?"

"Sure, but why?"

"I'm following the money. I promise to tell you everything later, but could you e-mail the financials to me now?"

"I'm sending them as we speak." More computer keys snapped.

"You're an angel." Sharon disconnected the call.

She dashed into her bedroom to grab her sneakers and socks while she waited for the transmission. If she was right about the money trail, she was going to share the news with Matthew right away.

Excitement pumped adrenaline into her system as Sharon hurried back to her laptop. She hit the refresh button and Allyson's e-mail appeared. Sharon opened the file and scrolled several pages before finding what she was looking for. She stared at the electronic document for several minutes, reading and rereading the information before she believed it.

Sharon dialed Matthew's number, tugging on her socks as she waited for him to answer. "Earl Stanton had financial interest in the lending company and the insurer of the businesses destroyed in the arsons."

"How did you find out?" Matthew voice conveyed surprise and excitement.

"I followed the money. You'll never guess where it leads." Sharon was almost drunk with the thrill of solving the mystery.

"Where?"

"Kurt Stanton's campaign financing account." She took Matthew's stunned silence as a standing ovation.

"You're kidding."

Sharon grinned as she tied her shoelaces. "I'll show you in a few minutes."

"Wait. Maybe I should come to you."

"I've got one foot out the door. Just wait for me." She ended the call.

She tucked the file folder under her arm, then grabbed her purse, car keys, and cell phone from the hall table before unlocking her door.

Sharon jogged down her front steps and strode to her car parked at the end of her block. It was just after seven o'clock. The shadows were growing longer as the day came to an end. A cool breeze tossed her jacket. Sharon slipped her cell phone into her pocket. She juggled her purse, folder, and car keys as she struggled to zip her coat.

Running footsteps closing in on her brought almost paralyzing flashbacks of her attack at the *Times* parking lot. Sharon forced herself to turn and face her fear.

Earl Stanton wrapped a fist around her upper arm. "Sharon, I was just coming to see you."

"Mr. Stanton. You startled me." Sharon had trouble breathing with her heart hammering in her throat. She was standing much too close to a killer.

"Did I?" Earl gave her his peculiar smile. The one that

hovered around his lips without touching his eyes. He must feel her fear through the grip he had on her arm.

"You did. You shouldn't rush up on people like that. I thought I was going to be mugged." She hoped that explained her breathless voice.

Earl stood so close. Sharon felt as if he were looming over her. His dark trench coat billowing in the late spring breeze added to the ominous impression.

His dark blond brows knitted as though in confusion. "I'm surprised you weren't expecting me."

Stop shaking and play dumb. "Why would I be expecting you?"

"Because, Sharon, you've figured out that I'm the Closer."

She hesitated just a second too long.

Chapter 32

Earl's smile broadened but didn't warm. "I thought as much. You're a very perceptive woman." He pressed his lips to her forehead. "Get into your car, Sharon."

"Why?" Sharon's skin crawled. She wanted to scrub her hand over the spot he'd kissed.

Earl angled away from the street beside them and stepped even closer to her. The hand that gripped her upper arm slid up to cup her neck. His body language was that of a lover having an intimate conversation in a public place.

With just the slightest pressure, he forced Sharon to tilt her head down. She saw him slip his hand inside her open jacket. A hard, metal object caressed the side of her waist. Sharon's eyes widened. She shook even harder. *Is that a gun?*

That's obviously what Earl wanted her to believe. And, since this man had shot and killed two people, the idea he'd pull a gun on her didn't tax her imagination.

"Let me help you with that." He tugged the arson folder out from under her arm. "Now get into your car, Sharon. The driver's side, of course."

Sharon turned in two jerky motions, weighted by her fear and Earl's grip on her arm.

Castigating questions further burdened her. Why didn't she let Matthew come to her apartment? But then he would have been facing the gun instead of her. She couldn't have lived with that.

Sharon deactivated her car alarm, which unlocked all the doors.

Earl waited until she slid behind the wheel. He stepped closer, letting her see the gun. "I know you're a runner, but can you outrun a bullet?"

He rubbed the gun up and down the side of her thigh. Fear was a metallic taste in her mouth. Could the gun go off accidentally? She was certain she'd seen documentaries about that on the Discovery Channel.

Earl finally stepped away. Sharon wiped her sweaty palms against her jacket—and felt her cell phone in her pocket. She had Matthew on speed dial. *Oh, please God, let this work.*

Earl slammed the driver's door shut. *Hurry.* She had to hurry. Sharon shoved her hand into her pocket as she watched Earl circle the front of her Civic. She slipped the phone out of her coat and brought an image of the command buttons to mind. Using her sense of touch, her frantic fingers pressed the keys to call Matthew. She pressed the speaker button and lowered the volume.

Her captor opened the passenger door as she tucked the thin cell phone tight against her left thigh.

He put the file folder on his lap and fastened his seat belt. "It's good you didn't try to drive away."

"I was tempted to run you over." *Please let this work. Please let Matt hear me.* Sharon took a deep breath and started signaling for help. "So, Mr. Stanton. I mean Earl. Where are you taking me?"

* * *

Matthew stopped pacing when he heard his cell phone ring. Who would call his cell when he was home? A disquieted feeling had been building almost since he'd said good-bye to Sharon. That feeling now spiked.

He took his cell phone from his end table. The caller identification showed Sharon's cellular number. "Hello?"

"Earl, where are you taking me?"

"What?" *Who is she talking to?*

"I don't want to just drive around." Her voice was unsteady and muted, as though she wasn't talking into her phone. "You have a destination in mind. Just tell me."

Matthew pressed the phone to his ear. His heart rate kicked up. "Sharon, can you hear me? What's going on?"

"And please be careful with that gun. I don't want it to accidentally go off."

Gun? Matthew grabbed his car keys and ran for the door. *Shit.*

It was just like Pittsburgh. Another person he cared about, someone else he was supposed to watch over, was in danger because he hadn't found the torch fast enough.

Where is Stanton taking her?

Matthew started his car and rested his hand on the gearshift. He pressed the speaker button and turned up his cellular phone's volume. He stared at the phone, willing Stanton to give Sharon a destination.

Sharon's voice came muffled over the signal. ". . . location in mind? Why won't you just tell me where we're going?"

Frustration rolled through Matthew as he strained but failed to hear Stanton's response.

Then, as though answering his prayers, Sharon repeated the destination. "Why Yeager Airport?"

Excellent. The airport. Matthew put his car in gear, heading for Interstate 64. Yeager covered a lot of ground, but hopefully Sharon could give him more specific directions when they got closer to the airport.

In the meantime, he had about twenty minutes to come up with a plan to save her. He reached into his glove compartment, hoping the battery still worked in the cellular the fire department had assigned to him.

He pressed the *power* button and expelled a relieved breath that the phone still had a charge, faint but sufficient. He entered Dunleavy's number. "I need your help."

Sharon wondered if Matthew were getting any of this. Was she speaking loudly enough? Had he even answered the phone or was she speaking to his answering machine?

She checked her rearview mirror hoping Matthew's Camry would miraculously appear. "Why are we going to the airport?"

Earl skimmed the papers in her folder. "How did you know it was me?"

Sharon shifted her attention to the front windshield, afraid he'd somehow sense she was sending messages to Matthew. "I didn't. But I knew whoever was behind the arsons killed Ray and Seth. What I don't understand is why."

Earl laughed, a remorseless sound, and turned another sheet in the file. "I had to do something to finance Kurt's campaign. I knew the fool would return the lobbyist's money."

"But why destroy people's lives? You burned businesses to the ground. Couldn't you have just written a check?"

Earl looked through the windshield, the gun braced against his lap and pointed at her. "Stay on the streets I don't want to get on the interstate." He returned his attention to Sharon. "There's a cap on how much I can contribute to my brother's campaign."

"The streets it is." She hoped Matthew understood the change of plans. She didn't completely grasp it herself. It took longer to get to the airport this way, but Sharon wasn't in a hurry. "You gave them the loans. Why didn't you just call them in?"

"Because the media would have gotten ahold of the story. The headlines would have read, STANTON TARGETS SMALL BUSINESS. But with my approach, fire would have been the villain. The headlines would have been, FIRE DESTROYS WEST SIDE BUSINESSES. Much better. I had it all planned."

Sharon glanced at Earl. He looked calm, unaffected by the consequences of his decisions. "What was your plan?"

"I convinced Chief Miller to hire an inexperienced firefighter with a checkered past as his lead fire investigator. And I convinced Gus Aldridge to replace you with my son. But your nosiness was a problem." He gave her a soulless smile. "I've tried to kill you before."

Sharon's heart froze. She clenched the steering wheel. "You were the man at the café fire. You dragged me into the building next door."

"I knocked you unconscious first. You would have died of smoke inhalation before you burned. But you're a hardheaded woman, literally and figuratively."

Sharon's eyes grew wide with amazement. She was trapped in a car with a gun-wielding psycho. She checked her rearview mirror again, searching for a familiar copper Camry. Was Matthew on his way? Or was she on her own?

"I also hired that upstanding young man to beat Payton's brains in. But you ruined that for me too."

"So sorry." The sarcastic words jumped out before Sharon could censor herself. In her peripheral vision, she saw Earl's narrow-eyed gaze. She didn't breath again until he continued talking.

"So I had him try to scare you off." Earl chuckled. The sound was genuinely amused, which made it even scarier. "You're either fearless or foolish. I think you're foolish for not realizing how serious I am about winning."

"You consider killing people winning?" She tried to strip any judgment from her tone.

"Whatever it takes." He spoke casually, thoughtlessly. "I value my position as a state senator's brother. I'm wined and dined just for the promise of passing a message to my brother. People will do anything for me. They're afraid to cross me. It's a heady feeling to have that much power, and I'm not giving it up."

Matt, are you hearing this? "But what made you think you could get away with arson, much less murder?"

"I am going to get away with it."

Sharon sincerely hoped not. "I'll turn left onto Barlow Drive."

"That's fine."

She wondered if Earl found her announcement odd. He didn't seem suspicious. Sharon kept him talking, hoping to distract him. "Is that why you killed Ray? To make certain you got away with your crimes?"

"I needed a fall guy. The insurance companies wouldn't process the business owners' claims until they knew who'd caused the fires." Earl paused and, when he spoke again, his voice was tired. "Lucas failed me there by running with the arson coverage. But he made it up to me with the stories on Ford's confession and Payton's criminal history."

Sharon struggled with her temper. "Ray didn't confess and Matt doesn't have a criminal history."

"Please don't interrupt me."

Sharon shivered at Earl's emotionless tone. She kept her attention on the road ahead. Not much farther to the airport. She needed a plan.

Earl shifted in his seat. "As soon as Ford was identified as the arsonist, the insurance company released the money."

"And you deposited it into your brother's campaign finance account."

"And now that we've come to the end of our story, you can turn left here."

Sharon heard the smile in his voice. She glanced at Earl, then back through the windshield at what looked like a grassy knoll to nowhere. "But we haven't gotten to the airport yet. We're not even to Keystone yet."

"Close enough."

She looked to the left. "There's no road."

"Please turn left. I don't like to repeat myself."

Sharon glanced in her rearview mirror before steering her little car down the hill along a man-made path through the grass and bramble. The Elk River was nearby. The feel of her compact cellular against her thigh was small comfort considering she still didn't see Matthew's car.

She was on her own. "Where are we going? The only thing here is the Elk River."

"Exactly. You can stop the car here."

Sharon stopped the car on the edge of the weed-infested clearing beside the Elk. She put the gear in park, cut the engine and turned to Earl.

A trace of a smile hovered at his lips. "I can't shoot you.

It's not that I don't want to. But, if another gunshot victim turns up, they'll never stop looking for the shooter."

She hated to ask, but his rambling was stretching her nerves. "What do you intend to do?"

He waved the gun toward the front window and the body of water on the other side. "You're going to drive into the river."

Sharon almost laughed. He'd lost his mind. "No one's going to believe I committed suicide."

"With the media's help, I have everyone believing Ford committed suicide."

Sharon shook her head, incredulous. "What makes you think I'm going to drive my car into the river and allow myself to drown?"

"Don't misunderstand. I don't want to shoot you, but I will if you don't do as I say."

Sharon's grip tightened around the steering wheel. "You won't get away with this."

Earl cocked his head to one side. "Why not? Is it because you think Payton is coming to rescue you?"

Chapter 33

Shock stole Sharon's breath. "What?"

"I knew you were up to something. You're much too intelligent to repeat directions like a well-trained parrot." Earl extended his free hand toward her. "Please give me your cell phone."

Sharon hesitated while Earl waited patiently. She was caught. But she didn't really need her cell phone any longer. Matthew knew where they were. Sort of. She handed her phone to Earl.

Earl snapped the phone shut, cutting her connection with Matthew. "Good girl." He dropped the phone into his coat pocket.

"He's on his way. And he's bringing help." She hoped.

Earl nodded. "Then you'd better hurry. If I'm gone before Captain Payton arrives, I won't have to kill him."

Sharon clenched her teeth with impotent fury. "He's heard everything, including your confession."

Earl chuckled. "Who's going to believe an incompetent fire investigator who was charged with arson in the past over an upstanding member of the community?"

"He has proof of your involvement."

Earl tapped the file folder on his lap. "Do you mean this neatly typed, well-organized folder of information?" He waved the folder. "Don't worry. Everything will be destroyed with the help of my shredder."

Sharon shook with fury. "Matt and I aren't the only ones who know about this. You can't kill us all."

"The choice is yours, Sharon. Drive into the river and save Payton's life, or sit right there and watch me kill him."

Sharon let her hands slip from the steering wheel. Her forearms rested limply in her lap. She wouldn't accept those choices. There had to be a third way. She stared at Earl, watching his every move, while she pushed her mind for a solution. If she tried to drive away, would he just shoot out her tires?

Taking her silence for acceptance, Earl unfastened his seat belt. "Good. You're saving lives with your decision." Keeping his gun trained on her, he opened the door. "I'll step outside. Try to be quick. I want to be gone before Payton arrives. His life depends on that."

Earl turned his back to her and climbed out of her car. Sharon seized her opportunity.

With one smooth movement, she unsnapped her seat belt, unlocked her car door and jumped out of her Civic. It was time to see if she could outrun a bullet. Or at least get a really good head start.

She stumbled out of the car, almost losing her footing as she spun to race across the clearing. Sharon heard Earl's shout and urged her body to a greater speed.

She had to control her breathing. Fear and flight were causing her to hyperventilate. If she couldn't regulate her breaths, she wouldn't be able to keep running.

Sharon thought of her mother. What would it do to Helen if her daughter were killed? That image made her faster. She thought of Matthew. He needed her help to clear his name. That knowledge made her stronger. She wasn't running for herself. She was running for the people she loved.

She ran toward the hill that led back to Barlow Drive. The hill she'd recently driven down. Sharon was still struggling to catch her breath. Beneath the pulse beating against her eardrums, she thought she heard heavy footfalls behind her. Was Earl getting closer? Sharon couldn't turn to look. That would slow her. She had to keep running, keep moving forward. Would he shoot her in the back? The thought chilled her. Almost made her stop.

The ground rose in a slow and steady incline toward the road. The soil beneath her sneakers was spongy and uneven. Night had descended. The path was entangled in shadows and shapes in the no-man's-land between her car's headlights and the lights of the street.

Divots grabbed at her feet, tugging her ankles. Stones grew from the ground, stabbing her soles. Sharon planted her right foot—and fell to her knees. She struggled to rise, almost sobbing with fear. A tug at her jacket ripped a scream from her throat.

Earl had caught her.

He yanked on her coat collar, dragging her upright. Primal fear triggered her basic instinct for survival. Without conscious thought, Sharon flailed her fists back, connecting with a bone on Earl's face. Her hand went numb with pain. Earl roared a short, guttural expletive as he released her.

Sharon bolted, digging for reserves to get her up and over the hill. She shortened her stride, muscling her way upward. Her chest was on fire. She could hear her wheezing breaths. And then she could see the streetlights.

She looked to the left and then the right, taking a

precious second to orient herself. She turned right, running along the sidewalk toward the oncoming traffic.

She waved her arms above her head and drew as deep a breath as she could. "Stop. Help me. Someone help me." Her throat was dry and her voice was rough with strain. She battled despair as one car after another drove past her. "Help me. Someone help me."

Sharon raced down the sidewalk—and then the sidewalk rushed up to meet her. Earl had tackled her from behind. He flipped her over like a rag doll. With the glow from the streetlight she saw the bottom half of his face was covered in blood. She must have broken his nose.

He drew back his arm. "You bitch."

Sharon covered her face, waiting for the blow. Instead his weight was lifted from her legs. She looked up and saw Matthew land a punch to Earl's face. Sharon sensed the fury behind the blow.

The campaign manager stumbled back against the nearby streetlight. He seemed to gather himself before he charged Matthew. In addition to anger, Matthew had the advantage of height and youth compared to the older man.

But Sharon knew Earl was insane in his rage. She and Matthew had foiled his grand scheme from the beginning. Matthew had led an investigation he wasn't supposed to be qualified to pursue. She had refused to relinquish the beat from which she had been replaced. They hadn't been the puppets he'd expected, and now they'd thwarted his last-ditch effort to salvage his big plans.

Earl swung his fists with a crazed fury that put Matthew on the defensive. Matthew blocked the blows, but slowly lost ground as the campaign manager drove him back toward the hill.

Matthew glanced around, then shifted his body,

changing course away from the hill and away from Sharon. He didn't want anything else to happen to her. She'd been through more than enough. He forced away the image of Stanton getting ready to punch her—a woman almost half his size.

Secure in the knowledge Sharon was a safe distance away, Matthew landed a solid blow to Stanton's face that rocked the other man several steps back. Matthew felt a rush of vicious pleasure at the look of shock on his adversary's face. He followed Stanton, using his body to herd the other man away from Sharon. He had to protect her as he hadn't protected Michelle.

Matthew dodged another wild punch. He landed a sharp jab that drove the air from Stanton's lungs.

Images from his past and present collided. The call telling him Michelle's company had been dispatched to a suspicious fire. The recollection spun away to be replaced by the memory of carrying Sharon from the smoking building. Sitting beside Michelle's hospital bed. Comforting Sharon after the attack in the *Times* parking lot.

Matthew caught a blow to his jaw. He countered with a fist to Stanton's face. It was the senator's brother who stumbled back, but Matthew wasn't sure who he fought any longer. The arsonist in Pittsburgh who'd killed his sister, or Stanton, the murderer who'd threatened the woman he loved. In his mind, those men had become one as he continued to fight.

Stanton tried to rally, swinging wildly. Matthew diverted the blows and, with two quick punches, drove Stanton to his knees. It was then he heard the sirens and knew the cops had arrived.

And Sharon was there, standing beside him. Matthew sensed her presence at the edge of his mind. Her arms, slender and strong, wrapped around him, urging him away from Stanton.

Her words came to him from a distance, growing clearer over time. "You saved me. It's okay. You can stop now. You saved me."

NPR's Saturday afternoon programming murmured from Matthew's car radio on the drive back from the police station the next day.

Sharon shifted again on her seat. With all the scrapes and bruises on her tush and thighs, it was hard to get comfortable. She'd had the same problem at the station while giving her full statement of Earl's attempt to kill her the night before.

"Are you okay?" Matthew's voice cut through the hum of the window defroster and the swoosh of the windshield wipers.

Sharon scowled at the bandage wrapped around her foot and ankle. "I still can't believe I sprained my ankle running from Earl." She hadn't realized it until she'd turned toward the police last night. Her body had moved forward, but her ankle had collapsed.

"Adrenaline kept you going."

Matthew had swept her up into his arms. They'd given the police a brief statement and secured her car before she'd asked him to drive her to her mother's house. Helen had applied the bandage.

Sharon frowned at Matthew. "Are you okay?"

He glanced at her before returning his attention to the traffic. "Why do you ask?"

"You've been very quiet since we left the police station." Sharon stared through the windshield at the gray sky and green mountains. The rain was light but steady.

Matthew broke the tense silence. "Do you want to talk about yesterday?"

Sharon started to decline his offer, but instead told the truth. "I was terrified. He was going to kill me."

"Thank God you got away." His voice was rough with his own fears.

Sharon got a glimpse of how afraid he must have been for her. Even if she hadn't wanted to talk about what happened, perhaps he needed to. "Thank you again for saving my life."

"You don't have to thank me." He still wouldn't look at her. "You thought to use your cell phone to let me know what was happening to you."

"You showed up when I needed you the most." Thinking about it made her shake again. She clasped her hands in her lap to steady them.

"I almost didn't. I didn't know where you were when he made you drive off the road. And when he took the phone from you and disconnected the call . . ." A tremor went through him. "I didn't know what was happening anymore."

Sharon's brows knitted at the deliberate understatement. Why was he holding back? When Earl had disconnected the call, Matthew must have gone out of his mind with worry. She would have. "It helped to know I wasn't alone. That you were nearby."

"Not near enough." He took the interstate exit that led to her mother's house too fast. "You scared me too."

Sharon's eyes stretched wide. "How?"

"You argued with him. You baited him."

Sharon took exception to that. She shifted in her seat, looking for a more comfortable position as she faced him. "I didn't bait him. But he did make me angry. He tried to kill us, Matt. Twice."

"So you *did* remember he was capable of murder."
Matthew's sarcasm wasn't lost on Sharon.

"He took advantage of two desperate men. Then,
when he was done with them, he killed them."

"The guy's a sociopath. Even more reason for you
not to piss him off."

Anger outweighed her physical discomfort. "What
was I supposed to do. Cry?" She'd wanted to, but she'd
refused to show Earl her fear.

Matthew clenched the steering wheel, reliving the
fear. His bruised and torn knuckles showed white as he
guided his Camry through her mother's winding
neighborhood roads. "I forgot. You don't back down
for anyone. Not some thug in a parking lot who warns
you off the investigation. Not even a murderer with a
gun pointed at you." Matthew felt Sharon's gaze burning into him.

"Why are you angry with me?" She seemed more curious than annoyed. And that annoyed him.

"Because you almost got yourself killed."

"No, someone almost killed me. Why are you angry
with me?" She sounded so reasonable repeating her
question. Meanwhile, he fantasized about tearing the
steering wheel out of its column and throwing it into
the street.

Matthew pulled into Helen's driveway, cut the engine
but made no move to leave. He wanted Sharon to himself just a little longer. "I can still hear you arguing with
him." His voice was low and reluctant as he made the
admission. "All the while he held a gun on you. I could
hear you, but I couldn't protect you. I couldn't even tell
you to stop trying to make him angry."

Sharon rested her palm on his thigh. Every muscle
in his leg tightened, although he supposed the gesture
was meant to comfort him.

"I'm all right, Matt. You saved me."

He slipped his hand under hers and held on. Tight. "No. You saved me."

Sharon slid closer, leaning over the gearshift and moving into Matthew's arms. Matthew held her slender body close in his arms and tucked his face into her neck. He breathed in her soft, powdery fragrance and listened to the rain fall gently against his car. It would be a while before he was able to release the last remnants of yesterday's nightmare. Holding her in his arms helped.

Chapter 34

The embrace wasn't long enough to satisfy Matthew's need for her, but he had to let Sharon go. Her mother was waiting. He carried her walking cane and helped her up the steps through the rain to her mother's house.

Helen's television was tuned to CNN. Sharon's mother and friends seemed to be dividing their attention between it and each other. Helen and Edison Scott, Allyson's father, shared the overstuffed love seat. Allyson and Andre sat in matching armchairs.

Matthew helped Sharon settle onto the sofa. She braced her back against the sofa's padded left arm and extended her legs along the plump cloth cushions. He tucked extra throw pillows under her right ankle, then sat on the opposite end of the sofa.

The other occupants watched him with various reactions. Helen and Edison looked amused. Allyson seemed suspicious. Andre appeared empathetic. Matthew pretended not to notice.

Andre's gaze swept from Matthew to Sharon. "How'd it go at the police station?"

Sharon shifted for a better view of her friend. "It was

long. Earl's lawyer's claiming Matt and I lured Earl to the Elk River. Although forensics found only Earl's fingerprints on the gun. And ballistics has matched his gun to the bullet the medical examiner recovered from Seth's chest."

Sharon heard amazement but not surprise in the murmurs circulating the room. It was one thing to suspect a prominent citizen, such as Earl Stanton, of committing heinous felonies. It was another to be confronted by the evidence. Would a jury feel the same way?

Matthew rested his right ankle on his left knee and sank deeper into the sofa. "Forensics is also going to compare Stanton's prints to those found on Ford's suicide note. And they're going to see if the gun found with Ford is registered to Stanton."

Edison frowned. "Why didn't they check the registration before?"

Matthew shrugged. "When they didn't find a record of Ford owning a gun, they assumed the gun wasn't registered."

Sharon nodded. "Add the information I've collected linking Earl to the lending company, and the state has a solid case."

Helen's eyes shone with maternal concern. "How do you feel about the trial?"

Sharon imagined reliving yesterday's experience for the court. "Nervous. I'll be the prosecution's key witness against Earl." Matthew's large palm settled over her shin below her linen walking shorts. His touch was warm, comforting. Too bad the court wouldn't let him hold her hand while she testified.

Andre rubbed his chin. "It'll be a high-profile case."

"You'll be hounded by the press."

Sharon quirked her brow at Matthew's comment.

"How will Earl Stanton's charges affect the investigation into your nonexistent criminal past?" Andre questioned Matthew.

Bitterness sharpened Matthew's words. "As far as I know, that investigation is ongoing."

"Meyer did a good job on the article on Sharon's abduction and attempted murder." Andre referred to police beat reporter Bill Meyer.

"Yes, and the copy editor's headline was inspired." Allyson quoted the text. "FIRE INVESTIGATOR FOILS SERIAL KILLER, SAVES REPORTER."

Sharon forced a laugh. "The headline's not quite accurate, though. I'm not a reporter anymore."

"You'll always be a reporter." Matthew's tone was somber. "It's part of who you are, and you're good at it."

He'd managed to fluster her. Sharon masked her uncertainty with humor. "Can I use you as a reference?"

"Yes." He sent an entire message with that single syllable. Was she interpreting it correctly? Or did she hear what she wanted to hear?

Andre nodded toward the television. "Listen."

The anchorwoman stared solemnly into the camera. "The West Virginia state legislature has ended its investigation into allegations of ethical misconduct by three-term state senator Kurt Stanton."

The young woman continued in sober tones. "Arson and murder charges have been filed against Earl Stanton, the senator's brother and campaign manager. Ethics Committee members believe the senator's brother was accepting the bribes without the senator's knowledge."

Matthew's voice ended the stunned silence. "Did Stanton just throw his older brother under the bus?"

Allyson shook her head. "Kurt Stanton idolizes Earl. No, this sounds like something the party leaders ordered."

On-screen, the news station rolled a tape of an earlier press conference with Kurt Stanton. The senator stood behind a podium. His movie-star looks had dimmed. He appeared strained and tired. Lost.

"My brother is innocent of these charges. This is an obvious attempt by our opponents to discredit my family." Kurt's voice carried the force of his conviction. "I will not be bullied out of this election. In November, the voters will decide whether I will continue to serve the great state of West Virginia."

Before his final word faded from the microphone, reporters fired questions at Stanton. But they spoke to his back. The senator left the podium without a backward glance.

Sharon turned to Allyson. "Henry Rush had been counting on that investigation. What do you think he'll do now?"

Allyson bit her lower lip, worry in her eyes. "I'd better call him."

Sharon had an uncomfortable feeling. "Do you think Kurt really didn't know what Earl was doing?"

Allyson frowned at the television. The anchor had switched to another story. "He certainly sounded sincere."

Andre adjusted his glasses. "There are too many loose ends. Who knew what? Was anyone taking bribes? If so, why?"

Sharon remembered a conversation she'd had with Earl during which he tried to sway her vote with Kurt's looks rather than his substance. "Kurt may have been as much a pawn in Earl's power play as the arson victims."

Helen shook her head sadly. "If that's true, I feel sorry for him."

Edison grunted. "Why? What is he, a windup doll who can't think for himself? So his brother wanted to be the power broker in the background. What did Kurt want?"

"Maybe he really wants to help people." Matthew's tone was measured and thoughtful. "To serve his community."

Sharon shifted again. Some of her scratches itched. "We may never know Kurt's motivation. But I feel sorry for his family. Innocent or not, they share the shame of what Earl's done."

Allyson gestured toward the television. "You saw the pain on Kurt's face. We don't know whether he took the money, but I'm beginning to think Earl took it in Kurt's name. And now Kurt's paying the price with his reputation."

"What about Lucas?" Helen looked at Sharon. "He may be an adult but, based on what you've told me, he doesn't act like one. He still needs guidance. With his father in prison, who'll give it to him?"

Edison grunted. "Kurt will."

Helen shook her head. "It's not the same."

Edison scowled. "It couldn't be worse than Earl's taking care of him."

Andre interrupted the debate. "The business owners, Sharon, Matt, Stanton's family, Rush, the firefighters. Those are the victims we're aware of. There may be more."

Edison glanced at his watch. "We should get going." He looked at Helen. "Are you sure we can't get anything for you while we're out?"

Her mother shook her head. "I'm sure."

Edison, Allyson, and Andre stood. In her peripheral vision, Sharon saw Matthew stand as well. She turned to him. He looked as reluctant to leave as she was to watch him go.

"Do you need anything?" His words sounded forced. Heavy.

You. But Sharon shook her head. After yesterday's ordeal, everything was upside down and turned around. She needed time to straighten herself out.

Matthew nodded. "Call me if you do."

Sharon's gaze tracked him as he walked to the door. Helen held the door open for their guests. Everyone exchanged choruses of good-byes and see-you-laters.

After locking the front door, her mother wandered to the picture window. She looked outside as she spoke to Sharon. "For an unarmed man to charge after a gunman to rescue a woman, he must love her very much. With that much love, there has to be trust."

Helen gave Sharon a pointed look—eyebrows raised and gaze direct—before leaving her daughter alone with her thoughts.

Sharon looked up from the Sunday *Times* when the CNN anchor announced a breaking news bulletin.

"State Senator Kurt Stanton was shot outside the Charleston Convention Center minutes ago." The young man sounded stunned. "He was rushed to the Charleston Area Medical Center where he was pronounced dead on arrival."

Sharon and her mother exchanged wide-eyed looks. Helen used the television remote control to increase the volume.

A file photo of the senator appeared above the anchor's left shoulder. "The senator was on his way to a breakfast speaking engagement when the gunman, identified as Henry Rush, shot him. Rush then shot himself and was pronounced dead at the scene."

A photo of Rush joined the image of Stanton

on-screen. "Rush was the father of one of the miners killed in a recent mining accident. More information will be provided as we continue to cover this breaking news story."

Sharon was swamped with regret. "What a waste."

Helen's sigh seemed a yard long. "A tragedy and a waste."

"Neither man got what he needed. The Ethics Committee should have completed its investigation and either charged Kurt or cleared him. And all Henry wanted to know was why his son died."

Helen lowered the television's volume again. "I don't think we'll ever get those answers. Kurt's party will run someone else for his seat, and Henry's questions will fade away."

"And he'll become another Stanton casualty. Just like the arson victims and those firefighters."

Her mother gestured toward her. "You and Matt almost were. So many innocent people."

"Someone needs to find answers to Henry's questions."

What a tragedy. Matthew watched the anchor wrap up the Sunday breaking news bulletin on Rush's murder-suicide involving Senator Stanton.

He wondered what Sharon thought. He was certain she'd watched it. She and her mother were news junkies. Matthew couldn't stop thinking about Sharon. He couldn't let her walk away from him. What was he going to do?

His phone rang. Again. It had been ringing insistently since Saturday morning. Reporters had left messages asking him to grant them an interview. Fat chance. But when would they get that message? He wasn't being coy.

He wasn't playing favorites with the *Times*. He had no intention of calling them. End of story.

His answering machine clicked on and Matthew recognized Naismith's voice. He strode to the phone and grabbed the receiver. "Payton speaking."

A startled hesitation. "This is Naismith."

"What can I do for you?" He checked his antagonism, which wasn't easy. His boss was playing games with him—with his livelihood. He fantasized about crawling through the phone line and punching the other man in the mouth.

"I saw the article in yesterday's *Times*. The one about you saving Sharon MacCabe."

Matthew sat on the arm of the sofa. "Sharon got away from Stanton on her own. I was there for cleanup."

"The article painted you as a real hero. I also saw the retraction the *Times* ran about you and the Pittsburgh fire."

"You've been doing a lot of reading. But what does all this have to do with me?"

Naismith coughed. He was definitely uncomfortable. "We've completed the investigation into claims of your criminal past. We haven't found anything that substantiated those claims—"

"That's not surprising."

Naismith continued. "Therefore, we're reinstating you effective Monday with no change in pay or position."

The silence was suspicious on both sides of the line. Matthew had nothing but contempt for the assistant chief's speech. "How long did the investigation take you, Naismith?"

"You want the truth?"

"I'm entitled to it."

"I didn't do an investigation."

Being right didn't cool his temper. Matthew stood, hoping to walk off the anger. "Then why the pretense?"

"I didn't want you here, Payton."

"I got that."

Naismith sighed, a quick inhale and slow release. "Miller forced you down my throat. I told him you were green, but he didn't care. Said Mayor West told him Kurt Stanton would consider it a personal favor. That you were a friend of the family and needed a break. But Stanton didn't want his name involved. Didn't want it to look like cronyism. Shit. Nobody ever gave *me* a break. Why should *I* give *you* one?"

Matthew remembered Sharon telling him the rumor about his father knowing Fred West.

Naismith continued. "I felt like you were sent to spy on me. I resented your ass the minute you walked into my station. Second-guessing me. Undermining me—"

Matthew interrupted. "I never second-guessed or undermined you. I just tried to do my job."

"I know." Naismith sounded indignant. "But I couldn't figure out why they'd sent some wet-behind-the-ears punk who used Daddy's connections to get a job to spy on me when I have men putting their lives on the line every day."

"I'm too old to be referred to as a wet-behind-the-ears punk."

Naismith ignored him. "Then I read the article in the *Times* and realized you weren't spying on me. Stanton was using you. He'd told West to have Miller put some untrained puppy in the fire inspector's position hoping you'd be too stupid to figure out what was going on."

Matthew felt the prick of annoyance. "You were the one who couldn't see what was going on."

"But now that I do, I want to apologize for everything

I put you through, including that bogus suspension."
Naismith paused. "I respect you, Payton. You stuck to
your guns even when I turned up the heat on you."

Matthew wasn't moved. "Thanks."

"Whatever." Naismith's tone was dismissive. "I'll see you
tomorrow. Eight A.M. sharp." He disconnected the line.

Matthew returned his cordless phone to its charger.
Looked like he and Naismith would have a new beginning. Gone was the paranoid assistant to the chief. In
his place was a dismissive, cantankerous leader.

There was never a dull moment in the Mountain State.

Chapter 35

She'd wanted to return to normalcy so, despite Helen's
objections, Sharon had gone back to her apartment that
afternoon. However, nothing felt normal to her. Not her
sprained ankle or the cuts and bruises on her sore body.
Or a weekend without Matthew. She finished her soup
and reached for the grilled cheese sandwich.

Her bell rang. Setting aside the sandwich, Sharon
slowly rose. She limped to the door with a mixture of
hope and dread. If it were Matthew, would she know
what to say? If it weren't Matthew, how disappointed
would she be?

The bell chimed again. Through the peephole, she
saw Wayne in the hallway holding a bouquet of spring
flowers. Well, that answered one question. It wasn't
Matthew, and she was very disappointed.

She unlocked the door and pulled it wide so her
former editor could enter.

It had only been four days since she'd quit her job,
but it felt so much longer. Looking at her former boss,
Sharon felt nothing. No anger. No regrets.

"Hello, Wayne."

Wayne crossed the threshold and handed her the bouquet. "These are for you."

Sharon couldn't hold back a smile. The flowers were too lovely. "Thank you." She gestured toward the sofa. "Have a seat."

"How are you feeling?" Wayne paced beside her, stopping at the sofa.

"Fine. I'll be right back." Sharon limped to the kitchen. She made quick work of transferring the flowers from the cellophane to a vase. Manners compelled her to offer refreshments. "Would you like something to drink?"

Wayne's response carried into the kitchen. "Ice water would be nice."

Minutes later, Sharon returned to her great room. She extended the serving tray, offering Wayne one of the glasses of ice water and a coaster. "How's everything?"

"Not so great." Wayne took a gulp of his drink. "Lucas quit. He said he doesn't need the job anymore."

Sharon sipped her water, studying her boss. Each time she'd asked Wayne why Lucas had been given her beat, he'd dismissed and/or threatened her. Now he wanted her to commiserate with him because Lucas no longer wanted her job? Latent anger stirred. "What do you want me to say, Wayne?"

Sharon wished she could read Wayne's thoughts as he sat silent and contemplative in response to her question.

He took a moderate sip of water this time, as though moistening his throat rather than quenching a thirst. "Aldridge told me if I didn't want Stanton on my staff, I could leave."

Sharon had suspected as much, and she could understand her editor's dilemma. He was married with young children. Losing his job would place him at great financial risk.

But there was something Sharon needed to know. "Why didn't you tell me that when I asked why you'd demoted me? I asked more than once."

Another slow sip of water. Another contemplative silence. "I didn't want to admit that I'd folded under Aldridge's pressure. That I could toss away my integrity so easily."

Sharon frowned into her glass. Wayne's response sounded like a white-gloved version of the truth. What wasn't he telling her?

He put his unfinished glass of water on the coaster. "Stanton and his father hated you. They said you were too smart for your own good. At first, I couldn't understand why that bothered them. But now I know why."

Sharon arched a brow. "They should have come up with a better cover story to explain why Lucas was replacing me."

Wayne laughed drily. "Didn't you believe Lucas wanted a job?"

"No. Especially since he never did any work." Sharon tensed, looking at Wayne from a different perspective. "Did they tell you about their plans?"

"No." He hurried to reassure her. "No, they never did. But it's easy to see now, isn't it? And you did expose them."

The silence that settled over them wasn't quite comfortable. Sharon continued to sip her water, wishing it was coffee.

"Sharon, with Lucas gone, would you be willing to return to the *Times* and take back your old beat? We need reporters like you who are willing to stick their neck out for the truth."

Her brows knitted. He wanted her to "stick her neck out for the truth" when he was still being evasive with her?

"Thank you, Wayne. I appreciate your personally offering me my job back. But I've already accepted a position with the *Gazette*."

Wayne's eyes widened with surprise. "When?"

"Yesterday."

"They called you on a Saturday?"

Sharon nodded. "I officially start in two weeks. My ankle should be better by then."

"What will you be doing?"

"Investigative reporting." Sharon would admit to the pleasure of sharing the news with Wayne. It was like reliving the excitement of the phone call from the *Charleston Gazette's* editor in chief all over again. "They're first going to publish a piece on the investigation into the serial arsons and murders, which led to Earl's charges."

"Congratulations. They're very lucky to have you." Wayne smiled but sounded disappointed. Maybe even worried. Or perhaps Sharon was flattering herself.

"Thank you. But, even if I hadn't accepted this position, I wouldn't have returned to the *Times*. I couldn't work for you again. Even now, I feel as though there's something you're not telling me."

Wayne nodded his acceptance and stood. Sharon followed him to the door. With his hand on the doorknob, he faced her. "I was promised the communications director position for Kurt Stanton's U.S. Senate campaign. If he won that bid, I'd go to Washington with him."

Sharon's brows knitted. "Did Kurt tell you that?"

Wayne shook his head. "Earl did."

The realization she was looking at another Stanton casualty saddened her. "Earl told me they were grooming Lucas for that position."

Disappointment, anger, and self-disgust rolled over Wayne's features. He turned and left.

Sharon closed the door. Even as Wayne had lied to her to further Earl's agenda, Earl had been lying to Wayne. There was a lesson here. Be careful who you hitch your wagon to. They might run right over you.

Matthew stared at Sharon's closed door. It was Sunday evening, and she was nursing a sprained ankle. He was sure she'd be home. But would she be any more receptive to giving him a second chance than she'd been before?

He checked his pockets, took a deep breath and pressed her doorbell. The nerves that had ridden with him to her apartment multiplied as he waited. He wiped his palms on the seams of his jeans.

Sharon opened the door, her eyes wide with surprise. "I was just leaving you a message." She held up her cordless phone and gave him a shaky smile.

"You were?" Matthew felt a wave of relief. She wanted to talk to him. That was half the battle.

Sharon pressed the phone's *off* button and stepped back. "Come in."

He crossed her threshold and watched as she locked her door. His gaze traveled from her tousled hair, over her blue Mountaineer T-shirt untucked over baggy gray sweat shorts to her bare feet.

He shoved his hands into his jeans pocket. "I know you don't believe I trust you, but I do. You think I'm just saying the words, but I'm not."

Sharon stepped toward him. "Matt—"

He raised his hand, palm out. "Just hear me out. Please."

Sharon stopped. But even standing still, she radiated energy. Was it impatience?

Matthew ran a hand over his hair, pacing away from

her. "At first, I told myself to stay away from you. Reporters had brought me nothing but trouble, and I was trying to start over."

Matthew went back to Sharon. "But I couldn't stay away. Instead, I got to know you." He took her hands in both of his. "The reporter who cares more about her readers than her byline. The woman who reaches out to people in need." His lips curved in a smile. "The warrior who won't back away from a fight."

Sharon spoke softly. "Not when I believe in the person I'm fighting for."

Matthew wiped the tears from Sharon's cheeks. "You were fighting for me. I'm sorry I didn't realize that sooner."

Sharon shook her head. "I don't think either of us was thinking clearly that day. Lucas's article rehashing the Pittsburgh arsons clouded your judgment. And your accusations against me . . . well, they really hurt."

"I'm sorry."

Sharon nodded. "I forgive you."

She'd forgiven him before but hadn't granted him a second chance.

Matthew walked to her entertainment center and inserted the disc he'd carried in his jacket pocket. "You have more courage and loyalty than anyone I know."

Sharon shook her head. "*You* inspired me, Matt. It took a great deal of strength to handle the tragedy of losing your sister and having people accuse you of causing her death. You not only coped, you rebuilt your life."

He inspired her. She admired him. Did that mean she believed he trusted her?

Matthew cued the CD and pressed PLAY. The strains of Patti LaBelle's "If You Asked Me To" rolled across the room. He approached her again, still afraid to pull her into his arms. He wanted to, but would she let him?

Sharon knew what Matthew was trying to tell her with this song even before she heard the familiar words, "I could love someone; I could trust someone."

Tension lined his features. Even now, she could see he wasn't certain of her. Matthew's voice was husky with emotion. "I love and trust you with all my heart and soul. Please. Give us another chance."

With his index finger, he traced a path down the side of her face. Just a whisper of movement with a tender touch. Her knees shook. The music built to a crescendo, and Patti LaBelle sang the words Matthew thought he couldn't express. Foolish man.

The emotions LaBelle crooned glowed in his eyes. This man who'd charged into danger to save her life now bared his heart and soul for her. As the beauty of the song wrapped around her, so did the power of his love.

Matthew put gentle pressure on her waist to bring her into his embrace. Sharon's lips parted as his mouth lowered to hers. It was a soft, persuasive kiss. A gentle lover's caress. Undemanding, but refusing to be ignored.

His tongue teased, aroused, tempted. His hands reacquainted themselves with Sharon's curves. His every touch expressed his feelings, broadcast his love. Strong, but tender. Everlasting. Sharon's heart was full to bursting.

She drew away to look into his eyes. "I love you too, Matt." His eyes widened with surprise and she nearly burst with joy. "Did you buy that CD just for this occasion?"

Matthew smiled. "I thought if I couldn't convince you, maybe the great LaBelle could. You once said your life had become a CD of her greatest hits."

Sharon was impressed he'd remembered that throwaway comment she'd made so long ago. "You were doing great on your own."

Matthew held her gaze, speaking his emotions. "I

can't imagine my life without you. Your love means that much to me. *You* mean that much to me."

Sharon blinked away tears. "I need you too, Matt." Recognizing the opening notes of the next song, she smiled and paraphrased Patti LaBelle. "You're the right kind of lover for me."